KERRY J DONOVAN

ON THE ATTACK

VINCI BOOKS

The Ryan Kaine series by Kerry J Donovan

To Colour Sergeant Glenn Gilmore, for letting me loose with an Accuracy AXMC sniper rifle. He didn't laugh at any of my efforts, even though I missed everything I aimed at.

Vinci Books

vinci-books.com

Published by Vinci Books Ltd in 2025

1

Printed and bound in Great Britain by Clays Ltd, Elcograf S.p.A.

Chapter One

Ocean Village, Southampton, Hampshire, England

Jerome "Teddy" Tedesco glared at the empty whisky glass in his hand. He'd have thrown the fucking thing at the wall, or at the Kraut, but his therapist kept telling him to meditate, to find his inner peace, not to vent his anger on others so readily. To do so wouldn't help relieve his underlying stress, or lower his blood pressure, or sort out his anger management issues, or whatever.

Well, screw her. Screw the overqualified, overcharging bitch into the wall.

She knew nothing.

So far, he'd paid the woman a small fortune to leave her Harley Street clinic and make weekly house calls and, after twenty-three sessions, the best coping strategy she could come up with was meditation?

Total bloody shit.

"Think things through before you act, Mr Tedesco," she'd said, before clocking up another fucking invoice. "You'll find it works."

Yeah, and what else had he been doing all his Goddamned life?

Fuck.

It was little better than the things Mother used to tell him as a boy.

"Count up to ten, Jerome. Count up to ten. If you do that, the anger will fade, and the world will seem a much happier place."

If he'd listened to Mother, he'd have saved tens of thousands of pounds worth of therapy over the years, but … sod it. If he'd listened to Mother, he'd still be working for the Shylock in the back street betting shop, and he wouldn't be the owner of all he surveyed—half of Southampton's seafront. He wouldn't own any of his businesses, the casinos along the south coast, the fishing boats, the pleasure cruisers, the stud farm on the South Downs, or the racecourse. Where would he be if he'd counted to ten and toed the fucking line?

Nowhere. That's where.

He let the Kraut on the other side of the desk, Schechter, sit and squirm a little longer before delivering judgement.

The moron would be doing plenty more squirming in a minute, but Teddy kept him dangling. He liked to see the minnows suffer. It suited his management style, and it made the ending all the sweeter. The two slabs of meat standing either side of the door already knew what he was going to say—he'd told them before they let Schechter into his office, his inner sanctum. They'd be ready for any reaction from the stupid Kraut.

German efficiency be fucked.

Teddy had to admit, Schechter looked the part. Tall, blond, square-jawed, broad-shouldered, intelligent, blue eyes. He was the archetypical Aryan—one of Hitler's supermen. But everyone knew what happened to Hitler and his bully boys. They bottled out and ended up losing a war they should have won. Schechter had come highly recommended by a man Teddy once trusted, but that hadn't worked out too well. Not so far. Not for the Kraut, and not for Grady, the Kraut's sponsor.

Fuck's sake, who did he have to screw over to get things done properly these days?

Teddy held up his empty glass and the nearer of the two guards, Ginger, rushed to refill it for him.

A good monkey. Well trained.

Teddy warmed the glass in his cupped hand and inhaled the rich vapours. Smoky, oaky, warm. The aroma of peat bogs, oak casks, and heather. Precisely the aroma a Macallan Speyside single malt should give off. Reassuringly expensive. He raised the lead crystal glass and touched the liquid to his lips, allowing his skin to absorb the moisture. He licked away the residue.

Very pleasant. Very rewarding. Well worth the price.

"Tell me, Schechter, how difficult should it be to dispose of a corpse?"

The Kraut stared back, said nothing. His open-mouthed expression, dumb and stupid. Not a good look for someone about to plead for his life. Plead and fail.

Teddy lowered the glass to the coaster in case he lost

control, which was on the cards. Wasting any of the glorious nectar wouldn't do. Wouldn't do at all.

Meditate. Count to ten.

To make certain, he rolled his chair further away from the desk, distancing himself from the glass and the Kraut. It gave him more perspective. More room to operate. More room to think.

"It isn't a rhetorical question, man. Answer me!"

Schechter stiffened. For the first time since he'd joined the organisation, the German showed real fear. Damn right, too. On the other hand, it was the first time he'd fucked up in all that time. Simple thing, but it had caused Teddy a monumental fucking headache.

"I apologise, Mr Tedesco," he said in his fucking annoying, stiff and precise accent. "It was the result of unforeseen circumstances. We thought—"

"You thought! Fuck off. You didn't *think* at all. When Grady recommended you, he said you were bright. A university graduate, no less. It's not like Grady to be so fucking wrong. A shame really. He used to be my go-to guy for new personnel, but not anymore. Timothy and Ginger have acquainted him with a hospital bed. The fucker's going to be drinking his meals through a straw for the next few weeks. He's not 'going-to' go anywhere for quite a while."

Ginger sniggered.

Teddy grabbed a book off the shelf behind him and hurled it at the redheaded fucker, who caught it mid-flight, in front of his nose. Good reactions. It reminded Teddy why he'd kept the bugger around for two years. Not as efficient or bright as Timothy, but acceptable. Although Teddy still needed to keep him on his toes. Didn't pay to let the hired help grow too comfortable or to have ideas above their station.

"What the fuck you laughing at, shit-for-brains? Your job is to stand there, look mean, and do as I say. Did I tell you to laugh? You're not laughing, are you, Timothy?"

The enormous, black South African at Ginger's side stared at a point above Teddy's head, giving it the thousand-yard stare.

"No, Mr Tedesco. Not at all, sir."

Good boy, Timothy.

"That's right. See that, Schechter? Timothy knows when to answer and when to keep his mouth shut. Pity Ginger doesn't learn from him. He doesn't know when to keep his ears open and his mouth shut. He will though, given time."

Ginger shut the book quietly and hugged it to his chest. A thick, leather-bound volume it was, something about the decline of the Roman Empire. Teddy's interior designer— the limp-wristed queer—had bought a truckload of the dusty books to build what he called the room's "ambience". In the end, Teddy approved of the look and had even started to read a couple of the monstrous tomes. After all, they'd cost enough. Might as well get some use out of them other than as fuck-off, expensive wallpaper.

"You can put it back where it belongs, Ginger. We all know you never learned to read. Yeah, you can laugh at that one. It's meant to be a joke and people can laugh at my jokes."

Timothy smirked as Ginger marched across the room, replaced the book with its mates, and returned to his post without so much as a snicker or a twitch in his expression.

Teddy sat still, giving Schechter the evil eye the whole time. What the fuck was he going to do? Things were beginning to slip sideways. If he didn't get business back on track, the London hyenas would rumble south and start circling the *veldt*, and he couldn't let that happen. Teddy valued his position in society—and his neck—too much to allow it. No way. Best to cauterise the dead tissue before the infection spread, and what better way than to make an example of a young, German smartarse.

Top of his head, Teddy could list a dozen ways to dump a corpse, and all of them would have been better than the one Grady and Schechter had chosen, stupid mutts. Most of the methods, he'd already utilised himself on his way to the top.

Dig a hole in the woods somewhere and plant the body as fertiliser. Chop it up into pieces with a woodchipper and feed it to the pigs. That was a good one, possibly the best. Pigs loved human meat. Ate everything—bones, teeth, hair, the lot, and then they crapped it out over the fields as manure. Wonderful. The circle of life.

Back in the day, you could drop a body into the foundations of a bridge or a new building and cover the bloody thing with a thousand tonnes of ready-mix. Couldn't do that easily these days, though. Not since builders became so bloody security conscious, fenced everything in, and rigged up surveillance cameras. Teddy blamed the Health and Safety Executive and all the other Nanny State, do-good bastards. Fuck them and fuck all the so-called terrorists who gave good, honest thieves a bad name. Ignorant, towel-headed cretins who blew themselves up for a pack of virgins. What use is a virgin to a fucker who's blown himself into tiny pieces? The lack of logic was hysterical. Comedians would write sketches about it if they weren't so shit-scared of the fallout.

Count to ten, Teddy. Savour the moment. Watch the Kraut squirm.

"Okay, Schechter. Let's have it. I gave you and Grady the simple task of losing Tubby Malahide's blubber-filled carcase and the whole thing ended up like a dog's breakfast. Tell me what happened in your own words, and tell me what you're doing to rectify the situation."

The Kraut clasped his hands together. Bubbles of sweat formed on his upper lip.

Yeah, that's right, Schechter. You should be sweating.

Teddy leaned forwards, retrieved his drink, and took a real sip, soaking up the golden liquid. He waited for a story that might just save the German's life—but he doubted it.

Schechter swallowed and took a breath.

"Come on, Schechter. I don't have all fucking day."

"I apologise, Mr Tedesco. I was trying to gather my thoughts. I need to make this as clear and concise as possible." The Kraut covered his mouth with a hand and coughed. "On Saturday, Grady called and told me we had a task to perform on your behalf."

"Yes, yes. I know all that bollocks. Don't think you can shift all the blame onto poor, old Grady just because he's not here to defend himself. I already have his explanation and want your side of things before making my final decision. See how generous and fair I can be? That's why they call me the nicest boss on the south coast. Isn't that right, Timothy?"

The South African dipped his head.

"That's right, Mr Tedesco," he said, in a deep, rumbling voice that could shatter bricks—and kneecaps. "Absolutely right."

"Good. Now get on with it, Schechter. I'm not a patient man."

The German shuffled in his chair. "Grady called me to his flat and told me to bring a tarpaulin and a car with a big enough boot to take the, ah, package—"

"Fuck's sake, man. We're all grownups here. Call a shovel a fucking shovel."

"*Entschuldigen sie?* Excuse me?"

"Tubby wasn't a brown-paper parcel headed for the post office. He was a corpse, a cadaver, a body, a stiff. He might have been dipping his hand in my till, but he'd already paid for it with his life. Show him some fucking respect!"

"*Jawohl!* Yes, sir." Schechter swallowed before continuing. "I drove Grady and the ... *body* to the quarry, under his directions. It was not a place I had visited before. He said it would be deserted at that time in the evening, but when we removed the body from the car, a dog barked."

"The mutt you shot?"

"Yes, sir. That's correct. A woman of middle-age, maybe forty-five, was exercising her animal around the lake that had formed from the quarry workings. The animal was brown and white, and stood about so high." He raised his hand about two and a half feet above the carpet.

"I don't give a shit how big the mutt was. This isn't Crufts, you fuckwit. Get on with the story!"

Teddy jerked his hand and some of the expensive whisky splashed onto his fingers. He licked them clean. Strike one for the Kraut. Any more errors and he was out. This wasn't baseball. No second or third strikes in Teddy's organisation.

"Grady yelled at me to get her. He can't run because of his bad knees and one of us had to stay with the ... corpse. I gave chase."

"How far away was this old biddy?"

"Across the lake on the other bank. No more than thirty, thirty-five metres straight across."

"So, this little, old lady was only a few yards away, but she was too fast for you, and you let her escape?"

Teddy squeezed the glass so hard, he worried it might shatter under the pressure.

"It was not like that, Mr Tedesco. Thirty metres in a straight line, but the shore was curved, and she ran directly into the woods. I could not run straight across, because the *wasser* was too deep. I had to run around the shoreline. The woman was faster than I expected, but I gained quickly upon her."

"And you had a gun, right?"

"Yes, sir. I was close enough to shoot her without missing when the dog attacked. Vicious. Look!" He rolled up his shirtsleeve and showed the bandage covering his forearm. "I shot the animal two times in the chest, but it landed on me. Took me down to the ground. By the time I threw it off, the woman had disappeared. It was dark and pouring rain, and I had no *taschenlampe*, ah, flashlight. And then I heard a car roar away."

He took a breath before continuing.

"All this time, Grady was yelling at me to come back, so I picked up the dog and carried it back to the car."

"You took the dog?"

"Yes, sir. I thought it best not to leave any evidence. You know, the bullets inside the animal?"

Teddy took another sip. Collecting the mutt showed initiative. The Kraut had just earned back his first strike. He might be on his way to earning a full reprieve, too. Although it was too early to tell.

"Also," Schechter said, growing more confident, his voice firmer, "the rain was pouring down. It was heavy enough to obscure our tracks, I thought. And there was one other thing, Mr Tedesco."

"Which was?"

"The dog was in good condition. Despite the rain, I

could tell it had been professionally groomed. Well looked after. Expensive collar, you know?"

"So what?"

For the first time since his arrival, Schechter's shoulders relaxed a little. A ghost smile stretched his thin lips. He reached into his pocket. Timothy and Ginger stiffened and started moving forwards, but Teddy raised his glass and shook his head to send them back to their posts. In his left hand, the one not holding the tumbler, he gripped a SIG Sauer P226—the weapon of choice for the US military. Good enough for the Americans, meant good enough for him. Teddy would never be without it and, with Schechter on the other side of the desk at a distance of less than two metres, he wasn't likely to miss.

Despite the state-of-the-art gizmos protecting his office —the body scanners, the x-ray and infrared cameras, the metal detectors, and the other electronic countermeasures —Teddy was not going to drop his guard. Too many high-ranking "businessmen" had grown lazy thinking they were Teflon-coated and died as a result. Well, not Teddy Tedesco. Nobody was going to catch him on the crapper with his trousers around his ankles.

The Kraut's hand came out of the pocket holding a white, plastic disk, no bigger than the lid of a jam jar.

"If that's a bomb …"

Teddy set the tumbler on the coaster, racked the SIG, and pointed it at Schechter's face. The Kraut's eyes bulged, and his jaw slackened.

"No, sir. I-It is a microchip reader. Given the dog's well-kept condition, I-I thought it a possibility that it had been microchipped. I bought the device at a pet shop this morning."

With his thumb, Teddy pressed the gun's de-cocker to

lower the hammer and make the weapon safe, but he kept it in plain view and Schechter's eyes stayed locked on the muzzle. Hardly a surprise. Teddy'd been on the wrong end of a gun a few times in his life. There were few things in the world more terrifying than seeing the black hole open up in front of you, especially when it was being held by a nut job with evil in his heart.

"And was it?"

"Chipped? Yes, sir," Schechter said, drawing his gaze from the muzzle back to Teddy. "It was, and I now have the name and address of the owner."

He turned the scanner to let Teddy read the screen.

> Mrs Angela Shafer,
> #3 Railway Cuttings,
> Old Mill Lane,
> Hampshire.

Teddy nodded and allowed himself a congratulatory smile. The kid had done well. Saved his own life even if it did upset Timothy and Ginger, who looked as though someone had opened their last Christmas presents by mistake. Not to worry, he'd be able to feed someone else to his murder monkeys soon enough. There were always plenty of people around who tried to put one over on Teddy Tedesco. So far, none had succeeded. At least, not for long —as Tubby's ghost would confirm.

"Nice one, Schechter. What's your first name? Grady told me you were smart, but never gave me your full name."

"Hardy, sir," Schechter said, swallowing after Teddy slid the SIG back into his top drawer. "My mother named me after the actor, Hardy Kruger. She had a girlhood crush—"

"That's enough of the back story, son. Don't get too

comfortable. You're still a fuck-up. All you've done with that"—he pointed at the scanner—"is bought yourself a little grace period."

The grin fell from Schechter's face.

"Yes, sir. Sorry, sir."

"I assume the old dear went screaming to the filth?"

Schechter worked a finger between his shirt collar and his neck, and pulled. Fucker must have found it difficult to breathe in such a tight collar and with the tie done up so high. Well, sod him. He needed to show some respect and all Teddy's employees knew the correct dress code. Professional attire at all times. The Kraut should have bought a shirt with a better fit.

"Yes, sir. I have been following the investigation on the police scanners," Schechter managed to say. "As I expected, they found nothing at the quarry. It would appear they have closed the investigation, more or less."

"Any press coverage?"

"Minor reports on the local radio and in the local newspaper, but nothing national."

The information tallied with his own research. Teddy paused for a minute before retrieving the glass.

"Okay, that's acceptable. What did you do with Tubby's carcase in the end?"

"Grady knew the location of a different quarry with a lake. Apparently, there are many such abandoned workings in the region. We weighted it down with rocks, sliced the body open from here"—he pointed to a spot below his navel and ran his finger up to his sternum—"to here, to vent the accumulating gasses, and threw it off the cliff into the water. It sank like a boulder. No one will ever see Tubby Malahide's mortal remains again, sir. I promise you."

Teddy took another sip. It tasted good again.

"They'd better not, Schechter. You won't survive for long if they do."

Again, the Kraut shot him a nervous smile.

"You want me to pay a visit to Mrs Shafer? Make sure she does not speak to the police again?"

Teddy was about to agree but had second thoughts and shook his head. "No, that won't be necessary. I have a better idea. Pony's been bored recently. I'll set him on the woman. He can have his fun."

Ginger shuffled his feet and shot a sideways look at Timothy.

Timothy didn't move. He knew better.

Colour drained from the Kraut's already-pasty face.

"Pony?" Schechter asked, his voice thin and scratchy.

Inwardly, Teddy smirked. The Kraut had definitely heard the whispers. Who inside the organisation hadn't?

"You've met my little brother?" Teddy asked, already knowing the answer.

"No, sir. But I know him … by reputation."

Teddy laughed and drained his glass. His eyes watered as the rich heat scoured the back of his throat.

"So, you've heard the stories?"

Schechter dipped his head. "I have, sir. Yes."

"All true. Every single one of them. But the stories everyone knows about aren't the half of it. I could tell you some that would turn your hair white, if you weren't already an albino."

Schechter raised his right hand and smoothed his hair into place in a reflex action he probably didn't realise he was doing.

"But if you really want to know, I'll get Pony to tell you himself. Would you like that?"

Schechter shook his head emphatically. "No, thank you, sir. That will not be necessary."

"That's a shame. He loves an audience. A special case, my baby brother. Very special. Now bugger off, but keep your mobile powered up. I might need you later today. One of my tenants is a few days late on her rent."

Schechter jumped to his feet, clearly unable to leave the room quickly enough. While the Kraut's back was still turned, Timothy looked at Teddy, a question formed in an arched eyebrow.

Teddy shook his head, confirming that the trick with the microchip scanner had saved Schechter's life. Timothy nodded but couldn't hide his disappointment. Spending the first fifteen years of his life under the apartheid regime, the big South African had every reason to hate blond, white men, but he'd have to pull in his horns, for the moment.

Timothy opened the office door and Ginger escorted Schechter from the room, probably about to tell the German how close he'd been to ending up lying alongside Tubby Malahide.

Teddy grinned. No value hiding the truth from the men. They needed to be kept in line.

"Don't worry, Timothy," Teddy said, reaching for his phone. "There's a little action on the cards in Lymington. A couple of trawlermen have developed sticky fingers. You'll have plenty of opportunities to flex those big muscles of yours."

"Thank you, Mr Tedesco. Looking forward to it. Want me to leave the room while you talk to your brother?"

"What do you think?"

The big *kaffir* tapped a finger to his forehead in the nearest action he would ever make to a salute.

"Be right outside when you need me, Mr Tedesco.

Don't forget your dinner with Mrs Tedesco. Roast chicken's on the menu tonight, sir. You asked me to remind you."

Fuck. He had forgotten. So many things to think about.

"Thanks, Timothy," he said, punching buttons on the phone number pad. "I did remember. And Mother can damn well wait."

Sorry, Mother. Didn't mean it. Just for show.

Timothy closed the door quietly behind him and the call connected.

"That you, Teddy?" Pony asked with his standard, girly voice.

"And who else would be calling you on this private line, baby brother?"

"You got something interesting for me at last?"

"Fancy taking a little trip into the country with that arsehole boyfriend of yours?"

"Which one?" Pony asked, his high-pitched giggle squealed down the phone line. "I have so many."

"I was thinking of the one with the beard and the muscles, Pavlovich. You still seeing him?"

In other words, "Is he still alive?"

"No. I have a new special friend. Johnno Ashby. The sweet boy needs an education though. What's the job?"

Teddy gave him the outline.

"Any constraints? Want me to make it look like an accident?"

Teddy snorted.

"Don't care what you do so long as the bitch doesn't talk to the filth again. You can make it quick if you like but, knowing you, it'll be slow and …"

He allowed the sentence to trail off, waiting for Pony to jump in. It didn't take long.

"You know me so well, big brother. I enjoy toying with them. How old is she?"

"No idea, bro. All I have is her name and address. Want me to put one of my investigators on her?"

"Nah. Don't bother, Teddy," Pony said, using his serious "down to business" voice. "Doing the deep background stuff makes it all the more fun. Adds to the enjoyment, you know? The excitement of the hunt tastes every bit as sweet as the kill itself. By the time I'm finished, I'll know everything about her from her favourite hairdresser to her daughter's bra size. Assuming she has a daughter."

Again, he broke off to giggle—a sound that prickled the fine hairs on Teddy's neck.

"Give me a few days and I'll have her begging for release." He let out the breathless laugh that must have made his victims wet themselves. "And I don't mean the sweet release of a good, long screw, if you know what I mean, bro."

Teddy wrinkled his nose in disgust.

"Spare me the details, Pony. Just get the job done and make sure no one finds the body. Disposing of a stiff is what gave us this problem in the first place."

"Ah, Teddy. You were always the squeamish one. But I don't think of this as a problem. Oh no. This situation is what I like to call an *opportunity*!"

The line clicked dead on Pony's intimidating laugh. Teddy dropped the phone in its cradle. For a brief moment, he almost felt sorry for the Shafer woman. He shuddered again.

Poor cow.

Still, business was business. Move on or move out. Time to dress for dinner. Mother did so love to see him in a smart suit.

Chapter Two

Friday 27th November – Angela Shafer

Spire Road, Andover, Hampshire, England

In the dark behind Angela, a door slammed. The hollow noise boomed through the near-deserted car park. Footsteps clacked, hurrying towards her. Was it *him*?

Oh God. Why can't he leave me alone?

The breath caught in her throat. She increased her pace, up on her toes, avoiding heel-strike, trying to quieten her footfalls.

Where did she park the car? There. Up ahead. The other side of Brian's Volvo.

She tried to calm her rapid gasping. Could he hear her breathing? Could he see her in the poor light? God, was he there, hiding in the darkness?

The chasing footsteps faltered, shuffled, continued. He hadn't seen her, didn't know where she was. She ducked, keeping below the roof level of the few remaining cars. She should have left with the others, but there was always one more thing to do. Brian needed the Brick Street property details for the morning's viewing, and she'd volunteered to stay late.

Stupid, stupid woman.

Still on the move, panting, heart thumping, shivering, she fished in her handbag for the car keys, gripping them tight. She reached the Volvo and ducked between it and her battered Fiat. The button on her key fob hadn't worked for years. Couldn't use it anyway. The flashing indicators would give away her position.

She pushed the key into the lock, turned, tried the handle. Nothing. Still locked.

God! The other way. Turn the key the other way! Idiot!

The footsteps drew closer, louder, echoing through the car park. *He* was there! Nearly upon her.

Angela tried again and turned the key anti-clockwise. The alarm disengaged, and the door buttons popped. More noise. Inside on her plastic seats, she slammed the door closed and pressed the security door lock. The buttons popped again.

Safe. Oh God, safe.

Angela sat, stiff but shivering, gripping the steering wheel with both hands, trying to quell the shakes. The keys dug into her palm, hurting, but she couldn't relax her grip until the panic attack faded.

Knuckles rapped on her driver's window.

Angela jumped. A short screech burst from her mouth.

She spun to face the noise. The hand tapped again. Its

owner bent at the waist. A familiar face appeared. Smiling. Friendly.

Brian! Thank God.

"Angela, are you okay?"

She breathed again.

"Brian, you ... startled me. I was miles away. Just a sec."

She jabbed the key into the ignition and turned it enough to feed power to the windows. She hit the button and waited for the glass to shudder down its channels in the doorframe.

Brian grinned at her through the opening.

"Sorry to scare you. Should have called out. Forgive me."

"No, no. It's my fault. I've had so much on my mind since ... well, you know. And with Bobbie away at university, I've been left on my own, stewing."

If only that were all. She tried returning his smile, but it felt unnatural—forced.

Brian stepped back from the car and stood up straight. Typical of the man, so thoughtful. He didn't want to crowd her.

"Yes, I know. Things have been tough on you recently, and I ... we ... I mean everyone at the office wants you to know we're here for you. If there's anything you need. You didn't take any time off after the ... after the plane crash. We all care about you, you know?"

Angela's face heated. Embarrassed by his gentle and supportive words.

"I do know. Thank you. Everyone's been so very kind. You and Alan in particular." She straightened her shoulders. "Was there something you wanted?"

Brian frowned in the way he did when trying to remember something lost and on the tip of his tongue.

"Ah yes, right," he said, fidgeting in his jacket pocket, still frowning, but less so. The ridges on his forehead softened. "You left this on your desk." His hand came out holding her mobile phone. "I thought you might need it tonight."

She sighed and took it from his hand, trying to show gratitude and hide the fear haunting her life. "Thank you, Brian. You didn't have to go out of your way."

He smiled his disarming, warm smile again. Her heart rate slowed a little, and the shakes diminished with it. If she confided in him, would he help? Could he? No, she couldn't do it to him. Brian had a family—Beatrice and the girls— and telling him would put them in danger, too.

Why was this happening to her? What had she ever done to deserve it?

"You might need it," Brian said, casting his eyes over her ancient, little Fiat, which was one more MOT failure away from the scrapyard. "You have a long drive home. And Old Mill Lane is awfully quiet this time of night. I'd hate for you to be caught without a mobile if this old wreck packs up on you."

A stab of fear returned to halt her heart, as the thought of the long drive home to her quiet, empty, exposed, little house suddenly terrified her.

How had *he* found her? How did *he* know where she lived?

Brian leaned back, still taking in the old car with its rust and its dings, shaking his head sadly. "Do we really pay you that poorly?"

"Excuse me?"

"Well, I might be stepping out of bounds here, but your car is a wreck. I hate the idea of you breaking down in the middle of nowhere. And it's not as though you can resort to public transport, not in that rural backwater of yours."

He laughed at his own joke—Hampshire hardly justified the tag "rural backwater".

"I mean, there aren't any buses out where you live. Why don't you upgrade? If finances are a problem, Alan and I would be happy to countersign a loan application. We might even consider some sort of leasing arrangement on the business." He paused and shook his head. "Oh, sorry, I'm being pushy again, aren't I?"

"No, no. Not at all."

Shocked anyone would care, Angela fought back the threatened tears. She so wanted to confide in him, but no. No. She couldn't take the risk.

"Well," she managed to say through her nerves and the sense of gratitude, "as it happens, money isn't an issue. In fact, I've been considering changing cars recently, but … it's just … I've been too busy."

Maybe she should leave the area. Up sticks and run. She had enough money now, but the man on the phone had found her once and she couldn't guarantee that he wouldn't find her again.

Dear Lord, what could she do?

"Is anything wrong, Angela?"

"N-Nothing. Why do you ask?"

He opened his hands in a shrug. "It's just that for the past few days you've been so distracted. Most unlike you. I know your sister passed away recently, but … Alan and I have been worried it's more than that. Is it something either of us have done or said? Or not done and not said?"

"You've been talking about me?" she snapped.

She didn't want to snap but couldn't help it. Her nerves had been shredded ever since Breaker's Folly.

"No, Angela. It's nothing like that. We're worried for you. Actually, we're being selfish. The office would grind to a dismal halt without you holding it together for us."

"Oh, I'm … really grateful, but there's nothing you can do. It's just that … I'm missing Jackie."

That's right, you coward. Blame everything on your dead sister when she has nothing at all to do with it.

"Sometimes," she continued, losing herself in the moment, "I see a figure in the street, and I call out, thinking it's her. Then I'll be sitting in front of the TV and remember watching the same show with Jackie and find tears rolling down my cheeks. No reason, no stopping it either. It kills me every time I see a news report of the crash."

Brian pushed a hand through the open window, breaking the barrier between them. He rested it on her shoulder. The first time they'd touched since hugging at Jackie's memorial. A funeral with no body. Jackie's remains still lay at the bottom of the North Sea. Divers had recovered the black box flight recorders and most of the aircraft, but not all the bodies. The risk and expense wasn't deemed worth the reward and she and Bobbie had ended up burying an empty casket.

Brian pulled his hand away. "It's only been a couple of months," he said. "Your emotions are bound to be raw, but they'll ease. I promise."

He meant well, but his words didn't help. She took a tissue from a packet stuffed in the pocket of her car door and wiped the tears. Turning her head away, she blew her nose and crushed the tissue into a tight, little ball.

"Listen, Angela, do you have any plans for tonight? We could have dinner if you like. Talk things over."

Angela looked at him in shock.

"What about Beatrice and the girls? Won't they be waiting for you?"

Brian's mouth dropped open and his eyes bugged. "My word, no. I didn't mean it that way. I meant for you to come home for dinner with the family. I'd call ahead. Beatrice and the girls would be delighted to see you again."

Angela threw her hand up to cover her mouth. How embarrassing. What was wrong with her?

"I-I'm sorry. Didn't mean it like that. I was just worried they'd wonder where you were. Thanks again for bringing my phone, and thanks for the offer of dinner, but I already have plans for tonight. I'll see you in the morning. Bright and early."

She turned the key in the ignition. The Fiat coughed into life and belched out a cloud of dirty, blue exhaust fumes. Brian stepped away, his nose wrinkled.

As usual, the transmission crunched as she engaged first gear and pulled the car slowly out of her space. She left the car park with the image of a bemused and waving Brian D'Costa burned into her memory.

He'd been completely correct about Old Mill Lane. Eight miles of winding, two-lane road, deserted and unlit after sunset, it would be one of the worst places in the region to break down. She'd never even tried dialling from her car—and why would she? Although a mere twenty miles from Southampton, for all she knew, the place was a communications black spot.

After a slow but uneventful drive, she crunched into a lower gear to negotiate the tight turn into Railway Cuttings and slowed right down to make the sharp corner into her driveway. A terrace of three Victorian cottages faced her. The one on the end bought by Mum and Dad in 1986. He'd been so proud of the place. His first and, as it turned out, only house purchase. He'd renovated it and lavished great care on it until Mum died. After that, he curled into a metaphoric ball and allowed the place to disintegrate slowly around them all.

No lights on in any of the windows.

Oh God.

She'd be alone in the Cuttings again.

The other two houses in the row were second homes, owned by London couples who only visited on weekends and during the holidays. Before *he* started calling, her cottage had seemed peaceful and safe, but now … it stood out silent, ominous, and scary.

She drove the wheezing Fiat onto her gravel drive and turned the ignition key. The engine spluttered on for a few more turns before coughing and dying. What did that mean? Why didn't it just stop?

Angela rolled down the window and strained her ears, listening for anything unexpected. The wind whistled in the conifers behind the cottages, a cat mewled, a motorbike roared along the nearby road, but nothing stood out as unusual. No strange cars filled the other drives. No unusual sounds. No smells.

She took a steadying breath.

Since Breaker's Folly, her life had been one long, waking nightmare. The police had found nothing and basically accused her of fabricating the whole story. During their final meeting before he closed the case, the silver-haired detective sergeant actually asked whether she was taking any medication. The fool indirectly suggested she'd imagined the whole affair.

"If I've been hallucinating, where's Lady?" she'd asked, slapping her hand on the desk between them in the cold, grey interview room.

"Perhaps your dog simply ran off. Did she like to chase rabbits?"

"She's a Border Collie. They are bred to herd sheep and cows. She doesn't chase rabbits. She was shot, I tell you. Shot dead!"

The policeman frowned impatiently at her before checking his watch.

"Mrs Shafer," he said in the condescending way officials often used when bothersome members of the public interrupted their tea break. "As I told you earlier, we searched Breaker's Folly thoroughly and found nothing. I'm sure your dog will find her way home. Have you considered posting a reward?"

He stood, pointed her to the door, and that was that. The policeman dismissed her as though she meant nothing. On her way home, she fumed, contemplating ways to punish the man for his laziness. She'd call the local paper, the radio. She even considered talking to her solicitor, the one handling Jackie's estate, but she didn't get that far. The man with the quiet, posh voice and the scary laugh started calling.

The first call interrupted her typing the email to her solicitor. At first, she thought it was a cold call, a man selling life insurance. He knew her name and address, and was very polite. Then he told her not to talk to the police again, threatening all sorts of harm to her and Bobbie if she did so.

He knew about Bobbie!

Morning and night, he called. Said he'd be watching her and would pounce when she least expected. Whenever she lowered her guard.

Dear Lord, what am I going to do?

Sitting in the car with her hands still gripping the wheel

tight, warm tears ran down her cheeks. She'd never felt so scared. Not just for herself, but for Bobbie, too.

Again, she listened to the night. Again, she heard nothing unexpected. Could she leave the car and brave the darkness? Her house stood no more than ten metres away, waiting for her, bathed in the Fiat's headlights. It offered sanctuary, but something stopped her moving.

Maybe the man had been bluffing. Maybe she had nothing to worry about. Bobbie was safe in Norwich, and she could move on with her life. After all, what had Angela really seen? What could she really do if the police wouldn't listen?

With teeth gritted, she unpeeled her hands from the steering wheel and turned off the headlights. She rolled up the window, removed the key from the ignition, and grabbed her handbag, clutching it to her chest as though it would protect her.

She reached for the door handle and pulled. The lock clicked, the door screeched open, and the courtesy light flashed a dim yellow. She sniffed the air, but the lingering stench of unburned exhaust fumes told her nothing other than her car needed a completely new exhaust system. Well, no, thank you. She'd waste no more money fixing a car that was so old and so tired. She was going to buy a brand-new car. A BMW or a Mercedes. A white one with leather seats.

Lord, how her mind wandered.

Concentrate, Angela.

She sniffed again, but no strange smells—no aftershave warning her of *him*—could have punched through the odour of partially burned premium unleaded.

Unsatisfied by her precautions, but unable to see an alternative, Angela unclipped the seatbelt and climbed out of the car. Ten more paces and she'd be home, safe again for another night.

The courtesy light in the car stayed on long enough for her to identify the Chubb key to the front door. The movement-activated security light over the front door would help, but she wanted the key ready to avoid delay.

A hand fisted in her hair. Before she could scream, a second hand clamped over her mouth. A hard body slammed into her back, forcing her against the side of the car.

Oh God!

"Told you I would come, Angela. Didn't think I was kidding, did you?"

He cackled.

A firm bulge, where a man's groin would be, pressed against her backside. Her knees buckled, legs unable to take her weight, but he held her mashed against the side of the car. Crushed and helpless.

Oh God. Please. No.

She tried to struggle but he was too strong. Too solid. Immovable.

She should have gone home with Brian and his family.

Family ... her family. Bobbie.

How was she going to save Bobbie?

Oh God. Please make it quick. Please make it be over.

Chapter Three

Friday 27th November – Angela Shafer

Old Mill Lane, Andover, Hampshire, England

Hot, nicotine-fouled breath scorched Angela's ear.

"Did you think I was lying, bitch?"

Tightening his grip on her hair, the man forced her face against the roof of the car. The freezing metal burned her skin. She whimpered as he ground his hips harder into her buttocks. The bulge felt bigger, more solid.

Her crying out aroused him?

Quiet, Angela. Be quiet. Don't encourage him.

If she stayed calm, maybe she'd find a way out. Her phone. Could she reach it? No, too dangerous.

Stupid woman, he'll kill you.

She had to stay alive. Stay alive for Bobbie.

"We're going to have some fun, you and me."

He chuckled, the same mirthless laugh he'd used on the phone. Angela closed her eyes and clamped her knees together, trying not to pee.

"Well," he continued, "not sure how much fun it'll be for you darling, but me? I'll be having a ball."

Car headlights snapped on, flooding her front garden in their harsh, white glow.

Saved! She was saved!

She struggled, fought, twisted around to face the car.

"Help! Please help!"

She bucked her head. Screamed again. Flailed her arms. Reached up and behind, trying to find the man's eyes with her long fingernails.

He jerked his head away, out of reach. His arms were too long, too powerful. She couldn't get close and turned her fingers to scratch the exposed skin at his wrists.

The animal, the pig, snarled. He cracked her head into the car's side pillar. Blinding lights flashed behind her eyes.

The pig's cruel laugh echoed through the night.

"Stupid bitch," he said. "No one's here to help you, and I don't need any assistance, thank you very much. I can do whatever I want to you all by myself. I'm going to take this slow and steady, and I'm going to enjoy every single second. Those headlights aren't from a knight in shining armour, darling. There is no Good Samaritan. Oh dear me, no. They're from my car, and that's Johnno driving it. He's my ride home. He likes to watch, too. Might even join in when I'm finished with you. If there's anything left of you for him to play with, that is."

He stopped talking long enough to lick her neck. She nearly retched.

"Now, let's go in the house. It's cold out here, and I do like my central heating."

Without warning, he dragged her by her hair, forcing her along the path with him. She caught sight of his face for the first time.

He wasn't one of the men she'd seen at the Folly. More than two people involved. A gang? God, how many of them were there? One of these people shot Lady. Why hadn't she kept her stupid mouth shut?

Pig's evil smile showed clean, perfectly aligned teeth. Dark eyes but pale skin, almost translucent in the harsh light of the car's full beams. A clear view. No mask. She could see his face, and he didn't care.

She was going to die. He was going to kill her!

Headlights bathed the scene bright as day. Yet her attacker didn't waver. His smile widened, and he nodded towards the other car.

Warm pee dribbled down her legs. Angela couldn't stop her lower lip trembling and her chin jumping. Tears rippled her vision, ran down her nose. She sniffled, and the man's eyes sparkled.

Showing fear *did* excite him.

Be brave, Angela. Show him nothing.

She had to stay strong. Stay alive for Bobbie. Keep him talking. Maybe it would help. Give her time to find a way out.

"W-Why are you doing this?"

Pig's evil smile broadened. "Haven't you got it yet, sweetheart? I'm doing it because I enjoy inflicting pain. Because I enjoy fucking people who don't want to be fucked. Men or women. Boys or girls. I don't care. Do you get it now, darling? I'm going to make you plead for mercy, and then I'm going to kill you."

"P-Please don't hurt me. I'll be good. You can do what-ever you want, but I'll—"

He yanked her hair again. Pulled her closer.

"You'll be good? You'll be *good*? Yeah, darling, you'll be excellent. This is going to be the best sex I've had for weeks. By the time I've finished with you, there won't be a hole I haven't rammed, or a piece of your flesh I haven't tasted. We've got all weekend, baby. You are going to be *so* good."

It wasn't happening. It couldn't be happening. She'd wake in a minute, sweating and screaming. She'd had panic attacks before, nightmares. But her scalp hurt where he'd torn it, and her cut cheek bled inside her mouth.

No, not a nightmare. Reality.

"Johnno! Get over here!"

The headlights snapped off. A car door opened and slammed shut. Footsteps crunched on gravel.

"W-What do you want me to do?" Johnno asked, meek as a kitten.

Pig wrenched her hair and rammed her head against his hip to hold her in place. She scrambled sideways. Bent at the waist, she had to grab the back of his jacket to avoid falling and losing more hair.

"Either kick the front door open, or find her keys, you fuckwit!"

They were going inside. The hall. What could she use? Something. Anything. The telephone table. She could swing it. Smash Pig's head in. But what about the other one? What about Johnno?

An open-handed blow clapped her cheek, rattling her teeth and slamming her head against the bony part of his hip. Once again, lights flashed behind her closed eyes.

"Where are your keys, bitch?"

Angela could barely hear him through the ringing in her

ears. It hurt so much. Maybe if he hit her again, she'd lose consciousness and miss the worst of what was to come.

He pulled her hair again. She squealed, scrunched her shoulders to protect her ears, grabbed his jacket. So much hurt. So much pain.

Don't cry. Don't let him hear you cry.

"Answer me or I'll smash the window open with your face. Don't try my patience, woman."

Although his words were vicious and callous, the only time he'd raised his voice was to call Johnno from the car. Somehow, the quiet, controlled speech was scarier than when he yelled. She answered. Couldn't help herself.

"By my ... my handbag," she said. It was all she could manage.

He pulled her head up until it was level with his once more. She had to stand on tiptoes and put her hands on his chest for balance. His pecs tightened, and his sneer turned to a smirk.

Petrified, she froze. She couldn't pull her hands away. She couldn't move.

"Where is it?"

"I-I dropped it."

"Stupid bitch."

Johnno moved in the darkness. Gravel scattered. Clouds rolled away.

"Here they are," he said quickly, sounding eager to please. "I have them."

The keys rattled on the ring.

More footsteps. The gate opened, hinges screeched. Somewhere in the back of her mind, she remembered the can of lubricating oil on the top shelf of the garage.

Why was she worrying about that now, of all times?

Johnno scurried along the path to the front door,

searching through the keys. The security light snapped on, blinding her.

"Come with me, you," Pig said.

He lowered his hand and started walking, forcing her to crab along beside him. She had no choice. His fingers tangled tighter in her hair, pulling, wrenching. Hurting.

Her hair would be such a mess. Would Geraldine be able to rescue it?

Hair? You're worried about your bloody hair?

Johnno reached the front door, pushed it open, and found the light switch. Her hallway. Her home. It should have been a sanctuary, but … the phone stand!

She reached out for it, but Pig moved too quickly, pulling her through the hallway, following his acolyte towards the front room. Johnno turned on more lights. The curtains would be open. Someone passing might see, might help.

But, no. At night, the lane would be quiet. Lonely. No one would drive past. No one would save her.

Pig dragged her into the front room, threw her on the single chair in the corner, and stepped closer. She kicked out. Landed a glancing blow to his shin.

"Fucking bitch!"

Angela barely saw his hand move before his fist smashed into her face.

———

SOFTNESS BENEATH HER. Nothing above.

Warm air. Quiet.

"Wake up, darling. Wouldn't want you to miss any of the fun."

Angela squeezed her eyes tight shut, but a slap stung her cheek and spun her head. She had to look.

"Awake now?"

Her front room. Still alive. Why?

Sore. Everything hurt.

Pig stood above her, a cruel smile twisting his lips. Lights on, curtains still open. He knew they wouldn't be disturbed. She was alone, helpless with a madman. No, two madmen.

Johnno stood in the open doorway. Watching, silent, face pale.

She was alone with two men. Totally vulnerable. She stared at Johnno. Dressed the same as the pig, but half the size and about ten years younger. He looked at her with what, pity? Could she use that information somehow? Would he help her?

"Yes, that's better," Pig said, rubbing his hands together. "Now we can get started."

He reached for her blouse, undid her buttons one at a time, slowly. What had happened to her jacket, her overcoat?

The blouse parted, exposing her bra, her skin. Her belly trembled. She moved her arms to cover herself, but he grabbed her wrists and twisted them outwards. It hurt, but she gritted her teeth, trying not to cry out. It was what he wanted.

Still smiling, Pig kept twisting. Pain.

He was breaking her arms.

"Stop, please," she whimpered.

He released her wrists and grabbed her hair again, forcing her head towards him, tearing more out from the roots. He stopped when her face was centimetres from his groin. The outline of his penis stood out clear through his tight trousers.

Oh God, no.

Pig's white shirt—starched and perfectly pressed—clung to his flat stomach. His free hand moved lower, its thumb hooked into his leather belt.

"Like what you see, darling? Want some of this meat inside you? Think you can take it all, do you?"

If she just allowed him to get it over with, gave him what he wanted, maybe he'd let her go.

Anything, Angela. Do anything. Stay alive. Survive.

"Don't hurt me. Please don't hurt me anymore."

Pig's grip on her hair tightened, his other hand reached for the zip, then pulled away.

"'Please don't hurt me anymore'," he mocked. "Darling, I haven't even started yet. I told you, we have all weekend."

Her cheek throbbed from where he'd hit her. She'd bitten her tongue and her cheek, and tasted blood. More than one tooth in her head was loose, but if he put his thing anywhere near her mouth, she'd bite down and bite down hard. Her stomach lurched at the thought of what he'd do afterwards, but she'd bite down anyway.

She turned to stare at Johnno, trying to lock eyes with him, but the creature looked away.

Coward. You filthy coward.

Pig slapped her again. Not as hard as before, but hard enough to rattle her teeth.

"Look at me, not Johnno. I'm the one in control!"

She lifted her eyes and stared into his.

Dark, they were. Empty of all, even hate.

"After I've fucked and killed you, I'm going to leave your body to rot. Got it?"

She tried to nod, but his fist in her hair was too tight.

"Yes, yes, I—"

"Then I'm going to pay a visit to Norwich."

Bobbie? He knows where Bobbie is? How?

Fear changed to terror. Terror became anger, rage.

"W-What did you say?"

"Yeah, that's right. Finally getting the message?"

Pig turned to his minion.

"Hear that, Johnno?" he said. "The bitch is finally getting the message."

He pulled her forwards on the chair and pushed his head towards her face.

"Oh yes, we know all about your daughter. Pretty, like you, only young and fresh. Nice, big tits, too. Bigger than yours and firmer. None of that middle-aged, wrinkly, drooping bollocks. And none of that flabby belly shit, either."

He punched her in the stomach, knocking the wind out of her. She gasped and pulled her knees up to her chest, struggling for breath. Darkness encroached at the edges of her vision.

Bobbie! Oh God, Bobbie. What have I done?

Pig continued. "When I'm finished with you, dearie, Johnno and I are going to pay darling Bobbie a little visit. We'll be able to compare notes. You or your brat. Which one's a better fuck."

"Bastard!" Angela gasped. "Don't you touch my daughter. I'll kill you!"

She struggled. Kicked out, aiming for his shins again, but she missed, and it only made him laugh louder.

"That's it, bitch. I love it when they fight back. Much more enjoyable. Johnno!" he yelled. "Time to have some fun. Come here."

Johnno didn't move.

Pig pinned her head to the back of the chair by her hair. He grabbed her breast and mashed it against her ribcage.

Angela tried to push his hand away. He punched her in the face and grabbed both her wrists, holding them together in one hand. He wrenched her arms over her head. Hot tears flooded her cheeks.

"Bastard!" she screamed. "Animal! Pig!"

She kicked out again, aiming for his groin this time, but he twisted, and her shoe glanced the side of his hip.

"Fucking bitch."

He hit her again and again, and the strength ebbed away. Vomit rose, burned her throat. She swallowed it back.

The pig took hold of her skirt and pulled up. The gash he had for a mouth spread into another grin.

"Now, open wide, honey ... this is going to hurt."

———

ANGELA STARED at the ceiling the whole time Pig was on top of her, grunting, tearing, thrusting, pummelling. Breathing on her. Hot, wet, foul air. Used air. Staring at her without blinking, his eyes empty, dead. He was waiting for her to react.

She didn't.

She was numb and sore and humiliated and angry and terrified. But she gave him nothing. The whole time he was on her, in her, Angela chewed her cheek, tasting blood. It reminded her she was still alive. She had to keep going—for Bobbie.

Fighting Pig had only brought pain and a few moments of blackness. He was too big, too strong. Nothing seemed to hurt him.

Angela crawled inside herself. She withdrew from the room. She visited Bobbie in Norwich. A beautiful city. Lots of flowers that smelled so nice in the warm, summer sun.

Clean and light and bright and happy. The cathedral with its spire pointing to heaven, reaching up to God.

Where was God now?

Why had he deserted her?

———

THE PIG GRUNTED AGAIN. Pulled out of her and punched her in the mouth, laughing.

"Not bad," he said. "I've had worse. Your turn, Johnno. I've warmed her up for you."

Oh God. No!

Her body responded and she screamed. Tried to sit up, but the pig held her down, slapped her again.

Johnno, still by the door, watched but did nothing. A strange expression clouded his face. Was he enjoying it? Getting aroused? He was going to be next. Take his turn. But did he want to? Why did she care?

God, stop this, please. Let it be over.

"No, I-I can't," Johnno said, shaking his head, waving his hands in front of his chest. "Don't make me."

Pig pushed himself to his feet and pulled up his underwear and trousers. "Get over here, fuckwit. I'm taking a breather. Your turn. Make her suffer."

Angela curled into a tight ball and covered her face with her hands. She cried through closed eyes, trembling. She wanted to throw up, but nothing happened when her stomach rippled.

No more. Please, no more.

Outside, a door crashed open.

An explosion and a flash of blinding, white light.

Johnno flew through the air, screaming. The coffee table splintered under his crashing weight.

Someone—a man—yelled, "Down on the floor!"

Another shouted, "Get down! Do it now!"

A man dressed head-to-toe in black raced through the open doorway. A second followed close behind.

Pig spun. His hand reached into his pocket.

Angela's eyes stung, and her ears rang.

A blue-white light flashed.

Rapid clicks followed, partially drowned out by Pig's agonised screams. His eyes rolled up into his head and he collapsed in a heap on the floor in front of her, twitching and convulsing. Blood dribbled from his mouth and his hands clenched into fists. Feet thrashing and legs flailing wildly.

Bastard!

Angela kicked out. The pointed toe of her shoe connected with Pig's jaw. He fell backwards, and his head cracked against Johnno's knee. He stopped moving. She jumped up, screamed, kicked him again, and stamped her foot into his groin. Something soft and squidgy moved beneath her heel.

"Bastard!' she wailed and stamped again. "Bastard, bastard!"

She raised her knee again but lost balance and teetered sideways. The first man in black rushed forwards, one hand outstretched.

Angela screamed and threw out her arms to fend him off. She fell, hit the carpet hard, and scrambled on her backside, hands and feet scurrying, pushing her into the corner of the room.

"No more. Oh God. Please, no more!"

Chapter Four

Friday 27th November – Angela Shafer

Old Mill Lane, Andover, Hampshire, England

The first man in black clipped a strange-looking, plastic gun into his black canvas belt and raised both black-gloved hands, palms forward, showing them empty. He squatted in front of her.

"Angela. Angela Shafer," he said, his voice quiet, but calm and gentle. Not at all like Pig's. "You're safe now. These men won't hurt you anymore, I promise."

The man with the soft voice and sad, brown eyes lowered his knees to the carpet and sat back on his haunches, keeping his distance, and blocking her view of Pig and Johnno.

"I'm so, so sorry we couldn't get here sooner. I can't

imagine what you must have gone through, Angela. But I promise you this, you're safe now."

Angela hugged her knees to her chest with one arm, while trying to pull her tattered clothing together with the other.

The man turned to his partner. "Corporal, run upstairs and fetch a cover from a bedroom. I'll watch these two."

The corporal rushed from the room and returned seconds later, carrying the quilt from her bed. He handed it to the first man, who'd done nothing in the corporal's absence but turn sideways and keep a steady eye on Pig and Johnno.

"Here you go, Captain," the corporal said quietly. "Mind looking after Angela while I deal with the rubbish?"

"Thanks," the man with the gentle voice, the captain, said. "You make a start. I'll give you a hand in a sec."

The corporal handed the quilt to the captain, who placed it on the floor by her feet. After that, he stood and backed away, giving her space to breathe. His actions calmed her, eased her panic.

Slowly, feeling returned to her hands and feet … and everywhere in between. Her body ached, her thighs stung, and her torn scalp burned.

"Take your time, Angela. There's no rush."

He knew her name. How? Who were they? Who were these men who'd saved her life?

Angela reached out a tentative hand, snatched the quilt, and tucked it around her body and under her backside. At first, the cotton was cold and made her shiver, but slowly, the warmth arrived. And with the warmth came the discomfort.

Don't think about it. Don't think about it. It never happened.

But it *had* happened, and she'd never be the same again. But at least Bobbie was safe. She was safe, wasn't she?

"Oh God. Bobbie!"

The words came out mumbled through swollen, painful lips. She spoke them half in her head, half aloud.

The captain turned. "What was that, Angela?"

She buried her face in the quilt and shook her head. The men had saved her life, but could she really trust them? They were men and men were evil bastards. All of them.

She'd never trust a man ever again.

But this man—these men—had saved her.

God! So confused.

The captain spoke again, still keeping a distinct gap between them. "Don't worry, we'll be here when you're ready to talk. Is there anything you need?"

Again, she shook her head, but she wanted to scream.

Bobbie.

What could she do about Bobbie? Should she tell Bobbie about the attack, warn her? Were they still in danger now that Pig and Johnno were under arrest?

Arrest? But were they under arrest?

There had been no proper police warning, just shouts and the explosion.

Corporal?

The captain had called the other one Corporal. Had the army come to save her? Why the army?

So many questions, but no answers.

And wouldn't the police have arrived in greater numbers? Where were the blue lights and the sirens and ... who'd called them? The police couldn't have arrived in time, not from Andover.

No, they weren't the police, but who?

God, she was rambling. Her mind flitted around, trying

to focus on anything, anything but what had happened. The sneering, grunting, smiling Pig with his … with his …

Stop it, Angela.

Keeping between Angela and her attackers, the captain and his corporal bound the men's wrists and ankles with the sort of plastic strips electricians used to bundle wires together.

Pig stirred and groaned.

Angela whimpered and tried to drive herself deeper into the corner.

Pig shook his head and strained against the bindings. "Cut me loose, you stupid fucker. Do you know who I am?"

"No," the captain answered, cold and menacing at the same time, "but I'm sure you're going to tell me in the end. And mind your language, there's a lady present."

"That fucking bitch is dead meat! Hear me? Fucking dead meat. You too, moron. I'm adding you to my fucking list!"

"That's more than enough from you, *mister*."

The captain unclipped the plastic device from his belt, rammed it into Pig's neck, and pressed a button. The arc of blue light appeared again, along with the clicking. Pig convulsed, squealed, and fell still and silent. Although Johnno hadn't moved since collapsing on the coffee table, the captain repeated the procedure on him. The smaller man juddered, frothed at the mouth, and, after the captain released the button, lay still.

For the briefest moment, Angela wanted to rush into her kitchen for a carving knife to hack off Pig's penis, but she couldn't force her legs to do anything but tremble.

The captain showed her the device.

"Stun gun," he said gently. "Fifty thousand volts to the jugular. He'll think twice about swearing for a while."

The military men dragged Pig and Johnno from the room by their ankles, allowing their heads to bounce over the threshold and crack on the floor tiles in the hall. They left her alone in a room, in a home she no longer recognised as her sanctuary.

Such a mess. Broken furniture. Dark stains on the pale chair in the corner—a chair she would never sit in again. Cushions thrown on the floor. Oh Lord, Bobbie's photo on the mantelpiece.

She'd never be able to stay there alone without being reminded of what Pig had done to her.

Her stomach churned. Bile rose to her throat, and she retched. She rolled over and grabbed the rubbish bin. Acid vomit surged, exploded, splashed. She lowered the bin to the floor, pushed it away, spent. Exhausted.

By the time the captain returned, Angela's tears had stopped rolling down her cheeks, and her stuttering breathing had calmed a little.

"W-Who are you?"

He smiled gently. "You know who we are, Angela. You asked for our help. I'm just desperately sorry we couldn't reach you sooner."

"What?"

"If you don't mind, we'll do the introductions later, when you've recovered a little more. For now, call me … Peter. My associate's name is Danny. Mind if I have a seat?"

She shook her head. "N-No, of course not."

He chose the clean single seater across the room from her, but leaned forwards, elbows resting on knees, as though ready for instant action.

"Is there anything I can get you?" He sniffed and his eyes turned towards the rubbish bin. "A glass of water?"

"N-No, I just need … time."

"Okay, I understand."

"W-What are you going to do to them?" she asked, looking first at the broken coffee table and then at the door.

"Don't worry about those two. As I said earlier, they won't be bothering you again." He paused and studied her. "Your face looks … painful. It must hurt like the devil."

Angela touched fingers to her cheek. It was swollen, but numb, and the bleeding inside her mouth had stopped. Other parts of her hurt more, much more. The captain, Peter, must have known that, but chose not to draw attention to it. Did he feel sorry for her, or disgusted by her?

Both?

After what Pig had done, Peter must think she was damaged, tainted.

She stared at his face, searching for contempt, and found nothing but calmness and … sympathy.

No, she wasn't being fair on him.

His actions had shown nothing but empathy. Others might show distain, but not Peter, and not his friend, Danny.

"Someone's on the way. She'll tend to your injuries but, in the meantime, would you like to take a shower?"

She stared at him. What was he getting at?

"Won't that destroy the, um …"

Angela squeezed her eyes closed. What on earth was it called? She'd seen a TV show about it only the other week. Her head was a mess. Couldn't concentrate. Her mind wandered about all over the place.

"Forensic evidence?" Peter suggested.

"Yes, that's right. Forensics. In the TV shows I've watched—"

"You want to take this to court, Angela?"

She paused, thinking about all she'd read about rape

trials—God she'd used the word "rape". The worst four-letter word imaginable. Couldn't even think it without quivering, let alone say the word aloud. She'd never use it again.

A court case.

Did she want a court case?

All the questions and the scrutiny. The thought of dragging Bobbie into the horror of legal proceedings hit her almost as hard as the blows Pig had rained down on her. Angela's belly, bruised and sore where he'd beaten her, fluttered.

"What are you suggesting?" she asked, forcing her voice to sound stronger, more normal. "Are you going to let them go? He threatened Bobbie."

Peter pursed his lips and fixed her with his warm, brown eyes. Like dark chocolate. Kind eyes. Nice eyes.

"As for those two, there's no need to worry about them. They won't hurt you or your daughter. You have my word."

God, he knows Bobbie's my daughter!

Angela fought to keep the remaining contents of her stomach down. The shivering returned.

"H-How do you know Bobbie's my daughter?"

"You told us, Angela. It was in your message."

Fear gave way to confusion, and in turn gave way to relief as the information fell into place like the pieces of the jigsaw puzzles Bobbie used to love as a child.

"You're from the website? The 83 Trust?"

His sad smile returned, this time it seemed more encouraging. "Yes, and we'd have been here earlier if our … transport hadn't been delayed by this morning's storm. You have no idea how sorry I am, Angela. We tried hiring a helicopter, but they were all grounded."

A helicopter? Where had they come from? Abroad?

Angela shook her head. The movement hurt her neck

and shoulders. Searing pain throbbed behind her eyes. She winced and bit her lower lip.

"Are you certain you don't need anything? Danny won't be long. He makes a half-decent cuppa these days. Taught him myself, and it didn't take that long. A couple of two-hour lectures. A fast learner is our Danny." Another smile softened his face. "Don't worry about Bobbie, either. I sent two of my friends to Norwich to protect her."

The emotions she'd been trying to hold back broke through the dam. Relief overwhelmed her. Angela dropped her face into her hands. She rocked back and forwards against the wall, bawling.

Words tumbled from her mouth, unbidden, uncontrolled.

"I was so scared. All the time he was … he was … all the time. Smiling. Leering. Speaking quietly. Vile words. He said he'd kill me and then he'd turn on Bobbie. I tried to fight … kicked and scratched but … Oh God … he was so strong. He … he enjoyed it. Then he wanted the … other one to take over … oh God. What am I going to do?"

She rocked and cried, releasing all the anger, the fear, the pain.

Peter let her rant until she ran out of energy, until she'd blown herself out like the morning's storm. He simply sat and watched and waited. He didn't offer words of sympathy. Didn't try to console her, or reach out and comfort her. She wouldn't have been able to take his touch. Not then, maybe never.

"Bobbie, I need to see Bobbie."

"You will, Angela. I promise. I've asked my people to bring her here. One of them is a woman, a medic. She'll look after Bobbie and tend to your injuries."

He stood slowly and backed away, still giving her plenty

of room. She breathed deeply, easily. Easier than she had done for hours.

A good man. A good, good man. Kind, sad eyes, in a rugged, bearded face. A face that had seen hardship. Angela could tell.

"If you like, I'll give them a call. Check their ETA."

"ETA?"

"Sorry. I'll check when they're due to arrive."

He reached into a pocket in his tunic and pulled out a small mobile, but before he could dial, Danny returned. He gave her an encouraging smile that made her want to cry again. They were both being so nice.

"Everything okay out there, Danny?"

"Under control, Captain," he answered quietly, his voice young but authoritative. He had a slight accent, but she couldn't identify its origin. "The big one wet himself. The other one soiled his trousers and is crying like a baby needing its mother. I'm surprised you can't hear him from in here."

Peter handed Danny his phone. "Call Rollo. Find out what's happening."

Danny turned his back, and Peter approached her.

"The floor is hard and must be cold. Would you be more comfortable on the settee? May I help?"

Peter held out his hand. She hesitated before taking it, but, despite the carpet, the floor made her hips ache. He helped her to stand, but she stumbled on jelly legs. He caught her, held onto an elbow, and led her the three short steps to the settee. She dropped into its soft embrace and cocooned herself in the quilt once more.

"Thank you," she said, barely able to form the words.

"You're welcome. Rest there for as long as you need."

Again, the tears formed, and she had to wipe them away. She sniffled a runny nose.

God, she must look a state.

Peter turned his head, searching the room.

"Do you have any tissues?"

Angela pointed to the occasional table on the far side of the second armchair, and he passed her the box. She took a couple and blew her nose, but placed the box on the arm of the chair, knowing she'd need more. Forgetting her torn lips, she wiped her mouth. Pain caused her stomach muscles to contract and force air through her nose.

The bile, when it arrived again, took her by surprise, and she found herself doubled over, vomiting into the plastic bin Peter held under her chin. His other hand held her hair back and out of the stream.

Once again, the tears flowed, and this time, Angela didn't even try to hold them back. She buried her face in her hands and let them flow.

What was wrong with her? Would she ever stop crying?

Peter took the bin away, holding it at arm's length.

"Sorry," she blurted out, "and thank you, for everything."

"No need to apologise to me, Angela. You've been through a terrible ordeal. Do you have a downstairs toilet?"

She nodded. "Under the stairs."

"Okay, back in a tick."

He returned with the bin emptied and rinsed, and placed it on the carpet close at hand. She felt better, more settled.

"Who are you?"

"As I said, I'm the man you contacted asking for help."

"You're from the website? The-83.com?"

"That's right. Didn't I say?"

"No. No, you didn't. Not exactly."

Danny entered the room and lobbed the mobile to Peter, who caught it with one hand.

"ETA, two hours, boss."

"Is he still on the line?"

"He is, but I put it on mute."

Peter turned towards her. "Angela, you heard Danny. Bobbie and my friends will be here soon. Would you like to talk to her?"

Panic surged from Angela's stomach and lodged in her throat. "Does she know what's happened?"

Danny fully entered the room.

"No," he said. "I told Rollo, the team leader, but Bobbie only knows you've both been threatened, and we want you together for security purposes."

"Thank God."

Peter held out the mobile.

Angela took it, stunned at the steadiness of her hand when she expected trembling fingers to drop the phone into the bin. She took a deep, controlled breath and let it out slowly before speaking.

"Hello, darling," she said, forcing a calmness into her voice she didn't really possess, "are you there?"

"Mum? Mum? Is that you? I've been worried sick."

"Yes, yes, it's me. I'm fine now," she said. Lies were sometimes necessary for the greater good. "Where are you?"

"We've just hit the M25. For once the traffic's light. We're not far away now. What's happening? These officers tell me you witnessed a crime and we're being put into protective custody."

Angela looked at Peter and mouthed the word, "Officers?"

He nodded and raised a finger to his lips.

"Yes, darling," Angela blurted. "That's … yes. I did see something, and we both need to be safe."

"Really? This isn't some ridiculously over-elaborate practical joke? I mean, Detective Inspector Allman showed me her ID card, but I've never seen one before. For all I know, she could have printed it on her desktop PC. Although it looks pretty impressive. Has a crest and a holographic logo and everything. I phoned the number on the card, The Hampshire Constabulary HQ in Southampton, and they confirmed the details."

Angela flashed a look at Peter, who again nodded his encouragement. He whispered, "I'll explain everything later. You have my word."

Bobbie continued talking, clearly having missed Peter's whispered promise. "I tried calling you, but your mobile and the house landline kept sending me to voicemail." She paused, took a breath. "Sorry, Mum. I know I'm rabbiting on like a lunatic, but this is so exciting. Nothing like this ever happens to people like us. Are you sure you're okay? You're very quiet."

"Can't get a word in edgeways, darling. But it's wonderful to hear your voice."

"So, what did you witness? DI Allman wouldn't give me any details. Is it something at work with the D'Costa brothers? Are they avoiding their taxes? Laundering money for the mob? I never did trust that Brian D'Costa. Shifty eyes, you know?"

Despite her bruised and split lips, Angela found herself smiling. Bobbie's enthusiastic rambling was exactly what she needed to hear.

"Anyway, Mum," Bobbie said, "the driver—strong, silent type—is looking daggers at me. Oh, just to say, they didn't give me much time to pack, so we'll have to put a wash on at some stage. Anyway, see you very soon, okay?"

"Okay, darling. Love you to pieces."

"Love you, too."

The phone fell silent. Angela stared at the digital clock flashing away on the display. It read 20:37. Bobbie would be hungry when she arrived. She never ate properly at college and had been looking ever so gaunt recently.

Peter beckoned for the phone.

"Thank you," she said, handing it over and sniffling away a tear. "I feel so much better."

His smile lit up his strangely familiar face. She'd seen him somewhere before but couldn't for the life of her imagine where. With all she'd suffered since Breaker's Folly, it was no wonder her memory was letting her down. Maybe it was playing tricks on her.

"She's a livewire, your daughter."

"No arguing with that." Angela laughed, surprised she had one in her so soon. "No arguing at all."

"We're both looking forward to meeting her," he said. "Aren't we, Danny?"

The younger man, who'd been standing in the doorway, combed his fingers through his wavy, blond hair. Surely he wasn't blushing?

"Yes, boss. It will be good for Mrs Shafer and her daughter to be together. And I bet you're looking forward to seeing the doc, too?"

Despite her skewed emotional state, Angela detected an undercurrent of friendship and respect between the two men that went way beyond work colleagues.

"What was she saying about ID and police officers? I thought you were soldiers?"

"Not soldiers. Not exactly, but I'm afraid your daughter's instincts were quite correct. The warrant cards are fakes. We aren't affiliated with the police, but we are former military personnel. And, by the way, the surly driver Bobbie talked about is Rollo. Former sergeant in the Special Boat Service, and one of the very few people in the world I'd trust with my life. Danny is another. Both Rollo and Danny are on your side, and you won't find better protectors."

"And Detective Inspector Allman? Not a police officer either?"

Peter coughed into his hand. "No, I'm afraid not. She's our company medic. Apparently, she's a fairly decent actor, too."

She sensed pride in his praise of the doctor.

"You and the doc are close? Is that why Danny said you were looking forward to seeing her again?"

"Hmm," he scowled at the younger man. "Military discipline can sometimes go awry even in the best-run unit. Much more of that insubordination, Corporal, and you'll find yourself on a charge."

Danny snapped to attention and shot a very smart salute.

"Yes, boss. Sorry, boss. Won't happen again, Captain," he said, winking at her.

Angela couldn't believe how easily their comfortable banter could pull her out of the horrible darkness and lift her towards the light. The banality was life-affirming. Perhaps, given time, and more doses of normality, she could survive this awful thing. No, she *had* survived. Thanks to Peter and to Danny.

"I don't know what the penalty for insubordination is, Captain, but I think Danny should get a pass this time. He —you both—are exactly what I needed," she said through a yawn. "I don't even know your full names."

"Peter and Danny will do for now. If you don't mind, I'll hold off the explanations and the full introductions until your daughter arrives. It'll save me having to repeat myself."

Angela yawned again, barely able to keep her eyes open.

"Okay, that suits me. If you don't mind, I'll take that shower now. Will one of you help me up the stairs?"

She hurt all over and stank of *him*. Much as she doubted it would ever be possible, and with the idea of going to trial firmly off the table, she needed to scrape every vestige of *him* off and out of her as soon as humanly possible.

Chapter Five

Friday 27th November – Angela Shafer

Old Mill Lane, Andover, Hampshire, England

Peter jumped up and offered his gloved hand yet again. This time, her legs were stronger and felt more like her own. Sore, but her own.

Why was he still wearing gloves?

Shouldn't he take them off?

Was it strange?

Stop asking so many questions.

Peter was a good man. Honesty poured out of him in waves.

She needed to stop being so jumpy. She needed to heal.

After a stop halfway to catch her breath, pulling on the handrail all the way, Angela reached the landing at the top of the stairs, but could go no further. Her legs simply stopped working. Holding the quilt in place with one hand, she clung to the top post with the other, sweating, panting, unable to move.

Peter appeared alongside, trying not to stand too close on the narrow landing. "What's wrong?"

"It's d-dark. I-I can't go up there."

He brushed past. She trembled at his proximity and shrank away, watching as he opened every door, turned on every light, and searched all the rooms before returning to her.

"The place is secure. I've drawn all the curtains. No one can see you and you're alone. If you want me to stand guard out here while you have your shower, I'm happy to do so. Likewise, if you want to be alone, I'll go downstairs and come running if you need me."

Her lower lip trembled again. His offer to stand guard over her in her own home made her feel useless.

"Sorry. You must think I'm pathetic."

His hand hovered over hers as it grasped the oval ball on top of the newel post, but it didn't touch her.

"I think no such thing. You are one of the bravest people I've ever met. Many women would be catatonic after what you've been through. The only thing I feel right now is fury at those bastards outside in the car and guilt for not arriving in time."

Tears flowed once more. How could there be any left?

"You are a kind man. Thank you ... for everything you've done. I'll be okay up here on my own, b-but please don't leave."

"We're going nowhere. Not until the others arrive. Call if you need me."

As he stepped aside, she pried her hand free of the

support and headed for her bedroom. Peter hardly made a sound as he descended the stairs. She turned and followed his every move, making sure he kept his word.

A slim man, he was so light on his feet, the tread fourth up from the top didn't even squeak as he glided over it. He planted his feet on the outside edge of each tread. Where had he learned that trick?

―――――

ANGELA SLID the bolt across the bathroom door and checked the handle three times to make sure it was secure. She closed her eyes and turned her back to the mirror while undressing, not wanting to lock in the memory of any marks Pig had left on her body.

After standing under the steaming-hot shower and scrubbing everywhere with the rough side of the cleaning sponge until every centimetre of her skin was red and raw, Angela filled the tub. She slid below the surface until everything was submerged but her face. It hurt like hell all over, especially whenever she moved her mouth or blinked too hard or wiped her nose. The Lord above knew what she looked like, but she still couldn't bring herself to brave the mirror.

Slowly, the moist heat soaked into her, and she allowed her mind to float. She followed the meditation techniques she learned in yoga, smiling at Bobbie's pre-adolescent, corny, old joke about not liking yoga on her breakfast cereal because she preferred milk.

Bobbie, her darling child. Her bright, intelligent, beautiful girl.

She'll be home soon.

How would she react? What could she tell her? The truth? All of it?

No. Think of the water. Think of the warmth. Let your mind float free.

Angela couldn't remember the last time she'd luxuriated in a bath since having the shower installed after Dad had passed away.

Had he really been gone five years and Mum eight? Had she really been an orphan for so long? If Peter and Danny hadn't arrived in time, Bobbie would be an orphan, too.

No. Think of the water. Let your mind float free.

She'd spent over half her inheritance upgrading the cottage. A new bathroom with its fancy, power shower, a new kitchen, and redecoration throughout. She'd even invested in a new tile roof and replacement double-glazed windows and doors. Stupid thing to do when she should have sold up and moved into town. As usual, her heart had ruled her head. Money wasted.

All that effort and now she couldn't live there anymore. It would never feel safe again. It would never feel like home.

Angela lay back, head resting on a towel, and allowed the heat of the water to seep further into her muscles and ease her aching joints. She covered her sore face in a wet flannel and breathed in the humid warmth, allowing it to cleanse her pores and warm her lungs. It felt so good after the … after the attack.

She sweated into the water. Expunging the stench of Pig. Cleansing herself from the inside. As the water cooled, she topped it up with more hot.

A sauna to cleanse her—body and soul.

Why hadn't she sold the house and moved? It wasn't as though she didn't have the money, not after the unexpected windfall from The 83 Trust. Nearly ten thousand pounds and the promise of much more. That, coupled with the money she had left from the family inheritance, would have been more than enough to cover the deposit on a lovely, modern apartment in Andover. She'd be in the middle of town, closer to her friends and to work.

When the banker's draft arrived, she'd phoned her bank and spoken to Tony, a man with a Liverpool accent. He confirmed all the numbers on the banker's draft as valid, and she nearly fell from her chair. She remembered the conversation clearly, almost verbatim.

"Are you certain?"

"Yes, Mrs Shafer," Tony had said. "Simply deposit the draft in your local branch and the funds will be credited to your account within three business days. No doubt about it. None whatsoever."

Angela had been too stunned to react.

"By the way," he continued, "you're not our first customer to have received a draft from this organisation and query it. In fact, the central clearing bank has notified all financial institutions that The 83 Trust is a legitimate charitable concern that is legally able to disburse monies as they see fit. And before you ask, the funds are tax-exempt. All you need to do is declare the income on your end-of-year tax statement using the reference code as it appears on The 83 Trust's letter and you're in the clear."

"The 83 Trust?" she asked.

"Yes," Tony answered. "They have a website if you want to investigate further. Would you like the URL?"

"No need. It's on their letter. I hadn't wanted to visit their site in case the whole thing was a scam."

Angela removed the dampened hand towel and opened her eyes. Steam wafted up from the water. Condensation coated the tiles and misted the mirror. She was in a fog, literally and figuratively, but the cleansing, hot water after the shower had worked wonders. She could almost imagine it hadn't happened.

She closed her eyes again and allowed her thoughts to drift once more. Who were her saviours, Captain Peter and Corporal Danny? Who were they really?

Should she trust them? Did she have an alternative?

After the call with Tony, and still hugely sceptical, Angela visited the trust's website and it all became clear, shockingly clear. Without knowing it, Jackie had reached out to her from beyond the grave.

Angela should have guessed from the name of the website and the name of The 83 Trust. It was so obvious. Eighty-three people had died when Ryan Kaine, the mad terrorist, blew Flight BE1555 out of the sky.

There had been no survivors.

Jacqueline Roberta Shafer, Angela's baby sister, had been one of the eighty-three.

Just thirty-two years of age. So young. So much life left to lead, she'd barely even started. The heart and soul of everyone's life, heading to a hen party in Amsterdam with the intended bride and seven other bridesmaids. All dead.

Murdered by Ryan Kaine.

Whenever Angela imagined what must have been the last few moments of Jackie's life, she cried. In the overly hot bath, she cried again. Tears of loss. Tears of frustration. Tears of dread. Tears of relief at having been delivered from death.

So many evil men in the world. Angela wished people could be more like Peter and Danny. Honest, caring men. The guilt on Peter's face when he apologised for being late showed how much he cared. And he must have come from far away to have considered hiring a helicopter.

She wiped her eyes with the cloth and sighed as her thoughts were dragged back to Jackie and the crash.

The website outlined how The 83 Trust had access to funds from generous corporate and private donors to support the families of the victims of Flight BE1555. The site even included a big, red, "call to action" button.

If you are in imminent financial or physical danger, **click here***!*

AT FIRST, she'd ignored the button. Angela didn't need any more and preferred to leave the money for others, but she'd bookmarked the site in her browser, in case her situation changed.

After Breaker's Folly and the first phone call, she returned to the site and clicked the button, which activated a drop-down questionnaire. She checked the relevant squares, filled in the text boxes, and expected nothing. She definitely didn't expect Captain Peter and Corporal Danny to burst through her front door and save her.

Since the bath had calmed her nerves and allowed her to think more clearly, Angela desperately needed to hear their story.

Finally, after three top-ups with hot water and what must have been forty minutes' soaking, the wrinkled skin on her fingertips confirmed it as time to drain the tub. Reluctantly, she twisted the knob to raise the plug and waited while the falling water exposed and cooled her skin.

Angela, lobster red and fully relaxed in the steamy

atmosphere, climbed out of the tub into the cold steam. She wrapped herself in her fluffy bath towel, tied her long hair in another towel, and padded to her bedroom. She dressed —fresh underwear, loose jeans, plaid shirt, baggy jumper, wool socks, and her warmest carpet slippers. She covered her dressing table mirror with the damp towel and dried her hair. The brush teased out the tangles, but she had to take it gently around the damaged scalp. Without the mirror, she had no idea what her hair looked like, but, by the time she'd finished, it was clean and tangle free, and held away from her face in a loose ponytail.

Her alarm clock showed twenty-three minutes to ten.

Bobbie and the others would be arriving soon. She half-stumbled down the stairs on weakened legs, using the handrail for support once again, but not leaning as heavily as before, and opened the door to the front room. Empty.

Where had they gone?

"Peter?"

Kitchen. Empty.

"Peter! Danny!"

They'd left her alone!

Chapter Six

Friday 27th November – Angela Shafer

Old Mill Lane, Andover, Hampshire, England

Angela raced along the hall and pulled open the front door. The shock of cold air stung her face, froze her damp hair, and burned her lungs. Her two saviours, still dressed in black, smiled apologetically.

Thank God.

"You said you wouldn't leave the house! You promised."

Peter rushed closer. "Sorry, Angela. I needed to check the ... rubbish."

Angela held tight to the door handle and beckoned him inside, desperate not to be left alone.

"I-I'm going to make coffee. Please come back in."

Downstairs in her warm kitchen, Angela busied

herself with the coffeemaker. A present from Jackie two Christmases earlier, it produced the perfect cup. Strong, rich roast, cream, no sugar. Her saviours chose the same.

Once she'd rattled the mugs and carafe onto the tray, hands shaking again, Peter insisted on carrying it and led them into the front room. She lowered herself carefully into her armchair—the unspoiled one—adjusted her position to make herself comfortable, which wasn't easy, and pointed the men to the settee.

Three friends having late-evening refreshments.

All very normal.

All very surreal.

The captain poured for them all, sank into the settee opposite, and waited. Danny remained standing and took a position close to the window.

She took a sip, trying to avoid scalding the cuts on her lips. No one spoke for ages. Between sips, Danny twitched the curtains, keeping watch. Peter leaned forwards, cradling his cup, but not drinking, perhaps waiting for his coffee to cool.

Get on with it, woman.

"So, who exactly are you?" she asked, rather more abruptly than she, or they, expected.

Peter recovered quickly and pointed to his man.

"I've already introduced Danny—the scruffy reprobate slurping his coffee too loudly. By the way, keep him away from your biscuits. He never could pass a pantry without diving in and helping himself."

"Slurping? *Moi?*" Danny asked, looking hurt and sticking out the little finger on the hand holding his big mug. "As if."

Tall, muscular, in his late twenties, and quietly spoken,

Danny filled the room with power and strength. And gentleness.

Unbelievable. There she was, talking with a man almost young enough to be her son after what had happened. Could things get any more weird?

Although Danny still looked offended, it didn't stop him asking, "Did somebody say something about bickies?"

Despite the bruised cheek and the fat lip, Angela smiled. "There's a biscuit barrel next to the kettle. Please help yourself."

The younger man strode towards the door, but not before glancing at Peter for permission.

"And you, Captain?" Angela asked, staring hard at the older man, really studying him for the first time.

She put him a year or two younger than her—early forties. Around average height and slim, sinewy almost, but powerful. She knew this from the way he'd dragged Pig from the room with one hand. Pig was a huge man, well over six foot tall, and heavy with muscle.

Angela shuddered as the memory edged its way to the front of her mind.

Peter's brown eyes were clear and honest. Dark brown hair, sprinkled with silver, and a full, but neatly trimmed, salt-and-pepper beard. He carried himself like a military man, straight-backed, square-shouldered, and had an air of quiet authority. Here was a man used to issuing orders and having them obeyed. Rugged. Not handsome, but certainly not ugly. Pleasant. Competent. Friendly.

"I'm just Peter. If you don't mind, we'll do without surnames. At least for the moment."

"Really?"

Peter—she doubted it was his real name—scratched at his beard as though it annoyed him.

"Well, Danny and I have just shot fifty thousand volts through two men, tied them up, and bundled them into the boot of their own car. I'm sure you understand, we're skirting around the perimeter of the law here. And judging by your option to take the shower, I don't think you want anything to do with the police. I'm right there, yes?"

She nodded and took another sip of her coffee. She'd made it too strong. Should have asked for more cream but didn't want to make a fuss.

Danny returned with a pile of biscuits on a side plate. "Digestives," he said, an edge of regret in his voice. "Want one, Captain, Mrs Shafer?"

Peter shook his head. Angela did the same.

"Sorry they're so plain," she said. "I sometimes buy chocolate-coated, but only for special occasions. If I'd known you were coming, I'd have …"

She allowed the expression to trail away. The situation was growing stranger by the minute, and she was only just managing to hold herself together.

"You'd have baked a cake?" Danny finished for her, his cheeky grin making him appear even younger. "That would have been nice, but these'll do well enough."

He walked his cup and plate to the window, still peeking through the curtains, but remaining engaged in the conversation.

"Earlier, you mentioned a helicopter. Why would you need one of those? Where did you come from?" she asked, giving up on finding out more about the men themselves.

Peter shuffled in his seat and finally sipped his coffee. "Best I don't tell you that. Security issues, you know? We received your form two days ago, but, as I said, it took a while to … organise transportation."

"You ... you wanted to check out my story, too. Didn't you?"

He lowered his cup to the coffee table and shuffled even closer to the edge of the settee.

"Mrs Shafer, you have to understand," he said, frowning and suddenly very serious, "we help a lot of people and, from time to time, we find ourselves working outside the law, as we have done tonight. The UK authorities take a dim view of vigilantism and would quite happily see us all behind bars."

"Us all?"

"Sorry?"

"You said, 'us all'. How many of you are there?"

His head pulled back. "That fluctuates depending on need. I really can't go into detail. For your protection as much as ours, you understand."

"You're definitely from The 83 Trust, though?"

"That's right. I'm head of the ... how can I put it?"

He rolled his eyes to the ceiling as though struggling to find the right words. Angela had the distinct impression he hadn't prepared the explanation ahead of time.

Interesting.

His warm, brown eyes found hers again.

"Let's just say I'm in charge of the practical, proactive side of the organisation."

"I thought The 83 Trust was a charity, responsible for disbursal of funds to the families?"

Peter nodded. "That's our primary role, yes."

From his spot by the window, Danny nodded before stuffing another biscuit into his mouth. How many was that now? Three? Four? Where did he pack them all?

"Your site says your aim is to support the families of all the victims. Eighty-three families, yes?"

"That's correct," Peter said. "All the families are of equal importance to us. It's one more reason for our late arrival. We had another … case to deal with. Sometimes, we can be spread a little thin."

Angela drained her coffee and refilled her cup. After talking with them for a few minutes, her shakes had nearly gone. Maybe learning more about The 83 was good therapy.

"And checking my CV would have taken time, too, of course."

Peter's apologetic smile returned. "Think of it as part of our due diligence. We can't just drop everything and leap into action. We have to prioritise, and there's always the chance of us being played for fools. The authorities have issues with our methods, if not our goals, so we need to take great care."

"Okay, that sounds … reasonable. Forgive me for being inquisitive, but I've not seen any TV adverts or bumped into any chuggers trawling the streets with their charity boxes. How do you raise your funds?"

Peter tilted his head to stare at her, clearly not a man to blurt out information without careful consideration.

"We've received a few unsolicited donations from the general public. The British are a generous people. However, most of our funding comes from institutional and individual benefactors."

Danny scoffed and hid his face behind the curtain.

"Why the twinkle in your eye, Peter?"

"Let's just say our initial benefactor was a tad reluctant to ante up with the money at first. But that was before I showed him the benefits of his generosity."

"What do you mean 'reluctant'? You stole from him?"

Peter's expression hardened. "I prefer to call it redistribution of a murdering thief's ill-gotten gains for the benefit of the people he wronged. Will that do?"

Angela took a breath, biting back a retort before it burst from her mouth, and nodded.

The seated man showed a harder edge, not that it was directed at her, but rather at the unseen enemy, the so-called individual benefactor. An icy blast of emotion reached her, and she shivered. Anyone standing in Captain Peter's way had better take care. But, at that moment, she felt nothing but gratitude for the self-contained military man and his biscuit-demolishing associate.

"What are you going to do with them?" Angela asked, glancing towards the window.

"That depends on a number of factors," Peter answered, checking his watch. "We have about thirty minutes before Bobbie arrives, and our two friends in the boot of their BMW aren't going anywhere until then. In the meantime, can you face telling us exactly what happened at Breaker's Folly?"

Angela closed her eyes. She hated the idea of reliving the scene, but it would take her mind off the more recent atrocity—an atrocity she refused to solidify with a name.

"It was horrible," she said, barely able to force the words through a constricted throat. "Like something out of a gangster movie."

She blinked tears from her eyes and dived into the story.

Chapter Seven

Friday 27th November – Angela Shafer

Old Mill Lane, Andover, Hampshire, England

Angela squirmed deeper into her chair, trying to make herself more comfortable, but nothing worked. Since the warmth of the bath had dissipated, everywhere Pig had assaulted started hurting again.

"As I wrote in the online form, it started last Saturday afternoon."

"Saturday the twenty-first?" Peter asked.

He took an old-fashioned, spiral notepad from his pocket. It had a pencil stuck in the wire. When Peter saw her expression, he smiled. "Don't worry, it's okay. Just taking a few notes to compare with any claims our friends in the

BMW make later—when the time comes for us to have our quiet, little chat. Please carry on."

"Okay, I'll do my best." She gulped before continuing. "Saturday started off quite nice, cold with a sharp breeze, but dry."

Peter stopped writing and looked at her. A question showed on his face, but he waited patiently, saying nothing.

"Sorry, the weather is relevant, I promise. Seven miles from here is a disused quarry, Breaker's Folly. A little-known beauty spot …"

Hardly pausing for breath, she told him everything that happened—the men in the car, the dead body, being chased through the woods. She managed to hold herself together, fighting back the tears, until she reached the part when the driver shot Lady, her baby. Her poor, brave, little dog.

"The next thing I knew, Lady's lead tore from my hand and she was gone. She must have turned to attack the man. I heard barking and growling, and the man yelled. Then the gunshots and the yelp, but I kept running. Too terrified to stop." Her lower lip trembled. "My brave, little dog saved my life, but I just kept running. Left her to die. I'm such a coward!"

Angela buried her face in her hands and let the tears run free.

Peter eased up from the settee and squatted in front of her—close, but not touching. Not intimidating.

"There was nothing else you could have done. If you'd stopped, you'd be dead, too."

He reached out and placed a hand on her forearm. The simple, human warmth of his touch gave her strength. Danny had taken a pace away from his station near the window, his jaw muscles tensed and released, anger darkened his expression. She hadn't taken him for an animal lover, but she knew nothing about the men who'd saved her life. Only that she trusted them.

"Please continue if you can, Angela," Peter said, soothing and quiet.

"I'm okay. Want to finish," she said, surprised at the steadiness of her words. "I reached the car and raced away. Luckily, it was facing in the right direction ... but I was in a real state. My poor Lady, gone. The other man, dead, too. Could hardly see the road through my tears. It wasn't until I nearly crashed into a hedge that I remembered to turn on the headlights."

She paused long enough to dab her eyes with a clean tissue before continuing.

"I drove straight to the nearest police station at Andover. Hysterical. They tried to calm me down and called for a doctor, but I kept crying and trying to explain what happened. It took ages for a detective to arrive."

"His name?" Peter asked, after squeezing her hand and returning to the settee. His pencil stood poised over the notepad, waiting.

"Detective Sergeant Shorebrook, I think."

Peter nodded and touched the pencil to the paper. "What happened next?"

"I gave my statement to the detective, but I don't think he believed me. He was very offhand. He told me they'd sent a patrol car almost as soon as I reached the station, but the officers had found nothing. No car, no dead body, and no Lady. He promised to send a proper search team at first light, but it felt as though he was dismissing me as a hysterical woman with an overactive imagination. The doctor arrived and cleaned up this scratch on my forehead"—she fingered the partially healed cut over her left eye—"from the branches in the woods. Then the sergeant brought in a young, female police officer, Jessica, to take me home. She stayed with me for a couple of hours and then left."

"Is that it?" Danny demanded, fists clenched tight, undoubtedly trying to control his anger. "Is that all they did?"

Angela nodded. "More or less. Jessica asked if she could contact a close friend or a family member to stay with me, but I told her I was okay. She gave me her card and an incident number and left when another police car arrived to take her back to the station."

Danny glanced at Peter and shook his head.

"Bloody hell, Captain. Talk about a useless waste of space."

Peter raised a hand to calm him and asked, "This happened on Saturday evening. Has there been any police follow-up since?"

"Detective Shorebrook called in the following afternoon, Sunday, and told me they'd searched the Folly and found nothing, and no trace of anything unexpected. Not even tyre tracks. Must have been the rain, you see. So heavy it kept me awake most of the night. A storm." She took a deep breath and continued.

"I offered to show him where everything happened, but he said they'd searched the area thoroughly and were convinced I'd been the victim of a prank. Kids trying to scare me. That's when I started shouting, demanding to speak to his superior. I'm afraid I lost my temper. I yelled, 'What about Lady? She wouldn't have run away and left me'. You know what Shorebrook said? Do you?"

Peter nodded. "I can imagine."

"He suggested I have 'Lost Dog' signs made up and attach them to lampposts. He also assured me that no bodies matching the dead man's description had turned up anywhere in the county, and no missing persons reports had been raised. In short, he closed the file and told me to carry on with my life."

"Did you return to the Folly and search it yourself?" Danny asked.

She shook her head rapidly. "No. I've been too scared."

"That's understandable. You've had a terrible shock," Peter said.

"I felt so guilty for not doing anything to find Lady. Even if she is only a dog, she deserves a proper burial, doesn't she?"

"Yes, she does," Danny said. "That brave girl might well have saved your life."

"Are you a dog person?"

He smiled gently. "I do have a soft spot for canines."

Peter cleared his throat and she turned to face him again.

"I imagine you didn't go to work on Monday?"

"Nor on Tuesday, I was too upset," she answered, throwing back her shoulders and trying to stop the tears flowing. "I lay in bed most of the time, feeling sorry for myself. I thought about calling Bobbie but didn't want her to miss any lectures. She loves Lady almost as much as I do … did." A sob broke her flow, and she wiped away more tears.

"Wednesday was the first time I felt strong enough to return to work," she continued. "Despite the money The 83 Trust sent me, I still need to work, and I've used up all my annual leave, so …" She shrugged and didn't finish her sentence. "It went okay. I told everyone at work I'd had a fall, and they were very supportive. No one knew about the police thing, and I decided to keep it to myself. Then, in the afternoon at work, the phone calls started, and I completely lost control."

"Phone calls?" Peter asked, nodding.

"Y-Yes. A man with a high-pitched voice. Pig. The man … the man out there …"

She threw a glance at the window and Peter nodded his understanding.

"What did he say?"

"Not much. At first, all he said was, 'Talk to the police again, and you die'. Simple as that. I ran to the Ladies Room and threw up in the toilet. The men from the Folly had found me. I have no idea how."

Peter and Danny exchanged glances.

"Do you know?" she asked the captain.

"I have an idea," he answered. "Was Lady chipped?"

Angela paused for a moment.

"Yes. Yes, the vet did it when she was a puppy … Oh my God. They found my name and contact details from Lady's registration!"

"It's a reasonable assumption," Peter said. "You can pick up a microchip scanner at most electronics shops. They might have ordered one online if they wanted to stay anonymous. Waiting for delivery might explain the delay in contacting you."

She nodded sadly. The slight hope she had of Lady being alive died with the logic of his words.

"What did you do after the phone call?"

"I was frantic. Left work early and drove home. Then I found a note posted through my letterbox. I-I couldn't believe it. They'd been to my house."

"Can I see it?"

Angela pointed to the cabinet in the corner of the room. "It's in the top drawer."

Danny retrieved the paper and read it before passing it across. She didn't need to read it again, she'd burned the words into her memory.

WE KNOW WHERE YOU LIVE. *Don't talk to the police again.*

"I HELD the paper at the corners and put it in that plastic folder. Is that okay?"

The captain smiled and shook his head. "Doesn't matter. We're not in the business of looking for forensic evidence to make a court case. Those two outside will furnish any information we need."

Danny winked at her.

"I can't wait," he said, smiling. "As they say in all those cool, gangster films, 'Payback is a bitch'."

Angela shuddered. A flash of pity surfaced for the men trapped in the boot of their own car, but the tender area throbbing on her scalp where Pig had yanked out a tuft of hair brought the horror back. They'd killed Lady, too, and they deserved anything and everything coming to them. Any slight sympathy she had for the evil creatures dissolved into a cold, hard anger.

Peter flipped a few pages on his notepad. "We received your contact form Wednesday night at eighteen-oh-eight. Was that right after you'd read the note?"

"Yes. I couldn't think of anything else to do. Even if I did have the courage to call the police, they wouldn't have helped. They might even have thought I printed the note myself to support my 'hysterical' story. If you look at it closely, you'll see it's on standard copy paper and could have been produced on any of a million inkjet printers. No, the police were useless, and I was desperate. Didn't know what to do. Then I remembered bookmarking your website. Thank God you came."

Peter lowered his eyes to the note, but said nothing.

"Are you going to … I mean, what are you going to do with them?"

"Not sure yet, but I'll think of something. In fact, I already have one or two ideas to run past Danny when we're alone. First though, we need to make sure you and Bobbie are safe. Do you have any questions before I ask you to pop upstairs and put some clothes in a suitcase?"

"I need to pack?"

The captain stood and slipped the notepad into his pocket. "Angela," he said, "you aren't safe here. We need you packed and ready to leave by the time Bobbie arrives."

Angela took a moment to work out the implications of his words before sighing. "Yes, I see that. I-I understand."

Peter stepped forwards, holding out his hand. "We've organised a safe place for you to stay while we work out what to do."

Angela fell silent, unable to think of anything to say. Life as she had always known it had probably come to an end. Nothing would ever be the same again.

Once more, the tears fell, and she could do nothing to stop them.

———

AS PETER PROMISED, the car arrived at a little after ten o'clock—a large driver alone in the front and two women in the back.

Bobbie. Her Bobbie!

Angela raced into the cold, night air and reached her

daughter almost before she had time to climb out of the back seat. She swept Bobbie into her arms as though they hadn't seen each other for years when, in fact, it had been less than a fortnight.

"Bobbie," she gushed, "let me look at you!"

"Mum, what happened to your face?"

Angela flinched as Bobbie reached up to touch her bruised cheek.

"I'm okay, darling. Thanks to Peter and Danny. What about you?"

"Confused but fine. What's going on? Your face is all swollen and that cut on your head looks nasty. Have you been in a car crash?"

Peter stepped forwards. "Sorry to rush you, but we need to take this inside."

He ushered them and the two others into the house, where Danny waited, guarding her suitcases and watching Pig's car.

Once in the front room again, and while Angela still clutched Bobbie's arm, Peter made the introductions.

"Angela Shafer, meet Lara, the doc."

The woman was tall, nearly as tall as Peter, and striking. Angela would have paid Geraldine a small fortune to replicate her wavy, auburn hair. Lara smiled and offered her hand.

"Hello, Angela," she said, her voice cultured, and her accent refined Home Counties. "Lovely to meet you. Sorry it has to be under these circumstances."

"Um, hello," Angela said, unable to think of a more interesting response.

Peter pointed to the other new arrival, a huge, clean-shaven fellow with short-cropped hair. With his craggy, weather-beaten face, he would have looked at home on the bridge of a ship.

"This monster is Rollo. Don't be frightened by his ugly mug, he's not that bad, not since we've managed to house-train him."

Rollo growled and shook his head slowly. "Don't listen to him, Mrs Shafer. I was housetrained when the captain was still soiling his nappies."

They shook. Rollo's hand was enormous and calloused, but warm, and his grip gentle.

The front room struggled to accommodate so many people, and Danny was forced to stand in his now-customary place by the window. Bobbie kept throwing side-ways glances at him until Peter finished with the introductions. Danny nodded to her, smiled, but said nothing.

"Okay everyone," Peter said. "We need to give Angela time and space to bring Bobbie up to speed. Angela"—he turned to her—"we should be out of here inside twenty minutes. That okay?"

"Mum, what on earth's happening? And where's Lady? She's normally all over me by now."

"Take a seat, darling. I have some bad news and there isn't much time."

Peter and the others left them alone and, once again, Angela told her story. It wasn't any easier the second time around, and ended with them both in tears, hugging each other tight.

Chapter Eight

Friday 27th November – Evening

Old Mill Lane, Andover, Hampshire, England

Kaine led Lara and Rollo into the kitchen, leaving Angela and Bobbie alone in the front room and Danny in the unlit porch, staring into the night.

"Does she know who you are yet?" Lara asked quietly after Kaine had closed the kitchen door.

He frowned. "I thought it best to keep that little gem from her for a while. She was in a hell of a state when we arrived."

"That's hardly surprising given what she's been through since Saturday and tonight. When I think of what that man did …" She closed her eyes and shivered before continuing. "I hope you weren't too gentle with them."

"Hear that, Rollo?" Kaine said. "All that self-defence and fieldcraft training you've been dishing out has turned our mild-mannered, country veterinarian into a firebrand."

Rollo made a face—a cross between a grimace and resignation. "Can't say I blame her, boss. Those bastards don't deserve gentle treatment."

"They didn't receive any. I doubt they're too comfortable hog-tied and lying on top of each other in the boot of that BMW. Not much space or air. And the smaller one, the one who watched, crapped himself. A stun gun will do that to a person now and again. Imagine waking up trapped inside a small, metal box with all that stench? Poor Pig." Kaine chuckled at the image. "Couldn't have happened to a more deserving pair of animals."

Lara stiffened. "Ryan Liam Kaine, that's more than enough of that. Don't you go associating those Barbarians with anything in the animal kingdom. Animals deserve more respect."

Kaine frowned at Rollo's snigger.

"Yes, Doc. Sorry, Doc. Won't let it happen again, Doc." Kaine winked.

Lara slumped a little, and a more serious expression drew lines on her face. "What's our next move?"

Kaine shot a look at Rollo, whose expression of wide-eyed innocence wouldn't have been out of place on an altar boy.

"Don't look at me like that, Captain. You were the one who agreed she should tag along to fetch the daughter. 'Good camouflage and it will put her at ease,' you said, if I remember correctly. And as usual, you were dead right."

Rollo opened the near-empty fridge and sighed. "We'll need to pick up some provisions along the way. I was hoping to rustle up some sandwiches for our trip north.

Without more food, Danny won't stop moaning the whole way."

"Don't worry about Danny. He'll be with me. And besides, the gannet's already munched his way through half a packet of biscuits and downed three mugs of coffee. He'll survive 'til breakfast. So, what happened when you picked up the lass?"

Rollo closed the fridge door and leaned against the kitchen surface, arms folded.

"I let the doc do all the talking—not that I had much choice in the matter, of course. Stood in the background like a squaddie on guard duty. Have to admit, she played it well. Born to the role of the detective inspector. I almost believed her myself. The fake warrant cards were pretty convincing, too." He smiled at the memory. "As for the combat training, she's a quick study. Won't be long before she knows which end of a throwing knife to hold. Wouldn't trust her with a rifle, though. Too hot-headed."

Lara scowled at Rollo. "You know I'm right here, don't you? I can speak for myself!"

"See what I mean, boss?" Rollo answered, wincing. "And yes, Doc. There's no doubt about that. You certainly can speak for yourself."

Kaine kept a straight face, waiting for her outburst.

Lara harrumphed and turned to face him.

"So, what now?"

"As I told you on the phone, our plans have changed. The two arseholes in the BMW present an opportunity to speed things up a little. We don't have to play defence anymore. They'll give us the edge, so we can move into attack mode."

"Did you get through to Mike?" she asked.

"Yep, he's looking forward to seeing you again. Apparently, his prize mare delivered a foal this year. Says he'd like you to give her the once-over. He doesn't like the local vet. Claims he's too smarmy—and expensive."

Kaine had developed the knack of reading Lara's emotions through her body language. Although she tried to mask the little tells and was learning not to be so transparent, hiding her emotions didn't come naturally to a woman used to being so open. Until she learned the trick, he'd be forever on protection duty. Not that he minded—he'd taken on far more onerous tasks in his time.

He read the battle going on inside Lara. Excitement at the prospect of examining a young horse and a temporary return to her old life, fought with the disappointment at him for side-lining her from the operation. Another emotion simmered below the surface, too. The unspoken attachment that had developed between them since the day they'd met.

After a second or two, Lara forced out the words, "That'll be great. Can't wait to see Mike again. I love his farm, and I'm sure Angela and Bobbie will love it, too."

"Excellent. Thanks Lara," he said, hating the accusatory look she threw him. "It's a massive wrench for them, and your being with them is going to help. Meanwhile, Danny and I are going to have a little fun with our new friends."

Lara sneered. "Stick the boot in for me, will you, Ryan?"

"Tut tut, Dr Orchard. That's so beneath you."

"No, it isn't. Those men assaulted a woman and shot her dog. I have nothing but contempt for them. Do your worst."

Kaine nodded and showed her one of his grim smiles.

"I plan to do just that."

Chapter Nine

Friday 27th November – Night

Breaker's Folly, North of Andover, Hampshire, England

After a thirty-minute drive in the country, following the satnav's directions, Kaine turned right and pushed Pig's BMW hard and fast over the bumpy and potholed lane. Danny followed close behind in their hired Ford.

If the lame-arsed bastards in the boot had woken, loosened their bonds, and were preparing for a fight, the buffeting would knock some of the stuffing out of them. Docile thugs would be easier to manage.

After half a kilometre, the headlights picked out a five-bar, metal gate blocking their progress. Kaine jumped out, opened up, and drove another two hundred metres until the track led into a deserted, gravel parking area.

He killed the engine and waited for Danny to nose up to the Beemer. Not one to mistreat a hire car—although they didn't need to worry about losing the deposit—he'd closed the gate and taken his time driving over the rough track.

Kaine climbed out into the chill night and stood still, listening to the BMW's engine tick as it cooled. Once Danny turned off the Ford's motor, the sounds of the country filled his ears. An owl hooted somewhere off to his right. Straight ahead, a cold bank of humidity pushed at his face and water trickled over rocks.

A stiff breeze whistled through naked branches and pine needles. Somewhere upwind a fair distance away, a fox barked at the moon, whose silver light flashed and rippled on the water, partially visible through the trees.

In short, the perfect, isolated place for a spot of rigorous interrogation.

The stench when Kaine finally popped the BMW's boot almost defied description. He'd smelled nothing worse since the last time Rollo cooked dinner. Apart from the evacuated bowels and the emptied bladders, both men reeked of sweat and vomit. Kaine could swear the Ford's sidelights showed the haze of a blue fug rising as he lifted the boot lid.

The luggage compartment's dim courtesy light cast a strange glow and deep shadows over a scene straight out of a crime movie. Stark, flat faces showed through the gloom. The one on top—the one Angela had named "Pig"—screamed through his gag and struggled to free himself.

As well as the cable ties binding the men's wrists and ankles, Danny had wrapped wide duct tape around each man's head at least three times. To help with breathing, he'd cut a tiny slit into each gag. There would be no value in having either man suffocate before they'd had the opportunity to answer Kaine's questions.

Neither man wore a beard, which was a disappointment. The idea of ripping facial hairs out when tearing off the duct tape wouldn't have upset Kaine one little bit. The thugs planned to murder a woman Kaine had vowed to protect.

Kaine's blood was up. Without the need for information, he and Danny might have torn the bastards limb from bloody limb, and neither would have wasted any sympathy on it. The men deserved everything coming to them.

Danny stepped away from the car.

"Bloody hell," he said, covering his nose with the back of his gloved hand, "that's a bit ripe."

"Not particularly pleasant, is it," Kaine said over the noise coming from the man on top.

Pig screamed, his cheeks puffing out like bellows against the tape. To emphasise his emotions, he writhed and squirmed against his bonds. He paid no attention to the damage he was inflicting on the even more unfortunate one underneath, who seemed dazed by the event and by his partner's actions.

"Reckon he's a little miffed?" Danny asked, lowering his hand, but still wrinkling his nose against the stench.

"Your powers of observation astound me, Danny. Grab his legs and dump him on the gravel. No need to be too careful. Drop him if you like. Doesn't matter to me."

Danny leaned in and took a glancing blow to the arm from Pig's booted heels.

"Careful," Kaine said, taking the big one's shoulders and heaving the body over the lip of the boot, "you've got dirt on your jacket now."

Danny smiled and took his share of the weight.

"Bugger's heavier than he looks, isn't he?"

They dropped their load, face down on the stones. Pig howled.

"Ooops," Danny said, "butter fingers."

Pig rolled onto his side, still howling through the gag, but fell silent when he looked at them in the red backwash from the brake lights.

"See that, Danny? I think he's just noticed we aren't wearing masks."

Still and quiet, their captive studied each of them in turn, no doubt trying to memorise their faces.

"Wonder what he makes of that?" Danny asked, raising his nose to take in the fresh air before bending into the boot again. "Want this one out, too?"

"Why not? They're going to share the same fate, after all."

The slim, smaller one, the main target of Kaine's psychological warfare, whimpered and kept his eyes squeezed tight shut. Kaine had assessed the pair before Danny bound and loaded them into the boot. Angela's horrific story painted the bigger one as the leader, and the other as the follower. Neither man's actions since Danny opened the boot had done anything to dispel the theory.

"Will you look at that, Corporal? Poor, little fellow's too scared to open his eyes. You can take the shoulders this time."

The man squealed as they lifted him from the car, but still refused to look. They lowered him carefully to the path, but kept him well away from his mate, who twisted his head to turn his angry eyes on the little one, staring in silent intimidation.

Sidekick must have felt the emotion emanating from his partner. He whimpered again and tried to writhe further away, closer to Kaine and Danny. The implication was clear. Sidekick was more terrified of Pig than his captors. The moment they changed his perceptions on that score, they'd be halfway home.

"Hey, you," Kaine whispered, "open your eyes."

The smaller captive shook his head and made a strangulated whimper that might have been words, but Kaine couldn't tell.

Kaine drew the Fairbairn-Sykes fighting knife from his calf sheath—the sound of steel sliding over leather unmistakable—and squatted in front of the smaller man.

"Don't be rude. Open your eyes, or I'll slice off your eyelids."

In the background, from his position in the half-light, standing guard over Pig, Danny sucked air through his teeth.

"Ouch," he said, offering scant sympathy.

Sidekick peeled back his lids and blinked hard, trying to find focus in the semi-darkness. Kaine twisted the blade to catch the moon's silver light and flashed it into Sidekick's eyes. Tears flowed as the blubbing man locked his gaze on the gleaming blade.

"Now for a few questions," Kaine said through a cold smile.

The terrified man shook his head and squealed. Pig looked on, impassive, apparently unmoved by his partner's looming fate.

Kaine lowered his arm and touched the blade's finely honed edge to the centre cable tie, the one holding the others together. It snapped open and Sidekick's legs and arms sprang apart.

The movement after such a prolonged stay locked in the same position must have been agonising and he squealed.

Danny and Kaine exchanged pained looks. Both knew what being hogtied for hours would do to a body. Each had undergone similar discomforts during SBS boot camp, and both could remember the agony of cramping muscles and locked joints. Although, if Kaine's emotions were anything to go by, Danny felt no empathy for the squealing man.

"Shame, eh?" Danny said, as if to confirm Kaine's opinion.

"Prop him up against the wheel," Kaine ordered.

Danny dragged the smaller man on his backside and jammed him into position. Once away from the knife, the terrified man's eyes never left Pig's glare.

Time to get to work.

Kaine took a knee in front of Sidekick. He raised the knife and twisted the handle. Once again, the stainless-steel blade glinted in the silvery light. He waved the knife around the deserted parking area.

"Recognise this place?"

The man didn't answer, his total focus was on the moonlight dancing on the blade. Kaine cuffed him on the back of his head.

"Concentrate, little man," he said, keeping his voice low.

In circumstances such as these, a quiet voice was often more terrifying than the howling of a madman.

"I asked if you recognised this place. Do you?"

He shook his head and mumbled something.

"What was that?"

More mumbling.

"Sorry," Kaine said. "This won't do. I'm going to cut off that tape. Keep perfectly still, or you might lose an ear. Ready?"

Sidekick's vigorous nodding made Danny laugh from his

position on the far side of Pig. His right hand rested on the handle of his holstered SIG. Pig hadn't missed the firearm and was no doubt trying to work out how to turn the tables on the situation.

Kaine had no concerns on that front. Danny had been one of his troop for years, and he'd never been anything other than first rate. Together, Kaine, Rollo, and Danny made a formidable team.

"I said keep your head still, fool," Kaine said, working the blade between the man's ear and hair, and slicing away from the scalp.

Kaine ripped at the tape until he'd exposed the man's mouth but left the rest in place.

Sidekick screamed and sucked in a huge breath. The cuts on his lips started bleeding.

"Now, what were you saying?"

Pig growled and tried to wriggle closer, but only succeeded in scuffing his highly polished shoes on the gravel. Terrible way to treat what looked like hand-tooled, Italian leather.

Danny drew his gun and fired in one continuous movement, keeping the trajectory well away from Kaine and Sidekick. The bullet ploughed into the stones centimetres from Pig's head and ricocheted into the night.

Pig stopped struggling, but his gaze found the gun. No fear, just calculation. A cold fish. A sociopath.

No room for negotiation with that one.

Danny lowered his aim. "The next one gives you a third eye."

Kaine patted Sidekick's exposed cheek.

"Well?

"What? Wh-What d'you say?"

Kaine emitted the growl of a man close to losing his

patience. "For the last time, I asked if you recognised this place."

"I don't know nothin'," he whimpered between shuttering breaths. "Haven't never been here before, honest."

"Those are double negatives."

"Huh?" he said, his bottom lip trembling, his chin dimpling, and his tears flowing faster.

Fresh urine darkened the patch in his trousers that had only recently started drying.

"Grammatically speaking you've just told me you do know something, but let's forget the English lesson. You're certain you don't recognise this place?"

The man turned his head, looking around as though for the first time.

"It's country. I don't do the country. Not never."

"Okay, ignoring the poor grammar again, let's say I believe you. Begs the next question. Who's he"—Kaine jabbed the blade in Pig's direction before resting it on Sidekick's right knee—"and why did he attack that woman?"

Sidekick shook his head.

"No, no. C-Can't tell you nothin'. They ... they'll kill me."

"They? Your friend and who?"

Sidekick clamped his jaws together. Kaine tapped the flat of the blade against the youngster's kneecap, but the kid shook his head and closed his eyes.

"You're more afraid of him than me. Is that it?"

A nod and another whimper.

"I see. You are a stupid, little man."

Still on his haunches, Kaine swivelled and smiled at Pig, whose eyes showed triumph.

"Let me see what I can do to change your mind. Corporal, remove Pig's gag, will you?"

Danny holstered the SIG and drew his dagger, the twin of Kaine's Fairbairn-Sykes. His stroke was less accurate than Kaine's, deliberately so, and he nicked the big man's earlobe. Pig howled. Blood ran down his neck and stained the collar of his once-white shirt.

A string of colourful expletives erupted from the creature's foul mouth when Danny ripped away the tape.

"Ooops, how clumsy of me."

"I'm going to rip your fucking head off you fu—"

Danny drove the heel of his left hand into Pig's face, splitting his upper lip.

"Rip my head off? How you gonna manage that, arsehole?"

Pig spat blood onto the gravel and started talking, this time controlled and quiet, eyes fixed on Danny, smiling through the split lip, teeth stained red with blood.

Danny stood back and chuckled while the man spewed his venom.

"You don't know who you're fucking dealing with, Blondie. You can't hide from me or mine. When I get loose, I'm gonna kill you dead, and I'm gonna do it slowly. After that, I'm coming back for that fucking slag, Shafer, and then I'll have her daughter. If she's really tasty, I'll string her out and force her to turn tricks to pay for her next fix. I've done it before, and I'll do it again. Then, Blondie, I'm gonna find your sister, if you have one, and do the same thing to her."

He paused for breath.

Danny scratched the back of his neck. "My sister's name is Michaela, and she scares the crap out of me. She'd eat you for breakfast. I'd happily give you her address if you like, but you won't be around long enough to use it."

Kaine kept a straight face. Danny didn't have a sister. He didn't have a brother either.

After a few seconds, Pig turned his wrath on Kaine. "As for you, you skinny, little fuckwit. You're the leader, right?"

Kaine took a bow. "I am indeed. I'd say it's a pleasure to make your acquaintance, but I'd be lying."

"Well, I've got a special place in hell for you. It's gonna take you weeks to die. Months. In the end, you're gonna beg me to kill you."

Danny fingered his lower lip and turned to Kaine. "Are you scared, boss?"

"By a man trussed like a Christmas turkey and talking through his backside? Yes, absolutely terrified. Are you?"

"Shaking in my boots, boss. Shall we let him go?"

Kaine scrunched up his face. "Let me think on that for a while." He turned to face Sidekick. "Does he mean all that?"

The younger man nodded. "I-I think so."

"Are you going to tell me his name and who he works for?"

Sidekick's eyes filled, and his lower lip quivered. His whole body shook as he bawled, "No. Please don't ask me. Please don't."

Pitiful.

"Nice one, Johnno," Pig said, success colouring his voice. "Keep quiet, and I'll see you're okay."

Kaine patted the lad on the shoulder. "Johnno, is it? Okay, Johnno. Just relax there for a minute while I silence this foul-mouthed bastard."

He rose and stood close to Danny. "What do you reckon, Corporal. Do you believe this creature?"

Again, Danny scratched the back of his neck. "You know what, boss? I think *he* believes it."

"I'll ask him to his face, just to make sure."

Kaine lowered his head, prepared for what he had to

do, but still willing to give their prisoner one last chance. He took two paces forwards and stood over Pig, arms crossed, looking down.

"What's your name?"

"Fuck off!"

"That stuff you said earlier, murder, rape, drugs, all that."

"Yeah?"

"Is it true?"

"Yeah!"

"Even if I let you go, you're going to kill everyone involved?"

Pig sneered. "Yeah, that's right."

"And your mate, Johnno? You're gonna kill him, too?"

"'Course. Snivelling snot-rag didn't have long, anyway. I was already getting bored with him. I need fresh meat."

Kaine stroked his beard as though trying to make a decision when he already had no doubt of his next course of action.

"You've given me a real dilemma here. What possible reason do I have to keep you alive?"

A moment of doubt flashed in Pig's dark eyes before the swagger returned. "You wouldn't dare kill me. I'm protected."

"You are?"

"S'right."

"By whom?"

"Protected. You can't touch me."

"I can't?"

"No, I'm untouchable. I get away with murder, always have, and now you're on my list."

Kaine bent at the waist and jabbed Pig in the right eye

with his index finger. Pig jerked his head back and roared. He bucked and howled and tried to roll away.

"You bastard. You fucking bastard!"

"Untouchable? Really? What was that, then?" Kaine said, after the noise died down a little.

Pig stared at him through the one good eye. The other eye was closed, but streamed tears that, to Pig, might have felt like blood or aqueous fluid.

"Who's here to protect you?"

Pig screamed and bucked against his bindings. "No one touches Pony Tedesco. No one! You're all going to die! Hear me?"

"Pony Tedesco? Thanks. That's all I need. Goodbye, Pony."

"Fuck o—"

Kaine slid the blade between the man's sixth and seventh ribs, canted upwards, towards the head, severing the ascending aorta. He twisted the handle.

Pony's eyes bugged, and a question formed. His jaw dropped open, but no words came.

"Sorry, son. But I believed every word you said. You gave me no choice."

Pony blinked three times, shuddered, and the light faded from his eyes. Johnno screamed at the trees, begging the night for help.

Danny stepped alongside Kaine, shaking his head. "Don't think you should have done that, boss."

Kaine wiped the blade on Pony Tedesco's expensive shirt. "What choice did I have? You heard what he said. No remorse. If we'd let him live, Angela and Bobbie would never have been safe. They'd have been running for the rest of their lives, and our job isn't to collect evidence for a court case."

Danny frowned. "Not what I meant, Captain. I meant a blade through the heart was too quick for the bastard." He tilted his head towards Johnno and raised his voice. "If it had been me, I'd have castrated the bastard and let him bleed out slowly and in agony."

Kaine took the message. This time he nodded.

"Ah, I see what you mean, Corporal. You make a very good case. Perhaps you'd like to deal with the accomplice over there? The one who keeps wetting himself."

"Oh yes, please, boss. Let me at him."

Johnno squealed, rolled onto his front, and tried to squirm away from the car and into the nearby undergrowth. Unfortunately for him, the bindings at his wrists and ankles slowed him down and turned him into a beached flatfish.

Danny rushed forwards, grabbed him by the scruff of the neck, and dragged him back into the glow of the Ford's sidelights and smiled into his face.

"Who are you more afraid of now, little man?"

Chapter Ten

Friday 27th November – Night

Breaker's Folly, North of Andover, Hampshire, England

Kaine stood back and watched Johnno lean away from the BMW and vomit next to the wheel. After heaving his dinner and retching through his tears, he sat back, eyes closed, shaking and hugging his knees tight to his chest. He didn't have the awareness to wipe his chin and snot ran around his mouth, mixing with the dribble of puke.

Not a pleasant sight.

"Don't hurt me," he snivelled at Danny. "P-Please don't hurt me."

"Why not?" Kaine asked, avoiding the mess and looking

into the cowering blue eyes. "You didn't do anything to stop Pony molesting Angela Shafer."

"What could I do? You saw what he was like. I couldn't save her, but I d-didn't touch her, I-I promise. P-Pony tried to make me do it … tried to make me hurt her, but I wouldn't."

"Bastard!" Danny snapped. "What do you fucking want, a medal? I'll pin something to your chest, you miserable bastard. You're as culpable as he is!"

He moved closer but stopped when Kaine shot out an arm.

"Easy, Corporal. You can have him in a minute."

"No, p-please. I-I'll tell you all I know, but p-please … please d-don't hurt me."

Kaine hesitated for a moment before nodding to Danny, re-sheathing the dagger, and sitting cross-legged in front of the pitiful wretch. He leaned forwards, resting his forearms on his knees.

"Good," he said. "Name? And don't tell me it's Johnno. I want your full name."

The terrified youngster swallowed hard, and his Adam's apple bobbed twice.

"Johnathan Ashby … Johnathan P-Peter Ashby. M-My drivin' licence is in my jacket pocket."

"No, it isn't," Danny said and lobbed a wallet to Kaine, who caught it one-handed and flipped it open.

The licence and bank cards confirmed the name.

"Okay, Ashby, let me make this crystal clear. You have one chance to live long enough to see daylight. I've heard of Pony Tedesco," Kaine said. Lying to a scumbag didn't count. He had no idea who Pony Tedesco was, but he was sure as hell going to find out. "Tell me one thing that doesn't tally with what I already know, and I'll let my friend loose. You heard what he wants to do to you?"

Ashby snapped his knees together, nodding vigorously. "I-I'll tell you everythin' I know. I promise."

Kaine twisted around and winked at Danny, his temporarily muzzled Rottweiler. "Corporal, fetch a bottle of water. This man needs a wash, and I can't stand to look at that mess on his face."

Danny snapped out a smart salute and hurried to the Ford, returning seconds later with three bottles.

"Here you go, boss. Enjoy."

He handed one bottle to Kaine and held out another to Ashby. When the snivelling coward reached to accept it, Danny pulled the bottle away in a childish game of "yes you can, no you can't". After two more fakes, Danny finally gave in and allowed Ashby his water.

"Corporal," Kaine said, sighing heavily, "that could be construed as cruel and unusual punishment. Consider yourself on a charge, and a day's wages deducted from your salary."

"Yes, boss. Sorry, boss," he said, not looking even slightly abashed, and added, "Salary? You mean I'm being paid?"

"Any more wisecracks and I won't let you have this crea-ture"—Kaine pointed at their prisoner—"when he tells his first lie."

Ashby's hands shook so badly, and the cable tie was so tight, he couldn't unscrew the cap on the bottle. In one lightning-fast action, Kaine drew his knife, slashed the plastic tie, and re-sheathed the blade.

Ashby gasped and dropped the bottle, staring at the red welts on his wrists. He scratched in the dirt around his still-bound ankles until his fingers found the bottle. He broke the seal, took a mouthful, rinsed out his mouth, and spat, before taking a long swallow. He poured some water over his face and dried off with the sleeve of his jacket, all the time staring at Pony Tedesco's slowly cooling body.

"T-Thanks for the water." Ashby filled his lungs and released a long, faltering sigh. "H-He really dead?"

From his position, standing over the body, Danny snorted. "Never seen anyone deader." He swung a foot back and aimed a kick at the dead man's head but pulled out at the last moment. Kaine knew his young friend well enough to know that kicking a corpse fell far outside his innate comfort zone.

The moon bathed the body in a flat, harsh light. The small, black mark on the silk shirt didn't look fatal. Barely a scratch. Precious little blood had left the body. It would have pooled in the chest cavity. They'd have to take care when moving the carcass or they'd end up covered in claret.

"Oh God," Ashby said, breathless as a whisper, "Teddy's gonna go ballistic."

Teddy?

Kaine wanted to ask, but didn't want to ruin his bluff. He removed his mobile from his jacket, selected the recording app, and hit run. No need for the spiral notepad he'd used as window dressing to reassure Angela Shafer.

"I imagine so. Tell me what you know about Teddy."

"I-I dunno know much. He don't never leave his tower block. He runs his operation from what Pony calls—called, 'Teddy's War Room'."

Ashby paused for another swallow, giving Kaine the opportunity to speak. "Describe him."

"I-I only met him once. He's older than Pony, but you can tell they're brothers. Same chin and … nose. Same voice, too. Maybe not so high-pitched. Good lookin', but scary. Teddy's eyes is different, too. Darker. Harder. He's closer to your height and build than what Pony were, and real tough. Cunnin'. You don't get to run an operation like his if you can't handle yourself."

Ashby was finally reaching the juicy stuff.

"Explain."

Ashby took another glug of water, before crushing the bottle flat and replacing the top. He kept his head lowered, eyes down, trying not to look at the corpse lying less than three metres to his left.

"Look up at me," Kaine barked. "I'm a human lie detector. I need to see your eyes, so I'll know when you're lying. Or would you like me to use the knife on those lids?"

Ashby shuddered. "Listen, M-Mister. I'm a queer what likes big strong men. P-Pony and me were special friends. That's it. We met at a club on the London Road. Hit it off right away. Pony were powerful and smooth. I-I didn't know what he was really like 'til later. He scared me shitless. I-I tried to stop seein' him, but he wouldn't have it. Got really jealou—"

"We don't need to hear about your love life," Danny said, sneering.

"S-Sorry, but I wanted to tell you what it were like. I didn't have no choice … tonight, I mean. Pony didn't say where we was going or what his plans were. When I-I saw what he was doin' to that poor woman, I-I were terrified. Couldn't move. And then … and then … he told me to do the same thing, but … but I couldn't, wouldn't. I can't do it with women …"

His voice trailed off. He looked from Kaine to Danny and back again as though realising what he'd admitted.

"But I wouldn't've done it, even if I could. Please, please

don't think me and him are the same. I'm not. I'm glad you came in and stopped him. I am. Really."

The last few words erupted from him faster than the vomit. Kaine was half-inclined to believe him.

"Okay, I'll take that as read. Get back to Teddy Tedesco."

Kaine took a gamble and assumed Pony and Teddy shared the same surname. They could have been half-brothers with different fathers, but it seemed a fair bet.

"I don't know nothin' 'bout Teddy's business." He raised a hand when Kaine reached for the knife. "No, no. It's true. All I know is what I heard on the streets. Gossip, y'know? Rumours."

Kaine rolled his empty hand forwards. "Okay, okay, give me the scuttlebutt."

Ashby frowned a question before working out what "scuttlebutt" meant and started talking again.

"F-From what I heard on the streets and from Pony, Teddy runs the biggest illegal operation on the south coast. Gamblin', whores—girls and boys—drugs, protection rackets, blackmail, traffickin' illegals, armed robberies. He got a small army for security, all big and beefy. All of them's armed."

The wind sliced through the trees. It ruffled the small man's long hair, pushing it across his face. Shivering, Ashby tugged it away with the little finger of his left hand in a peculiarly feminine gesture and hugged his knees to his chest. Kaine let him sit, rocking and twitching for a minute. Then the kid looked up.

"M-Mister," he said in a quiet, pleading voice, "that's all I know. Honest."

Kaine shook his head. "No, it isn't, not by a long way."

Ashby's chin trembled. "It is. I'm tellin' the truth."

"You met Teddy one time, right?"

"Yeah. Only once."

"In his office?"

"Yeah, that's right."

"How did you get in?"

"Huh?"

"You heard the question," Kaine said, allowing a hard edge into his voice. "I don't like repeating myself."

Ashby's chin trembled. Once again, he came close to tears.

"Oh, right. Pony took me through all them electronic gadgets. You know, like the crap they have at airports. Scanners, metal detectors, x-ray machines. There's two sets. One on the ground floor, the other on the top floor, before we got into—"

"Teddy's War Room?" Danny interrupted.

"Yeah, yeah. That's right," Ashby said, lifting pleading eyes to Danny, clearly desperate to make a connection. "After the lift opened, they done the same searches. And after all that, one of the security guards, a black man, patted me down. I'm tellin' you, the place is a … a fortress. Like the Bank of England. Ain't no one gets in Teddy don't want in. I mean, the bloke's paranoid." Ashby closed his eyes and scrunched up his pale face.

"Paranoid or just security conscious?" Kaine asked.

"Nah, paranoid. Pony told me Teddy's been shot a few times. Ambushed, y'know? Last time, a couple of years back, it nearly killed him. One of the bullets grazed his head. He ended up in hospital for a month. Once they discharged him, Teddy turned the whole tower block into a stronghold. He moved his mother into the floor below to keep her safe. Apparently, he loves his mother. Proper loves her, y'know? Durin' the visit, he kept tellin' Pony as how he should call on her more often. Pony kept noddin', sayin' he would, but I could tell he were lyin'. To keep Teddy sweet, y'know?"

"Very touching," Danny sneered. "A criminal who loves his mummy. Heart-warming."

Kaine waved Danny into silence. "Keep going with the story. Tell me what else you know about Teddy's paranoia."

Ashby shrugged. "There ain't much else to tell. He runs his organisation through, what d'you call 'em, intermediaries, yeah? Electronic tags on everythin'. I mean, he employs a team of IT geeks all the way up the wazoo. Has eyes and ears all over the city and inside all his clubs. Apparently, whenever somethin' special's goin' down, Teddy makes his men wear earpieces, like secret agents? Some even have body cams, like them ones the cops wear, y'know. Teddy likes to see and hear what's goin' on. Pony once boasted if someone so much as farts on any street in Southampton, Teddy can analyse the gas and tell you what the guy had for lunch."

Ashby paused long enough to wipe more dribble from his chin before rattling on at machine-gun speed, trying to save his life with a barrage of random information. Happy to let the man rant, and hoping at least some of the information turned out to be useful, Kaine listened patiently.

"Teddy's outer office, the one where Elizabeth sits—"

"Elizabeth?" Kaine asked.

"Teddy's secretary, or PA maybe. She's protective of him, like there's somethin' more goin' on between them, y'know? I notice stuff like that. It's one of my skills. Anyway, her office is like one of them newsrooms. TV monitors all over the walls. She's got three desks in there. I reckon it's where the bodyguards sit when Teddy wants some privacy, like. And in Teddy's big room, the screens are hidden by bookshelves that slide back like somethin' out o' James Bond. Teddy's proud of the setup. Even showed me how everythin' worked." Ashby paused for breath before racing on.

"Then, as we was leavin', Teddy went ape-shit when Pony spilled some of his whisky on the carpet. He wasn't pissed about the carpet, but on account of the whisky. Expensive stuff it was. Straight off of the top shelf. Pony laughed in his face. Said he was more into beer. I had a—"

"Okay, that's enough." Kaine tapped his watch. "You're not giving me anything of value."

"Sorry. I'm nervous. Makes me talkative. Oh yeah, this one time, Pony took me to a restaurant, The Lobster Bisque. Posh place. Michelin star. We wore suits and ties, and Pony came over as Lord of the Manor, y'know. Talkin' like he owned the place, rather than Teddy, which likely pissed Teddy off. Like I said, Teddy owns loads of businesses, some dodgy, some legit. He sees and hears everythin'. Got his fingers in a lot of … a lot of …"

"Pies?" Danny offered, ever so helpfully.

"Yeah, pies," Ashby said, shuffling his backside closer to the car.

"Anything else?" Kaine asked.

"No, no. Of course"—he raised an index finger in the air—"you want to know where he lives." He hit his forehead with the meat of his hand. "I'm such a dummy. Pony lyin' just over there, dead, don't help my concentration, y'know?"

Ashby's face paled. He threw a hand over his mouth and looked ready to hurl whatever was left of his dinner into the gravel once again.

"Breathe through your mouth. You'll get over it."

Ashby sucked in a lungful of air through his mouth and his colour returned.

"The address?"

"It's the buildin' next to Genting's Club on Oxford Street, Southampton. Pony took me past it loads of times. Once, he looked at the block and laughed. The lights on the top floor were still glowin'. Pony said Teddy were probably watchin' us right then and there. I remember askin' why Pony were laughin'. He slapped me round the back of my head, and it hurt."

Ashby's lower lip jutted out, making him look like a schoolboy.

"That were the first time he hit me when I didn't want him to, y'know? When I weren't expectin' it."

"Get on with it," Kaine said, having no interest in the pitiful man's sexual peccadillos. "Did Pony tell you why he was laughing?"

Ashby jerked up his chin, sniffled, and used his sleeve as a handkerchief again. Kaine wouldn't have wanted his cleaning bill.

"Yeah," Ashby said, turning his eyes to the stars. "It was gone midnight and Pony said, 'If you must know, it's because I'm down here about to gamble usin' his money, and he's still up there at work, earnin' it. Dozy fuck should get a life instead of workin' the whole time.' I remembered bein' really scared 'cause it were the first time Pony dissed his brother, y'know. Until then, Pony talked as though Teddy were the best thing since … since …'"

"Sliced bread?" Danny butted in again and started pacing behind Kaine's back.

Kaine could number maybe ten people on the planet he'd allow to guard his back, but Danny's pacing made him antsy. Not that Kaine could blame Danny for his unease. Time was motoring along.

A pale pre-dawn cut a sliver of light into the eastern horizon, promising a dry, fresh day. They needed to leave the area. No telling how soon the first visitors would begin stomping their way through the undergrowth. Although Angela said the Folly was poorly utilised as a beauty spot, Kaine couldn't discount the idea of being interrupted. It would be bad luck for a coach-load of twitchers to arrive, hunting a rare African Goldfinch, while he and Danny were loading Pony's body into the boot of the BMW.

Ashby nodded vigorously. "Yeah, that's right, sliced bread. Somethin' must've happened to piss Pony off, 'cause that night he lost money like he didn't care, I mean, thousands and thousands. And when we got back to his flat, I … well, let's just say I was scared he'd beat me to death, y'know? I mean, I've been with some powerful and angry men, but that night, Pony were an animal. I ended up bruised and … sorry, I … I can see you don't want details."

Ashby broke down. Tears fell again and Kaine could tell by the pause in Danny's pacing that even he was starting to feel sorry for the ineffectual, little creep. Danny always was a sucker for a sob story, and a single look at Ashby and Pony would confirm that one was no match for the other.

"Stay right where you are," Kaine said, pointing a finger to the ground. "The corporal and I are going to discuss what to do with you. Understand?"

The abject man nodded and buried his face in his hands, crying quietly.

Kaine stood and motioned for Danny to join him out of earshot.

"Believe him, boss?"

"Do you?"

Danny wagged his head from side to side in the approximation of an indecisive nod. "On balance, yes."

"Agreed. The kid's a lightweight. I don't think he's an instigator or a killer, but he didn't lift a finger to help Angela, and I can't forgive him for it."

"What d'you want to do with him? You said yourself we aren't cops or prison guards, and I don't really want to kill the little jerk."

Kaine stood still, staring at, but not really seeing, their captive. After a moment he nodded, decision made.

"You've got a plan?" Danny asked.

"I have."

"Am I gonna like it?"

Kaine flashed Danny an encouraging smile. "Let me answer that with another question."

Danny rubbed his hands together. "Ooh, do like a nice pop quiz."

"Given what Pony said about being protected, and what Ashby just told us, I'm assuming Teddy pointed Pony at Angela Shafer in the full knowledge of what he planned to do. Do you think a little payback is in order?"

"Let me get this straight," Danny said. "Are you planning to start a war with a mobster called Teddy Tedesco, who, according to that pipsqueak"—he tilted his head towards the silently weeping Johnno—"runs the biggest crime syndicate on the south coast?"

Kaine nodded. "That's pretty much it. Tedesco's going to have a meltdown when he learns what I did to Pony."

"What *we* did, sir," Danny said through a grim smile. "I'm here, too."

"Fair enough. We both know how men like that operate. He can't allow his brother to die without showing a reaction. Angela and her whole family will be targets until we've neutralised him as a threat."

Kaine paused for a moment before offering Danny a way out he already knew the youngster would refuse.

"Listen, Danny, I'll understand if this is more than you signed up for. Things are likely to get a little hairy over the next few days. You can take a pass if you want. I won't think any less of you."

Danny delivered an instant response with a hurt frown.

"Kidding aren't you, boss? After what Teddy set in motion, if you weren't going to do anything, not only would I be very disappointed, I'd have had to pay the bastard a visit myself."

Kaine clapped Danny's shoulder.

"Excellent. Knew I could rely on you. Now, let's send Teddy a message, eh?"

"You going to call and tell him where he can collect the body?"

"And leave a corpse lying around here for anyone to stumble over? Not likely. I think we'd best have it hand-delivered, don't you?"

Kaine returned to Ashby and sliced through the cable tie binding his ankles.

"Right then, young man," he said, smiling. "Fancy earning yourself a few extra hours of life?"

Chapter Eleven

Breaker's Folly, North of Andover, Hampshire, England

The second Kaine gave Ashby his instructions, the kid fell apart.

"No, no. Please don't ask me to do that. Teddy's gonna kill me."

Feet scrambling on gravel, he tried to bolt, but Danny, expecting the reaction, clipped him across the back of the head and he settled down.

"Listen to me, Ashby," Kaine said, voice cool, quiet, "you don't have any choice in the matter. Either do as I tell you or die right here, right now."

Kaine stepped aside for Danny to approach and show the kid his knife. He waved the blade at the kid's groin and allowed the silence to extend until Ashby'd had enough time to digest the news.

"So, what's it to be? Do I let my friend loose on you, or are you going to be reasonable?"

"Y-You're sendin' me to my d-death. You know that, right?"

"You never know," Danny said, grinning like a maniac, "Tedesco might even thank you for bringing his brother's body home for a proper burial. Might even give you a tip."

"That's not funny. Teddy's going to beat me to a pulp."

"Maybe you'll enjoy it, eh?"

Ashby's face disintegrated.

Danny grabbed his lapels, yanked him to his feet, and pulled him close. The blade, still in Danny's hand, grazed Ashby's cheek, drawing blood.

"Listen to me, you snivelling bastard. I saw the results of what you and Pony did to Mrs Shafer, and I heard what you had planned for her daughter. Captain?" he said, turning to Kaine. "I've got a better idea. Why don't we call Teddy and let him know how helpful Johnno's been in answering our questions?"

Ashby wriggled.

"No, no. Oh shit, no. P-Please … please don't."

He tried to break Danny's iron grip, but he'd have had greater success trying to open a can of beans with his teeth. After another futile struggle, his hands fell to his sides in defeat, and resignation crumpled his bleeding face.

"W-What exactly do you want me to do?"

"First, you're going to help me load Pony's carcase into the boot of the BMW."

"What? N-No, I couldn't."

Danny cuffed Ashby's ear.

"After that, you're going to drive the body to Teddy's bunker and deliver the captain's message."

Ashby wallowed. He tore his eyes from Danny, and let his gaze fall on Pony's corpse.

"Look at me, Ashby," Kaine said. "Look at my face."

Reluctantly, Ashby dragged his gaze from the body and turned it on Kaine.

"Make sure you can describe me to Teddy."

"What?"

Kaine snatched Ashby from Danny and dragged him into the glow from the Ford's sidelights to allow him a better view. "I know after what I did to Pony, Teddy's going to be out for my blood. Make sure he knows what I look like. Okay?"

Confused but compliant, Ashby nodded.

"Tell him Angela and Roberta Shafer are under my protection. They will not be harmed. Got that?"

Kaine released Ashby's lapels and he slumped back against the car, looking Kaine up and down, taking in every detail.

Kaine took out the notepad he used earlier and jotted down a number. He tore out the page, folded it in half, and handed it to Ashby, who took it with trembling fingers.

"That's my mobile number. I know Tedesco will never let the matter drop, but tell him I'm giving him the same chance I'm giving you now. He has one week to disband his organisation and leave Southampton. If he doesn't, mine will be the last face he ever sees."

Ashby stuffed the page into his trouser pocket.

"I'm giving him time to bury his brother. See what a

nice person I am? But tell him if I don't hear from him within the week, I'll be coming for him. I'll tear down his organisation brick by brick, man by man. Tell him I'm going to retire him with extreme prejudice. Do you need me to write any of that down for you?"

The kid shook his head. "No, no. I heard what you said. You've got a death wish. Teddy Tedesco's gonna go ape. Please, you can't make me do this. I'll be dead by mornin'."

Kaine shrugged. "Well, I'm not sure what Teddy's going to do with you, but at least you'll leave this place alive. Now, help the corporal with the body, and then off you toddle."

Danny dragged the body to the back of the BMW and made the weeping Ashby take the feet—the lighter end. With Ashby grunting and straining under the load, they hefted the corpse to the lip of the boot and rolled it into the stinking luggage compartment. Pony landed with a dull, wet thud. Danny folded the legs and arms inside and slammed the lid into place.

Seconds later, Ashby hit the accelerator and the BMW took off in a wheel spin of flying gravel and a wagging rear end.

Danny sidled across to Kaine, shaking his head. "Really, boss. 'Retired with extreme prejudice'?"

Kaine smoothed his beard. "Yes, sorry, Danny. Heard it in a film once. Always wanted to find out if it sounded as naff in real life."

"And does it?"

"You tell me."

Danny gave him a lopsided grin. "It does."

They stood watching the BMW's tail and brake lights bounce and wobble along the track, stop at the gate, and continue on their way. They turned left, heading towards the main drag into Southampton, and were soon lost to the darkness.

"Driving a little fast for these roads," Kaine said. "Hope he doesn't have an accident."

"Did you plant the bug on the Beemer?"

Kaine nodded. "Yep. We'll know exactly where Pony's body ends up. By the way, what was all that hopping from one foot to the other and pacing?"

"Just trying to make out I was itching to kill him. You know, I was being in the moment. I was 'emoting'."

"Looked like you needed the toilet."

Danny sighed. "Everyone's a critic."

"Much more of this covert ops stuff, and I'll have to enrol you in a drama class. Anyway, I wonder what Teddy will do when he hears my message?"

"No telling. I know what I'd do if someone killed my only brother."

"Even if he was a rapist and a psychopath?" Kaine asked.

"Good point, but I doubt a gangland leader will make that distinction. I trust you know what you're doing, boss. I mean, it might have been better to hide the body and keep Pony's death a secret."

"But we'd never have been able to trust Ashby not to talk."

"Another good point." He nodded. "What now?"

"Now, Danny, we tidy up and find ourselves a nice breakfast."

"Best thing you've said all day. I'm starving."

"Thought you might be."

Five minutes later, Kaine stood back and scanned the car park for signs of their presence.

Danny had cleaned up most traces of a disturbance

using a branch he pulled out of the bushes. As an anti-forensics measure, Kaine took a jerrycan from the Ford's boot and splashed a couple of litres of petrol over the patch of Pony's blood and Ashby's vomit.

"And now breakfast, boss?"

"Yep, and on the way, I'll leave a message with Sabrina. See if she's available to run a deep dive on Teddy Tedesco and his organisation," Kaine said, heading to the passenger seat of the Ford and pointing Danny to the driver's side.

"And if she isn't, you'll ask Corky?"

"Yes, Corky. We need good intel and fast. Can't be too fussy how we acquire it, either." Kaine patted his pockets. "Got any matches? A lighter?"

"Sorry, boss. Gave up smoking when I joined the service. What about the"—he searched on the dashboard—"bloody hell. No cigar lighter. The world's gone mad."

"No matter, I have the equivalent of rubbing a Boy Scout's legs together. The petrol will have started to evaporate by now and the gravel's a combination of flint and granite. Drive on."

Danny keyed the ignition and pumped the throttle, and the sporty Ford roared into life. As Danny pulled the car away, Kaine drew his SIG. It took three shots before the glancing ricochets ignited the fuel, but it went up in a pleasing ball of blue-and-yellow flame.

"Don't you just love fireworks?" Danny said and added more weight to the accelerator. "M1 to Northants? Motorway services will be opening for brekkie soon."

"Yes, Danny, I haven't forgotten your bottomless pit of a stomach. You're almost as bad as Larry Kovaks."

Danny threw a hand up to his chest. "Eat more than Fat Larry? *Moi?* You're kidding, right?"

Kaine ignored Danny's interruption and continued

with, "And after breakfast, we'll head straight to Long Buckby. We need to prepare for a small war."

The fireball behind them lit up the inside of the car and Danny's smile. "Extreme prejudice?"

Kaine didn't respond. He was already deep into campaign planning mode.

Chapter Twelve

Saturday 28th November – Jerome Tedesco

Ocean Village, Southampton, Hampshire, England

Teddy stood over the battered and bloody remains of the miserable, little creep, wiping down the leather-bound cosh he'd taken his time to do most of the damage with. The wet sponge would suffice for the time being. He'd sterilise it in the autoclave later.

To make certain, Teddy kicked the body in the head a couple of times with his special boots. The steel toecaps crunched the skull, but the fucker didn't so much as twitch. Dead meat, just like poor, departed Pony.

"That'll teach you to let my brother die. Fucker." He snapped his fingers and pointed to the mess on the Clean

Room floor. "Timothy, clear that away and call the under-taker. Pony needs a proper burial."

While Timothy loaded the soggy remains into a plastic garbage bin borrowed from the janitor's cupboard, Teddy washed his hands and face in the sink. Hot water, carbolic soap, paper towels. He repeated the process for good measure.

"After *this* is taken care of, we start looking, yes?" Timothy asked. "The man who did that to Pony needs teaching a lesson."

Teddy wadded up the damp towels and threw them into the bin with the queer, destined for the basement incinerator. Then he tore off his paper suit and the booties, and dropped the lot into the bin alongside the corpse. No trace. No danger of police reprisals.

Try getting forensics on me, Little Piggies. You've got no chance.

"Yeah. Too bloody right he does. Put every man in the organisation on it. This so-called captain wants a war, I'll give him a fucking war. I'm gonna crush the bastard with my bare hands. He's going to regret crossing me and mine."

Timothy's face screwed up in his version of looking thoughtful.

"I know that look," Teddy said. "What's on your mind?"

"Sorry, Teddy. It's a bit … delicate. I, er, I don't want to upset you any more than you already are."

Teddy pulled back his shoulders and glowered at the big South African. "You'll piss me off big time if you don't spit it out. I don't pay you the big bucks to be timid. Or are you losing your bottle?"

Timothy's jaw muscles expanded and contracted as he ground his teeth.

"That's better," Teddy said. "Now, spit it out."

"Did you take a close look at Pony's wound?"

"No, 'course not. He was my baby brother, and I'm not a fucking ghoul. Why, what d'you see?"

"It's clean. One precise cut, between the ribs and into the heart. A real pro did that. It would have left very little blood at the scene. This captain knew how to handle a knife, that's for sure. If you want my guess, the man had special forces training." Timothy's expression hardened. "Thought you needed to know, Mr Tedesco. If you're going to draw this man out, you might want to think about drafting in some serious ex-military types. The boys we have on staff are okay for a little intimidation and in a brawl, but if you need real firepower, they'll probably come up short."

Teddy contemplated his chief minder's words. In all the years he'd been on the payroll, Timothy had never spoken as much in one go. It proved the man's advice had been thought out and deserved serious consideration.

"You don't think he got lucky then, this 'captain'?"

Timothy shook his shaven head. "Not a chance, and from the way Johnno described the ... takedown, it shows they were serious pros. Highly skilled. As I said, Special Forces—Black Ops."

"You reckon some braindead soldier with ten weeks' military training is gonna make me sweat?" Teddy slammed the side of his fist against the white-tiled wall. "Black Ops? I'll show him fucking Black Ops. Let's see how brave he is. Where's that sheet of paper with the fucker's phone number?"

Timothy took the captain's note from his jacket pocket and handed it over, together with one of the firm's burners. For a black bastard, Timothy was a good man. He wouldn't let Teddy's anger outstrip his judgement. Not that Teddy would ever drop his guard and use his contract phone or a land line for non-legit activities.

Teddy punched the phone number into the mobile and waited. Each time the ring tone repeated, Teddy's heartrate ratcheted up another five beats.

"Not answering. The fucker's turned tail and run. So much for Black-fucking-Ops. This arsehole's found out who he's dealing with and run off with his tail—"

"Hello, is that Teddy Tedesco?" piped up the cheery voice on the other end of the line. Teddy hit the speaker icon and the man continued.

"Is that the man who used to have a brother called Pony? You know, the rapist. The would-be killer? The snivelling coward?"

He sounded relaxed, calm, as though he was booking a table at his local restaurant. Not running scared at all. Timothy stared at the phone, concentrating hard on the smug bastard's words. In the background of the call, birds twittered and a horse whinnied.

In one form or another, Teddy had been around horses all his life. First as a stable hand, then as a bookie's runner, and finally as an owner. His stables currently housed some of the finest racehorses in the UK. Teddy knew horses when he heard them. The captain was in the country somewhere. Teddy'd give a million in cash money to find out where.

"Yeah, this is me, you fuck—"

"Oh dear. No need for the expletives, Teddy, dear boy," the smooth voice said. "For that show of disrespect, I'm hanging up. Ring me back in two hours."

The call disconnected. Teddy stared in disbelief at the silent phone in his hand, wondering what had just happened.

"Did the bastard hang up on me?" he asked Timothy.

"Sounds like it, Mr Tedesco."

Christ Almighty!

"How fucking *dare* he?"

Teddy hit the redial button, but the ring tone kept buzzing, unanswered. He thumbed "cancel" and had to stop himself from throwing the phone at the wall.

"Who does he think he is? Disrespect? I'll show him fucking disrespect!"

Blood pounded in Teddy's ears, and the Clean Room grew dark as his vision clouded. He dropped the phone on the ceramic draining board, leaned against the wall, and closed his eyes.

Count to ten. Count to fucking ten. Breathe, man. Breathe.

Slowly, the pounding in his ears faded and his breathing settled. He let out a long sigh and opened his eyes again to find Timothy standing to attention.

Teddy scowled at the black fucker. "You still here?"

Timothy grabbed the handle of the plastic bin. "I'll get Ginger to dispose of the rubbish."

Teddy shook the last of the anger from his head. "Yeah, okay. Make sure he does it properly. Make him stand over the incinerator for at least an hour. I don't need another cock-up like the one that started this whole shit storm."

"You can rely on Ginger, Mr Tedesco."

"Thought I could rely on Grady and the fucking Kraut, too. But look where that led. Pony's dead and this arrogant prick"—he waved an index finger at the silent mobile—"is threatening my livelihood."

"Like I said, Mr Tedesco, I'm sorry for your loss."

"Spare me the platitudes, *boy*. We both know Pony was a fucking liability, but he was *my* fucking liability. My family. My blood. If he ever got too far out of hand, I'm the one who should have done the business, not some jacked-up soldier boy trying to make a name for himself."

"I'll be right back, Mr Tedesco."

"See that you are. You're going to do some recruiting, and I'm putting a price on Captain Arsewipe's head."

Timothy rolled the bin through the back door, and Teddy locked it behind him.

Teddy stood by the sink and scanned the room—two steel doors, white tiles on the walls, floor, and ceiling, a ceramic sink, and a drain in the centre of the floor. Although currently spattered with the queer's blood, vomit, and shit, it wouldn't take long to sanitise.

Teddy sniffed, enjoying the aroma of death.

His Clean Room was notorious. Put the fear of God into his minions and his enemies alike. It made people toe the line even though he rarely used it these days.

Careful to avoid treading in the gore, Teddy picked up the mobile and walked through the second door, the one leading to his adjacent office. He dropped the mobile on his desk and slid into his leather chair.

Teddy eyed the silent mobile. He'd give Captain Arsewipe his two hours all right. He'd humour the bastard and calm down in the process. Assuming the fucker deigned to answer his bloody phone again, Teddy would finesse a meeting with the Black Ops moron. Oh yes. And after that, he'd introduce the bastard to the delights of the Clean Room.

Captain Arsewipe would take days to die. Weeks maybe.

Teddy snapped out of his daydream, leaned forwards, and pressed a button on the intercom.

"Elizabeth?"

"Yes, Mr Tedesco?"

"Call in the sterilisation crew. The Clean Room needs a scrub."

"Very well, Mr Tedesco," she said, switching to her

sultry voice—a real turn-on. "Do you have time for a massage? I know how tense you get after a ... workout."

"As it happens, I do have a couple of hours to spare. Get in here and bring all the oils."

As usual, Elizabeth's throaty chuckle made Teddy's heart rate double.

Chapter Thirteen

Saturday 28th November – Morning

Mike's Farm, Long Buckby, Northants, England

Kaine and Danny reached the farm as the sun broke through the thin mist of a late-autumn morning. Mike—a septuagenarian former sailor with the strength and vitality of a man twenty years his junior—met them at the door and ushered them into the dining room for a "meet and greet".

Kaine eased Lara to one side while Danny, Mike, and Rollo discussed the previous day's events with growing excitement and increasing volume.

"How's Angela?" Kaine asked, turning his back to the others.

"Her physical injuries are largely superficial, but

emotionally?" Lara spoke quietly and shook her head sadly. "Although, she's a strong woman and having her daughter close is a good thing, only time will tell."

"Understood." Kaine nodded. "Does she need anything? Medication?"

"No. That's covered. We dropped into the local pharmacy on the way here to pick up some supplies. Among other things, I've given her an *ulipristal acetate* tablet. It's an over-the-counter medicine you'd probably know as the morning after pill. It's the best I can do for her under the circumstances. Ideally, I'd recommend she visit a counsellor, but given the situation, that's impractical."

She paused for a moment to catch her breath before grabbing his hand and looking at him through tear-filled eyes. "Ryan, what that man put her through was ... awful."

He pulled her close, cupped her cheek gently, and wiped away a tear with his thumb.

"He won't hurt anyone else again."

Lara held his hand and pressed it harder against her cheek. "You ... killed him?"

"There was no other way."

Darkness clouded her eyes. "I ... understand, but ..."

"Lara, I know what you think of my methods. But I promise you, if I could have delivered him to the police with enough evidence to put him away forever, I'd have done it in a heartbeat. You know that, right?"

"Yes. Yes, Ryan, I know."

"Besides, no barrister is likely to call me or Danny as witnesses, even when I am cleared of the ... other matter. Odds are, Pony would have walked free sooner rather than later. And where would that have left Angela and Bobbie? Running and hiding for the rest of their lives. I couldn't let that happen."

He tried to drop his hand, but she held on and pulled it close to her chest, hiding the action from the room. Kaine found the gesture compelling and intimate, and wondered how he was going to survive without her when she finally returned to her own life.

"I know," she whispered, "but I'm worried about what's going to happen next."

Reluctantly, Kaine pulled her hand from his.

"Don't be. Next," he said, "Danny and I are going to make a few calls. Then we'll wait."

"Wait for what?"

He turned to face the group and spoke loud enough to break through their chatter. "We'll wait to find out who acquires the necessary intel first, Sabrina or Corky. What do you reckon, guys?"

Rollo answered first. "My money's on the French lass. Despite his mouth, Corky's all bluster."

"Dunno about that, Sarge," Danny piped up. "Sabrina's one of the best hackers in the business"—he held up a hand to forestall Rollo's interruption—"but my money's on Corky."

Rollo raised a dark eyebrow. "How much are you prepared to lose on the little weasel?"

"Twenty quid too rich for your blood?" Danny's cheeky grin held enough power to lighten most moods.

"Too rich? You young puppy. Double it. No, treble it."

Ordinarily, Kaine would have frowned on gambling in the ranks, which could lead to bad blood, but Rollo and Danny were long-term friends. They paid their debts quickly and didn't take things too seriously. He let them shake hands on the sixty-pound wager.

When Sabrina called back first, it earned Danny a heavy, Rollo-sized thump on the shoulder and an "I told you so" swagger. But when her response turned out to be a recorded message containing a brief apology, Danny shot Rollo a smug grin.

They broke for lunch while waiting on Corky's call. Unfortunately Kaine received the initial irate call from a worked-up gangster first. He strode outside to the courtyard before connecting.

"Hello, is that Teddy Tedesco?" he asked, putting on an upbeat, customer service voice. "Is that the man who used to have a brother called Pony? You know, the rapist. The would-be killer? The snivelling ..."

———

WHILE THEY WAITED for Tedesco's return call, Kaine took Rollo and Danny to the room above the barn—the soon-to-be-equipped operations centre.

While Danny, as Chief Recruitment Officer, made a series of phone calls, Kaine and Rollo worked up a solid foundation upon which to build a battle plan. Halfway through the conversation, Corky called to add his extraordinarily detailed information to the mix.

Danny whooped and held his hand out to Rollo. Without pausing or grumbling, Rollo dragged his wallet from his jacket pocket and slapped three twenties into Danny's eager palm.

Ten minutes before Tedesco's deadline, Kaine and Rollo joined Mike in the backyard sun trap to wait, leaving Danny in the middle of another call.

Kaine placed his burner on the oak garden table, and they basked in the rare warmth of a bright and calm, late-autumn day. An almost-imperceptible zephyr barely had the strength to move the haze, birds chattered in the bare chestnut branches and overhead, and a few white clouds dotted the sky. Kaine soaked up the tranquillity.

Mike filled his pipe, but struggled to keep the thing lit. He had to keep attacking it with the lance-like flame of a pipe lighter. A huge pall of blue smoke hung around his shaggy head, partially obscuring his Captain Birdseye beard. It forced Kaine to cough, wave a hand in front of his face, and move upwind of the fug.

At least that was his excuse.

Kaine's relocated position allowed him a better view of Lara, who stood a few metres distant, inside the main paddock. She was holding the reins of a black horse so huge, its shoulders reached as high as her head. One false move from Lara and the beast, if startled, could easily grind her into the mud, but Lara patted the animal's neck and spoke quietly into its ear. The joy in her smile was something Kaine could only watch and revel in. Horse riding was one of the few physical activities he'd yet to attempt. Maybe one day, when things settled down a little, he and Lara could …

Enough of that, Kaine.

As Kaine checked his watch, Danny emerged from the house and took his place on the bench between Mike and Rollo.

"What do you reckon?" Kaine asked, powering up the mobile. "Think he's stewed enough?"

"You're ringing him?" Danny asked. "I thought he was supposed to call you?"

Kaine winked. "It always pays to keep the enemy off balance."

He dialled the number and hit the speaker icon.

Lara climbed the fence and straddled the top rail. The

horse rested its head in her lap. A vision of perfection—Lara, not so much the horse.

Tedesco answered immediately and spewed out a string of invective.

Kaine cut the call.

"Teddy needs to learn some manners."

"So, now we wait some more?" Mike asked, dropping the uncooperative pipe into an ashtray in annoyance.

Before Kaine could respond, the mobile buzzed, and he declined the call.

"Yep, now we wait. We need another call from Tedesco to give Corky a chance to home in on his location."

"But we know where Tedesco is," Mike offered. "The bug you placed on the BMW tells us that."

Lara climbed down from the fence, rubbed the animal's nose, and hurried across the yard to join the conversation. She sat next to Kaine—the extra space on the bench being yet another reason for his earlier move. She smelled of lavender soap and horse musk. The former was nice, but the latter took some getting used to.

"No," she said, "that only tells us where the *car* is. Isn't that right?"

She aimed the question at Rollo, not Kaine. Probably for the sake of appearance, but Kaine had no doubt everyone knew what was really going on between them.

"That's dead right," Rollo answered, smiling his encouragement. "Ashby could have dumped the car and run, or he could have parked somewhere safe and legged it to Tedesco's fortress."

Kaine took up the mantle of storyteller. "Corky's monitoring both the bug's location and this mobile. If Tedesco and the BMW are in close proximity, he'll have a pretty accurate fix on Teddy's permanent location. It'll save us a bit of time if we can get confirmation."

"Also," Danny said, not to be left out of the conversation, "Corky needs time to do his stuff."

"What stuff?" Lara asked.

Danny, the most technologically savvy of the group, took the floor. "He'll try to piggyback on Tedesco's mobile phone signal and splice into his electronic footprint. If it were me and I had all the right equipment—and half-decent, ninja, IT skills—I'd have set up a search algorithm to identify any activity related to Tedesco and his organisation. If Corky's as good as he claims to be, it shouldn't take him long to give us access to Teddy's surveillance systems and his data and comms lines."

Danny stopped talking and stared into the distance, lost in thought for a moment. An evil smile creased his face.

"What's wrong now?" Rollo demanded.

Danny snapped his attention back to Rollo. "Nothing, but I was thinking. If Teddy has one of those integrated smart homes with a centrally controlled metering system, by the end of today, Corky will probably be able to control everything—including his central heating." He looked around the table and laughed. "Maybe the captain could ask Corky to override the safety systems on the boiler and turn up the hot water. We could boil Teddy's nuts the next time he takes a shower."

Mike grimaced and made a sucking sound with his teeth.

"Good idea," Rollo said. "Why not add it to Corky's to-do list."

Kaine rapped the table with his knuckles. "Okay, let's bring this mothers' meeting to order, eh? And keep the noise down." He shot a look up to one of the bedroom windows, behind which Angela and Bobbie rested. "Let's remember why we're here. Okay?"

Lara followed Kaine's glance and shuddered. The others nodded, and the group fell into a short silence.

"Would you like me to go check on them?" Lara asked, pulling away and leaving a cool gap next to him on the bench.

"I'm sure they'd appreciate that," he said, nodding. "They'll probably have a load of questions, too. And I'd rather they didn't overhear what I have to say to Tedesco."

She squeezed his hand and left. Mike winked as she passed him and said, "You've a good lass there, Ryan. Look after her. Anyone who can handle Dynamite ..." He tilted his head towards the black horse, who snorted and pawed the Northants clay in its paddock the moment Lara entered the house.

"Dynamite?" Kaine snapped. "You let Lara near a horse called Dynamite and have the gall to tell *me* to look after her?"

"Don't be daft, Ryan," Mike said, his bearded cheeks plumping, and his deep voice resonating around the yard. "You saw what she was like with him. She's got greater control over the beast than I have. And anyway, his name comes from the size and force of his droppings, not his temperament. All I'm saying is, don't stand downwind of the beggar after he's had a nosebag full of oats."

Danny tried hard not to laugh and had to cover his mouth with his hand.

Rollo shook his head sadly. "Careful, Mike. Even though we're your guests, the captain here doesn't have a sense of humour as far as the doc's safety is concerned."

Kaine rose and stood over them, staring the two older men down. "If you two jokers have quite finished, we've an operation to plan. Chief Petty Officer Procter, do you mind if we decamp to your office? I'd like to see how Corky's doing before I call Tedesco in"—he checked the screen of his mobile—"let's say thirty-five minutes."

Mike jumped to his feet with every bit as much fluidity as Kaine and snapped out a smart salute. "Certainly, Captain. Follow me."

He ruined the military effect by ending the salute with a wink.

"You old codger," Kaine said, clapping the man he considered a second father on the shoulder. "As for you, Sergeant Rollason, wipe that smirk off your face."

Rollo didn't exactly wink, but his twitching left eye came very close to it.

During stand-down time between ops, Kaine usually liked to allow his senior men a certain tolerance, knowing they'd all snap-to when the need arose. But the operational parameters had changed. Currently, everyone he called on was a civilian, a volunteer. As such, he needed to loosen his tight hold a little. That being said, during an active operation he would accept nothing other than total professionalism, and the men knew it. The time to put their game faces back on was fast approaching.

"Danny?" Kaine called.

The blond corporal had approached Dynamite, but kept on the safe side of the fence, well out of range of his hooves and his rear end.

"Yes, boss?"

"Any luck contacting our errant colleagues?"

"A little, boss. I emailed Cough but haven't had a reply. As for Stinko, he seems to have dropped off the planet. Fat Larry and Slim are on their way and should be here by tomorrow afternoon."

"Okay, fair enough. Tried the VSC for the others?"

"Yes, boss."

"When they do reply, tell them we have a nice, little contract for them. If they're abroad, get them First Class travel back to Blighty and we'll cover any expenses and losses they incur, provided they can supply an itemised invoice."

Danny pulled in his chin. "Itemised invoices from a bunch of mercenaries? Are you kidding, Captain?"

Kaine nodded and smiled. "You aren't the only jokers on the farm. Right, time to make the office our home for the afternoon."

Chapter Fourteen

Saturday 28th November – Lara Orchard

Mike's Farm, Long Buckby, Northants, England

Teary-eyed, Bobbie sat in the comfy chair a thoughtful Rollo had carried up to the fourth bedroom from Mike's lounge. Angela lay in bed, trying to rest.

Lara stood over her patient, not feeling as much an absolute fraud as she might have done.

As part of her work designing The 83 Trust's website, Sabrina had produced a detailed legend for Lara which included a medical degree, doctor's ID, and an authentic prescription pad. In her spare time at the villa—between the physical training and the IT management—she'd spent hours and hours boning up on human anatomy and physiology, and learning the human equivalent of animal medications. As a result, she had been able to supply Angela with a gentle sedative, but the poor woman fought it all the way, and who could blame her?

Every time she closed her eyes, Angela would wake soon after, calling out and fighting the demons attacking her in her sleep. Although mother and daughter held hands and hugged the whole morning, true rest would come to neither woman, not until enough time had passed.

The way Bobbie looked after her mother, the love between them was clear. Tears blurred Lara's vision.

Lara had always wanted to be a mother, but she and Ollie had kept putting off getting pregnant and the right time never materialised. His first posting to Helmand Province, Afghanistan, happened so soon after their wedding, they had little appetite to start a family. After all, why rush? They were both young and had plenty of time. When he returned from his first tour of duty, they decided to delay having kids until her veterinary practice became better established and he'd recovered from the traumas of war.

Whenever the subject arose—often on a rare Sunday morning while they lazed in bed after making love—Ollie would laugh and say, one day, they'd have a whole basketball team's worth of kids. To which, she made the standard reply, "That's okay for you, buddy. I'm the one who'll have to carry them all to term. Nine months of swollen ankles and backache? One baby will do, and maybe a second to keep the first company!" What was meant to be a joke turned sour when he received orders for a third tour to Helmand—and never returned.

Damn it, Ollie. Even with Ryan by my side, I still miss you so much.

Despite the passing years, Ollie's loss still had the power to twist her guts and rip out her heart.

But what of Ryan? Her heart was always trying to rule her head whenever she was around him, and her initial gut instinct to believe him had turned out to be correct.

The way they met was like something out of an action movie, something she could never tell her friends—not that she ever expected to see them again. The thought of his injuries, the men who came and burned down her farm, and everything that came afterwards still caused chills and sometimes, the occasional doubt.

But the heart wanted what it wanted, and hers wanted Ryan Liam Kaine, damn it.

And she knew he felt the same. The hug at the ferry port in St Malo, and the brief, wonderful, yet-to-be-repeated kiss promised so very much.

But ...

Oh God, there always has to be a "but".

But they could never really be together, not in "that" way. Not in the full-blooded, marriage, kids, and happy families kind of way, even if they both wanted the same thing. It seemed as though events outside their control would forever conspire to keep them apart. First the work in London, then the dangerous visit to Haarlem and the other in Exeter, and now they were protecting Angela and Bobbie. And what about next week, and the week after that?

Sometimes, at night in the villa, she lay awake, imagining what it would be like to have Ryan in bed beside her, and for him to do more than just sleep. Considering the way they had fallen into a comfortable, symbiotic working relationship, she had absolutely no doubt they'd be good together elsewhere.

Lara shivered and nodded an apology to Bobbie, who'd been disturbed by her movements.

Lara sighed. What the hell was wrong with her? She should be ashamed of herself.

To think of romance while tending to the victim of a vicious attack was wrong in so many ways, but whenever she tried to distract herself from the awfulness of Angela's situation, every thought and feeling led her back to him. It was no wonder she felt the way she did. Lara loved Ryan Liam Kaine, and yet she'd done nothing about it.

Since meeting and, yes, saving Ryan's life, Lara had lived on the edge, with danger at every turn. And yes, again, it did sound melodramatic, but the truth was often laced with melodrama. At any moment, bad men could find them both and end their lives. Ryan constantly placed himself in danger and one day, his luck would run out. Almost inevitably.

The regular bursts of adrenaline shooting through her system affected her in ways that were impossible to quantify.

Or maybe she was simply randy after so many years of celibacy.

Being physically close to Ryan for so many weeks yet being unable to touch him had become almost too much to bear.

Bobbie's eyelids drooped, and Angela's breathing grew ever shallower. Lara had done nothing since walking in the room, but perhaps just her presence was calming enough.

Time to allow sleep to work its healing magic.

She drew the curtains closed but left a narrow gap to allow some light in—Angela wouldn't like waking to a darkened room. She rested the back of her hand against Angela's forehead, which was warm and dry—good—and turned towards the door.

"Who are you?"

Angela's words, although whispered, made Lara jump.

Breathing deeply, she returned to the bed and smoothed the bedding in a way she'd seen nurses do on TV. Animals didn't require the same bedside manner as humans and, for that very reason, they didn't teach hospital etiquette at veterinary school.

"I'm Lara, the team's … medic."

Bobbie stirred. Her eyes opened, she yawned, and stretched her arms to the ceiling.

"You already told me your name," Angela said, louder since Bobbie was awake, "but who are you and what do you want?"

"We're here to help," Lara answered softly.

She reached out to touch Angela's hand, but Angela jerked it away and held it up to her chest.

Bobbie leaned forwards in her chair and held Angela's other hand in both of hers.

"Mum," she said quietly, "we're safe here. It's going to be okay."

Angela worked her way into a seated position without releasing her daughter's hand.

"Don't treat me like a fool, Bobbie. I've been molested, not beaten senseless. My mind is fully operational. Now, Lara, if that's your real name, tell me why you're here, who exactly is Peter, and why is he somehow familiar? And who are those other men? I need more than you've all told me so far."

It had to happen, and Ryan had agreed to full disclosure, but—there was that "but" again—how could she tell two frightened women the real identity of their saviour?

"They deserve to know, Lara," Ryan had said when she'd broached the subject over lunch. "The way they've reacted to the situation so far, it's clear they can handle the truth."

Rollo and Danny overheard the conversation, and both laughed quietly, to avoid disturbing Angela.

"Bloody hell," Danny said through the tears, "the boss thinks he's Jack Nicholson."

Rollo nodded. "Or maybe he sees himself as Tom Cruise and the doc here as Demi Moore?"

Danny shrugged. "They're about the same height."

"Who, the boss and Tom Cruise?"

"No, the boss and Demi Moore."

Ryan shook his head and shrugged at her, clearly not getting the reference. At that moment, Lara vowed to ask their go-to girl for internet security, Sabrina, to sign them up for a safe streaming account at the villa. She needed to introduce Ryan to some of Hollywood's greatest recent output. As well as relieving some of her night-time boredom, it would help her to get to know him better. She knew a great deal about his military skills and some details of his family background, but nothing about what made him tick as a person. Watching films together would help. Lara could think of worse things to do than spending time in the dark with Ryan Kaine, sitting close, eating popcorn … cuddling.

Now that was an interesting question. Did Ryan Kaine eat popcorn?

Focus, Lara.

She studied Angela closely. Was she ready? Lara reached for her medical kit, and carried it and the spare chair to the side of the bed.

"Before I answer your questions, let me check you over."

Angela held up her free hand. "My heart rate is normal, my blood pressure is a little elevated—a chronic condition for which I take tablets—"

"Jesus, Mum! You have high blood pressure?" Bobbie interrupted. "Since when? Why didn't you tell me? Too much butter on your toast and not enough exercise. For goodness' sake. I keep telling you. Why don't you ever listen? Remember what happened to Dad?"

Angela and Lara let Bobbie rattle on. She needed to vent.

"If you're quite finished, young lady," Angela said after Bobbie flopped back into her chair, spent from the effort. "I'm the parent here. I'm the one who looks after you, not the other way around. And if you must know, strenuous exercise is what put us in this situation in the first place. If I hadn't taken poor Lady for a walk …"

Angela let her words trail off into silence. Lara allowed her a moment to gather herself and spent the time operating the pressure cuff—one thirty-five over eighty-five. As Angela said, slightly higher than normal, but not dangerously so.

"So," Angela said, "are you going to tell us who you are?"

Lara took a breath and packed away her equipment. She had to do it right, to maintain Ryan's honour and for Angela and Bobbie's safety. If she got things wrong, it would put everyone in danger, including Mike.

Okay, Lara. Out with it.

"Before I tell you anything, you need to know two things. My name *is* Lara, and Peter is the most honest, honourable, and genuinely caring man I've ever known."

Sorry, Ollie.

Her departed husband was all those things, too, but to bring him into the story would only confuse the issue.

Angela nodded. "I-I could tell when he was listening to me at the house he's a good man, but it doesn't answer my question. Who is he?"

Here goes. Please do this right, Lara.

"The captain's full name is Ryan Liam Kaine and he——"

"Ryan Kaine!" Bobbie gasped.

"Oh my God. He can't be!" Angela shouted. She threw back the covers and eased herself out of bed. "Bobbie, we have to get out of here."

Lara stood, but gave them plenty of room. She didn't want to block their way.

"Are we prisoners?" Angela asked, reaching for Bobbie and shielding her from Lara. "Are you going to kill us, too?"

Footsteps raced up the staircase. Lara surprised herself by recognising Ryan's light tread.

"Ryan," she called, "it's fine." The footsteps stopped. "Give us a moment, please."

"Are you sure? Is everyone safe? Are you okay?"

"Yes, honestly. But I imagine we'll need drinks in a little while." She smiled soothingly at the trembling women. "I've yet to meet a college student who wasn't ready for a drop of booze."

Bobbie stepped to the side of Angela, but they still held each other tight.

"Okay, Doc," Ryan called through the door. "There's beer in the fridge, wine in the cellar, and something stronger in the drinks cabinet if needed."

Ryan's footsteps retreated to the ground floor and Angela's shoulders relaxed a little.

"See?" Lara said. "His only concern is for the safety of the people under his protection. I promise you, he's the best person in the world to have on your side at a moment like this."

Angela blinked. "Is it locked?" she asked, looking at the bedroom door.

Lara shook her head. "Of course not. You aren't prisoners. Try it."

She stepped aside and waited for Bobbie to cross the room. The hinges squeaked as she pulled open the door.

Lara tutted. "Oh dear, I'll have to remind Mike to oil those hinges. You met Mike as we arrived. This is his farm. You'll like him. Lovely man."

Bobbie peered out into the well-lit hall, checked to make sure no one was standing there on guard duty, and returned to her mother's side.

She felt safe enough to close the door again.

A good sign.

Lara continued, speaking calmly as though chatting about the weather. "I wouldn't advise it, but you're free to go any time you want. If you like, we'll call you a taxi, or drive you to the local railway station but, as I said, I'd advise against it. You're safe here from the people who want to hurt you, but whether you stay or not is entirely your decision."

Angela exchanged glances with her daughter before sitting on the edge of her bed. Bobbie sat beside her, and Lara took her place on the chair in front of them.

Lara relaxed a little. They'd overcome the first hurdle.

Now for the next part.

"I'll answer all your questions to the best of my ability, and Ryan will fill in any blanks."

Every time she mentioned Ryan by name, both women tensed, but it was only to be expected. They'd been told a pack of lies by the media. Neither knew the real Ryan Kaine or why he was part of what happened to the plane, and Lara saw it as her job to put them right.

"Where are we?" Angela asked.

"You're on a farm in Midlands. I can't tell you any more than that until you decide to stay."

"And if we demand to leave?" Bobbie asked, still holding tight to her mother's hand.

"We'll take you to the nearest taxi rank or station and you can be on your way. We'll even give you all the cash you need to get anywhere you want to go, but, as I said—"

"Yes, yes, we know," Angela interrupted. "You advise against."

"For your safety," Lara said.

Angela kept demonstrating plenty of fighting spirit, which would serve her well over the upcoming days and weeks.

"So," Angela started hesitantly. "Are you trying to tell us Ryan Kaine *didn't* shoot down Flight BE1555, and he *isn't* responsible for my sister's death?"

Here it comes. The truth only.

"No," Lara said, locking eyes with Angela, "that's not what I'm saying at all. Ryan did fire the missile that destroyed the plane and killed everyone on board, but—"

"It was an accident?" Bobbie asked, scepticism written on her face. "He killed eighty-three innocent people by *accident*, and you expect us to believe that bollocks? And then ... then you want us to trust our lives to a secretive, military non-cop who won't even tell us where we are? Excuse my language, Mum, but you, *Doctor*, and everyone else here can get fucked. We're leaving!"

She jumped up and tried to pull Angela to her feet, but Angela resisted.

"No, Bobbie," she said quietly, tugging her daughter's hand, "I've seen him in action, remember? The captain doesn't strike me as a man who makes many mistakes. I want to hear what the doctor ...what Lara has to say before we make a decision."

Lara relaxed into her chair and nodded her thanks. "Ryan was set up by some very nasty, very greedy men. He'd worked with one of them for many years and had considered him a friend. It's complicated, but when he retired from the military, Ryan joined his best friend's consultancy business. One of their tasks was to certify new military equipment. They worked under licence for the Ministry of Defence and various European armaments companies. It was all completely legal and above board. At least that's what Ryan thought."

Lara's voice cracked, and her eyes watered. What his so-called friend, Major Graham "Gravel" Valence, tricked Ryan into doing was nothing less than barbaric. She still found it impossible to think about it without being overcome with emotion.

"The plane crash," Angela said. "It was part of one of these trials?"

Lara nodded and wiped her eyes with her fingertips before answering. She told them everything she knew. She told them about the weapons test, what happened aboard *Herring Gull*.

She paused to swallow before continuing.

"Eighty-three people died that night, including your sister"—she looked from Angela to Bobbie—"and your aunt, because the head of an arms manufacturing company wanted to increase his company's share price. He targeted one man and hid the death amongst dozens of others."

Lara paused again and let the silence swell to fill the room.

Angela shook her head and covered her mouth with her free hand. "This is too much. After all that's happened recently I really can't …"

Bobbie leaned closer and they hugged. "Where do you come into the story? Are you and … the captain married?"

"No. Before the plane crash, Ryan and I had never met."

"Really? You two look so close," Bobbie said.

Lara smiled sadly and tried to think of a decent response, but Angela peeled Bobbie out of her arms and straightened her sweater again.

"So, how *did* you come to know each other?" Angela asked.

"When *Herring Gull* blew up, Ryan swam nearly ten miles to shore, only to be ambushed later the same morning. He was seriously injured in the attack and stumbled into my clinic. I sewed him back together and—"

"And fell under his spell?" Bobbie asked, arching an eyebrow.

"Not at all. He was dirty, looked like a rough sleeper, and wore clothes that didn't fit. To be honest, I was petrified of him, and I shouldn't have treated him at all. But without me, he would have bled to death. ... I had no choice. Then the armed men in the police helicopter attacked us."

"What?" both women asked together.

"I didn't believe it either until bullets drilled dozens of holes in my barn and set it on fire. Without warning, too, which told me they weren't police at all. What they did to us confirmed Ryan's story. And they weren't only after him. Just because I was there, they tried to kill me, too. But Ryan saved me when he could have simply run away and left me behind. He's been protecting me from them ever since."

"A farm?" Angela asked. "Your clinic was on a farm? What sort of doctor are you?"

She paused for a beat before answering, trying not to look apologetic. "I'm a veterinarian. That's another reason why I didn't want to treat Ryan's wound at first."

"A vet? You're a bloody vet?" Bobbie said, shaking her

head in shock. "But those men downstairs keep calling you 'Doc'. And you treated my mum."

Angela patted her daughter's leg and nodded at Lara to carry on.

Lara shrugged. "Ryan and his men don't always have access to a GP. When absolutely necessary, I treat their injuries. That makes me a medic in their eyes. It's the way military people behave. Pragmatists, the lot of them."

"So, how often do they get injured?" Angela asked quietly.

"Less often that you'd think, given what they put themselves through. Listen," she said, leaning forwards and resting her elbows on her knees, "If you've nowhere else to be, I think you need the whole story. Will you listen?"

Angela glanced at a frowning Bobbie before nodding.

"Yes, we'll listen."

Lara started talking.

Chapter Fifteen

Saturday 28th November – Lara Orchard

Mike's Farm, Long Buckby, Northants, England

Lara spoke for twenty minutes straight, pausing only to answer their questions. She told them how Ryan had gathered proof of his innocence and how he'd sent it to an unnamed senior contact in the police. She also told them how the government refused to clear Ryan's name because the company at the heart of the conspiracy, SAMS Plc, was deemed too important to fail. According to the Ministry of Defence and the Home Office, SAMS was essential for the "defence of the realm" and had to be protected. The company had to survive and thrive. The only thing the authorities *had* done was arrest the SAMS Chairman, Sir Malcolm Sampson, for "tax fraud and misappropriation of company funds". With him out of the picture, they allowed the company to continue operating more-or-less as normal.

When Lara finished, Angela and Bobbie stared at her, each clearly lost in thought. Angela sat so still, she barely even breathed while Bobbie's right leg bounced and her fingers twitched.

Eventually, Bobbie broke the awkward silence.

"So, you have proof of Ryan Kaine's so-called innocence?" she asked, still looking, and sounding, unconvinced.

"Yes," Lara said, "I've seen the digital proof of Ryan being beaten nearly to death and of Sir Malcolm himself admitting to ordering the destruction of Flight BE1555."

"So, why don't you release the evidence to the media? Wouldn't that clear the captain's name?" Angela asked.

"I want to," Lara said, "and I've been trying to convince Ryan to go public, but he won't let me."

"Why ever not?" Angela asked.

"It's complicated."

Bobbie scoffed. "It's bloody obvious, isn't it? This whole story's a pile of crap. You don't have proof at all. Ryan Kaine murdered Auntie Jackie and all those other poor souls, and you're protecting him because you love him. Go on, tell me I'm wrong."

Lara sighed. The girl was dead wrong in the first instance, but completely accurate in the second.

"I know it sounds fantastical, but it's the truth, I swear it."

"Yeah, right," Bobbie said, shaking her head. "I don't know what your game is, but I don't believe a word of it. I've seen Sir Malcolm Sampson on the news. He's got all the charisma of a dead fish, but a mass murderer? Total bollocks."

"Just because he wears a business suit and appears on

TV occasionally, you dismiss his guilt, but at the same time, you're happy to believe Ryan's a mass murderer because of a few vague news stories? Is that fair?"

"But … it's been all over the media and the press. More than a few stories." Bobbie's sudden uncertainty showed in her hesitation and the way she looked to Angela for support. "The police are still looking for him."

"Are they?" Lara asked. "Are they really? And the police have never arrested the wrong suspect for a crime either, have they? By the way, when was the last time you saw a news item with a police officer saying Ryan's still a person of interest in the disaster?"

Bobbie's mouth snapped shut. She looked up at the ceiling as though trying to access a memory.

"You're right," Angela said. "It's been weeks since anyone's mentioned Ryan Kaine."

"That's because the police know he's innocent."

"Lack of interest more like," Bobbie mumbled. "The news cycle keeps … well, cycling."

"No, it's because our contact in the police, a well-respected senior officer, has spoken to every chief constable in the UK and told him what he knows. Also, the last Home Secretary offered Ryan immunity, but the current two-faced cretin reneged and insisted Ryan presented his case in public court. I suspect the man has his own agenda, but I don't have any proof of that."

Bobbie stared at Lara for a moment before nodding. "That, I can believe. Never did trust a politician."

"Now, Bobbie," Angela said, patting her daughter's hand. "I don't think we need to bring your Trotskyist beliefs into the discussion."

"Trotskyism is an intellectual paradigm, Mum, based on

well-thought-out tenets. It's not a belief system. Not a bloody religion."

Lara held up a finger to interrupt their chat. "Just because Ryan won't let me share the evidence with the public, doesn't mean I can't show it to you. Perhaps this might help convince you."

She pulled a digital tablet from her handbag, tapped in the access code, and opened the heavily edited movie file. It showed some, but not all, of Ryan's mistreatment at the hands of Sir Malcolm, Adam Akers, and his pet thugs. It also included the arrogant monster's blasé confession. In his own slimy, self-serving words, Sir Malcolm boasted of how he'd paid Ryan's friend, Gravel, to set him up and how a few insignificant deaths would add so many zeros to the company's bottom line. Ryan had her remove the part of the recording where he coerced over three hundred million Euros from SAMS' slush fund—money SAMS had earmarked to oil the machinery of commerce, particularly in the Third World. The money was a factor in Ryan's decision not to release the video proof. Apart from putting himself at risk by giving himself up to the police, he'd be required to hand the money to the government. Even though he was absolutely putting it to better use, he'd still taken it. Angela and Bobbie didn't need to know all the details.

Some information was best left undisclosed.

She handed the tablet to Angela, climbed out of her chair, and hurried to the door, unable to watch the torture again. Every time she forced herself to play the recording, she died a little inside. Its only saving grace was that the images also reminded her of what Ryan went through to prove his innocence and what they were all doing for The 83.

Ryan's refusal to release the information to the media was, of course, honourable and selfless, but she still hoped one day to convince him he was wrong. Fat chance of that, though. Amongst Ryan's faults, his stubbornness could be the most frustrating.

Lara reached for the door handle but stopped and turned to face the bed.

"Play the recording from start to finish and return the tablet later." She addressed her next words to Bobbie. "After you've seen the kind of man who's risking his life and his freedom to protect you, perhaps you can take a moment to decide your next move." She opened the door and stepped into the hallway. "In the meantime, I'll be downstairs if you need anything. By the way, if you do decide to leave, Ryan *will* make it happen. I can promise you that."

Lara closed the door quietly, leaned against it, and exhaled heavily. She'd done all she could. The rest was up to them and the evidence they were watching.

Every part of her hoped they'd decide to stay. If they left, it would likely mean their deaths.

She pushed away from the door and descended the stairs with a quiet tread. Halfway down, her stomach rumbled. Lunch was a distant memory and exercising Dynamite had given her a huge appetite, but the Lord alone knew what kind of a hole the guys were making in Mike's larder. If a hungrier pair than Rollo and Danny existed on the planet, they'd probably be worth an entry in the Guinness Book of Records. She'd have to ask one of them to escort her into town in the morning to stock up on groceries.

She headed to the kitchen. Mike would need a hand preparing supper.

Chapter Sixteen

Saturday 28th November – Lara Orchard

Mike's Farm, Long Buckby, Northants, England

Lara set her empty cup on the coaster protecting the surface of Mike's polished-oak occasional table. She couldn't hold back a yawn. Although it was still early evening, she was surprisingly relaxed, and Mike's strong, dark blend of cocoa had really hit the spot.

An alluring log fire crackled in the wood burner. It felt good, comfortable.

Mike, snoozing across from her in his favourite wing-back chair, snorted and shook himself awake. His shaggy, white beard, scrubbing-brush hair, and craggy face always reminded her of a film pirate. With a peg leg and a parrot on his shoulder, he'd pass any audition for a panto of Treasure Island as long as it was a non-speaking role. His gentle manner, quiet voice, and cultured, Scottish accent would have ruled him out for the role of Long John Silver.

He rubbed the sleep from his eyes and groaned gently while arching his back, playing up the "old man" aches and pains for all it was worth.

Lara wasn't having any of it. Despite his age, Mike Procter was as fit and sprightly as any seventy year old she'd ever met. When asked, he put it down to healthy living and having been in the service long enough to remember receiving his daily tot of rum.

The last time Lara had the pleasure of spending time on the farm, she and Mike had grown unexpectedly close. They'd spent the quiet times, after finishing the farm's daily chores, chatting and swapping life stories. Lara talked about her vet practice and Ollie, and learned more about how Mike and Ryan had met. The old sailor turned out to be a great storyteller. One night, he described Black Tot Day, 31st July 1970. The last time the Royal Navy issued sailors with their daily rum ration.

"Horrible it was," Mike said. "End of an era. Every sailor in the fleet acted as though the Admiralty had banned Christmas."

Despite his general health and vitality, sleeping in a chair wasn't good for a man of his advanced years, but he refused to turn in until Lara did.

"Hullo, love. Still awake, then?" Mike rolled the crick out of his neck and groaned again. "It's been a long couple of days. I thought you might want to turn in early tonight."

"It's too soon for me, and Ryan's still up. Sleep well?"

"Never better, thanks."

"Liar," she said, smiling.

Without rising, he reached into the fuel basket at his

side, added another log to the fire, and settled it with a poker before closing the glass-fronted door.

"Should have left the boiler running, but I've always liked a real fire. Makes the place more homely." He cocked an ear and listened to the wind whistling through trees bordering his stable yard and the rain hammering against the windows. "Wild night, but the storm will pass by morning."

"You can tell that just by listening to the wind?"

A knowing smile puffed out his beard. "After thirty-five years at sea, a crusty, old sailor learns to read the weather," Mike said, and rubbed his left knee. "The old arthritis plays up when the air pressure drops. That … and I listened to the evening's shipping forecast."

"You old fraud," Lara said, shaking her head. "Thought I heard the radio earlier."

"Are you warm enough, lass? I could bank up the fire a bit more if you like."

"No need. Not for me. It's toasty in here. … I love this place."

Mike cast his eyes around the comfortable sitting area. Oak beams, wood-burning stove, solid-oak furniture. It reminded Lara of her farmhouse and, for the first time in ages, she felt a twinge of regret.

"Ellie furnished it, and I've tried to keep it going since she left."

Patch, Mike's black-and-white sheepdog, raised his head at the mention of his former mistress' name. Mike tickled the old dog's ruff. Patch yawned and settled back down again, his misty eyes reflecting the orange flames. Mike no longer tended sheep and Patch had worked his last flock. At the old dog's side, Petra, a dark mongrel, remained sleeping.

The door to the staircase creaked open. Angela timidly poked her head into the room.

"C-Can I speak to him?" she asked, barely above a whisper. "Can I speak to ... the captain?"

Mike stood, pointed to the fire, and said, "Come in, lass. It's always parky in that stairwell."

Angela opened the door and stepped further into the room. She wore a white, terrycloth dressing gown wrapped tight up around her neck, but it didn't hide the bruising to her throat. The legs of her jeans showed beneath its hem, and she wore socks and trainers.

Lara eased out of her chair. "Do you want to leave?"

"No, no, it's not that," she said, frowning as though in surprise. "I-I actually wanted to thank him again and apologise to you for the way I reacted to his name, even after what he did for Bobbie and me."

"You believe me?"

"Of course. How could we not, after seeing the video? It was hideous."

"And Bobbie?"

Angela glanced behind her at the closed door. "When she saw how badly the captain was beaten, she cried. She's disappointed with herself for the way she spoke to you. Guilty, you know? She'll be down in a minute. We both want to speak to him. Is he here?"

"Last I heard, he was in the office, on the computer," Mike said, pointing the way.

"Is he?" Angela asked, glancing at the clock on the mantelpiece, which showed twenty-five past eight.

"He's doing some research," Lara answered. "Shall I fetch him for you?"

"No, no, don't disturb him. It can wait until morning." She moved into the centre of the room, edging closer to the fire and to Lara. One hand gripped the lapels of her dressing gown, pinching them together at her throat. "Um, earlier, someone mentioned a drink?" She held her free hand out to the warmth of the fire.

"I know and I'm sorry, but after the sedative I gave you, alcohol wouldn't be a good idea," Lara answered.

"No, I was thinking a cup of something warm would be nice."

"Cocoa?" Mike asked, grabbing Lara's mug and pointing Angela towards a three-seater settee.

She smiled but winced and placed a hand on her split lip. "That would be wonderful. If it's not too much trouble."

"No trouble at all, lass. In fact, I'll join you," Mike said, hurrying towards the kitchen. "Three steaming mugs of cocoa coming right up. Oh, and what about Bobbie? She'll probably like one, too. Maybe the lads will join us when they've finished their business."

"He's a lovely man," Angela whispered when Mike disappeared and started rattling saucepans, "to open up his home for a pair of women in distress."

"Keep this to yourself, but he thinks of Ryan as the son he never had. He'd give up his life to protect him, as would all his men. That's a measure of the man."

"Okay, Doc," Angela said, "you've sold him to us. We believe you. No need to use a ladle."

Lara laughed. "Sorry, I do tend to lay it on a little thick. It's just that I hate what people have been saying about him. Ryan doesn't deserve it, and he'll never speak up for himself."

"I don't deserve what?" Ryan asked, pushing through the kitchen door, but keeping his distance once he spotted Angela.

"You don't deserve any sympathy," Lara snapped. "Anyone eavesdropping on other people's conversations won't ever hear anything nice about themselves."

Ryan sighed. "Guess I deserved that. Evening, Angela. I expected you to be in bed. How are you feeling?" He winced and raised a hand. "Sorry, I should know better than to ask stupid questions by now. Is there anything you need?"

"No, thank you, Captain. Mike's making us cocoa."

"Did, um …" Ryan shot a look at Lara before continuing. "Did Lara brief you?"

"Yes, Captain Kaine. Lara explained everything."

Ryan stiffened a little, his brow wrinkled.

"And what's your decision? Can you bring yourself to trust a man like me?"

"Yes," she said without hesitation. "We owe you our lives, our thanks, and an apology."

Ryan lowered his head a fraction. "You owe me nothing. I'm the one who should be apologising for what happened to your sister and for arriving so damned late."

Lara had never seen Ryan look so uncomfortable. She felt for him, but he wouldn't appreciate her rushing to his side to offer her support.

Silly, obstinate man.

Ryan pointed to the spare seat near the fire. "Please. Sit. If Mike's making his world-renowned cocoa, you're in for a treat. Farm-fresh milk, dark chocolate, and a generous tot of rum for anyone not on duty, which rules me out I'm afraid, but you'll love it."

"Afraid not," Angela said, easing into the sofa beside Lara, "I'm under doctor's orders. Or is that vet's orders? Either way, no alcohol for me, but Bobbie will no doubt claim my share."

"Claim your share of what, Mum?" Bobbie asked, entering the room, her face freshly scrubbed and glowing with vitality.

"Our host is offering to add a tot of rum to our drinks. Perhaps he'll let you have my share if you ask nicely."

Bobbie stared evenly at Ryan.

"Mr ... sorry, Captain Kaine," she said, "may I have my mum's share of rum, please?"

Ryan smiled an apology. "Sorry, Ms Shafer, not my call. Mike's the host, not me. But if I know him, it won't be a problem."

Bobbie took three long strides forwards and stood in front of Ryan, breathing heavily. She matched him for height and stared him down. Ryan lowered his eyes and seemed to be waiting for a verbal hammering.

Tension's cold weight filled the room.

"September tenth," she said, quietly.

"Excuse me?"

"That's the day the police released your photo, and the media denounced you as the terrorist who shot down Flight BE1555."

"Ms Shafer ... I—"

"No," Bobbie said, her voice cracking, "please hear me out. I loved Auntie Jackie. Ever since that day, I've hated you. I sometimes dreamed of what I'd do if I ever met you. I-I've wished you a horrible death so many times, and ... Oh God. I'm so sorry. Can you forgive me?"

Lara released her breath.

Angela slumped back into the sofa, her sigh matching Lara's. Ryan's shoulders lost some of their tension.

"Nothing to forgive, Ms Shafer. I'm the one who needs to apologise. I'd do anything to change what happened to that plane."

Bobbie brushed aside his offered hand and pulled him into a brief hug. She pecked his cheek and pushed away.

"No, after what you did for Mum last night, I don't need your apology. I don't know how I'd have coped without her."

Again, Ryan shook his head and cleared his throat. "Look, can we take the apologies as read? This is truly unnecessary, and a little … embarrassing."

Bobbie nodded. "Okay, Mr Macho. I can see you don't go in for the touchy-feely stuff."

How right you are.

Lara did her best not to roll her eyes.

Ryan arched an eyebrow theatrically. "That's *Captain* Macho to you, Missy."

Bobbie laughed, and the hint of a smile appeared on Angela's bruised and swollen face.

"Good to see everyone's getting along swimmingly without me," Mike said, walking in from the kitchen, carrying a tray with seven steaming mugs, a half-full bottle of Old Navy rum, and a biscuit tin. "What have I missed?"

"Nothing exciting," Ryan answered, clearing room on the coffee table.

Mike set the tray down, handed around the mugs, and removed the biscuits and the bottle, leaving two mugs on the tray. "For the lads," he said. "They'll be a little chilly about now, I'd have thought."

"Where are they?" Lara asked and grinned. Of the group, only Mike was old enough to refer to Rollo as a lad.

"Rollo's patrolling the perimeter," Ryan said. "And Danny's volunteered for guard duty in the porch."

Angela sat bolt upright and cast a worried glance at her daughter. "Guard duty? Is that strictly necessary? Are we in danger here?"

"Standard operating procedure," Ryan said. "There's no reason to think anyone knows where you are, but I don't believe it's possible to be too cautious."

Ryan leaned one elbow on the mantelpiece and blew across the top of his mug before taking a sip. He shook his head when Bobbie scooped the rum from the table and offered to perk up his cocoa.

"That's right," Mike said, picking up the two remaining mugs. "No one ever accused the captain of complacency."

Bobbie unscrewed the top from the rum and tilted a healthy tot into her drink. "Anyone else? Doc?"

Lara held up her mug. "A dribble, please," she said, adding, "to keep out the chill."

"I imagine the troops aren't allowed alcohol while on duty?" Bobbie asked Ryan, replacing the top on the bottle. "Which is a shame on a cold night like this. Mike, can I help? I'll take one of those out to, what's his name … Danny, is it?"

Mike handed her one of the mugs and kept hold of the other one. "Thanks, lass. Why don't we leave the grown-ups to chat? I'm certain Danny will appreciate waitress service. Follow me."

He smiled at Angela and Lara, and led Bobbie through the door to the front hall. Ryan closed it behind them.

The moment they'd cleared the room, Angela turned to face Ryan.

"What happened when you took those … creatures away in the boot of their car? W-What did you do to them?"

Ryan took another sip before answering. Lara knew him well enough to tell he was searching for the right way to answer. He never blurted things out without thought, and he always tried to avoid lying.

"I'm sorry to be blunt, but you don't want to know the details."

"You killed them?" Angela asked, her voice a mix of shock and relief. Her hand shook so much, she was in danger of spilling her cocoa down the front of her dressing gown.

"No," Ryan answered, "I let the little one go. But, don't worry, he's no danger to anybody."

"But Pig ... the one who ... who attacked me, he's dead?"

Ryan took a moment before answering.

"There was no other way to keep you safe. The kind of man he was ... and after what he did. I had no choice."

Angela gasped, and the mug nearly slipped from her hands. Lara took it from her and placed it, and hers, on the coffee table before throwing an arm around the distraught woman's shoulders.

"Sorry, Angela, but——"

"You don't need to apologise to me, Captain. I'm glad."

"Really?"

"Yes, really."

Lara had expected an eruption, but a calmness softened the worry lines on Angela's face, and she let out a long, relieved sigh. "Good riddance. That man was pure evil. I saw nothing behind his eyes, not even hate. I know you did the right thing. Except ..."

"Except?" Ryan asked, defensively.

"Except, I wish I'd been there to see it."

Ryan tried hard to hide his surprise, but Lara had been around him long enough to read his body language. A very slight widening of the eyes and a stiffening in the muscles of his neck were enough to give it away. "Do you need any details, for closure?"

Angela shook her head. "All I need is to be sure I'll never see him again. Except in my nightmares."

"You can believe it, Angela," Lara said, resting her hand on top of Angela's. "If Ryan says the man is dead, there's no doubt."

"In that case," Angela said, looking up at Ryan through hope-filled eyes, "Bobbie and I are safe? We can go home?"

Ryan shook his head. "I'm sorry, but it's not as simple as that. You're still in grave danger. You'll have to stay here until we can ensure your safety."

"Why? If Pig's dead, why do we still need your protection?"

Ryan set his mug on the mantelpiece and dropped into Mike's comfortably worn armchair. He sat on the edge of the seat and leaned forwards.

"Listen, Angela," he said, holding her attention with a calm gaze, "I won't sugar-coat this. As payment for my letting him go, the second man, Johnathan Ashby, told us everything. Pony Tedesco was acting under the direct orders of his elder brother, Teddy."

Ryan leaned even closer to Angela. "It turns out, Teddy is responsible for the death of the man you saw being dumped at Breaker's Folly. Teddy sent his baby brother to kill you and left the method entirely up to him."

Before continuing, he glanced at Lara, as though asking for permission. Lara nodded.

"When Pony woke from his enforced snooze, he boasted that his brother had power and a long reach. He also said he was untouchable and said you, Bobbie, and every member of your extended family would never be safe. That's why I had to … silence him permanently. So, with his brother also knowing who you are and where you live, you can see why there is no alternative."

Angela stiffened. "Bobbie and I can't stay here on the farm forever. I have a job and she has to study."

"I understand, but for the short term it's safer for you to stay here. However, I think I'm able to promise you it's only temporary."

"How temporary?" Angela asked, throwing a worried glance at Lara.

"It's okay, Angela. Ryan has a plan. Don't you, Ryan?"

He tilted his head to the side and raised a shoulder in a half-shrug, half-nod. "I'm certainly working on one."

Angela looked hard at him. "Can you tell me what it is?"

Ryan scratched at his beard. "The details are a little … flexible right now."

"Meaning?" Angela asked.

"It's a work in progress, Angela. But if you agree to stay here with Mike, the doc, and my two most capable friends, it will give me a chance to pay a flying visit to the south coast."

"Ryan," Lara said, glaring at him, "I really don't like the sound of that."

"It's okay, Lara. I plan to phone ahead and arrange a meeting first." He smiled and double hitched his eyebrows.

"Oh God, Ryan," Lara gasped. "You don't mean what I think you mean?"

"Possibly. I fancy meeting Teddy Tedesco face-to-face. Easier to gauge a man that way."

Lara jumped to her feet. "Ryan, that's suicide!"

"Not necessarily. Perhaps if I deliver my condolences in person, he'll warm to me. As you know, I can be quite charming when I try." He grinned. "We'll maybe come to an arrangement whereby he promises to leave Angela and Bobbie alone."

Angela shook her head. "You think he'll agree to that?"

Ryan shrugged. "Doubt it. The likelihood is he won't even agree to a meeting, and I'll have to opt for the alternative."

"Which is?" Lara didn't want to ask but couldn't stop herself.

"If he doesn't do as I tell him, I go to war with Tedesco and his whole organisation."

Angela gasped, and for Lara, the temperature in the room plummeted.

Chapter Seventeen

Saturday 28th November – Evening

Mike's Farm, Long Buckby, Northants, England

Kaine prepared himself for Lara's reaction to his bombshell announcement. She looked ready to explode, but his mobile phone buzzed and saved his blushes. He pulled the phone from his jacket pocket and glanced at the screen.

"Our friend with the Australian twang."

"Who?" Angela asked.

"Corky," Lara answered. "One of our IT hackers."

"Oh dear," Kaine said, wagging a finger at her. "Don't let him hear you say that. According to Corky, he's a world-class 'information acquisition specialist'." He winked.

Lara stared at the still-ringing mobile. "Has he been successful?"

"Only one way to find out." He smiled apologetically at Angela. "Sorry, I have to take this outside."

Kaine retreated to the kitchen before accepting the call.

"Hello, Corky, you're up late. Or is it daytime wherever you are?"

"Whatcha, Mr K. How ya diddling?" Corky asked, as forcefully cheerful as ever. "As for where Corky's living, you'll never find out. Corky keeps his own timetable, and you did say you was in a hurry."

If anything, his Aussie twang had increased since the first time they'd spoken. It made Kaine suspect Corky's subterfuge went deeper than simply hiding his location.

Kaine dropped into a hard-backed dining chair and rubbed his eyes. Sleep was long overdue, but Corky's information would likely prove invaluable, and he needed to stay awake until the rest of the team arrived. Rollo and Danny had been awake for the best part of three days and needed their rest as much as he did.

"Yes, Corky. That I did. So, what do you have for me?"

"No, 'Well done, Corky, thanks very much, Corky'?"

"Sorry, Corky. Things have been a little fraught here but, as you insist. 'Well done, Corky, thanks very much, Corky.' Now, what do you have?"

"Well, it weren't easy, Mr K. Corky had to jump through a load of hoops and limbo under even more poles."

"But you managed brilliantly, of course. Otherwise, you wouldn't be calling me so late in my day. Stop milking it, son." Kaine smiled as he spoke, softening his voice. "You volunteered to help, so help. Please."

"Alright, Mr K, alright. Don't get shirty." Corky chuckled through his words.

A kookaburra chuckled alongside him, but it didn't necessarily mean the hacker was anywhere near Australia

—the bird's call might have been a recording. For all Kaine knew, Corky could be parked in a van on the lane to Mike's farm. Equally, the guy could be bouncing his phone signal off a dozen satellites from an origin in South Korea.

Suffice it to say, Kaine was delighted Corky had decided to work with rather than against him.

"Right," Corky said, "Corky sent an email with all the details to your system at the villa, but do you want the management summary?"

"Yes, please."

"That's one of the things Corky likes about you, Mr K. Right down to business as always. First off, Corky cracked the password of that mobile you liberated off of Pony Tedesco. Piece of cake for a man with Corky's skillset. It gave him access to all Teddy's personal numbers. So, guess what Corky did then?" Corky paused, presumably expecting an answer.

Kaine obliged. "You tapped all Teddy's phones?"

"Yep," Corky answered, "especially the one he keeps private for family matters—the one Pony marked in his contacts as 'War Room'. Now here's a thought, Mr K. How's about calling him on that number? Can you imagine how he'd react? On top of that, it'd make Corky's job easier to record all his ranting and raving."

"That's a great idea. You are a genius," Kaine said when Corky paused again, no doubt needing his ego stroked —again. The fact that Kaine had already planned to do that very thing was beside the point.

"Yeah. Too right Corky is," Corky said through another chuckle. "And he's already picked up some bits of info as will come in handy when you want to take the evil arsehole down. It's all in the file Corky sent."

"Thanks, Corky," Kaine said, because he felt he had to. "That's brilliant."

"Anyway, this dude is real heavy, Mr K. His psycho brother was bad enough, but Teddy's worse on account of him being more sly. More careful. Like what Johnno Ashby told you, he's built a huge organisation along the south coast, centred in Southampton. Deals in all sorts of nastiness. You name it, Teddy's got his fingers all over it. Like Corky said, Teddy's one bad dude and out for blood since you topped his baby brother. Spitting nails ain't the words for it, Mr K. Some of the language he's been using even makes ol' Corky blush."

"He's being open about his business on the phones?" Kaine asked, slightly surprised. Most experienced villains kept the specifics for face-to-face meetings.

"Nah," Corky said, chuckling again, "he ain't that dense, but he ain't that clever, neither."

"Corky, I feel a revelation coming. You have ears on Tedesco, don't you?"

Corky's high-pitched laugh was starting to grate, but Kaine let him continue unchecked.

"Yes, Mr K. Corky most certainly does."

"Care to explain?"

"Corky's one totally brilliant dude. There ain't no doubt about it."

"Tell me."

The hacker let the kookaburra finish snickering before answering. "Well, it's like this. Teddy's a bit paranoid, right. Keeps his offices, apartments, and main buildings under full digital surveillance, cameras, mics, the lot."

"And you've tapped into it?"

"Nah, not exactly. See, the surveillance system is closed circuit. Works on a sealed loop. To tap into it, Corky would have to break in and physically splice into the wires. Ain't no way Corky's about to do that kind of shit. Too risky. Corky's happy where he is. Safe too. Corky's bestie, Sean, could do it, no probs, but he's occupied looking after his new baby. Cute, little thing she is, but cries all the time, y'know? Anyhow, Corky found a weak spot in Teddy's defences, and you'll never guess where."

"Go on," Kaine said, "you have my undivided attention."

After allowing yet another chortle to die out, Corky spoke again, almost breathless. "Despite what he does for a living, Teddy loves his dear, frail, old Mumsie. So, he's set her up in the flat on the floor below his business-cum-office-cum-home penthouse. Teddy pays for round-the-clock healthcare and has a baby alarm hardwired into the phone lines. He even added a failsafe satellite system as backup. No prizes for guessing what Corky did, Mr K."

"You tapped into the baby alarm?"

A loud cackle made Kaine wince and pull the phone away from his ear.

"Sure did, Mr K. First time he used the baby alarm intercom at the same time he was speaking on the mobile, Corky dived in faster than a koala up a gum tree. Corky broadcast a 'screech burst' he designed himself. It's a clever patch app what keeps the baby alarm permanently open through a virtual relay, only the system functions as normal as far as Teddy's concerned. Brilliant, right?"

Kaine had no idea what the IT genius was talking about, but it sounded clever enough.

"So, you can pick up everything Teddy says from his office?"

"And from anywhere in his property that has an intercom for the baby alarm. Corky can tell you, Mr K, old

Teddy gets up to some strange shit in the bedroom. Would make your toes curl. Likes his girls and boys young. Real young if you know what Corky means. And his main squeeze, Elizabeth's her name, joins in, too. Some of the kids don't speak any English, neither. Corky thinks he takes first pick of the kiddies he smuggles into the country. Horrible piece of filth is our Teddy Tedesco. You're gonna take him down, aren't you, Mr K?"

With images of Angela's bruised face and battered, exposed body, and the memory of Pony's threats playing on the screen in his head and turning his blood to lava, Kaine answered quietly. "Yes, Corky. I'm taking him down. No quarter. No bargaining." He hesitated a moment before asking, "Is there anything else I need to know?"

"Teddy posted a reward for any information on what happened to Pony and, you ain't gonna like this part, Mr K." Once again, the IT specialist paused.

"Okay, Corky. Spill it."

"Johnno Ashby, you know, the bloke you sent to Teddy with Pony's body …"

"What about him?" Kaine asked, but already suspected the answer and the familiar weight formed in the pit of his stomach.

"Teddy beat him to death in his so-called Clean Room, after the bloke delivered your message. Took his time over it, too. If you like, Corky can tell you what his men did with the body."

One more fatality on Kaine's conscience, but this one weighed less heavily than many of the others. Although Ashby hadn't been active in the attack on Angela, he'd done nothing to prevent it. In time, he would have bowed to Pony's will and joined in the brutality, if only to protect himself from another beating. No, Ashby's passing generated little guilt.

"That's a terrible shame," Kaine said, barely meaning it. "And yet another thing Teddy's going to answer for. If you add the recording to the file, I'll consider sending it to our police friend at a later date. Ashby's family will want to know what happened to him, but it's best not to tip our hand to Tedesco for the moment. So, any other information I need right now?"

"Only that Teddy has an army of thugs on his payroll, and all are armed, some ex-military. Thirty-three in total. Calls them his 'security team'. Corky's built a dossier on the ones he's managed to trace, but it's incomplete. Still working on the rest, but Corky figures you'd want what's available so far."

"Any intel is useful, as long as it's accurate."

"You can bet your life on Corky's info being accurate, Mr K."

I do, Corky. I really do.

"By the way," Corky continued. "What's your other information gatherer doing? Can't see no signs of her in the digits."

"She's still busy on a separate project. You're all I have right now, and I really do appreciate your help. I doubt even Sabrina could do what you've done in the time frame."

"If you're trying to butter ol' Corky up, Mr K, it's working," Corky said, laughing again. "Laters."

Kaine plugged the phone into the universal charger on the kitchen windowsill. He'd fire up his Sabrina-protected tablet and read Corky's email as soon as he'd had some sleep. If he tried reading anything before then, nothing would stick, and he'd hate to miss something important.

While at the kitchen window, Kaine unplugged Pony's

mobile and slipped it into his pocket. He'd use it once only, but not until well clear of the farm. Corky's intel would tell Kaine whether Tedesco's organisation was sophisticated enough to trace Pony's mobile, but until he read the files, Kaine would leave the mobile powered down.

The handle on the kitchen door squeaked. Kaine spun around to see Lara opening the door, with tray in hand.

"Can I come in?"

Kaine smiled. "Sure, I was just coming to talk to you."

"Really," she said, her voice sceptical.

He fitted the plug into the drain hole on the old-fashioned, butler's sink, opened the hot tap, and added a squirt of washing up liquid. She unloaded the mugs into the sudsy water and grabbed the dishcloth, confirming it was his turn to wash.

Although Mike had a serviceable dishwasher, doing the dishes had become one of their nightly rituals at the villa. Kaine had come to think of it as a sort of detox therapy. A degree of normality in an otherwise abnormal existence.

Being close enough to Lara to smell her body scrub, see the light dancing in her eyes, and feel the warmth from her skin didn't hurt, either.

"What were you going to say?" she asked.

"Sorry?" he said, working the scouring pad over a particularly stubborn cocoa stain.

"You said you were coming to talk to me. What were you going to say?" She took the mug from him and attacked it with the dishcloth.

"I wanted to apologise for dropping that 'going to war with Tedesco' line on you. And … maybe explain my logic."

"You don't have to explain anything to me, *Captain* Kaine. It's not that I have any say in the matter. After all, I'm just the little woman. My role here is to patch up everyone's injuries and to keep my mouth closed—and to do the dishes."

"Lara," he said, turning to face her, "stop that right now. I value your input in all things. You are the only person on the planet who can turn my insides to jelly, and you know it, but—"

Lara lowered the mug to the drainer and faced him square on. She grinned. "I'm messing with you, you great, big idiot. I know you have to deal with Teddy Tedesco, or Angela and Bobbie will never be safe, but promise me one thing, will you?"

"I'll try my best."

"Don't take any unnecessary risks."

Kaine allowed his eyes to bug open.

"*Moi?*" he said, hand on heart. "Take risks? As if."

She scooped a handful of suds from the sink and splatted them on top of his head.

"Oh, how childish."

"*Moi?* Childish?" she said and stuck out her tongue.

"Touché."

He took a dry dishcloth and wiped the suds from his hair. She laughed—a sound he loved—and they carried on cleaning dishes and mugs, standing close enough to touch. Kaine had rarely been happier.

"Where's everybody else?" he asked.

"Mike escorted Angela to bed. She wanted to stay up to thank you again, but I told her you were a grumpy, old man and wouldn't appreciate it. Bobbie's still in the porch with Danny. They seem to be enjoying each other's company."

Kaine nodded. "Hardly surprising. They're about the same age and Danny always had an eye for a pretty girl. And she did seem unusually keen to take him his cocoa."

"You think Bobbie's pretty?"

"A little young for me, but yes, she is attractive."

"As is Danny."

"You think Danny's pretty?"

"Don't be ridiculous," she said, playfully slapping his arm—his recently injured right arm.

He tried not to wince.

Lara didn't seem to notice his discomfort and clarified her comment. "Danny's good-looking in a boyish, floppy-eared puppy sort of way."

"Are you trying to make me jealous? Because it won't work. I'm immune to your womanly wiles. And I can understand what Danny would see in Bobbie. It'll be a damsel-in-distress kind of thing."

She turned to face him again. She edged even closer, staring at him. "Is that the way you see me, Ryan?"

Crap. How can I answer that?

He struggled to swallow past a drying throat.

"Maybe at first," he whispered, "but no. Not now."

"Then how *do* you see me, Ryan?"

The white light of the ceiling fixture glistened in her eyes and the emotion pouring out of them drilled a hole through his heart.

He wanted so much to tell her the truth. If he could guarantee their safety together, he'd whisk her away back to the villa in a heartbeat and spend the rest of his days just trying to make her smile.

"For God's sake, Ryan. Answer me, will you."

She clutched his arm and squeezed. He gritted his teeth and sweat popped on his brow. This time she did notice.

"Oh my God. Your arm. I forgot. How is it?"

"Fine, thanks," he said, putting on his "brave soldier" face, "but it'd probably heal faster if people didn't keep slapping and pummelling the hell out of the bloody thing."

Apart from her being such a delight to his eye and his heart, one benefit of having a medic on permanent standby was the care she gave to his injuries. They were all properly treated and monitored, and healed even faster as a result.

The five-inch gash on his arm, for example, acquired during his most recent escapade helping a member of The 83 in Exeter was a case in point. After receiving the knife wound in a brawl, he'd resorted to his usual, stop-gap measure of wrapping the forearm in duct tape to staunch the blood flow until he reached safety. Although the wound had been deep, the man who'd given it to him—a murderous and devious bugger—hadn't lived to brag about it.

The whole incident had been a bit of a shock to Kaine's system, in that he'd learned a valuable truth. Just because he'd vowed to protect The 83, didn't mean they all deserved it. Some deserved Kaine's harshest judgement.

Kaine wasn't too old to learn lessons. He'd have to be even more careful to check out the people to whom he offered his services. Unfortunately, his reticence led to their delay in helping Angela. At some stage, he'd have to find a more efficient decision-making process.

In Mike's kitchen, with the concerned frown creasing her face, Lara once again turned into the administering angel.

"Come on," she said, beckoning with her fingers, "let me see."

Feigning reluctance, Kaine sighed and allowed her to lead him to a dining chair. He sat, pulled up the sleeve of his shirt, and flexed the forearm gently. Although he appreciated Lara's concern and her proximity, he couldn't help groaning at the way she prodded and poked at the livid scar.

"Ow," he said, tearing his arm from her grasp. "For pity's sakes, girl. You're not kneading bread."

She laughed.

"Big baby. It's healing well, as usual."

"Yeah, I know. But have a heart, will you?"

"If you're going to war with Teddy Tedesco, you'll probably suffer worse than that."

"Yeah but I won't have to sit still, and I will be able to fight back."

She rolled down his sleeve and patted his arm again, this time gently.

"So, can you tell me what you're planning? You said something about calling ahead and making an appointment. You can't be serious, surely."

"Bloody hell, Lara. First you pummel a severe injury so hard the wound nearly splits open, then you accuse me of being a baby, and now you're calling me Shirley. Is there no end to your cruelty?"

It took her a moment to get the "Shirley" reference and when she did, she actually resorted to an eye roll and a face palm, but Kaine stood on shaky ground, and he knew it.

"Ryan Liam Kaine, if you can't be serious for one minute, I'm going to … to …"

"What? Scream?"

"No, I'm going to bed."

"And leave me all alone in the middle of the evening? As I said, you can be such a cruel woman."

She harrumphed a huge sigh. "It's cold in here. At least let's go sit next to the fire and you can tell me what you're planning. If I know you and your tactics, I think I'll need a hug."

He sprang to his feet, a gazelle in the guise of a tired, old man.

"That's the best offer I've had since we left France."

She took his hand and led him towards the sitting area.

Safely ensconced on the settee after adding another two seasoned, oak logs to the dying fire—with Lara in his arms, her head resting on his chest—Kaine outlined his plan for the morning. She allowed him to speak without interruption and barely moved. At one stage, he suspected she'd fallen asleep and stopped talking but she urged him on with an annoyed grunt.

When he finished, he asked, "Well, what do you think?"

Lara spoke into his chest, her breath warming the skin through his heavy shirt. "You seriously think you can end this tomorrow?"

"To be honest, I doubt it, but it'll be worth the risk, don't you think? Tedesco's just lost his brother. He's mad as hell right now, and if he's as arrogant and irrational as Pony was, he might just go for it. If he does, I'll be able to end this with one swift, surgical strike."

Lara lifted her head to look at him and left a cold patch over his heart. Her eyes were red-rimmed with fatigue and one small step away from tears. He hated seeing her upset and hated himself for dragging the beautiful woman into his crap-ugly world.

"You can't trust Teddy Tedesco," she said, her voice hushed. "Why don't you take Rollo and Danny with you?"

"And leave Angela and Bobbie, and you, unprotected? Not a chance. Mike used to be one of the best, but he's slowing down, and it wouldn't be safe for you or him."

"You just have to do everything on your own, don't you?"

She sat up, pulling herself away from him and letting even more cold air force its way between them.

"You're good, Ryan. Highly skilled, but how are you going to fight a war like this on your own?"

He reached up and cupped her face in his hand. She looked so fragile and scared, and all he wanted was to kiss away her fear. "Tomorrow afternoon, a few of my most trusted former troop will start arriving. I'll designate two to stay at the farm for the duration. The rest will form my private army. Hopefully, they won't be needed, and they'll be part of the first guerrilla unit ever to have been formed and disbanded inside a couple of days. Might even make a new world record."

Quiet laughter rippled from the direction of the front porch.

"Sounds like the younger element are enjoying the moonlight," Kaine said.

"Is there a moon?"

He shook his head. "Nah. A heavy fog bank rolled in about half an hour ago. To be honest, there's no real need for Danny to be outside anymore since Rollo set up the infrared cameras."

"Aren't you going to call them inside?"

"Nope. By now, Rollo's in the barn's comms room. Nice and warm in there. As for Danny? Sounds as though he's appreciating Bobbie's company. It would be cruel to break up their little party. Oh, and talking about being cruel," he said, raising a finger, "perhaps that's a job for Cruella de Orchard? Whatcha think, Doc? Are you going to ruin the youngsters' evening?"

He smiled when she did.

"I'm not cruel, Ryan," she said, scrunching back into his arms, "I'm worried for you, that's all. Don't blame me for caring."

"No, I won't," he said, stroking her hair.

Damn it, Kaine. You are a soppy, old Marine.

Lara folded her arm around his waist, squeezed, and relaxed. He continued stroking her hair until her breathing settled into the steady rhythm of sleep.

"I'd die rather than see you hurt," he whispered.

She purred in her sleep, and he smiled and wondered what it would be like to live a normal life.

Fat chance.

Chapter Eighteen

Sunday 29th November – Jerome Tedesco

Ocean Village, Southampton, Hampshire, England

Teddy's private landline rang. Only Mother and Pony knew the number. Mother was in bed, asleep, and Pony wasn't ever going to use a phone again.

Fuck!

"Timothy!" he yelled.

Moments later the office door opened, and the black bugger popped his shiny head into the room.

"Yes, Mr—"

"Trace this fucking call," he said, pointing to the phone.

"You want me to monitor your private line?"

"Don't fucking question me, you ingrate. Do it! It's Captain Arsewipe."

"Keep him talking as long as you can, Mr Tedesco."

"I know what I have to do, fuckwit. Get on with it!"

Timothy left the room without saying another word. The door closed with a soft click.

Teddy snatched the squawking phone from its cradle. "Who the fuck's this? If you're telesales with a random dial program, I'm gonna find you and send someone round to tear your fucking throat out."

The caller laughed. A sarcastic, drawn-out chuckle.

The fucking captain!

"Hello, Teddy, is that how you always answer your calls on this line? What if it's your sainted mother?"

Captain Arsewipe spoke quietly, gently mocking.

I'll teach you to mock Teddy Tedesco.

"How'd you get this number?"

The bastard didn't answer right away, but the wind and traffic noise in the background suggested he was in a car, driving fast, perhaps on a motorway or a dual carriageway. Not much help and a fast-moving car was almost impossible to trace.

Fuck.

"Answer my questions or I'm hanging up."

"Don't give me that crap, Teddy. You and I both know you're trying to trace this call. Who's running the trace? Let me see. Is it the fellow you call Ginger? Hardly an original name for a redhead. Or would it be Timothy Khumalo?"

Christ, how much did the bugger know?

"My money's on Timothy," he continued. "He lives in your guest apartment and will be around this time in the morning. So, let's make this a little easier on Timothy. I'm on the M3, heading for Southampton, and I'm alone. All alone."

The walls started to close in around Teddy. He wanted to smash something. Anything. Grind it into powder.

"Hello? … Are you still there, Teddy? … What's the matter, cat hacked out your tongue?"

Teddy couldn't breathe. Sweat soaked his scalp.

Count. Start counting.

He made it all the way to three before the words spewed out. "When you killed Pony, you signed your own death certificate, you arsehole. Why d'you do it? Why d'you kill my brother?"

"He gave me no alternative, Teddy. You see, the Shafers are under my protection. Now and forever."

"Fuck off. I'm gonna kill them all. Mother, daughter, aunts, and uncles. I'm gonna wipe that family off the face of the earth."

"Hmm. That's pretty much what Pony said before I stuck my knife through his heart. Empty promises must run in the Tedesco family."

"Yeah? Well you can bet I'm going to murder the Shafers, but I'm gonna do you first, fucker. You first. So, you call to gloat, or what?"

That's it, Teddy. Keep the soon-to-be-dead fucker on the line.

Captain Arsewipe started up again with his snivelling, goading words. "Everything's rushing through your head right now, I bet. Questions a-plenty, no doubt."

Teddy couldn't believe his ears. The bastard was crowing. Actually fucking crowing.

"How did you get my private fucking number?"

Another laugh.

"C'mon, Teddy, ask me a difficult one. I'm using Pony's mobile. He very kindly said I could have it. Not in so many words, you understand, but I'm sure he doesn't mind. Not where he is at the moment. Anyway, fact is I killed Pony, and I'm planning to kill you. You see, I'm an exterminator, Teddy. In the greater scheme of things, Pony meant less to me than the last rat I tossed in the bin. I kill vermin and I'm very good at it. Want to find out how to avoid being next on my list?"

Teddy stared at the photo on his desk, the one with Mother, Pony, and him outside the cemetery when they'd buried Father. Fifteen years ago, almost to the month. At twelve, Pony was staring into the camera smiling that vacant smile of his. Mother was crying, while Teddy, at twenty-two, the new head of the family business, looked steadily into the lens, showing a tough face to the world. Father died because he got over-confident. A firm from Portsmouth tried to muscle in on the family business, and Father didn't take it seriously enough. Well, Teddy learned his lesson. Ever since then, he'd been on guard. Nobody was going to make a move on his patch and get away with it. Wasn't happening, not while Teddy drew breath.

"You're threatening me?"

"Well worked out, Teddy. You're faster than your idiot brother, but before I say anything else, let me just offer my condolences for your loss. Although the truth is Pony's death is no loss to the world, I do like to follow standard social etiquette in these matters."

Cool head, Teddy. Hear the fucker out. Find out what he wants.

"I don't give a flying fuck for your condolences, *Captain*," Teddy said, trying to dial back his temper. "I want your head on a spike sticking out of my window, but not before I have some fun. See, when I find you, I'm gonna kill you slowly."

"Thought you might say something like that," the snarky bugger said, a smile still in his voice. "And I have no doubt you're going to try. So, why don't we get it over with?"

Captain Arsewipe scoffed.

The fucker actually scoffed at Teddy Tedesco! The phone creaked under the pressure from his iron grip.

"You'll die slowly!"

"You've already said that, Teddy. You're being highly colourful, my friend, but those are empty threats. How are you going to do that, do you think? You don't know who I am or who—"

"But I will, you fucker," Teddy said. "Right now, every man in my organisation is looking for you. Every man, hear me? I've put a bounty on your head. One hundred grand. Every lowlife in the country will be in on the search. You can't hide for long. And when I do find you, I'll—"

"One hundred thousand? That all? What a cheapskate. Is that all Pony was worth to the great Teddy Tedesco?"

"You fucker, I've just doubled it. And I've just doubled the length of time it'll take you to die!"

"Oh stop it with the moronic threats, you plankton. Unlike you, I don't make threats. I make promises. Are you prepared to listen to my terms?"

"Terms? Terms! What fucking terms?"

"The terms of your surrender."

"My what? Are you insane?"

Again, the man laughed.

He is. He's fucking insane.

How could anyone reason with a madman? Pony's face stared out at him from the silver-framed photo. This conversation was worse than trying to talk sense into Pony.

"Some have called my sanity into question in the past, and I grant you, it may be open to debate, but I'll take into consideration your recent bereavement and not take offence. So, my terms are as follows. Number one, you disband your whole organisation with immediate effect. Number two, you hand over any accounts and document books you might have to the tax man. Number three, you walk into the nearest police station and confess to the last ten crimes you've committed and provide all the evidence needed to ensure a conviction."

What the fuck was he on? Speed?

"And let's be absolutely clear on one point," he continued. "One of those ten crimes must include culpability in the murder of the poor soul whose body Angela Shafer witnessed your men trying to drop into the lake at Breaker's Folly."

The nutter finally stopped talking, but Teddy couldn't think of a thing to say. He allowed the silence to drag on for ages. A big, diesel engine drowned out the rest of the noise on the other end of the phone. Maybe a haulage truck on the M3.

"I'm sure you don't need me to repeat those conditions, Teddy. I know you're recording this call."

The bizarre nature of the man's demands struck Teddy like a kick in the nuts.

"Alternatively …"

"What? You have an alternative?" Teddy demanded.

Was there no end to the fucker's lunacy?

"I do indeed. Alternatively, we can end this right now, this morning. Man-to-man, just the two of us. Fancy that?"

"You're fucking kidding, right? You expect me to turn up to a fucking duel in the sun like a couple of cowboys?"

"Apart from the fact it's cloudy, why not?" Captain Arsewipe said, calm as anything. "My background check says you're quite handy with a gun. You talk a good fight,

Teddy, but do you have the stones to face me? What do you say … are you man enough?"

"And what if I don't turn up and don't hand myself over to the police? What then?"

"Oh that's simple," he said gently. "If you don't agree to every one of my conditions, my men and I will pay an extended visit to Southampton. We'll take everything from you, piece by piece. Money, resources, men, and your reputation. After that, when you're all alone, you and I will meet, face-to-face anyway. And then … you will die. And, as you are so keen to say, you will die slowly."

Christ, the balls on the fucker. Does he actually believe that bullshit?

Teddy considered counting to ten, but he couldn't be arsed. The anger boiling in his guts felt good.

"Okay," Teddy said. "I'll meet you. And I'll wipe you from the sole of my shoe like a piece of dog shit."

"Really?" Captain Arsewipe shot back. "You're actually going to leave your fortress? I'm honoured. If I wasn't holding onto your dead brother's phone, I'd give you a round of applause. Didn't think you had the nerve. Nice one, Teddy. But you will come alone, won't you?"

"Yeah, I'll be alone. You can trust the word of Teddy Tedesco. Name the place and time."

Yeah, you can trust me, dickhead.

"You're a man of your word, eh Teddy? Really? Let's see. You know Yellow Diamond Fabrications, of course."

Teddy gasped.

The fucker did know everything.

Captain Arsewipe spoke again. "Didn't think I needed to jog your memory. It's where Jerzy Harrow's mob euthanised your father. The factory's abandoned now, so we'll be all alone. No one to disturb us. Meet me there at eleven o'clock. You have two hours. I'll be in the main car park at the rear of the factory. Don't be late."

The call clicked into silence, leaving Teddy to stare at the dead phone.

Timothy returned.

"Did you fucking hear all that?"

"Yes, Mr Tedesco."

"Trace it?"

"No, sir. The call was too short. What are your instructions?"

"Get the boys. As many as you can find, and make sure they're loaded for hunting bear," Teddy answered, slamming the phone into its cradle. "The fucker's on the M3 right now. The boys are going to have plenty of time to reach the factory ahead of him. They can set up an ambush, on the off chance the fucker actually shows. I want the place saturated well ahead of the deadline."

"You want him taken alive, so you can question him?"

"Nah. Kill the fucker. Take as long as they like over it."

"Will you be going, sir?"

"Don't be fucking stupid. 'Course I'm not going."

"Want me to go and take charge?"

Teddy shook his head and leaned back in his chair. "You stay here with me. Ginger was in the army, right? He can lead the slaughter. Send the Kraut, too. 'Bout time he showed us more than how to read a dog's collar. Let's see if he's got the bollocks for the job. And I'll want pictures. Don't want to miss a thing. Send Pickford with his camcorder."

Chapter Nineteen

Sunday 29th November – Morning

***Yellow Diamond Fabrications, Southampton,
Hampshire, England***

Kaine powered down Pony's mobile, removed the battery, and threw it behind him. He also turned off the digital recorder, silencing the background traffic noise he'd recorded during his journey down the M1 from the farm.

He'd borrowed the recording idea from Corky. It seemed the IT specialist had more than one use.

Kaine's watch showed 09:07. It always paid dividends to arrive early for a rendezvous with an opponent, especially a sneaky one with no moral code.

"Okay, Teddy," he muttered to the pigeons strolling past his sniper's nest. "Let's see how true you are to your word."

One of the birds, a big, plump male, stopped. It tilted its head and looked at him through one eye as though to ask, "What are you doing on my roof?"

Kaine stared back, whispered, "Won't be here long, little buddy, no need to fret," and allowed the bird to wander off after opening its beak and cooing a warning.

Kaine settled down to watch and wait.

He didn't really expect Tedesco to expose himself to risk, but on the off chance the crime boss made an appearance, Kaine would be ready to take him out, clean and simple. He'd have preferred an honest, face-to-face show-down rather than the surreptitious, cowardly sniper approach, but if he could end this with a single shot, it would save lives, and it wasn't as though Tedesco deserved any leniency. In his research, Corky uncovered nearly three dozen disappearances directly attributable to Tedesco and his organisation. Not one of the disappearances had led to an arrest, trial, or conviction. Yes, Kaine might be a self-appointed judge, jury, and executioner, but in this instance, and to save the lives of Angela and Bobbie Shafer, he was prepared to assume the roles. He'd take no pleasure in the act but could at least justify it to himself.

"Protect The 83" had become his life's mission and his mantra.

The merest huff of moving air brushed his left cheek, a light, south-westerly zephyr less than five kilometres per hour. The sun, a low and watery glow through the light cloud, sat behind his right shoulder. It made spotting his target easy but blinded anyone looking towards him from the north and west—his kill zone. Atmospheric conditions couldn't have been much better in November.

Five storeys up on an abandoned office block, Kaine had a perfect, panoramic view of the meeting place. He lay on a flat, asphalt roof, hidden beneath a grey tarpaulin, one of many pieces of rubbish that broke the roofline. Only the pigeons could see him.

Three hundred metres away, the four-storey, concrete hulk of a building spread out below him in a U-shaped block. It surrounded an empty, rubbish-strewn, courtyard car park. Shattered windows showed black and jagged within the dirty, grey, concrete walls. The brilliant reflections of the few with unbroken glass shone like spotlights in the gloom, and a paved path ran around the foot of the building. It acted like an apron separating concrete walls from the tarmac courtyard.

Graffiti besmirched the lower walls, but none of it had any creative merit. The complex must have been too far out of town for the more accomplished taggers to waste their time and their spray paint.

The courtyard car park was full of the usual human detritus. Rubbish piled high in the corners—a mattress, discarded cans and bottles, plastic bags, used nappies, and fast-food containers. Filth and grime everywhere. The place hadn't seen a refuse collection in years and the solitary "Trespassers will be Prosecuted" sign on the fence clearly didn't frighten anyone into avoiding the place.

North End Way, a lightly used, two-lane, feeder road, ran north to south between Kaine and the warehouse complex. An access road split off from the way and led to broken gates that hung open and failed to block the entrance.

The building's seclusion happened to be one reason for it being Kaine's venue of choice. Another was its association with the death of Tedesco's father.

The breeze barely had enough strength to ruffle the pieces of torn plastic hanging from some of the broken windows, which he used as wind strength indicators. They were perfect for a sniper acting without a spotter.

Apart from his camouflaged Accuracy AXMC sniper rifle—chambered for 7.62x51 mm, 155-grain, NATO cartridges held within a ten-shot magazine—he had two other essential pieces of equipment to augment his ears and eyes.

The first device, a Pro-Optique Laser Rangefinder, calculated the distances to four predetermined target points —the central warehouse doors, the building's two gable ends, and the drop-off zone in front of the loading bay. With those four points plotted and the distance to each memorised, Kaine had triangulated a comprehensive kill zone within the heart of the complex. Nobody approaching on foot would escape his bullets.

With the second device, a military-grade, collapsible, GMX parabolic microphone, he'd be able to pick up any conversation within line-of-sight up to five hundred metres away.

At the range he envisaged—less than three hundred metres in near-optimal weather conditions—he'd expect a conservative ninety-nine-point-six percent hit rate.

Good enough for government work.

Kaine smiled at the expression everyone in the military used but nobody believed.

Within minutes of his arrival on the roof, Kaine had set the minute of angle on his scope to allow for his elevation. He also set the veer angle to allow for the minimal windage, and he targeted each area of the compound in turn to confirm the scope's range finder with the readout from the Pro-Optique. They tallied to within five centimetres.

As for the AXMC itself, he'd used the model before, but the particular weapon in his hands was brand new and had never been fired except on the range. Rollo, the team's Quartermaster, had obtained it courtesy of … God only knew. Kaine had spent the previous afternoon on the farm familiarising himself with its peculiarities—weight, balance, trigger tension, recoil, and accuracy. Each individual weapon had its own characteristics. The sleek beast laid out before him on the rooftop pulled half of one degree to the right on a target ranged at six hundred metres. It took Kaine a dozen shots to zero the scope and compensate for the weapon's inbuilt drift. After adjusting the scope, two further shots gave him the confidence that he'd hit whatever he chose to aim at. Three more shots at a tree some seven hundred and fifty metres distant—all dead-centre hits—rounded off a highly successful familiarisation session.

After he'd cleaned the broken-down rifle and packed it, and the ammo, into its canvas carrier, Rollo, his spotter for the afternoon, clapped him on the shoulder.

"Not lost any of your skills, I see."

Kaine shrugged. "A little rusty. Took more ranging shots than usual to find the right balance and pull pressure. Nice bit of kit, though. Clean and light. Where'd you find it?"

As usual, Rollo shook his head, said, "Sorry, Captain, I promised my supplier I wouldn't let on, not even to you," and Kaine allowed the matter to drop.

Apart from the wind-driven rustling, the rumble of the occasional vehicle passing in the distance, and the cooing pigeons, the parabolic mic picked up nothing of interest. No radio chatter. No casual human conversation. No human intervention of any kind.

Kaine scanned the target zone with his Zeiss field glasses, using the minimum of movement and keeping the lenses well back inside the flap of the tarp to rule out the possibility of glare flashing off the glass. Gentle sweeps through the north-south arc showed nothing to spark his internal warning sensors.

It had been years since his last operation involving sniper tactics and, despite the growing stiffness in his lower body brought on by lying still for over an hour, the familiar techniques returned. Once, as a younger man, he'd spent three days in a mud-and-water-filled ditch, wallowing in his own filth to take out a Taliban tribal leader. He'd survived on liquid nutrition from a ten-litre bag sucked up through a straw. Not a feat he ever wanted to repeat, but he would if necessary.

The current operation in Southampton would last no more than a couple of hours.

He reduced the potential for cramp by isolating, tensing, and relaxing each skeletal muscle group in turn, from feet to shoulders and back. The exercise encouraged blood flow to and from the lower extremities and maintained optimal mobility should the need arise for a rapid evac.

Kaine lowered the binoculars and took a wider view.

Still nothing.

He breathed easily, slowly, keeping his heart rate low and his senses alert. Minutes passed with the flowing speed of cold molasses.

They arrived at 10:09.

Movement flickered on either side of his peripheral vision, to the north and south.

"Morning, gentlemen," Kaine whispered.

He drew up the field glasses again and focussed on the side closer to him, the factory's north-facing gable end. Team Zulu, five men dressed in black, approached the building on foot, moving cautiously—bent forwards at the waist, scanning the area ahead and around them. They clung tight to the wall, following the military hand signals given by their leader, a powerfully built guy with wiry, flame-red hair. Four of the men carried a semi-automatic handgun, pointing it to the ground. The last one carried an AK-47 with an extended magazine. Although inaccurate over any great distance, it had a combat firing rate of over four hundred rounds per minute. Deadly in enclosed spaces.

Kaine swung the binoculars to the south and picked up the second phalanx, Team Yankee. Another five, similarly dressed, men approached in the same manner as their colleagues in Team Zulu. The blond leader, with a slighter build than Red, operated the same way. The only difference between the teams was that instead of an AK-47, the tail-end Charlie of Team Yankee carried a professional-looking video camera bolted to a Steadicam. The rig looked expensive enough to be used by a BBC outside broadcast unit.

Kaine's parabolic mic picked up the occasional stumbling footfall from the cameraman, who had to split his concentration between filming and where he placed his feet. He tripped over an oilcan and nearly fell into the man in front, and the blond leader hissed something in German. Kaine salted the information away for later use. Intel, no matter where it originated from, could come in handy.

Kaine watched in cold amusement as Red and the German led their squads in a coordinated pincer movement. They moved like former-military men with moderate skills, but made too much noise to be special forces. Infantrymen. Still dangerous.

A strategic retreat would have been advisable, but Kaine wanted to see whether Tedesco would turn up to spring the trap, despite his rumoured agoraphobia. During their phone call, Kaine had set the bait with his insults and jibes. If all that wasn't enough to lure the man from his self-imposed prison, Kaine would need to roll out Plan B—after developing one.

The presence of the cameraman suggested the crime boss would be nowhere near the rendezvous, but on the off chance he presented himself as a target, Kaine would stay until well after the deadline.

Again, he waited.

The men in black spread out on either side of the court-yard, taking cover behind rubbish bins and bushy weeds, and setting up a crossfire pattern no one standing in the courtyard could survive. They even interlocked and over-lapped their firing positions to avoid friendly fire incidents. Kaine's estimation of Red and the German climbed a few notches up the competency scale. However, from his elevated position, Kaine could see each man clearly. If he wanted to, he could probably have taken out every last member of the ambush teams before they found him. His suppressed shots would echo around the U-shaped building, which would likely make locating his sniper's nest by sound alone nigh on impossible.

He'd already calculated the optimal target order. Under normal operating conditions, Red would die first. Next, Kaine would target the man with the assault rifle and follow with the German—kill the leaders first, confuse the enemy. He'd leave the unarmed man with the camera alive to make a permanent record of the massacre. But this wasn't war, and these weren't normal operating conditions.

He quickly dismissed the option.

The men in black were hired guns, no more. They had mothers, wives, children, and he bore them no undue malice. Kaine had enough deaths on his conscience. He could kill in self-defence and in the defence of others, but, at that moment, Teams Zulu and Yankee didn't fit either scenario.

On the other hand, Tedesco deserved no such clemency. He'd sealed his fate the moment he'd set his demented brother on Angela Shafer. And Tedesco's demise would fill another purpose. Remove the head from the snake and the body would writhe around for a while, but eventually, it would wither.

Red raised a mobile to his mouth. Kaine pointed the parabolic mic and listened into one side of the phone conversation, while simultaneously scanning the courtyard for signs of movement, still hoping for Tedesco to make an appearance.

"...all set, Mr Tedesco," Red said, leaning around the side of an abandoned car—a Mini. "If the fucker shows, he's a dead man. ... No, sir. No chance of him getting away. I have a spotter on the main road into the site ..."

Kaine added another mental note to his growing knowledge base.

Red continued. "That's right, Mr Tedesco, we're totally secure. ... Hold on, sir. Something's happening inside the warehouse. ... Voices. ... A man and a woman by the sounds of it. They're having a right barney."

Red lowered the mobile and cocked an ear to listen for a moment before continuing the call.

"Yes, sir. ... No, the warehouse is a rabbit warren. We only just got here. Haven't had a chance to search the place yet. ... Okay, I'll send someone in. Stand by."

Red lowered the phone again, turned to his left, and pointed at two men. He summoned them by tapping his fingers to the top of his head and hurried them with a fist-pump. The men scrambled forwards, keeping below the height of the bushes lining the weed-strewn pavement that ran around the base of the warehouse. Each took a knee in front of their ginger-haired leader.

The first man—a six-footer with broad shoulders and narrow hips—wore a beard the image of the one Rollo had shaved off at Marie-Odile's behest. Red addressed his instructions to Blackbeard. "Find out who's making all that fucking noise. Be quick about it. The target's due inside thirty minutes."

Blackbeard nodded to his sidekick—a strong-jawed man with a Superman cowlick—and they took off at double time. Still keeping low, they headed towards a part-rotted, wooden door.

Red spoke into the mobile once more, "Mr Tedesco, I'm on it, sir. Won't be long. … No, it definitely ain't the target."

Before Blackbeard and Cowlick covered half the distance, twenty paces, the rotten door shuddered open, its hinges creaking so loudly, Kaine wouldn't have needed the mic to pick up the noise. A man, a woman, and a filthy, flop-eared dog squeezed through a narrow gap between the door and the jamb. The humans were of indeterminate age and blinked against the bright daylight. All three were in need of a good grooming. Their threadbare and grubby clothing gave away their status as rough sleepers.

"I told ya, love," the man insisted, "I don't have no fags left."

"Selfish bastard. You could of saved me one. Where we gonna find—"

Blackbeard and Cowlick cut short her words by slamming her and the "selfish bastard" against the wall. The man threw his hands up to his face and whimpered. The woman screamed, swore, and kicked out. The dog barked and snapped at his mistress' attacker.

Cowlick booted the animal in the ribs. It yelped and

slinked away, whimpering, tail between its legs. The woman swore a blue fit until Cowlick slapped her so hard across the face the back of her head cracked against the wall.

"Shut your fucking mouth, bitch," he snarled, grabbed her hair, and pinned her to the wall with it.

Blackbeard gut-punched the man, who doubled over and collapsed to his hands and knees, retching and gasping for breath.

On his rooftop, Kaine boiled. He detested bullies with a passion. No bloody way could he let this continue. He raised the butt of the Accuracy and rammed it into his shoulder.

"Who else is in there?" Blackbeard growled, but the man shook his head, unable to answer.

Blackbeard turned to Cowlick, his lips pulled back in a sneer. "Ask Lady Muck, and don't take no more lip from the bitch."

Cowlick yanked the woman's hair, pulling up her head. "Okay darling, who else is in there?"

"Fuck off," she yelled and spat in his face.

Kaine gritted his teeth. The woman showed spirit, even if it was misplaced.

"No," Cowlick said. "You fuck off, bitch."

He raised a fist in preparation to strike.

Bastards.

Kaine's right hand curled around the textured grip, and his finger caressed the gentle curve of the trigger. He selected a fixed target—Cowlick's right ankle—and lined it up on the mil-dot reticle. He used the second dot on the left horizontal to allow for the slight increase in wind speed. The cold metal of the stock against his cheek slowly warmed.

Sound faded.

His vision closed into the scope, blocking out external distractions.

Kaine breathed out steadily, lowering his heart rate. At the end of the breath, he paused and squeezed the trigger, applying the pressure slowly and evenly.

The rifle coughed—its full roar reduced by the sound-and-flash suppressor attached to the muzzle.

The butt punched into his shoulder.

Two hundred and seventy metres away, Cowlick's ankle exploded in a cloud of boot, bone, and blood. He collapsed in a writhing, screaming heap, pulling the woman with him until she wrenched her hair from his faltering grip and kicked him in the kneecap. Cowlick's Ruger SR45 clattered to the paving slab at his side.

Blackbeard spun. Confusion rippled across his face. Cowlick rolled onto his side and curled into a ball, hugging his crippled leg to his chest, writhing, his face creased in agony. The right foot dangled loose, held in place by a few scraps of tendon and boot leather.

"What the fuck?" Blackbeard screamed. "What happened? Anybody see what the fuck just—"

The second 7.62-calibre bullet shattered Blackbeard's right shoulder, stopping him mid-rant. He pirouetted, collapsed, and face-planted the concrete beside his writhing partner. The gun fell from his hand. The vagrants and their dog dived back inside the warehouse.

Kaine leaned away from the rifle and scanned the target area. The earbuds from the parabolic mic enabled him to hear Red's panicked, "Jesus fuck. Someone's shot Randy and Chukka! Anyone see anything?"

Kaine's third shot destroyed the video camera and with it, the filmmaker's right hand. If the camera had captured any telling images by accident, Kaine didn't want Tedesco seeing them. As far as Tedesco was concerned, Kaine would remain a phantom. At least for a while.

He settled back to watch, keeping the wide scene in full view.

Red cowered behind the Mini, yelling questions that became more and more strident and garbled.

"Where is he?" ... "Anyone seem him?" ... "Boomer, you got a location?" ... "Anyone got a shot?" ... "Fucking answer me, you bastards!"

While the three injured men cried out, pleading for help, six of the remaining seven kept their heads down. Only the blond with the German accent reacted with anything like bravery. Three times, he popped his head out from the side of his battered-oil-drum safety screen, took a quick look around, and ducked back into safety again, trying to identify Kaine's position.

After a few minutes without shots fired, Red seemed to find his courage.

"Schechter!" he called across the courtyard. "You got anything?"

"To your left, Ginger," Schechter answered, his accent thick. "The shots were from your left and high up, I think."

"You sure?" Red—Ginger—yelled. "Could have sworn they came from the right, inside the warehouse."

"This place is an echo chamber. The shots could have come from anywhere. What do we do? The injuries look serious, *ja*? So much blood. The men need the ambulance, right away."

"Hang on, I'll ask the boss."

"But they are dying! We need the ambul—"

"No. Cut your fucking whingeing. Phone the ambulance and the cops are gonna be all over this crap-hole like the fucking pox. Don't do nothing 'til I speak to the boss, get it?"

Schechter shook his head but didn't reach for a mobile. Instead, he lowered himself to the ground and slithered, snake-like, along the path towards the cameraman. In doing so, he exposed himself fully to Kaine, making himself an even easier target, one Kaine would never take advantage of. Schechter showed concern for his teammate, and the action saved him from taking a bullet.

Kaine trained both the mic and the rifle at Ginger—a much less savoury character.

"You there, Mr Tedesco?" Ginger whispered into his mobile. "We're in deep shit here. ... Three men down. ... No, not dead, but at least one's in a real bad way. Blood's pissing from his leg. Whoever's shooting at us damn near shot off his foot. What d'you want me—"

Ginger stopped talking and listened, nodding occasionally, grimacing once. "You certain, Mr Tedesco? ... What about the other men? ... Okay. No problem. The sniper? ... Yeah, right. No shots for at least five minutes. My guess is he's buggered off, but who the fuck knows? ... Yeah, okay. You can count on me, boss." He nodded and slid the mobile into a pocket.

"Ginger?" Schechter called. He'd reached the cameraman and dragged him behind a pile of rubbish, out of sight of the redhead, but not out of danger. Kaine could see their upper bodies and rotten wooden pallets would do little to stop a 7.62 NATO round. "Pickford's hand is shattered. Two fingers and his thumb are gone."

He gripped Pickford's wrist and held it up to reduce the blood loss, covering his own hand in red for his pains.

"Can he walk?" Ginger called.

Schechter spoke quietly to the injured man, who shrugged, then nodded.

"Yes," Schechter called. "Why?"

"The boss says he's called for the ambulance, but anyone who can walk has to go now," Ginger said. He raised his voice to a roar. "We've got to go before paramedics get here and bring the cops with them."

He turned to face the two remaining fit men on his side of the courtyard.

"Everyone move on my mark. Gather where we parked the cars. Ready your side, Schechter?"

The German nodded to his men, draped the cameraman's arm over his shoulder, and helped him to stand. They leaned against the wall, bent at the waist, keeping low.

Schechter shouted, "Ready."

"Okay," Ginger called. "On three. One …"

The men shuffled around, turning to face the main gates. Most took up a sprinter's stance, as though on the starting blocks, their weapons held like relay batons. All except Ginger himself.

"…two …"

Schechter, maintaining his tourniquet grip on the cameraman's wrist, started moving. He didn't wait for the end of the count.

"…three! Go, go, go!"

Five men broke cover, sprinting along the paths. Once in the open, they zig-zagged.

Away from the protection of the building, Schechter and the cameraman took a direct route. Maybe the German sensed a lack of danger. Maybe he was more concerned for the man under his care and wanted to take him to safety as fast as possible. Either way, he half-dragged, half-carried

Pickford across the open car park, in an act of selfless bravery that impressed Kaine.

Ginger stayed hidden, crouched behind the relative safety of the abandoned Mini, a sly smile cracked his ruddy face.

"Coward," Kaine muttered.

The redhead allowed his men to go first, drawing any possible fire. After witnessing the German's courage, Kaine's disgust at the actions of the team leader made him consider taking a fourth shot, but he dismissed the thought. After all, cowardice in the face of the enemy was no longer a capital offence. At least not in the UK.

Schechter and Pickford reached the gate, lagging far behind the others. The German yelled for help between laboured breaths. The last of the group—another tall blond —stopped. He turned, hesitated, looked around him, and hurried back to the struggling pair. He grabbed the cameraman's free arm and together, he and Schechter helped Pickford to safety.

Kaine salted away another piece of information.

Movement at his periphery caught Kaine's attention. In the far distance, two figures and a dog emerged from behind the main building. They scampered towards the rusted, chain-link fence surrounding the plot, climbed through a gap, and disappeared around the side of a crumbling tower block. Heading towards the main road into the city, they were no doubt looking for another abode. Kaine couldn't blame them. In their position, he'd have done exactly the same thing, and he took his cue from them. Time to skedaddle. Tedesco was clearly not going to make an appearance, not after Kaine had been forced to show his hand.

He slithered backwards from the lip of the roof and

made sure he was well out of sight before kneeling to break the rifle down. After covering both lenses with the flick-down caps, he loosened the two wingnut screws and released the scope from its bedding plate. He unscrewed the knurled nut holding the barrel into the stock and slid it into its sheath in the canvas carrier. The bipod stand unclipped easily from its groove in the stock and slipped into the bag's side pocket. As he removed the magazine, the indicator light on the mic flashed red.

What now?

He replaced the earbuds.

"…right, Mr Tedesco. They're gone. The place is clear," Ginger said, speaking into his mobile and talking loud enough to be heard above the groans and cries of an injured man.

Kaine lowered the stock of the Accuracy onto the carrier and belly-crawled to his original position, with the mic and binoculars in hand.

"Nah, boss," Ginger continued. "Ain't heard nothing from the shooter since he opened up. I reckon he panicked when he saw us and got off some lucky shots."

Kaine scowled. Ginger was either an idiot, or was trying to convince himself with his own words.

"Nah, he's long gone by now, I reckon. Otherwise he'd have picked off them others. … So, you definitely want me to do 'em? … Usual terms? Not bloody likely, they're friends of mine. I've met Randy's wife. Nice woman, big jugs. … I'll want double. Yeah, that's right. Twenty grand a piece. Not too much to pay for your piece of mind, is it? … Nah, I thought not. Consider it done, boss."

Ginger ended the call and stood. He removed the maga-zine from his handgun, a SIG P220, judging by the angled notches on the muzzle end of the barrel. A wicked smile cracked his pockmarked face. In that instant, Kaine understood.

Oh Christ. No!

Too late. Too bloody late.

Ginger turned, replaced the mag, cocked his weapon, and walked at a crouch towards his injured friends.

"No! You bastard. No!" Kaine yelled, but the wind in his face whipped his words away, and Ginger didn't react.

Kaine snapped his head around to check on the rifle. How long would it take to rebuild? Fifteen? Twenty seconds? Too long. He didn't have five. His SIG was useless at the range. All he could do was watch.

Blackbeard lay on his back, hand clamped to his damaged shoulder. Blood soaked his jacket and painted his fist dark red. His face was white and contorted in pain. Cowlick lay still and silent. He might have bled out already.

Ginger kneeled close to Blackbeard, arm extended, weapon cocked. "Sorry, Randy. Can't be helped. Teddy's orders. I'll sort out your missus if you see what I mean."

Randy cried out, "No! You fucker," and tried to scramble away, but Ginger shot twice. The back of Black-beard's head exploded, and he stopped moving.

Bastard. You callous bastard!

The redhead slithered to his left and crawled towards the second downed man, Chukka.

Kaine pulled out his SIG and fired three times into the air. Ginger dived behind Randy, using the dead man's body for cover, his red face showing terror.

"Be seeing you later, Ginger," Kaine said through gritted teeth. "You can count on that."

Kaine scrambled backwards, away from the edge once more, and finished packing the rifle. He collected the spent casings—three were still warm. He raced down the rusty fire escape and jogged the mile to his car. The image of the callous way Ginger had finished off his so-called friend would remain with Kaine for a long while.

Time to create a Plan B.

No mercy.

Chapter Twenty

Sunday 29th November – Jerome Tedesco

Ocean Village, Southampton, Hampshire, England

Teddy kicked a rubbish bin across the office and sent its contents flying. It twirled and settled in the corner before Teddy could bring himself to speak.

"How the fuck did he get there before us?"

Timothy knew better than to answer, but Ginger wasn't quite as smart.

"Not so sure he did, boss," the redheaded fucker said.

Teddy spun and sneered at the killer. "Oh, you're not so sure, are you?"

Ginger shook his head. "He could've arrived at the same time we did. Got off a couple of lucky shots and—"

"Lucky shots? Lucky fucking shots? You moron! Far as I can tell, the bugger hit exactly what he wanted to. Took out three men with three shots and then hung around long enough to see you take down Randy and Chukka."

Ginger wilted under the outburst. "But he missed me with three rounds, boss."

Timothy grimaced.

"If you've got something to say, Timothy, say it."

The black bastard waited a beat before answering. "The last three shots, Mr Tedesco."

"What about them?"

"Sounded like they came from a pistol. First three were from a rifle. A big rifle."

"So?" Ginger asked.

"Yeah," Teddy said. "What about it?"

"I think the pistol shots were warnings. The sniper was trying to warn Ginger off. He missed because no handgun could hit anything from the same distance as a rifle."

Teddy sniffed and unclasped his fists. "Yeah, I guess you could be right. So, it confirms what I was thinking about him being Black Ops. Not only that, but he's a fucking sniper, too?"

Ginger shuffled his feet uneasily. His ugly, red face grew uglier and redder by the second. For a ten pence piece, Teddy would have shot the useless fucker where he stood, but he'd already lost the use of three men that day and couldn't afford to weaken his army any further. No, he had too many jobs planned over the following few days, and he'd already spread his people way too thin. Still, it wouldn't always be this way. The second the pressure came off, Ginger was toast. He'd join Pony in the eternal sleep of the damned.

Timothy nodded. "Guess so, sir."

"Yeah, I'm right. I'm always fucking right. That's why I sit in the big chair, okay?"

"Yes, Mr Tedesco," both slabs of muscle said together.

"What happened to the Kraut?" Teddy asked, returning to the big chair.

"He took Pickford to the clinic," Timothy answered. "The poor bugger might end up losing the hand."

Teddy dropped into the soft, leather chair and leaned back. He'd conceded the high ground to the two giants, but not the authority.

"Yeah well, should have taken more care to keep his fucking head down. Bastard cost me an expensive camera, too. I should charge him for the price of a new one. So, I didn't get any shots of the action?"

"I think it was the point, Mr Tedesco," Timothy said.

"What d'you mean by that?"

"I was speculating, sir."

Teddy pointed him to one of the chairs on the other side of the desk. "Well, speculate from there. I'm getting a crick in my neck from looking up."

The bodyguards moved forwards at the same time.

"Not you, Ginger. You can fuck off out of it. Go find me some more men."

The redhead's upper lip curled as he asked, "How many, sir?"

"Half a dozen. Military. Make sure they know what end of a gun to hold and what they're up against. You'll be responsible for them. Understand?"

The redhead nodded. He didn't look all that happy to be side-lined from the powwow, or being made responsible for the men he hired, but fuck him. He was lucky to still be drawing breath.

"What terms and for how long? I mean, what quality of men you looking for, Mr Tedesco? How experienced?"

"Good foot soldiers. Two hundred a day plus the standard bonus. Fortnight minimum."

"I'll put the word out. Contact some of my old unit. They're always up for a scrap."

He left the office and closed the door quietly.

Bet the fucker wanted to slam it.

"Okay, Timothy. Spit it out. What does your speculating tell you?"

The black fucker sat up straight in his chair. Not one to relax around Teddy. Not Timothy. He had more sense than that.

"The first two shots disabled Randy and Chukka when they were beating up on a couple of tramps and their dog. The third bullet took out the camera." He stopped talking and looked up at the ceiling, lost in thought.

"Go on."

"It seems to me, the sniper was waiting for you. He set up an ambush in case you showed. But he only broke cover to protect a couple of hobos, and then he destroyed the camera in case it caught a shot of him."

The hairs on the nape of Teddy's neck started tingling.

"What exactly are you saying, Timothy?"

"Nothing other than, why would he do that? Why would a paid killer give a fuck about a couple of filthy *rondlopers* and their mutt? Given what he said about Angela Shafer and her daughter, he could be one of those vigilantes with a superhero complex. But, then again, there's the camera ..."

"Continue," Teddy said, slowly, although he already knew what Timothy was getting at.

"The fact he didn't want you seeing him on film might mean he thinks you'll recognise him."

Teddy nodded slowly. Timothy was making sense.

"You think he's from one of the London mobs? You reckon Big Gino's trying to muscle in on my turf again?"

Timothy hiked a shoulder. "Killing your brother might have been the first salvo in the war, Mr Tedesco. It's certainly weakened your position. And why didn't he kill anyone else at the warehouse? From his position on that roof, he could have wiped out the lot of them. It's interesting … no, no, it's nothing. I might be wrong, *ya*?"

"What's interesting, Timothy? There's only you and me here, you can speak freely."

Timothy's hand came up to wipe his shaved head. Sometimes, for such a powerful monkey, he could be a little timid, but Teddy knew better than to chivvy the bugger along too fast. If he did, Timothy would just clam up.

"How come Ginger survived? If the sniper's protecting the weak and defenceless, like the Shafers and those vagrants, why didn't he do the same for Randy and Chukka? I mean, given the fact he could have killed them outright with the first two shots, I'd have expected him to target Ginger, too. How come Ginger's still walking around fit and healthy? Maybe Ginger's working an angle."

It was worth the wait. Timothy wasn't just muscle. A brain lurked behind the brown eyes and the black skin.

Teddy nodded. "I was thinking the same thing. Maybe it's time to turn off Ginger's air supply. Let me think on it for a bit."

Timothy stood. "Yes, Mr Tedesco."

Before Teddy could wave him away, the private phone rang again. "What the fuck? It's the bastard sniper."

"Want me to hang around, boss?"

"Yeah, listen in. Elizabeth's running the trace on this phone, but it's probably another waste of time."

Timothy crossed to the other side of the office, picked up the extension, and nodded.

Teddy grabbed the handset. "Yeah?"

"Hi, Teddy, how are you? I missed seeing you this morning. Didn't expect you to be such a mealy-mouthed coward."

The smug bastard was taunting him again. Teddy wanted to reach into the phone and tear out the fucker's throat.

"Yeah, well. I got caught in traffic."

"Liar," he said, calmness itself. "Your men made it in plenty of time for the rendezvous. Admit it, Teddy, you bottled it. Then again, I should have expected that from someone who makes war on women and children. Ought to be ashamed of yourself."

"Yeah?" Teddy said, matching his intensity with the captain's—two could play the cool, intimidation game. "And if I'd done that, you'd have put a bullet in my head. So, who's the real coward? Me for protecting myself, or you for hiding on a rooftop and playing sniper?"

After a moment's silence, where the background noise down the line faded to nothing, Captain Arsewipe said, "No, Teddy. If you'd arrived alone as per our arrangement, I'd have made the meeting and we'd have faced off like real men. Then I'd have killed you face-to-face. Unfortunately—"

"Bollocks. You're a liar."

The fucker continued, ignoring Teddy's interruption. "—we're going to have to do this the hard way."

"What does that mean?"

"I'm going to tear your organisation down around your ears and expose you for the pitiful, lowlife coward you are. After that, I'll let the carrion crows peck at your flesh. That stunt you had Ginger pull on Randy and Chukka was completely unacceptable. What are the rest of your men going to think when they learn how you treated them? What price do you put on loyalty?"

Timothy shot Teddy a look he couldn't interpret. Did he give a fuck about Randy and Chukka? He'd been there when Teddy gave the order and didn't even blink. Nah, Timothy knew who paid his salary. He was cool with a bit of housekeeping.

"Don't talk to me like that, you miserable shit!" Teddy snapped.

The line clicked dead.

"Hello? Hello? Explain yourself, dammit!"

Timothy replaced the extension in its cradle. "He's hung up, Mr Tedesco."

"I can tell that. Go see if Elizabeth traced the call."

"He'll have used a burner, sir."

"Do as your fucking told, man!"

"Yes, sir."

His face an unreadable mask, Timothy stood and left the room. The door closed behind him. A moment later the phone rang again, and Teddy snatched it up.

"You really need to curb your language, Teddy. So, where were we? Oh yes, Ginger's act of cold-blooded murder. I guess you expected to blame their deaths on me."

"My men know what they signed up for. Anyone who takes a bullet while working for me knows I'll look after their families."

"Yes, of course you will. But what's going to happen when they learn you ordered the hits? How long before they start turning on you?"

"It'll be your word against mine and Ginger's. You're a

sniper who takes pot shots at them, and I'm their paymaster. Who are they likely to believe?"

"And what if I have proof?"

Teddy gasped. Couldn't help himself and tried to hide it with a cough.

"Ah now, Teddy. That hit home, didn't it."

"Proof? You can't have. There is no fucking proof!"

"Really? I wonder."

Fuck, no!

Teddy waited for a sign, a recording, anything, but the fucker rang off. His laugh cut in half.

Bluffing? He had to be bluffing.

The fucker has nothing.

Teddy slammed the phone into its cradle. His hands were shaking, rage mixed with fear. It was early, but he needed a drink.

As he reached for the decanter and glass, the main office door crashed open. Timothy pushed into the room, the anger clear on his flat face. Easy to read. Nothing inscrutable about the fucker now. He held a huge Glock steady in his right hand, pointing at Teddy's heart.

"What the fuck you doing with that gun?" he snarled.

Slowly, Teddy lowered his hand to the desk, reaching for the drawer.

The Glock boomed. The corner of his desk exploded. The black bastard shot at him!

Fuck it!

Teddy threw up his hands.

"Timothy, what are you doing?"

Even to himself, he sounded scared. Terrified.

Timothy sneered. "I figure your time is up, boss man. When the captain releases his evidence, you're finished, and I'm too close to you. I'll likely be a target, too."

Sweat leaked from every pore, sticking Teddy's shirt to his body, restricting movement.

"No, Timothy. It was a bluff. If the fucker had anything, he'd have used it by now. We're safe."

Timothy shook his head. "Can't take the risk, man. And even if the captain doesn't have proof, I don't think it'll be long before you put a target on me and Ginger. No, I think I'll take off, but before I go …"

He raised his gun and took aim.

Teddy gagged.

"No, no, don't. You want money? I'll give you money. There's two hundred grand in the safe. It's all yours. You can have it right now."

Timothy's big lips peeled back to bare his teeth—a dog snarling.

"I-I can get you more. How's half a million sound? Good?"

Timothy stepped further into the room. Behind him, Elizabeth looked on, eyes wide, hand covering her mouth. Why didn't she do something? Call Ginger? Anything.

The South African kicked the door closed behind him and raised the Glock a little higher. The muzzle's huge, black hole yawned wide, pointing at Teddy's face.

Oh Christ.

Teddy whimpered and backed his chair away from the desk until it bumped against the bookshelves. Bile rose from his gut. He wanted to puke but swallowed it down.

If he could convince the black bastard to take the money, he might still get out of this alive.

Survive. Stay alive.

"The money. You can have it all!"

Timothy's deep brown eyes wavered. He reached a

hand up to wipe sweat from his shiny, bronze head. Must've taken him ages to shave it every morning.

Let me open the safe, Timothy. Let me open the safe.

"It'll only take a few seconds, Timothy. A few seconds to change your life. You'll be rich, Timothy, rich."

A few seconds.

Yes, Teddy. Savour every single one even if it's your last.

Chapter Twenty-One

Sunday 29th November – Timothy Khumalo

Ocean Village, Southampton, Hampshire, England

Timothy Khumalo stood over the snivelling piece of white trash. The blubbing, whining runt he'd served for the best part of five years.

He was going to kill Teddy Tedesco. How good did it feel to call the man "Teddy"?

As for the captain, Timothy didn't feel any real animosity towards him. Nor did he care too much about what happened to Randy and Chukka, but if the news got out, the men would turn on Teddy and Timothy both. And how long would it be before Teddy took him out and maybe Ginger, too?

No, he couldn't afford to wait for the inevitable. He'd

been around the lunatic Tedescos long enough to know better.

Teddy, the arsehole in the posh, leather chair and the fancy, white, Egyptian-cotton shirt, had cash money at hand and Timothy wanted it. All of it.

He'd given five years of his life to the *bliksem*. Five years of bowing and scraping and for what? To be treated like an errand boy, a *kaffir*, the same way the whites back home treated him. Enough was enough.

The white boss man will die here, today.

"What do you say, Timothy?" Teddy pleaded, snivelling like a baby. "Half a million pounds would buy you a new life anywhere in the world. Anywhere. What do you say?"

Timothy thought about it. Five hundred grand—nearly ten million rand. With that much, he could live like a king in Durban in a high-rise looking over the Indian Ocean. Everybody there would kiss his black arse.

Hell yeah.

"There's two hundred thou in the safe, you say?"

Teddy blinked and lowered his hands a fraction, his breathing slowed a little. He could see a way out. He could see a tomorrow, but he was going to be disappointed.

"Yeah, yeah. It's all there, I promise."

"And the rest? The other three hundred?"

Timothy lowered the Glock a little and aimed it at Teddy's belly. If he made a sudden move, Timothy would gut-shoot him. The bastard wouldn't die right away. He'd live long enough to disclose the combination but wouldn't be a further threat.

"T-The rest is downstairs, in Mother's pantry. It's my exit money. Take me there and it's yours. All of it, I promise, but please … don't shoot."

Teddy winced and curled his lips in fear. What little

colour he had in his face drained away. Sweat popped out on his forehead and dribbled down his face, and he started shaking. The onset of shock. He'd be puking his guts up any moment.

Timothy raised the gun again and pointed it at Teddy's left eye, holding it rock steady.

Teddy's face crumpled. "P-Please, I'm begging you. Take the money and let me live." Tears mixed with the sweat and rolled down his white cheeks. His chin dimpled, and he whined. "Please don't."

"Open the safe," Timothy said, stepping to one side to cover both the door and Tedesco more easily, "but do it real careful, man. Any tricks and you die."

Teddy took a while to lever his skinny, white butt out of his posh chair. He staggered, nearly fell, but righted himself and leaned a hand against the bookcase until his breathing steadied. His eyes flicked towards the door and then locked on Timothy.

"Stop delaying. No one's rushing to help, and Elizabeth's nothing but eye candy. You're on your own, man. Move, and no monkey business, or this monkey's gonna puncture you with hot metal."

Teddy stiffened.

"You think I never heard you and Pony call me a monkey? You racist prick! You think I didn't have this planned when you finally fucked up, man? Yeah, I've been waiting for the day I could take you out with impunity. When Pony's body arrived, I knew it was only a matter of time. Without your brother, you are nothing, you arrogant piece of *kak*. I've been bowing and scraping to mothers like you all my life. But not now. Not anymore. Open the fucking safe!"

He jerked on the trigger. The Glock barked again and

one of the books behind Teddy blew apart. He squealed as confetti showered his head and shoulders.

"Next one goes through a kidney. Now move!"

Teddy grabbed the top edge of one of the leather-bound volumes and tugged. The whole row of books clicked open like a cabinet door and revealed a built-in wall safe. Timothy knew of its existence but had never seen it.

The door stood a metre wide and the same height as the shelf. In its centre, a digital number pad stood out black against the brushed steel.

Teddy punched in six numbers—his mother's birthdate. How sweet. How fucking obvious. He pressed the green "enter" key, and the door popped open, hinged on the right. Timothy couldn't see inside. He leaned to his left for a better look.

Teddy raised a hand to reach inside.

Timothy pushed the gun forwards. "Nah, man. That ain't happening. Step away."

Teddy's expression flipped from wrinkle-faced pleading to deep scowl. Timothy was right. The mother had been going for a gun.

"What you got in there, Teddy? Another of your fancy, chrome-plated SIGs already locked and loaded? I know you, man. Move away or die."

He added a little more pressure to the trigger.

"Won't take much to rid the world of another lowlife Tedesco."

Teddy raised his arms high and took two paces to his right, away from the open safe and closer to his drinks cabinet. He swallowed hard. "Kill me and you'll lose out on the rest of the money. Three hundred thousand pounds. Think about that, Timothy. Think how far that'll go in South Africa."

"I don't need you to open the other safe. I'm sure your mother can let me in. Wouldn't take much to persuade the empty-headed bitch."

Anger flared on the face of Timothy's former boss.

"Don't you hurt Mother. She's frail. She's not part of this."

"Better be on your best behaviour then, hey, man?"

Timothy flicked his gun again and edged closer to the safe. Teddy backed further away. Typical. He talked a good fight but like most bosses, once he reached the top, he'd grown soft and flabby. Maybe not on the outside, but on the inside. Success bred laziness. At heart Teddy was a coward, getting others to do his dirty work. People like Ginger, who would do anything to earn a few rand, even turn on their friends.

"Well, fuck me," he said, staring into the stainless-steel box, his heart thumping hard. "You weren't lying about the money, only the amount."

Timothy was rich. Rich!

The safe was crammed full of fifty-pound notes. Bundles of them, all neatly bound and stacked. Much, much more than two hundred thousand. And yeah, he was right about the trap, too. On top of one stack sat a Glock 17, locked and loaded, ready for instant action.

He hadn't studied Teddy's methods for the past five years to let the miserable fucker put one over on him.

"How much is in there?"

The edge of Timothy's vision blurred. He tore his eyes away from the cash. Teddy jerked his hand out of the drinks cabinet and the huge, chrome-plated SIG in his fist exploded twice.

Something hard slammed into Timothy's chest. White-hot fire blew his ribs apart. A second bullet thumped into his belly. He fell backwards. His trigger finger spasmed. The Glock bucked in his hand. The bullet clanged into the safe door and ricocheted up into the ceiling.

On the way down to the floor, Timothy's head cracked on the shattered corner of the desk.

The room swam, and daylight faded into blackness.

Chapter Twenty-Two

Sunday 29th November – Teddy Tedesco

Ocean Village, Southampton, Hampshire, England

Teddy stared down at the piece of garbage as it fought for life, its breathing wet and strangled, and its blood seeping into the rug. Shame he couldn't have finagled Timothy into the Clean Room, but Elizabeth would order a new carpet and the specialist cleaning crew wouldn't mind a second well-paid contract that week.

Teddy needed a new rug and a new head of security.

Timothy's mouth slackened. Frothy, pink phlegm bubbled through his lips. Dark, confused eyes stared up at the ceiling, losing focus. Fat lips moved but formed no words. His right hand still held the gun, but the arm didn't have strength enough to lift it, and the finger couldn't pull the trigger.

"Thought you could turn on Teddy Tedesco, did you?"

Teddy kicked the carcase in the ribs. Bones crunched, but the big, black fucker didn't so much as groan.

"Thought you could come into my office and threaten me, threaten Mother? You piece of shit!"

More bones disintegrated under the pointed toe of his expensive, handmade shoes as he kicked again and again, only stopping when he bruised his big toe and fatigue took over.

The shoes would have to go as well. Impossible to polish blood out of fancy, Italian leather. Sure, you could make them *look* clean and shiny, but the hand-stitched seams would always retain a taint of the victim, their DNA. Couldn't risk anything coming back on him.

Whooping air into greedy lungs, Teddy leaned against the bookcase and studied the mess.

"Tried to lay the blame on Ginger, didn't you, fucker? But you were the one working with Captain Arsewipe and Gino, not him. Always plotting against me. Didn't work though, did it? I'm cleverer than you, see? A nigger couldn't ever get the better of Teddy Tedesco!"

At some stage during the booting, Timothy had stopped breathing. Good fucking job, but fuck, all that blood. He'd maybe need to give the cleaners a bonus. Yet more fucking money down the pan.

Still breathing hard from the exercise and the exhilaration of another personal killing, Teddy replaced the chrome-plated SIG—his life preserver—into its hidey-hole in the drinks cabinet and turned to the safe. He tried to close the door, but the bloody thing wouldn't shut. He inspected the edges closely.

Fuck.

One of the tool-steel locking pins had a fuck-off, big groove in it. The damaged pin stuck out proud and caught on the side of the safe. Shit. The safe was broken.

Probably from Timothy's bullet. What the hell did the bastard have in his Glock? Cop-killers? Armour-piercing shells?

Didn't do Timothy any good, though. Did they.

Teddy sneered down at the bloodied and battered corpse.

"Couldn't help yourself, could you? Hey? One sniff of all that cash and you were mine."

He tried closing the safe door again, but one of the bolts kept catching on the side. Slamming it hard might work the pin past the obstruction, but the door might jam, and he'd be left without his emergency stash if something really serious happened.

Teddy took a few deep breaths to settle his breathing and his excitement. Apart from Johnno Ashby, who wasn't a challenge and didn't really count, he hadn't personally killed anyone in years. Recently, he'd been leaving the wet work to others—especially to Pony—but, like riding a bike, the skills came back easily when needed. He'd forgotten the euphoric sense of achievement. God, he missed the hands-on side of the business. He'd been too long in management.

The carpet, the books in the shelf, the ceiling, and now the safe, were all ruined. But he was still standing. Captain Arsewipe and the bitch with the dead dog, Shafer, were costing him time, money, and men. What the hell was he going to do about it?

Captain Arsewipe said he wanted a war. Well, he'd get his fucking war.

After one last kick to Timothy's groin—just to make

sure—Teddy strolled to his desk and dropped into his chair. He slumped back and relaxed for a couple of recovery breaths. Then the arousal hit and hit hard, as it always did when he killed someone.

Grunting from the effort, Teddy leaned forwards to press the intercom button. "Elizabeth?"

No response.

"Elizabeth, are you there? Answer me, woman."

Still no response. If the fucking cow had buggered off, she'd regret it.

"Yes, Mr Tedesco?" she answered, breathless.

"Where've you been?"

"On the telephone. Thought you'd need the clean-up crew. They're on their way. After hearing the shouting, I watched you on the screen and knew you could take Timothy, which is why I left you to it. Are you okay?"

Teddy stopped to consider her words. How could he have thought she'd desert him, too? The woman loved him with a blind passion and wouldn't do anything but help.

"Yeah, I'm fucking aces. Horny as fuck, too. Get in here and help me celebrate."

She chuckled. "Yes, Teddy, dear. Are you up to the challenge?"

"'Course I'm up to it. You know what I need after a good killing, and you'll be doing all the fucking work anyway."

"Yes, Teddy. I'll be right in. I'll bring the medicine. The real stuff."

Teddy grinned. If she didn't give the best blowjobs in the world, she might have ended up on the carpet like Timothy years ago. Although, thinking about it, she'd be on her knees on the same carpet very soon.

The door opened, and Elizabeth arrived carrying her

bag of chemicals and wearing a warm smile and very little else. She'd stripped down to her favourite uniform—G-string, corset, and peek-a-boo bra.

"Does little Teddy need his medicine?" she asked through pouting lips.

"Yeah. Get over here right now and make me all better."

Chapter Twenty-Three

Wednesday 2nd December – Morning

Mike's Farm, Long Buckby, Northants, England

The men mustered in the operations centre—a recently equipped space in the attic of Mike's barn. With Lara and Bobbie's help, Mike had laid on refreshments—tea, coffee, sandwiches, and enough sugared doughnuts to satisfy a police convention.

Kaine gave the men—all eight of them—time to eat and get reacquainted and, in the case of the most recent additions to his volunteer troop, newly acquainted.

Peter "Cough" Coughlin—former army sergeant and current mercenary—carried his left shoulder slightly higher than his right—the legacy of a Taliban insurgent's bullet. It made him look slightly awkward, but didn't hamper his movement, or reduce his accuracy with a rifle or a hand gun. Beside him, Private Stefan "Stinko" Stankovic—nicknamed after his surname, not his personal hygiene habits, which were impeccable—sat wide-eyed and keen. The last time Kaine had seen either man had been at night on an abandoned RAF airfield in the middle of Lincolnshire. Both men had proven their honour and their trustworthiness by not acting against Kaine even though they'd been hired to kill him. He'd maintained contact with them through the Victory Services Club, and they'd both jumped at the chance to work with, rather than against, him.

Although he'd already introduced the newcomers to their new comrades-in-arms, for operational purposes, he planned to keep friends together wherever possible. It took time to develop trust in colleagues under fire, and the operations he'd been planning didn't allow much time for trust-building.

The two other recent arrivals, Corporals Nathan "Nate" Montero and Jeff "Bandit" Baines, two members of his former SBS troop, were outside, patrolling the farm and would remain on personal protective duty for the duration. No way would Kaine lower his guard while Lara, Mike, and the Shafers faced potential danger.

The rest of the men—also members of Kaine's old troop—had arrived in dribs and drabs over the previous couple of days, each one keen to join the party.

Kaine stood in front of a large easel—a relic of Mike's failed attempt to become a landscape artist—in briefing mode. The easel held an A1-sized flipchart pad. He'd yet to reveal the full operation to anyone except Rollo and waited for the men to settle into their chairs with their coffee mugs, teacups, or soft drink bottles and plates. The fact some of them used plates at all surprised him and he put it down to the positive influence of having women around.

He tapped the wooden trestle table separating him from the men with the fat end of a marker pen and called the inaugural meeting of the ad hoc "83 Defence Brigade" to order.

The only things missing from Kaine's standard presentation equipment were a full military uniform and a laser pointer.

Earlier that morning, Danny had laughed when Kaine sent him into town to buy the pad and marker pens, saying, "Ever heard of these things called 'smartphones', boss? Why not create a document and email it as an attachment?"

"Happy to do that, Danny," Kaine shot back, "but then I'll have to confiscate everyone's mobiles and put them on the bonfire instead of sheets of A1 paper."

"Are you kidding, boss?"

"How else are we going to maintain security?"

"You know you can delete the files after you've created them?"

"Yes," Kaine answered with enforced patience, "but what about automated, cloud backup and all the time it takes to ensure every device's memory is wiped? We can't risk any sort of data trail coming back to us. We're about to break the law, Danny. Quite a lot of laws, actually. Burning a few sheets of paper is a lot easier in the long run, believe me."

Danny eventually caught the point and toddled off to town with Lara, Mike, and a fistful of cash to cover the added grocery expenses. With the influx of hungry military men, the farm's larder was taking a real hammering.

Kaine flipped over the cover page. The line written on the top of the sheet read, "*Mission Alpha*". It dealt with an attack on *Andros Freeway*, a fishing boat used by Tedesco's organisation to smuggle drugs and other "merchandise" into the UK from continental Europe.

"Okay, guys," he said, "read and inwardly digest."

He gave them a full five minutes to absorb the information before tapping the table again.

"That should be long enough. Even for the slow ones who move their lips when they read—Danny."

Everyone laughed, including Danny. He'd studied English Literature in university and had even passed a few modules, and was more than competent in his literacy skills.

"No fair, Captain," Danny moaned. "I'm having trouble with those wonky hieroglyphs you call writing."

Kaine waited for the second peal of laughter to fade. "Anyone have any comments or questions?"

He waited, but the room fell quiet.

"Come on, lads, don't be shy, I'm open to suggestions. If I've forgotten something, or screwed up, I need to know. Tell me. We're all in this together."

Corporal Petrov "Peewee" Ricardo, one of the quietest and most restrained marines Kaine had ever met—when not in an actual firefight—pushed up a tentative hand.

"Boss? If you don't mind …" Every head in the place turned towards him, and deep red flushes coloured his cheeks. "I … have a question." His voice faded, but with Kaine's nod of encouragement, he continued. "You want to board a fishing boat in the middle of the Channel. A boat crewed by an unknown number of heavily armed men—"

"According to Corky's latest intel," Kaine said, "it's likely to be four men and one woman. Tedesco appears to be an equal-opportunity employer."

More laughter, but this peal had a tinge of nervousness. Military men ahead of a mission didn't tend to relax much.

"Okay," Peewee continued, his voice growing stronger as the words tumbled out. "You want two of us to board a fishing boat and then subdue a crew armed with automatic weapons, AK-47s it says there." He pointed to the easel. "In my experience, drug smugglers aren't afraid to shoot. Why not just attach a limpet mine to the hull and sink the boat with the evil buggers still aboard? In my opinion, it'd be a lot faster, a lot safer, and it won't be any loss to humanity."

A timid Peewee looked around the table for support and received nods in reply. The loudest approval came from Corporal Patrick "Pat" O'Hara, the team's explosives specialist. After receiving his mates' support, Peewee sat back, allowing a relieved smile to form on his gaunt face.

"You won't get any argument from me on that score, Peewee," Kaine said after locking eyes first with Peewee and then with each man in turn. "These aren't innocent fishermen and women hauling in their nets and trying to make an honest living from the sea. They are smugglers and killers, but"—he paused to ensure he had their undivided attention—"who's to say drugs are the only thing they're smuggling? Tedesco is known to traffic in human cargo, and *Andros Freeway*'s hold is plenty big enough to carry a couple of dozen illegals."

"Aren't we going to use that nifty infrared scanner, boss?" Danny asked, pointing to a device on one of the shelves bolted to the back wall—one that looked like an oversized, digital camera. "That'll show up heat signatures and tell us how many people are aboard."

"I considered that, but what if the scanner breaks down? And what if the cargo hold is heat shielded? Are you prepared to risk innocent lives on the gamble that it isn't?"

Corporal Anthony "Slim" Simms threw up a hand.

"Corky's intel suggests they're only carrying a few kilos of coke and maybe a couple tonnes of fish, sir."

At his side, Corporal Laurence "Fat Larry" Kovaks snorted. "Fish. Yeah, right."

Slim countered with, "For camouflage, bozo."

Larry pointed a bony finger at him. "Now, that's a fair comment."

Kaine allowed the men time to settle before shaking his head. "And intelligence is never wrong, is it? People like Teddy Tedesco never make any last-minute changes to their 'inventory', do they? And of course, Teddy hires all his staff for their honesty and openness. None of them would dream of doing anything other than follow Teddy's orders, right?"

The men exchanged looks that showed the questions had hit home.

He continued. "One of Pat's limpet mines attached to the hull beneath the engine room would make the task easy, but I want to make sure there aren't any innocents aboard first."

Rollo pursed his lips but kept his own counsel. Kaine and Rollo had been through their own private discussions and Rollo was in full agreement, and he knew they had other operations in the pipeline.

Danny sighed. "I suppose you're calling for volunteers, boss?"

"I am. Boarding that boat instead of destroying it outright increases the risk immensely. I'd understand if none of you wanted to accompany me on my night-time dip, but I'm going ahead, even if I'm alone."

"Are you kidding, boss?" Pat said, looking hurt. "You think I spent all morning creating this little beauty in line with your specifications"—he lovingly traced his fingertips over a sleek, grey, metal object the size and shape of an

'80s-era mobile phone—"just to have you stuff things up by planting it in the wrong place? I mean, that would be positively criminal, and it wouldn't do my artistry any justice, now would it?"

"That mean you're volunteering to join me, Pat?"

"Indeed it does, boss."

"You certain? It'll be dangerous."

"Ah now," the Irishman said, a grin lighting his face, "wouldn't be any fun if it was easy, would it. Don't want to miss the *craic* if I can help it."

"Excellent, that makes two of us," Kaine said, looking pointedly at Larry, the best RIB pilot in the group.

"Three," Larry said instantly. "I can't leave you and Pat to have all the fun."

Slim, who'd spent most of the past decade joined at the hip with his skinny mate shouted, "Four," and the others added their numbers to the total. Rollo was the only former-SBS man not to volunteer and, in the current company, only Kaine and Danny knew the reason.

Rollo's days as one of the UK's best deep-sea divers ended when his equipment failed during a relatively simple training exercise in the Mediterranean. The accident led him to suffer decompression sickness. The three-day emergency recompression-decompression treatment on board the dive ship, and the subsequent two-month hospitalisation and rehabilitation left Rollo strong and healthy, but medically unfit to dive. The consequent loss of his dive certification led to Rollo's honourable discharge from the SBS and his availability to act as Kaine's right-hand man. Against all the odds, silver linings had poked out from behind even the darkest storm clouds.

Cough spoke out. "If I may, sir. I have a question." His voice held the trace of a Lancashire accent.

Kaine nodded, giving the latest addition to his diverse unit leave to speak.

"There's no mission date on the board," Cough said. "When's the off?"

"*Andros Freeway* is scheduled to make her next rendezvous in the early hours of Monday morning."

"That gives us the rest of today and four more days to finalise the op?" Cough asked.

Kaine nodded. "Should be plenty of time, but I sense another question."

"That's right, sir," Stefan said, sitting to Cough's left at the end of the table. He had to twist his head to see his mate. "Come on, cough it out." On realising the pun, he winced and raised a hand in apology.

Cough ignored the guffaws and kept his expression serious. "Thing is, sir, there are seven of you booties in this room. Why not even the odds and increase the attack force from two to, say, four?"

Stefan jumped in to answer. "SCUBA gear's expensive, and there are only two units." He pointed to the dive gear spread out over the shelving unit bolted to the rear wall.

"Lord, save us from ignorant squaddies," Slim said, laughing to cut the impact of the insult. "That's CCUBA gear—Closed-Circuit Underwater Breathing Apparatus—not SCUBA."

"So?" Stefan asked, a deep frown working its way onto his youthful face. "What's the difference?"

"Bubbles, communications, and dive duration," Slim returned, quick as a flash.

"Huh?"

Kaine grinned. He'd opted for closed-circuit rebreathers to extend their dive time and avoid the tell-tale trail of bubbles produced by a standard, open-circuit kit.

To avoid unnecessary casualties, stealth was a prerequisite of any waterborne operation. Ironically, had the state-of-the-art CCUBA equipment been available to Rollo on his ill-fated dive, he'd probably still have his certification. Fortunately for operations in support of The 83, money was not a restricting issue. They could afford the best equipment on the market, and Rollo knew how to source it at very short notice. He'd naturally been given the role of Quartermaster, and he took the work extremely seriously.

"Sorry, Slim. We don't have time for a diving lesson," Kaine interrupted. "You can explain the difference between SCUBA and CCUBA to our land-based friends over supper. But Cough and Stefan have made valid points. I'm surprised none of you so-called expert divers asked the same question."

Stefan's happy smile and Cough's knowing nod confirmed to Kaine he'd made them feel more at home.

"And the answer to your excellent question, Stefan, is no. It has nothing to do with finances. We're pretty well-funded. In fact, Sergeant Rollason, the Quartermaster, has equipped us rather well. He'll take you through the inventory tomorrow morning, to give you time to work them into your plans." He took a breath before continuing. "I'm afraid we can't beef up the numbers for Mission Alpha, because we have other missions to occupy our forces. And that's why Rollo isn't going swimming on Sunday night. He has other things on his plate."

Rollo's relaxed face said he wouldn't mind at all. "Anything that means I don't have to drink the English Channel's vintage slop is fine by me, boss."

"Thought you'd feel that way."

"What's Corky, our useful little hacker, come up with

now?" Danny asked, for the benefit of the men who knew nothing about the team's intelligence-gathering methods.

Kaine corrected his third-in-command. "Our 'information acquisition specialist' has picked up some other interesting pieces of chatter relating to our target."

He turned over the sheet of the flipchart to reveal "*Mission Bravo*". Again, he allowed the men a short time to read and digest.

The Andover and District Racecourse, one of the many legal and public faces of Teddy Tedesco's business empire, was holding its final meeting of the year. Expected crowds numbered in the tens of thousands and cash flowing through the on-course bookies' hands would total in the millions. At the end of each race day, the money—augmented by millions more in laundered cash from Tedesco's illegal operations—needed to find its way into a bank.

As mandated by his insurance company and following the advice of the Gambling Commission, Tedesco hired a security company, Post Call Ltd, to provide an armoured truck and three guards to transport the cash. Four of Tedesco's men accompanied the Post Call security guards during the drive to the headquarters of the Southern Counties Trustee Bank in Southampton.

After reading the notes, Danny's expression turned sceptical.

"If you don't mind my saying, boss. The security details look bogus to me."

"In what way?" Kaine asked, almost certain Danny was going to cover a point he'd already discussed with Rollo.

"See, the meet's four days long, from today through to Sunday."

"Yes, and?" Kaine asked.

"Each night, the armoured truck convoy leaves at exactly the same time and takes the same fastest and shortest way. Doesn't seem likely, does it? Shouldn't they vary the routes?"

Kaine smiled, happy to be proven correct.

"I raised the exact same point with Corky. He tells me Tedesco is so confident no one would dare interfere with his business, he uses the minimum protection required by the Gambling Commission and his insurers. The armoured truck has kept to the same timetable and the same route, without variation, for the past eight race meetings."

"Bloody hell, he's just asking for trouble, isn't he?" Danny said.

Kaine dipped his head. "That's what I thought. And Rollo's team is going to give it to them. Isn't that right, Rollo?"

Rollo crossed his arms. He didn't need to answer.

"And now for you, Danny," Kaine said.

"Me, boss?" Danny turned his head towards Rollo, who kept playing the game and shrugged.

"Yes, Danny, you'll need something to keep you out of trouble."

Kaine rolled back the top sheet of the flipchart once more and exposed the notes for "*Mission Charlie*".

"Have a good look everyone," he said, and allowed them time to absorb the information. "Danny, see if you can come up with a plan to interfere with the robbery. Okay?"

Danny's eyes lit up.

"Happy to, boss," he said, and stared at the page. "Assuming I can read your scribbles."

Mission Charlie related to a planned robbery at Garrett & Stimpson Ltd, a bonded warehouse in Southampton's dockland. A gang of professionals from London, with help from an inside man at the warehouse, were due to help themselves to a cache of antique jewellery awaiting inspection by HM Revenue and Customs. Not surprisingly, the officials had questions regarding the jewellery's provenance.

"How on earth did your IT man come up with that intel, Captain?" Slim asked. "That's pure gold. If you'll pardon the pun."

Kaine rubbed the back of his neck. "Corky has ears plugged into Tedesco's office and is running an illegal phone tap or two. Anyway, the London mob contacted Tedesco and asked for permission to do the job on his 'manor'."

"That must have cost them," Larry suggested.

Kaine grinned. "Got that right. It seems that our favourite gang boss demands twenty percent of the estimated take. He calls it a 'tribute'."

"Arrogant prick must fancy himself as a senator in the Roman Empire," Cough piped up.

At his side, Stefan nodded sagely. Kaine wondered whether the kid truly understood the reference but wouldn't dream of calling him on it.

"As I said, Danny's the team leader for Mission Charlie. He and his men will work out the details of the take down."

Pat cleared his throat. "Can I ask a question this time, Captain?"

"Fire away."

"There's no date on this briefing sheet either. When are the Londoners making their move?"

"That's where things get a little tricky," Kaine said, scratching his beard and waiting for the reaction. "The warehouse job is set for Sunday night."

"What?"

The effect of Danny's stunned question rippled around the room.

"Are you kidding, sir?" Cough asked, his tone incredulous.

"They're all on the same night?" Slim asked. "We're hitting all three operations simultaneously?"

"We'll be awful stretched, boss, don't you think?" Pat said.

"Possibly," Kaine answered, standing taller and raising his voice over the excited chatter. "But there are three things to consider. First, Tedesco's also spreading himself thin and is unlikely to have enough men to cover all three operations fully. Second, he won't expect us to attack so soon after his abortive ambush at the factory, and he lost the services of three men during that fiasco. And don't forget, his brother's dead, and so is his right-hand man, Timothy Khumalo."

"They're dropping like flies, boss," a smiling Slim said to another chorus of muted approval.

"And the third thing, boss?" Larry asked, after demolishing his third doughnut and the men had settled.

"We're going to hit him where it hurts most. In his wallet. A triple-whammy attack will cripple him financially and make him look weak in front of his men and his competition. He's going to have to react, and he could make a mistake. It might even draw him out into the open. Who knows, we might end this thing in one quick, three-pronged operation."

"And talking about the financial side," Danny said. "We get to divvy up all the spoils, right, boss?"

"Always looking on the bright side, Danny?" Rollo asked.

"One of my most endearing qualities, Sarge."

Danny's laugh drew a grumble of irritation from Rollo. "It wasn't meant as a compliment, son."

Once again, Kaine tapped the table for silence. "Okay. The three operations are going ahead and here are the teams. I'll lead the attack on *Andros Freeway*. Larry and Pat are with me. Slim and Peewee will join Rollo at the race-course. And finally, Danny's going to lead Cough and Stefan. That okay with you, Cough?"

"Of course, Captain. Why wouldn't it be?"

"You were a sergeant in 2 PARA. Sure you don't have a problem taking your lead from a former-SBS corporal?"

Cough shook his head definitively. "Absolutely not, sir. If you put him in charge, Stefan and I will follow. Not a problem."

Stefan nodded enthusiastically. "What he said, sir."

"By the way, for future reference, I'm giving Danny a field promotion. Take a bow, *Sergeant* Pinkerton. And Rollo is now Colour Sergeant. Everyone okay with that?"

"Yes, boss. Thank you, boss," Danny said, his words part-drowned by the cheers.

His powerful frame disappeared under a barrage of backslaps and hair tousling.

"Doesn't make a blind bit of difference to the pay reward structure, though," Kaine called out. "Any finances we liberate from Tedesco's organisation will be divided evenly within the troop—after deductions for equipment and other expenses, of course. That right, Q?"

"If I'm Q," the newly promoted colour sergeant said above another happy group roar, "does that make you James Bond or M?"

Kaine sighed and allowed the rowdiness to fade before rubbing his hands together and cracking his knuckles.

"Okay, men … and woman," he added as Lara entered

the office to appreciative gazes and frowned gently at him. "Get down to business. Unit commanders, take your men and come back in two hours with a fully structured mission plan. If possible, I'd like to synchronise the timetable as of twenty-one hundred hours, Sunday. Pat, you and Larry can carry on for a moment, I'll be right with you. Dismissed!"

The men separated into their operational groups and pored over laptops, tablets, and sheets of paper. Kaine turned to Lara.

"So, you finally have your own little army, Captain Kaine?" she said quietly.

Her eyes shone, and her cheeks were flushed as they always were after she'd exercised Dynamite.

"How about, *General* Kaine? My army, my rules. I can give myself a promotion if it'll impress a certain veterinarian."

"No need. I'm already impressed. But …" She glanced towards the men.

"But?"

Kaine placed a hand in the small of her back and led her gently into a quiet corner.

"This is really serious, Ryan. All that equipment"—she nodded to the small arsenal covering the table and chairs, and filling the metal shelving along the rear wall—"you weren't kidding about waging a war."

He shook his head and leaned a little closer but took care to maintain a decent distance. "How are our guests coping?"

"Traumatised, but Angela's strong. Physically, she'll recover quickly, I'm sure."

"Good. When I think what I let that animal do …"

Lara took his right hand and made him unclench it.

"You reached her as soon as you could. This is not on you, Ryan. Teddy Tedesco's to blame. You remember that."

"I will."

Damn right I will.

Kaine ground his teeth and tried not to dwell on what he'd have done to any man who treated Lara the same way that monster had treated Angela Shafer. He squeezed her hand and forced a change in the subject. "I can see you're interested in the range of gadgets Q has sourced. Anything in particular pique your interest, madam?"

Her hazel eyes, more brown than green in the dim light, scanned the shelving. "The dive gear. Looks a bit more complicated than the gear I've used on holiday. It's the sort of equipment I'd expect to see on the International Space Station."

He smiled and drew her closer to the shelves.

"Closed-circuit rebreathers," he said, grabbing one of the headsets and handing it to her.

Lara turned it over for inspection.

"Internal breathing ports. No mouthpiece," she stated.

"That's right. It forms a sealed unit with the drysuit, leaving the mouth free to use normal radio comms. Unlike SCUBA, the recirculating air warms and moistens during use. It prevents dry mouth. The system helps reduce diver fatigue, too. Fully configured, military-grade systems like these are a little over half the weight of a standard, open-circuit system."

Lara returned the headset. "Sounds interesting," she said, even though her expression told him it was anything but.

He tried again, hoping to impress. "Unlike using open-circuit regulators, high-pressure air isn't shoved down the diver's throat with every breath. It makes breathing under-water as natural as breathing on the surface."

"Natural breathing? Hmmm. Fascinating." Her eyes twinkled, and she closed the slight gap between them. "Please tell me more."

"Doc," he whispered, "are you humouring me?"

She nodded, and her dark hair shimmered in the low light shining through the east-facing window. "Just a little."

Pity's sake.

"One day soon, when we're home … I mean, when we're at the villa, I'll take you diving. You'll be able to see first-hand the difference in the equipment."

"Letting me loose on your equipment sounds wonderful, Ryan," she said, arching an eyebrow, "but let's wait for the summer, when the seas are warmer."

Not only had she ignored his minor "when we're home" gaff, she'd also let it slip that a long-term relationship didn't scare or upset her one little bit.

With that one simple statement, she'd given him a little hope and lifted his spirits so much he almost forgot the dangers his team faced that weekend.

Chapter Twenty-Four

Sunday 6th December – Daniel Pinkerton

Heading South, A34, Oxfordshire, England

Danny found it hard to settle. He gazed through the windscreen at the oncoming headlights and tried to appear cool, but his heart pounded against his ribcage, and he had to make fists to stop his fingers shaking. If Cough and Stinko noticed his tension, they had the good grace to ignore it.

From the safety of Mike's farm, everything had seemed easy and straightforward. Danny and Cough, both far more experienced than Stinko, worked out a plan of attack which the captain agreed to—after some discussion and a little tweaking—and off the three of them toddled to Southampton, in their average-looking car, keeping at or below the speed limit.

The fly in Danny's ointment came with Corky's last-minute update. Apparently, the London gang would be tooled-up even though they had a man inside the warehouse to give them easy access. On reading the news, the boss' first reaction was to abort the op, but Danny and Cough convinced him their plan would still work. After all, they had surprise on their side, and the London boys, having paid Teddy his up front "tribute", would consider themselves bulletproof.

Danny also assured the captain that he'd abandon the op if it started looking the least bit iffy. In the end, the captain agreed, saying, "Bring your men home safe, Danny."

His immediate response, "Of course, boss," echoed through Danny's head as they headed south.

Arrogant bugger, Danny.

He should have known better. Things were different in the field, so bloody different. The old military saying, "No battle plan ever survived first contact with the enemy," hadn't become a cliché without reason. Danny's careful plan might barely even survive the bloody drive to the location. Not with the heavy traffic and Stinko's snoring adding to his jagged nerves.

With Cough driving and Stinko sprawled across the back seat—the bloke was clearly nerveless and could sleep anywhere—Danny had so much time to think, he couldn't switch off his mind. First question, how could Stinko sleep through his own snoring? Danny wanted to slap the guy awake, but that would hardly enhance his profile as a caring leader.

Working against the grumbling snorts emitted by his slumbering colleague, Danny tried to memorise the Google Earth pictures of the warehouse district on his tablet, and ran through the proposed operation in his head a couple of hundred times.

"What's your speed?"

"Below seventy, Sarge," Cough said, without a hint of sarcasm.

A tremble ran up and down Danny's back. Although not an officially sanctioned promotion, the use of his new rank still gave him a buzz.

"We're cool," Cough added, giving him an encouraging smile. "First op in charge is a stomach-churner, yeah? Mine came in Fallujah. Hairy shit, but you'll be good. Stefan and I know our stuff, you know yours, and we'll have each other's backs. A bunch of London tough guys are no match for two fully trained, fully equipped British soldiers and one half-decent marine."

He turned his head long enough to wink, before refocusing on the road ahead.

Danny pointed to the warning sign flashing from the motorway gantry. "Fifty miles an hour up ahead."

"I can see it, Sarge," Cough said, a clenched jaw displaying his first signs of mild annoyance.

Inwardly, Danny kicked his own arse. First rule of command—trust your men to do their jobs.

"Sorry, Cough."

Cough's jaw muscles relaxed, and the car's digital speedometer fell a fraction below fifty mph and stayed there.

Danny powered down the tablet, settled into the seat, and closed his eyes, but listening to the roar of cars passing in the opposite direction without being able to see them was somehow worse. He woke the tablet again and studied the map until he knew the name of every street and lane within a half-mile radius of the Garrett & Stimpson warehouse.

Corky hadn't been able to learn the route the Londoner's planned to take from the Smoke, but only three roads led into the warehouse district, each pretty much from a cardinal point of the compass, north, east, and west. The sea protected the southern approach and, unless the gang were sailors and prepared to approach for the shoreline—unlikely according to Corky's intel—Danny's small unit would have all the access points covered.

The A34 turned out to be unusually traffic-free except for the almost obligatory snarl-up through Oxford and the Newbury bypass. They hit real trouble when they reached the M3. The final twelve miles of the trip, in nose-to-tail traffic, took nearly as long as the rest of the journey altogether.

Danny sat in the passenger seat, quietly fuming. Road-works and an accident had partially closed a stretch of the southbound carriageway and threatened to completely derail their timings. He tried deep-breathing exercises, but they only threatened to cause light-headedness through hyperventilation.

Bloody idiot, Danny. You know better than that.

"It's okay, Sarge," Cough said, calm as you like. "Plenty of time." He pointed through the windscreen. "Taillights are moving up ahead. We'll be through this soon."

Danny grunted. Without the illegal equipment in the boot of the car, he'd have ordered Cough to beat the jam by using the hard shoulder and to hell with the consequences, but that sort of manoeuvre was completely out of the question.

The thing of most concern to Danny during the drive south was being stopped by the police for a minor traffic offense. How would they explain a boot filled with military hardware?

As they bumped along at little more than walking pace, Danny imagined the conversation between Cough and the traffic cop.

"What's all this then, sir?"

"Excuse me, Officer?"

"All these guns and uniforms and bulletproof vests."

"What guns and uniforms and bulletproof vests, Officer?"

"These things in the boot of your car, sir."

"Oh, those little things."

"Yes, sir. Are they yours?"

"Of course they are, Officer," Cough would say, and he'd probably smile while doing so.

"What are you going to use them for?"

"They're Hallowe'en costumes, Officer," Cough would answer. "We went trick-or-treating."

"Ah, I see," the officer would say. "Hope you didn't eat too many sweets."

"We didn't, Officer. Bad for the teeth."

The officer would close the boot lid, salute, and say, "Very good, sir. Mind how you go, now. There'll still be some ghosts and ghouls about this weekend."

Yeah, right.

They'd call in an Armed Response Unit and not only would Danny and the others be whisked off to a cell somewhere never to be seen again, but worse still, they'd have let the captain down.

"What you smiling for, Sarge?" Cough said, snapping Danny out of his musings.

Danny yawned. "Nothing. Ignore me."

Cough nodded. "You're the boss. ... At last." He slipped into third and then fourth gear, and the car shot forwards.

249

Danny relaxed. Stinko let out another huge snort and twisted in his seat.

"Noisy bugger," Danny said.

"You get used to it," Cough said, dropping into fifth. "Can be quite comforting in the field, unless he gives away our position."

"Thank fuck I don't snore. How embarrassing would that be?"

Cough shot him a quizzical look Danny couldn't quite interpret and faced forwards, concentrating on the road.

"Fifteen minutes to the target, Sarge. Best wake the lad. Give him time to stretch."

Chapter Twenty-Five

Monday 7th December – Daniel Pinkerton

Industrial Area, Southampton, Hampshire, England

Despite the maddening delay on the motorway, Cough parked out of sight but within a short march of the warehouse units a few minutes after midnight—fifteen minutes ahead of schedule. The butterflies in Danny's belly were drowning in his gastric juices. Normally, he didn't have many pre-op nerves. He'd simply trust in Rollo or the boss and concentrate on his job, but the responsibility of command was a new and debilitating artefact. Basically, he was bricking it.

What if he screwed up?

What if Cough or Stinko copped it as a result?

Keep cool, Danny. Trust your instincts. Trust your men.

The captain wouldn't have put Danny in charge if he didn't think him capable. He closed his eyes. Found his quiet space. Swam in the clear, blue waters of the Mediterranean for a count of twenty heartbeats and settled.

Once out of the car, they checked each other for camouflage makeup and reflective surfaces, and jumped up and down on the spot to confirm nothing rattled. Danny pronounced them fit to deploy.

He checked their surroundings. The light levels couldn't have been better and matched the run-down nature of the area. One in every three streetlights was dark and two near the main warehouse block flickered in their last hoorah before permanent extinction. The remaining operational lights cast deep shadows. In short, perfect conditions for a clandestine approach.

Their target, Garrett & Stimpson's bonded warehouse, occupied one corner of a sprawling brownfield site ten miles southeast of Southampton City Centre. Apart from the dock at the rear—an inlet of the Solent—the estate complex was protected by a double-skinned, chain-link fence topped with curls of razor wire.

The warehouse, a single-storey, flat-roofed, concrete bunker of a building, had only two points of access. Access Point One led from the main road, the A3024, to the front entrance, which was guarded by an electrically operated gate and watched by Cough. Danny's post covered Access Point Two, the rear entrance, and Stinko took care of the coastal side in the unlikely event of the robbers arriving by boat. It never paid to underestimate the enemy.

On the drive down, and before starting his visit to Snoreland, Stinko offered two-to-one odds against the Londoners using the front entrance. Danny placed a tenner to win, just to be friendly. Cough declined the wager, saying that money was hard to come by and he'd hate losing it to, or taking it from, a mate.

By 00:23, they'd found their optimal positions and settled down to wait.

And wait.

———

PAST MIDNIGHT ON A BLACK, December night, sheets of ice-cold rain driven on a south-westerly gale chilled Danny's face.

Crap. Does it have to be so fucking bitter?

At least the freezing weather would discourage anyone from taking a late-night stroll, either dog-walking or security-patrolling. Not that the estate was close to anything residential.

Although his black battledress offered plenty of protection from the weather, his face was still frozen. The insulated gloves provided warmth, but he'd have to remove them if he needed to shoot with any accuracy. Hopefully, it wouldn't come to a firefight. The captain would prefer them not to resort to violence, but his crew's safety was paramount.

He peeled back the elasticised cuff of the top-of-the-range, insulated jacket—provided by the newly designated Q, who was clearly well suited to the role—and checked his watch. 01:58.

Shit.

The Londoners were running twenty-eight minutes late. They'd either been held up in the same God-awful traffic, or they'd called off the raid for some reason. Perhaps they were just useless gits who couldn't read a watch or a map.

They wouldn't last long in the military with such shocking timekeeping.

Danny lowered the boom mic attached to the earpiece of his short-range, closed-loop comms unit, which left his hands free to operate his weapon of choice—a Colt C8 carbine.

"Charlie Two from Charlie One," Danny whispered. "Report. Over."

"*All quiet here, Charlie One. Over,*" Cough answered.

"Charlie Three from Charlie One. Report. Over."

Stinko's reply took a moment. "*Nothing over here but water and more water. Bloody cold, too. I used to like the seaside. Over.*"

"Everyone keep your eyes peeled. Charlie One, out."

Danny raised the boom mic enough to wipe the rain from his face. He'd found an elevated position on a third-floor fire escape of an office supply depot seventy-odd metres from the rear entrance to the warehouse. It gave him a perfect view of the road servicing both the industrial estate and the lane to the warehouse's delivery entrance.

02:03.

What the hell's taking them so long?

Waiting was a killer on the nerves. Danny had never been the most patient of blokes, but this was chuffing terrible.

He closed his eyes for a second. While he fretted about the safety of Cough and Stinko, the boss was responsible for all ten men under his command, plus the doc, Mike, and Angela and Bobbie. On top of everything else, he'd taken on the role of guardian for the hundreds of people in The 83. All that responsibility. All those lives on his mind.

Christ, how does he cope?

Danny should have been nervous, but not terrified of screwing up. Nerves were good. They kept a marine on his toes, on his guard, but Danny struggled to steady his breathing, and his hands trembled like an old man with a terminal fever.

What they were about to do was simple enough, but even the simple things could go wrong, and he didn't want to let the captain down. Didn't want to let his men down. Didn't want to let himself down.

The live static in his ear snapped him from his thoughts.

"Charlie One from Charlie Two. They're here. Over."

Danny punched the railing he was leaning against. It gave out a low ring.

About chuffing time.

"Charlie Two from Charlie One. Details. Over."

"Black Mercedes G-Class. The automatic gates have just opened. Car pulling in. Buggers are parking out the front entrance. Confident arseholes. There are four inside the vehicle. All wearing black ski masks. Hold on. Car doors opening. Three men out, driver still inside. Front passenger's carrying something … could be a weapon but I can't make it out. Over."

Good news piled upon good news. Not only had Danny won twenty quid on the bet, the Mercedes had parked in full view of Cough, and it gave them time to consolidate their actions.

"Charlie One to Charlie Three. Did you copy that? Over."

Stinko clicked his comms unit twice to confirm hearing Cough's message.

"Charlie One to Charlie Three, gather at Charlie Two's location, ASAP. Charlie One, out."

Danny raised the boom mic again and, gripping the C8 in his right hand and using the guardrail for balance, he raced down the fire escape. On the ground, he used the neighbouring buildings and low hedges as cover and reached Cough in double-quick time, but breathless. Stinko beat him to the RV point, which wasn't an issue since he didn't have as far to travel. Danny took a moment to recover his breath.

"Want me to disable the driver, Sarge?" Cough asked. "It'll be simple enough to sneak up on him."

Stinko nodded. "I'll do it, if you like, sir. Need to do something to keep me warm. Perishing out back, it was. Bloody water."

Danny considered the option for all of a second and a half.

"No," he said, shaking his head. "We'll stick to the mission plan and wait for them to leave the building."

"Why?" Cough asked. "This setup is perfect. The driver won't know what's hit him."

"We leave the driver alone in case he's a lookout and they've set up a signal. I want the gang outside and in the clear. There are three night-watchmen in there and only one's the inside man. I don't want them ending up as hostages. Understood?"

"Yes, Sarge," Cough and Stinko whispered in unison.

"Mind you," Danny said, "now we know where they've parked, nothing stopping us finding better locations for the ambush, eh?"

Smiles greeted his suggestion.

"Stinko, see that dumpster?" Danny pointed to an over-full, rusted, green container parked near the loading bay along from the warehouse's front entrance. It provided solid protection and had a clear line of sight to the Mercedes and the entrance to the warehouse. "Reckon you can make it over there without the driver seeing you?"

"Does the Pope crap in the woods?" Stinko answered and took off without another word or sound.

"Fast and silent," Cough muttered. "He knows his stuff."

"Good," Danny said. "I'd expect nothing else from a member of 2 PARA. Now, let's see." He paused to scan the front of the building before saying, "One of us should stay here to cover the gang's exit, the other can take an attack position behind the entrance porch. You have a preferred option?"

Cough glanced at the brickwork projecting from the entranceway and shook his head.

"I'm easy. You choose." He paused for a moment. "Fun this leadership lark, isn't it?" he said, smiling.

"I'll take the porch, you stay here."

"No probs, Sarge. I'm happy staying here as tail-end Charlie. They shall not pass." He finished the statement with a straight face and a fast salute.

———

02:23.

The rain eased to a light drizzle.

The Londoners had been inside for ages and again, the wait was crippling. Danny had taken an extended route from the front gates, through the visitor's car park, hugging the shadows. He made the brickwork and, from a one-kneed shooting stance, levelled his weapon on the driver in the Merc. The C8 was light and its balance perfect. If necessary, he could have maintained the "ready" position all night, but stuff that for a game of soldiers. The raiders didn't have the whole night.

He released his grip on the rifle and lowered the boom mic once more. "Charlie One to Charlie Three," he whispered. "Got anything? Over."

"Charlie Three, receiving. Did you hear that metallic crashing a couple of minutes ago? Sounds like our guys are having trouble opening a storage cage. Over."

"I heard nothing. Charlie Two, can you see anything from there? Over."

"That's a negative. The driver's looking a little agitated. Can't tell much through the fogged windows but he might be in touch with his mates. ... Wait a sec, torchlights are flashing behind the warehouse windows. ... Looks like they're moving towards the front doors. Here they come. Over."

"This is Charlie One. Wait until they're inside the car. Wait for my mark. Over."

The warehouse doors flew open. Three dark-clothed and hooded men raced into the open, heading for the Mercedes. Two were carrying a heavy holdall between them, one handle each. The third man, short and squat, brought up the rear. He carried a sawn-off shotgun—double-barrel.

"Wait," Danny said.

As the two men struggled under the weight of the holdall, the driver popped the boot lid from inside the car.

"Took you long enough," he yelled, clearly not bothered about keeping his voice down.

"Couldn't find the fucking keys," Shotgun answered.

"Where's Jonah?"

"Got greedy, demanded a bigger cut." Shotgun mimed smashing his gun butt into a man's face. "Miserable fucker ain't askin' no one nothing no more."

Shotgun continued backing towards the driver, his weapon now pointed at the entrance doors, while the other two half-carried, half-dragged the holdall to the rear of the car. They heaved it into the boot, and the Mercedes' suspension sagged under the added weight. The driver gunned the engine.

Danny bided his time, waiting for the perfect moment.

A sawn-off shotgun spread the lead shot wide, but over a short distance. It was almost useless in an open area—the weapon of a man who valued fear over accuracy. Danny didn't want him getting nervous and letting loose a random shot.

"Wait."

Danny raised his carbine and took careful aim.

"Ready."

Once the boot lid slammed shut, the leader raised the shotgun, shouted, "Let's go!", and slid into the front passenger seat. Three doors slammed shut almost simultaneously, the engine raced, and the Mercedes fishtailed away from Danny in a squeal of burning rubber.

"Now!"

Danny fired. The Mercedes' front nearside tyre exploded. Five more shots, three from Cough, two from Stinko, blew out the other tyres. The Mercedes slewed sideways and …

Jesus, no!

…careened into the dumpster.

Stinko's dumpster!

The Mercedes shunted the huge bin forwards, before spinning anti-clockwise and slamming into the warehouse wall.

Oh shit. Stinko!

An orange flash lit the inside of the Merc. Then another. The windscreen exploded. Men screamed.

The engine cut out. Silence spat into the night.

Danny barged out from behind his pillar. He advanced quickly but kept under control. The Mercedes had come to a stop with its passenger side jammed against the warehouse wall. Nobody was getting out that way. He brought up his C8 and pointed it at the driver's window, aiming at where the man's head would be.

From his left, Cough broke cover, yelling Stinko's real name—Stefan.

No reply.

Oh shit. Oh shit.

Movement inside the Mercedes. Danny stopped, hooked his finger around the trigger.

The driver's door popped open, and the man tumbled out onto the concrete. Shot holes peppered his face and blood spurted from the stump of an arm, shot off below the elbow.

"Stefan!" Cough yelled again. "Where are you, mate?"

Silence.

Chapter Twenty-Six

Sunday 6th December – William Rollason

**Andover and District Racecourse, Andover,
Hampshire, England**

Rollo had a hard time believing anyone transporting millions of pounds in readily disposable, used notes and coins could be so blasé about the operation. Following four days of checking and rechecking the equipment and practising their takedown drills, he and his small team spent the final afternoon scouting the route provided by Corky. Where and how the round-faced tyke found his information, God alone knew but, so far, he'd been top-dead-centre accurate. A real, if weird, asset to the troop.

Although the captain had signed off on his strategy for an on-course raid, Rollo, as always, looked for a Plan B and, wherever possible, backed it up with a Plan C. Belt, braces, and safety pins, as he used to say in the old training days.

Over the years, he'd drilled the need for backup plans into all his rookies and wouldn't alter his SOP at this late stage of his career. To Slim and Peewee's quiet annoyance, they drove the route from the racecourse to the bank and back, twice. The second time turned out to be redundant. Rollo had answered his own question during the first run.

The armoured car's route turned out as expected, fast and direct. After departing the racecourse, the convoy—the armoured truck with lead and tail SUVs containing Teddy Tedesco's armed men—would travel west along the B3400 and another couple of miles south along the A3093. Both roads were minor and quiet, little more than two-lane, country blacktops. From there, the three-vehicle convoy would join the A303 and head east before turning south onto the A34. After that it was more or less a straight run south all the way to the bank in Southampton, taking in around twenty miles of exposed motorway and dual carriageway. Once in Southampton, any form of ambush without collateral risk would be close to impossible.

When he started on the second trip, he half-expected the "youngsters" in the back of the car to start asking, "Are we there yet?". But no, the young beggars spent most of the time tapping away on their mobile phones.

Kids these days.

Take the internet away from the youngsters, and they'd fall apart, but he'd expected more from his highly trained men. Rollo had half a mind to confiscate the bloody devices. Still, at least they seemed to take notice during their run through the less-exposed part of the route.

"We're not going through the whole route again, are we?" Peewee asked, for once putting his mobile down and lifting his head to look at Rollo through the rear-view mirror.

Boredom showed on his face. The fool even yawned.

I'll give you "yawn", Marine!

"Waste of time, Colours," Slim said, adding his voice to the discussion. "If we're looking for an alternative attack point, it has to be before the convoy reaches the A34. The country stretch between the racecourse and the A34, right?"

"So, you *were* paying attention?" Rollo asked.

"Of course we were, Colours. There's no point wasting time driving the main roads. Too exposed and it's too difficult to control all the variables. Passing civilians and all that malarkey. But"—he shot a furtive look at Peewee—"there's a place on the B3400 with potential."

Rollo glanced at the dashboard clock. 15:23. If they got a chivvy on, they still had plenty enough daylight left for a final recce of the minor roads. He fed more diesel into the engine, their Volvo leaped forwards, and the A34 rolled beneath the tyres at a little under seventy mph.

The ultimate decision fell to him, but what sort of a leader would he be if he didn't take notice of two experienced subordinates?

Peewee leaned forwards and rested his arms on the back of the passenger seat. "Slow up a little here. … See that lay-by? Yep, that's it. Pull in there and I'll run you through my thoughts."

Rollo stopped where Peewee indicated. The road ran through a stretch of ancient, oak woodland. It was quiet and, although not ideal, the area showed some promise as a backup attack point. Rollo sized up the area. The trees offered decent cover and, more importantly, no cars had passed in the two minutes since they'd stopped.

"See that corner?" Peewee pointed ahead to where the

road dipped down and disappeared around a seventy-degree left-hander. "That's where we could hit the truck."

"Okay," Rollo said, immediately seeing the pitfalls. "Walk me through it."

Peewee reached for the door handle.

"Stop. Don't be a bloody idiot!"

Cool it, Rollo. Kid gloves, remember.

He coughed. "I mean, talk—*talk* me through it. What'll it look like for the three of us to wander down a country road in the middle of the afternoon? A shade suspicious, don't you think?"

Slim punched Peewee's shoulder. "Dumb-arse."

"Sorry, Colours." Peewee's expression turned sheepish. He pulled the door closed and lowered his head. "Wasn't thinking. Getting a little ring rusty."

"Okay," Rollo said, "what's the plan?"

"See that oak right next to the road? The one with the damaged bark sticking out from the hedge?"

"What about it?"

Inwardly, Rollo sighed. He guessed what was coming but tried not to let the disappointment show on his face, even though it bubbled below the surface. With growing impatience, he heard Peewee out.

"There's a similar tree around the corner on the opposite side of the road. Right?"

"Right," Rollo answered, trying not to growl his response.

"So," Peewee continued, nodding in his eagerness, "this evening, after dark, we attach a small charge of C4 to the outside base of each tree, see? After that, we wait for the convoy to pass the first tree, and then, 'Boom'," Peewee said, simultaneously snapping open his fingers to indicate an explosion.

"I got you," Slim said, eagerly taking over from Peewee. "After that, we lob a couple of flashbangs and CS gas grenades. The guards don't have a clue what's hit 'em. They think World War Three's started and are crapping themselves. We step in, incapacitate Teddy's men, and blow the rear doors off the armoured truck. After that, it's bish, bash, bosh, we make off with the dosh."

Peewee backed up his mate with, "Yeah, piece of cake." They high fived and turned to face him.

"Simples," Peewee added and made a face that reminded Rollo of the leads in the film Dumb and Dumber.

"Whatcha reckon, Colours?" Slim asked.

Yep, Rollo knew it. Bloody idiots. What was it with SBS men and explosives? Boys with their toys.

"Are you being serious?"

They looked at each other, and their smiles fell.

"Of course."

"That's the most ridiculous plan I've heard since Danny tried to chat up the CO's daughter at that SBS Christmas party. This is leafy Hampshire, not bloody Helmand Province. We can't go blowing up trees and letting off CS gas. You never heard of keeping it simple? Your plan is far too complicated."

He shook his head sadly.

"And another thing," he added. "Armoured trucks are sealed. The CS gas wouldn't penetrate, and we couldn't factor in the weather. Wind direction, rain, cold. They all affect gas dispersal. No, it's right out of the qu—"

He stopped talking when both men burst out laughing and slapped a high-ten.

"Your face, Colours," Slim said through his wails of laughter. "A picture. As if either of us thought the captain would let us kill a couple of innocent oak trees that never did anyone any harm."

"Yeah, and all those squirrels and owls and things. The boss would have kittens. Besides," Peewee added, "we'd never get the timings right for blowing the trees. We'd need Pat for that and he's a smidge busy tonight."

"So, it's back to Plan A, 'kay?"

The mobiles!

"Christ, that's what you were doing on the mobiles? Hatching this ludicrous plan?"

Slim nodded. "Yeah, it was obvious from the first run through that Plan A is the only option available to a three-man team. Mind you, give us a few more men and a couple of police uniforms and we could easily organise a take-down on the M3. Right, Peewee?"

Slim's quietly-spoken mate nodded enthusiastically. "Too right, buddy. I can see it now, Colours in his reflective vest holding his hand up to stop the armoured—"

"Okay, okay. That's enough. You two are a couple of real comedians," Rollo said, scowling. "Going to book you into the Comedy Store."

"Oh," Slim said, "there's a real reason we got you to stop here."

"Really? Do tell."

"A couple of hundred yards around the corner is The Coach & Horses. Don't know if you noticed on the last run, but there's a board outside advertising pub grub. I could murder a pie and mash supper before the balloon goes up. What d'you reckon?"

"Either that," Peewee said, "or we could pop into the racecourse for a bag of chips. If we get a shuffle on, we could make it in time to have a little flutter on the four-fifteen." He raised a finger in the air and hitched his eyebrows as though he'd just come up with an idea. "We could use it as an opportunity to make a proper recce of the counting house."

"And have our mugshots all over the on-course CCTV cameras?" Rollo asked. "Not bloody likely. The Coach & Horses it is."

"Now you're talking, Colours," Slim said, during a fist bump with Peewee.

"Need I remind you, no alcohol?" Rollo stated in a tone that brooked no question.

"Colours," Peewee said, sitting a little straighter in his seat, "I'm mortified you felt the need to mention it. Me and Slim are nothing if not true professionals. Water and diet cola only. Maybe a coffee with pudding? We'll keep the booze for the after-game celebrations."

Shaking his head even more slowly than before, Rollo fired up the Volvo and pulled into the empty road.

"Excellent," Slim said, smiling wide. "Hope they do chips."

———

BY 23:55, Rollo had settled into his lookout post and waited. Arriving early gave him plenty of time to check his special toy. He assumed Peewee and Slim were performing the same task.

The first time he saw the Safe-Shock Police Stun Baton in action, a decade or more back, Rollo knew it would come in handy one day. Using his position as a procurement officer in the Royal Marines, he'd made it a point to develop a close relationship with the baton's manufacturers. Before his breathing regulator let him down during that rat-arsed training dive in the Med and buggered his ears, he'd visited

Safe-Shock's development labs regularly and had made a couple of suggestions to modify it for military operations. The MK2 version, the Safe-Shock Military Stun Unit, was shaped like overlarge knuckle dusters and incorporated an off switch for an integrated, LED torchlight. Rollo couldn't see any value in having lights blazing away during night-time, clandestine operations.

On leaving the marines and setting up his consultancy service, Rollo naturally maintained contact with his military supply chain. When the boss fell into his bit of trouble and asked for Rollo's help, the same supply chain came in handy. Hence his ready access to specialist equipment the likes of the Safe-Shock MSU.

In operational terms, the unit carried 50,000 volts and delivered a charge of 1.8 microcoulombs, which packed more than enough punch to incapacitate anything with less beef than a rhino. In all the trials and demonstrations he'd witnessed, no man or woman had remained vertical after being on the receiving end of a belt. Once—and only once —Rollo had volunteered to be a guinea pig. The test officer touched the unit to Rollo's left thigh and fired. The next thing Rollo remembered was being helped up from the dojo mat with everyone around laughing their silly, civilian faces off.

Yeah, yeah. Very funny.

They showed him the video of his "test" and repeated the part where he'd squealed like a little girl before hitting the mat.

So very, bloody funny.

From Rollo's perspective, the charge had induced an instant, debilitating cramp in every muscle in his body. He'd collapsed like a paper house in a thunderstorm. Even if he hadn't blacked out for a second, the charge would have overridden every aggressive impulse he had. In any event, the thing rendered him useless as a fighting force for a few seconds. Without doubt, the MSU was the fastest and most effective, non-lethal way to drop an opponent. Brilliant, but nothing could be considered perfect, and in the field, Rollo had identified two minor drawbacks—the unit had a four-second recharge delay, and the terminals had to be in contact with the opponent. No long-distance takedown. Other than that, the device ticked all the right boxes.

Rollo checked the MSU's readiness and revised the operational setup. They'd reached the racecourse early and had taken up their predetermined positions after setting their surprise presents according to Pat O'Hara's detailed instructions—under the cover of darkness.

Slim and Peewee flanked either side of the cashier's door on the grandstand, out of sight and in good cover. Rollo had chosen the entrance to the paddock—the most exposed location. He found a deep shadow between a low box hedge and the gatepost at the main entrance, but it would only give him cover part of the way. When he advanced, he'd be horribly exposed for the final few paces, but the background din would mask his sloshing through the mud—at least theoretically.

Rollo deactivated the LED light, hit the charging button, and felt the vibration through his palm as the aggressive, little darling prepped itself for action.

Although the unit only provided a single, five-second burst per charge, when delivered into the nerve bundle at the side of the neck, it would be "lights out for Larry".

For their raid on the racecourse, Rollo, Slim, and Peewee each had a unit and had made sure the batteries were new and fully charged.

Using the MSU, a concerted attack would incapacitate

the first three of Tedesco's men. Brute force and surprise would account for the others. Again, theoretically.

As for the hired help in the armoured truck, they were little more than drivers and porters. The three men weren't paid well enough to put up a fight. In fact, according to their employment contracts, Post Call's security guards were instructed not to fight back in the event of an attack, but to hunker down inside their highly secure vehicle and wait for the police.

Rollo had laughed when he read that piece of intel. Nowhere did, "We won't do anything to actually protect your valuables," appear on the Post Call's glossy, all-bells-and-whistles website.

Nope, that wouldn't be particularly good for business, now would it?

Their role was little more than window dressing designed to appease the insurance companies, a fact which suited Rollo immensely.

Whatever the outcome of the night's endeavours, no way would Teddy Tedesco claim for the losses on his insurance. No way at all. Lose all that face and admit someone had made a fool out of hard man, Teddy Tedesco, the Scourge of the South Coast?

Not a chance.

As the time ticked by, Rollo absorbed the natural rhythm of the night.

And then the rain started.

Chapter Twenty-Seven

Monday 7th December – Daniel Pinkerton

Industrial Area, Southampton, Hampshire, England

Desperate for news of Stinko, Danny stood over the squealing driver, left foot pressing down hard on the man's damaged arm, restricting blood loss, and not worrying about the pain he caused. From his position, Danny could see through the Mercedes' open door. As well as removing the driver's left forearm, the double-barrel blast at close range had taken away the top of Shotgun's right thigh. The man stared silently at the gaping, pulsing wound, eyes wide in shock. Face deathly pale. Silent but for the panting.

A severed femoral artery meant he'd bleed out in

minutes. No hope for him without immediate medical attention. Medical attention he wouldn't receive.

"Cough!" Danny yelled. "How is he?"

"Still looking!"

Still looking? What the fuck does that mean?

Danny turned his attention to the two men in the back. They were painted in red. One had a serious gash to his forehead, and blood flowed in a sheet down his face. Head wounds spewed blood and often looked worse than they were. The fourth man groaned, but Danny couldn't see any obvious injury.

He released the pressure on his foot. Claret pumped from the driver's arm. He considered letting the fucker suffer the same fate as his mate with the sawn-off, but that would be cold-blooded murder, and how would he explain it to the captain?

Shit.

Danny de-cocked his C8, slipped it around to his back, and kneeled near the man's head.

"Hold up your arm, arsehole. Press here."

He pointed to a spot inside the crook of the elbow.

The driver snivelled, but pressed his remaining thumb into the arm, and the blood flow reduced. Danny unclipped the buckle of the driver's leather belt and pulled it free of the trouser loops.

"My ... hand's gone. My fucking ... hand's gone. Hurts. Oh Christ, it fucking hurts."

"Shut up."

"Am I dying?"

Danny slid the end of the belt through the buckle to form a loop, which he slid up the driver's damaged arm close to the armpit. He pulled tight. The blood flow reduced from pumping, to seeping, and then to oozing. He wrapped the belt around the arm twice more and held the end near the driver's mouth.

"Bite on this."

"Huh?"

"Bite on this and keep the belt tight. I'm not hanging around, and this might just keep you alive until the ambulance arrives."

The man whimpered and bit down hard, narrowly missing Danny's fingers.

"Don't move now," Danny said, slapping the man's cheek, "and don't fall asleep." He waggled his mobile at the driver. "I'm calling the ambulance now. They won't be long … I imagine."

He threw another glance inside the Mercedes. Shotgun's head was down, chin slumped against his unmoving chest. The blood no longer spurted from his wound but trickled—driven by gravity rather than a pumping heart. The sawn-off, his weapon of choice, lay in the driver's footwell, its twin barrels resting on the throttle pedal. One of the men in the back of the car, the one without the blood-red mask, showed signs of recovery. Danny leaned into the car, removed the three weapons—two Glock 17s and the shotgun—unloaded them all, and threw them out of reach.

"Cough," he called again, "where are you?"

"Over here!"

Danny gave up his ministrations and raced towards Cough's voice. The wide shadow formed by the warehouse wall and dumpster, together with the inadequate street lighting, made it difficult to see any detail until he drew right up to them. Cough kneeled over a horizontal Stinko, his index and middle fingers pressed into his neck.

"Alive?"

God, please tell me he's still alive.

Cough looked up, a relieved smile accompanied the nod. "Pulse is strong. There's a bump on the back of his head where he hit the wall." He held up Stinko's helmet. "Must have lost this in the crash. He's out cold."

Danny exhaled and collapsed into a squat. "Thank Christ for that. I was going to miss his snoring on the drive back to the farm."

Stinko, the man himself, groaned. He slapped away Cough's fingers. "Get off. What happened? Did the arsehole shoot me?"

Danny and Cough laughed.

"Nah, mate," Danny said, dialling back on the relief and playing it cool, "you just took another nap. Slept through the whole bloody thing. I ... do have some bad news, though."

Stinko groaned as Cough helped him sit up and leaned him against the wall.

"What's that, Sarge?"

Danny stood and glanced at the wrecked car and its less-than-feisty occupants. "They used the front entrance. You owe me twenty quid. And don't think a little bump on the head lets you off. No sympathy in this man's army."

"Shit," Stinko said, still a little groggy but his voice had strengthened. "Hoped you'd forgotten about that. Well, don't just stand there, Cough. Help me up, buddy"

He held out a hand, climbed slowly to his feet, and leaned against the wall. After a few seconds, colour returned to his naturally florid cheeks.

"Cough," Danny said, "can you help him back to the car?"

"No probs, Sarge. Are we out of here now?"

"In a sec. I'll take a look inside the warehouse. Make sure everyone's safe. You have a burner phone on you?"

Cough nodded. "Of course."

"Call for an ambulance. The poor Londoners are a little banged up."

"Will do," Cough said, "just as soon as I pour Sleeping Beauty into his carriage. Mind you, it struck midnight ages ago. Hope it's not turned back into a pumpkin."

"Yeah, yeah," Stinko said. "How long are you planning to keep that up?"

"Until it gets old, mate. Maybe next Christmas? Come on, let's go."

Cough draped Stinko's arm around his shoulders, and they shuffled off towards the side street where they'd parked the car.

Danny returned to the carnage. Nothing had changed. The driver leaned against the Mercedes' front wheel arch, the end of the belt still clamped between his teeth.

As he rushed past, Danny shouted, "Good job you don't wear dentures, mate."

The driver's response was lost behind his clenched jaws and Danny's chuckle.

The warehouse's double doors opened into a dark reception area, but enough streetlight filtered through the frosted windows for him to make out a grey, metal desk and the chair behind it. The domain of a receptionist or office honcho.

He barged through a pair of internal doors and narrowly avoided stumbling over the body of a man wearing a dark blue, serge uniform. The insignia embroidered on the breast pocket read, "G&S Ltd – Bonded Security". The greedy inside man, Jonah, no doubt. No doubt he was dead either. Not many men would survive the butt of a gun repeatedly smashed into his face. Shotgun had clearly gone to town with a sustained attack. Little remained of the unfortunate man's features. Brain, blood, and other matter splodged over the floor and around his head. Danny hoped the police had the unfortunate guy's fingerprints on file. They sure as hell wouldn't identify him through dental records—at least, not without paying for facial reconstruction.

If Danny had any sympathy for Shotgun's demise, looking at the pulped remains of Jonah's noddle blasted it away. The bastard deserved his punishment.

A dark thought floated into Danny's mind. If Shotgun had treated a friend that badly, what had he done to the other two guards?

Oh crap!

Guilt gnawed at his guts. He'd made the decision to allow the gang into the warehouse. If innocents had died because of his fuck-up …

Shit, Danny. Don't go there.

He let the thought fester and, worry mounting, he pushed further into the cavernous storage area. Dim nightlights allowed half-decent visibility and he worked his way along two-metre-wide passageways formed by the metal security cages. As he drew close to the centre of the warehouse, muffled sounds reached his ears.

The groans of dying men?

Keeping his senses wide open against a possible attack, he increased his pace, turned a right-hand corner, and nearly laughed in relief at the sight of two security men sitting back-to-back on the floor, in the halo of a single spotlight. Bound together with cable ties at the wrists and ankles, and gagged with duct tape and a cloth, they didn't look at all comfortable—or happy.

Danny closed on them and squatted in front of the older, and significantly fatter, man. His embroidered label read, "Chief Security Officer". Confident neither man would recognise him through all the camouflage makeup and beneath his helmet, he smiled and removed his Fairbairn-Sykes from its calf sheath.

The grey-haired chief's eyes opened wide, and his nostrils flared. He leaned away, forcing his mate to bend forwards at the waist.

Danny shook his head.

"Don't worry, matey boy," he said, laying on a thick, West Country accent. "I'm only here to help."

Taking care not to nick the man's cheek, Danny sliced through the tape and peeled back the gag. He did the same for the second man.

"There you go, me ducks. Be much more comfortable while waiting for the police."

"W-What?" the chief spluttered. "You can't leave us here."

"Are you injured?"

The chief looked stunned, but after a moment to think, shook his head. "No."

"What about you, my lovely," Danny asked, tapping the other one on the shoulder.

"Yeah, I'm good. What about Jonah? Those bastards took him away. I heard him scream."

"Don't worry about him, old son," Danny said. "He were working with them buggers."

"Really?"

"Yep, really."

"W-Who are you?" the chief asked.

"UK Ports Defence Authority," he answered, making it up on the spot. "We're here to protect the country's docks."

The older man scoffed, clearly not believing a word. "I heard gunshots and a crash. What happened?"

Danny pursed his lips, trying to decide how much to tell them. "You'll find out when the police and ambulance arrive. Suffice to say, they're still around. But don't worry, me ducks, they ain't in no condition to hurt no one else."

He stood.

"You're really going to leave us like this?"

"Won't be for long, me ducks." He turned to leave, but only took a few paces before stopping and turning back. "Afore I go, any idea what they stole?"

The chief shook his head.

"Okay, not to worry. It's still in the boot of their car. Cheerio, now. And don't worry, me ducks. You'll be dining out on this story for years."

He left the warehouse with their angry calls ringing through the cages.

Outside, he found the team's car parked alongside the crippled Mercedes. The driver still sat upright and awake and still munching on his belt. He might well survive the night, which was better than could be said for two of his mates.

"What you waiting for, Sarge?" Cough shouted from behind the wheel of their inconspicuous, but intact, ride. "Get in. Can't you hear the sirens?"

"Only now you pointed them out."

Danny jumped into the passenger's seat but hardly had time to settle before Cough floored the accelerator and the car sprang forwards. The front passenger door slammed shut under the force of a sharp, left turn, throwing Danny to his right. Cough straightened and drove through the front gates at warp speed—or at least the car's nearest equivalent.

Danny shrugged his C8 around to his front, clamped it between his knees, and fastened his seatbelt. Only then did he have the chance to twist around and check on his men.

Both wore beaming smiles and practically hugged themselves with glee.

"You both okay? Stefan how's you?"

Having come close to losing him, Danny would never call him "Stinko" again. The guy deserved a better nickname.

"Dumpster", maybe?

"Never better, Sarge. You?"

"The head?"

Stefan made a fist, knocked it gently against his temple, and shrugged. "Can't feel a thing. Next time, I'll strap my helmet on a little tighter."

"Cough? Everything cool?"

"Not bad, Sarge," he said. "Not bad at all. A good night's work, I reckon. What do you think, Stefan?"

The lanky man in the back seat held his head and burst out laughing. So much so, Danny worried for his mental state. A crack on the head could result in serious, long-term damage.

Cough turned right to exit the industrial estate and hung a left onto a slip road joining the dual carriageway. He eased his foot off the throttle, slowing the car to a more sedate speed when he spotted a forty-mph roadworks sign. An ambulance and two police cars passed on the opposite carriageway, blue lights flashing, sirens waking the neighbourhood, scaring away the light traffic.

"Good timing," Cough said, turning to look at Danny, beaming.

In the back, Stefan's belly laugh had softened into a chuckle. Danny turned and tried to see the giggling man's eyes.

"He's hysterical, Cough. The head injury's worse than we thought. Where's the nearest hospital?"

"Sarge," Cough said, "he's okay, I promise you. Isn't that right, mate?"

Stefan stopped chortling long enough to say, "Yes, never better. Cough, you want to tell him or can I?"

"You found it, mate," Cough said, glancing in the rear-view mirror. "You give him the news."

"Tell me what?" Danny asked, fast losing patience with the inane double act. "For God's sake, tell me what!"

Stefan leaned forwards, straining against his seatbelt. "It's like this, Sarge. I've always been a nosey bugger. Can't help myself, see? Gotten me into loads of trouble ever since I was a boy."

Danny sighed. "If you don't get to the point soon, I'm going to give you a bump on the eye to match the one on your head."

"Sorry, Sarge. Well, I wanted to find out what the Londoners lobbed in the back of their Merc, so I forced Cough to stop and take a gander. Wanted to check out that antique jewellery they nicked."

Danny shot a glance at Cough and then looked back at the delighted Stefan, whose eyes were afire.

"You didn't!"

"Didn't what, Sarge?" Cough asked.

"Steal the jewellery. What the hell are we going to do with a load of antique contraband?"

Stefan's mouth opened wide in mock horror. "Me? Nick a load of gold and jewels? Never, Sarge. Scout's honour." He threw up a two-fingered salute. "Cash money, on the other hand, now that's different."

"Cash?"

Cough nodded. "Money. Bundles of used, fifty-pound notes stuffed on top of the trinkets. All wrapped up in plastic. Untraceable."

"How many bundles?"

"Twenty," Cough said. "One hundred notes per bundle. Sarge, we just picked up one hundred grand!"

"God alive! We can't keep it."

"Why not, Sarge?" Stefan asked, throwing his hands up and barking them on the roof panel. He swore and kissed the knuckles of his right fist.

"It's not ours."

Cough slammed his hand into the steering wheel. "Hear that, Stefan? Listen to Mother Theresa. Of course it's ours. We've got it. Possession is nine-tenths—"

"I meant we have to share it with the rest of the men."

"Bloody hell, Sarge," Cough spluttered after a quick double-take. "What do you take us for? 'Course we're gonna share it with the rest of the guys. We aren't thieves!"

"Technically, you are, even if you steal from other thieves, but ... where did it come from? The warehouse?"

"It's Teddy Tedesco's tribute."

"How the hell did you work that out?"

Cough took his eyes from the road long enough to wink. "The parcel with the money inside was addressed to Teddy. Bold as brass. I swear. Show him the packet, Stefan."

The still-chortling Stefan stopped sucking on his knuckle long enough to reach into the footwell and drag out a package wrapped in brown paper. He handed it to Danny. It weighed more than he expected. Although that was hardly surprising considering he'd never been as close to so much cash before.

He examined the package. They'd torn open one corner to reveal the neatly wrapped money, and there was writing scrawled on the front.

To: Teddy T,
Paid in full,
Gino D.

"Bloody hell," Danny said. "Looks like this Gino D mutt was expecting a receipt."

"Maybe he wanted to claim it as a legitimate business expense," Cough said and started laughing again. Stefan joined him.

Danny rewrapped the money and returned it. "You can look after it, mate."

"What's up, Sarge?" Cough asked. "For someone who just earned the best part of ten grand for one night's work you don't look all that happy."

Danny faced forwards. "Tired, I guess. Been a long few days."

The rain started again as they reached the entrance to the M3. Danny's eyes glazed over from watching the metronomic sweep and his mind dulled from listening to the whump-thump of wipers as they struggled to clear the windscreen. Before long, Stefan's rumbling snores fought for superiority over the noise of tyres on wet tarmac.

"There he goes again," Cough announced. "No danger of me falling asleep behind the wheel."

"I can take over if you're tired."

"Nah, I'm good for another hour or two. By the way, I'm starving. Always am after an op. Mind if we take the M1 and stop at the Toddington Services for breakfast? It'll save waking everyone at the farm."

Danny nodded.

"Sounds like a plan."

He fell quiet.

Whump-thump, whump-thump.

A few minutes later, between bouts of Stefan's snoring, Cough spoke again. "Wonder how Rollo and the captain are getting along."

"Radio silence, remember. We won't know until we're all back at the farm."

Whump-thump, whump-thump.

"Tougher than you thought?"

Danny yawned and blinked away the image of the wipers. "What's that?"

"Leadership," Cough said. "Tougher than you thought, yeah?"

What is he, a mind reader?

"A little."

"Been there, Danny. Want to talk it through?"

"Not really, mate."

"I'm here when you need to."

Whump-thump, whump-thump.

"Bugger it. How do you cope?" Danny asked the wipers, unable to look away from the hypnotic swiping.

"You do. Or you don't."

"Thanks, Yoda. That really helps."

Cough grinned. "Aim to please, I do."

Danny rubbed his face hard, trying to wipe away the fatigue and the negative mood.

"Christ, when I saw the Mercedes plough into the dumpster, I was paralysed. I thought Stefan was a goner."

"Me too. Luckily, he's a squaddie. We all have thick skulls."

"It was almost as bad when I tripped over Jonah's corpse."

"Jonah?"

"The Londoners' inside man. The arsehole with the

shotgun smashed his face in. I expected to find the other guards dead, too, and it was my decision to wait for the gang to exit the warehouse. At that moment, I thought I'd been responsible for the deaths of two innocent men. A horrible feeling."

"Listen to me, Sarge," Cough said, dragging his eyes from the road again and locking them with Danny's for a moment. "You did well back there. Made all the right calls. You've nothing to fret about. Stefan and I will follow you into battle again, no probs."

"Cheers. That means a lot. You both did well, too."

"Fuck off, Sarge. Don't get all soppy on me. This isn't a chick flick, and we aren't about to start hugging it out, right." He held out a hand and they fist-bumped.

The rain eased enough for Cough to put the wipers on intermittent. It helped Danny's mind settle for a while, but the silence grew, and his mood became more sombre.

With the sun nothing but a future hope and the eastern horizon still a barely seen black line, they reached a relatively traffic-free M1. Cough stepped up the speed a little above the limit, to match the pace of the vehicles streaming past in the overtaking lane. He yawned and shuffled in his seat.

"Sure you don't want me to take over?" Danny asked.

"Nah, I'm good. Thought you were asleep. You've been quiet long enough."

"Couldn't get one thought out of my head."

"What thought?"

Danny scratched an itch behind his ear. "It's a bit girly emotional, you might not want to hear."

"Go on then, I can take it."

Cough hitched his shoulders and scrunched up as though preparing for an incoming artillery barrage.

Such a comedian. Who knew?

"Right then, you asked for it. If Stefan and those security guards *nearly* dying fucked with my head so badly, how's the captain coping knowing he actually pulled the trigger that killed eighty-three people?"

"Good bloody question, Danny. Must cut him up big time. If I'd done the same thing I might have swallowed a bullet before now. He's a strong-willed man."

Danny nodded. "No wonder he's spending all his time and energy protecting the families."

"Yep, he's a bloody good bloke. That's why I'm here, happy to risk my life for him," Cough said, in a rare moment of sincerity, but he spoiled it by adding, "and the money helps."

Stefan spluttered and sat up, stretching his arms out. "What's up? Did I interrupt a special moment?"

"Fuck off, Stefan," Cough said, lowering his window and letting in a blast of refreshingly frigid air. "'Bout time you woke. Couldn't hear myself think with your snoring."

"Bugger off," Stefan shot back. "I don't snore."

Danny exchanged amused glances with Cough, and all was right with the world.

Forty miles of quiet introspection and growing daylight later, Danny became aware of Stefan shuffling around on the back seat. He turned in time to see the man sneaking a fifty out of the newly opened top stack. Grinning, he offered the banknote to Danny. "Here's the twenty quid I owe you, Sarge. You can keep the change … but only if you pay for breakfast."

"Mate," Danny said, smiling, "you've got yourself a deal."

Chapter Twenty-Eight

Monday 7th December – William Rollason

Andover and District Racecourse, Andover, Hampshire, England

As the weather forecast predicted, the heavens opened shortly after one o'clock. It hammered down. Monstrous raindrops exploded on the tarmac path surrounding the paddock with the force of mortar shells, quickly waterlogging the grass on the inner oval of the winner's circle.

Snug, dry, and warm inside his breathable and waterproof battledress, Rollo didn't bat an eye.

Rain suited his plans. A wet and miserable security guard was a less alert creature, and the dark-jacketed beefcake hunched in the entrance to the cashier's office trying unsuccessfully to light his cigarette, demonstrated the point to perfection. The man looked as dismal as anyone Rollo had seen in a while. Even better, wet skin conducted electricity with even greater efficiency than dry.

He couldn't have asked for more.

Rain ran down his face, tickling his chin where his beard would have protected him. He missed his beard, his old friend. He'd have to work on Marie-Odile, to talk her around. No marriage could work without give and take on both sides. On the other hand, the woman's other attributes more than compensated for her stubbornness—and for her interfering mother.

Deal with that later, Rollo. Head's up.

The time on his diver's watch read 01:23. Mission Bravo would go live at any minute.

The racecourse's alcohol licence only allowed them to remain open until 00:30 on a Sunday night. That left the staff sixty minutes to empty the tills, carry the money to the cashier's office, and count and bag it before the armoured truck arrived at 01:30.

As per expectations, the VIPs had been dribbling out of the corporate boxes and into chauffeur-driven limos since before midnight. At 01:12, the final party of six heavily inebriated "hoorays" gave their driver mouthfuls of aggressive verbals as he helped a smartly dressed, umbrella-toting bouncer pour them into the back of a pearl-white, stretch Lincoln. They clearly had no self-control or class, and Rollo didn't envy the driver his task of mopping up the pools of vomit they'd likely deposit on the red-leather upholstery.

"Hope it's not your Lincoln, mate," Rollo muttered to the driver. "And I hope you've shield-guarded that leather."

01:28.

Rollo lowered his boom mic into position.

"Bravo One to Bravos Two and Three," he whispered. "Report. Over."

"Bravo Two here," Slim responded. *"I'm wetter than a wet thing standing in a puddle on a rainy day. Apart from that, things are on plan. Over."*

Slim's "on plan" meant that from his position near the grandstand, he could see Tedesco's guards and the money sacks waiting in the atrium.

"Bravo Three," Peewee said, coming across as almost bored. *"Funny, but I'm toasty here. Protected by a lovely awning and next to a heating vent. ... Hang on. ... Yes. Target vehicle approaching. Over."*

Headlights raked the grandstand and lit up the lancing rain in dazzling silver. Gone was Rollo's hard-won night vision, but he wouldn't be needing it anyway. The rumble of a big, diesel engine added to the sound of the hammering rain, drowning out all other noise and forcing Rollo to raise his voice.

"Bravo One to Bravos Two and Three," Rollo said, unable to keep the urgency from his voice, "it's a go. Repeat, the mission is a go. Wait for my signal. Bravo One, out."

The automated gates swung open. The armoured truck rumbled into the paddock and roared past Rollo, its over-sized tyres and double rear axle throwing out a cascade of muddy spray. Movement-sensitive floodlights exploded into life, bathing the apron in front of the main entrance in a sheet of brilliant, white light.

Nope, definitely no need for night vision goggles.

Rollo smiled in anticipation of the action.

The side doors leading from the cashier's office cranked open. Two men he named Goons One and Two barged through and stood guard on either side of the doorway. They carried a wooden baton each, but Corky's intel suggested they'd be carrying handguns in concealed holsters. Goon One, the taller of the two and the one closer to Slim, spoke into a wrist mic like a proper security guard. Seconds later, Goon Three appeared, pushing a trolley loaded with well-stuffed postal bags.

The money.

Unexpectedly, Rollo's heart rate spiked.

Goon Four exited the building and stood guard behind Goon Three—Teddy Tedesco's four-man army had revealed themselves. The drivers, Goons Five and Six, would arrive in two SUVs after the money was safely locked inside the truck.

Goon One stepped out into the rain and banged on the side of the armoured truck. The rear doors opened, and two Post Call security men jumped out, splashing puddled water over Goon One. They started lobbing the sacks into the back of the truck.

Loading wouldn't take more than a few seconds, and everyone's attention, even that of the truck driver, would be on the money.

Bent low to minimise his profile, Rollo broke cover, dashed across the open space, and stopped in the shadow of the truck.

"This is Bravo One," Rollo whispered, "I'm in position. On my mark. Three …"

With his back against the side of the truck, Rollo slid towards the rear.

Men shouted above the noise of the pummelling rain.

"Hurry the fuck up, will you?" one said. "I'm getting bloody soaked."

"…two …"

"Nearly there," an older man answered. "You'll need to sign the docket."

"Fuck the shitting docket, we'll do it at the bank."

"Sorry, son. More than my job's worth to break protocol. Here's the last one. Four sacks, two with coins, and two with—"

"...one. Go! Go! Go!"

Rollo darted around the rear door, stun unit outstretched. His target, Goon Three, half-turned. Rollo pressed the firing button. A crackling. A blue-white flash. A girlie squeal. Goon Three crumpled to the rain-washed tarmac.

Two further crackling flashes forced Goons One and Two to kiss concrete beside their mate. Goon Four, the last man standing, gawped open-mouthed at his fallen comrades. After what seemed like forever to Rollo, Goon Four made his move. His right hand scrambled to reach the gun holstered under his left armpit. He didn't get halfway before the barrel of Peewee's SIG P226 touched his temple. He froze without having to be told.

Peewee and Slim got to work securing the Goons with heavy-duty cable ties—the modern warrior's first choice restraints. They were nearly finished before Post Call's Jobsworth found his voice.

"W-What the hell's—"

Rollo put a finger to his lips. "Shush. No talking." He showed the man a Glock 17, but pointed it at the Goon groaning in the puddle on the ground. "Be quiet and no one will get hurt. Tell your driver to get out of the cab. No, don't argue." Rollo twitched the Glock and Jobsworth changed his mind about interrupting. "I'm not interested in your operating procedures. If he stays in the truck, he'll get hurt and no one wants that. Especially not Post Call's board of directors. Personal injury claims can be extortionate."

Jobsworth blinked repeatedly but didn't make a move towards his personal radio.

Rollo turned to Jobsworth's buddy, a white-faced, gawky kid barely out of his teens. The youngster had raised his hands high above his head the moment Rollo shouted. He trembled and looked close to joining the Goons on the ground but wouldn't need the help of a stun gun.

"You tell him, son," Rollo said, "Or I'll make you and your officious leader get in the back when we torch the money."

"You're going to do w-what?" Jobsworth spluttered, taking a pace forwards until Rollo drew his attention to the Glock once again.

"You heard me right. Bravo Two, are you done?"

Slim stood and nodded.

"You have the incendiaries?"

"Yep."

Slim shucked off his backpack and removed two of Pat's "slim specials".

He climbed into the truck and whistled a merry tune while piling the sacks neatly and setting the charges.

Rollo turned to the kid. "Your driver has ninety seconds to vacate his cab. It's up to you."

The kid said, "Oh God. Oh God," and looked up at his hands.

"It's okay, son. You can lower your arms. Run to the driver and then keep running out through the gates. It isn't worth taking a bullet for minimum wages."

The kid dropped his arms and took off. It didn't take the driver long to make his decision, and the two men headed for the safety of the exit road. The kid showed a good turn of speed and easily outsprinted the lumbering driver, but it still only took a few seconds for both to disappear into the rain-spattered night.

Goon Four, the only one of Tedesco's men still *compos mentis*, looked up from his place in a large puddle. Peewee had dragged him into the middle of the winner's circle and attached him to the stanchion alongside his mates. "You're shitting nuts, you morons. Do you know who your fucking with? That's Mr Tedesco's money. Two-point-three million quid. For *Mr Tedesco*."

Rollo ignored the man's bluster and watched from a safe distance as Slim jumped out of the truck, slammed the rear doors, and took Jobsworth to one side. Slim studied his watch and held up his open hand. He counted down with his fingers and when his hand became a fully closed fist, a muffled whump rocked the truck on its stiffened springs. Rollo nodded.

Pat O'Hara didn't do things by halves. Ask him to build something to torch a couple of million quid's worth of marked cash and that's exactly what he provided. Knowing the Irishman's skills, the coins would probably be fused into one solid lump of metal within minutes.

"Shit!" Slim said. "All that dosh."

He led an unresisting Jobsworth to the steps in front of the main entrance and helped him to sit before he collapsed. Rollo wondered what Post Call's employee terms and conditions said about allowing their armoured trucks to be turned into cash incinerators. No doubt Jobsworth would find out when his line managers arrived to collect their damaged vehicle.

Rollo checked his watch. The whole operation had

taken less than three minutes. He squatted in front of Goon Four.

"What were you saying about Teddy Tedesco?"

"All that cash," the man said. "Why didn't you take it? You'll need it to try and get away from Mr Tedesco. Won't work, though. He'll find you."

Rollo made a bitter face. "What? Take the money and get covered in blue dye from the explosive packs when we open the sacks? No, thank you. I don't like blue."

"Mr Tedesco's gonna fucking kill you," Goon Four said, hushed awe in his voice.

"Well, no doubt he's going to try," Rollo said, smiling. "We have to go now, but when the great man gets here, will you give him a message?"

"I ain't your fucking messenger boy."

Rollo slapped him hard enough to spin his head. "Shut up and listen, it might save your life. When Teddy gets here tell him the captain says hello."

"Who?"

"Teddy will know. The captain also says, the next time they agree to a rendezvous, Teddy's to come in person and not send inferior lackeys."

"Bravo One," Peewee called, pointing towards the employees' car park, "we've got company."

Undulating headlights lit the dark, bouncing as the cars traversed an overspill car park that had turned into little more than a muddy field.

Goon Four smirked. "That's my backup. You're fucking dead meat."

"Really?"

Rollo touched the stun gun to the man's neck and hit the trigger, keeping it pressed for the full, five-second charge. The man squealed, shivered, and clenched into a tight ball. Blood spurted from his mouth. The foul-mouthed ignoramus must have bitten his tongue.

Remembering his time as a guinea pig, Rollo had to admit, watching a man receive a full dose really was bloody hilarious.

Two dark, Mercedes SUVs turned the corner from the muddy car park onto the smooth surface of the road, moving slowly. The drivers clearly had failed to notice anything untoward in the pickup area. Jobsworth sat, head in hands, oblivious, but out of range and safe. Likewise, the Goons were well clear of the upcoming blast area.

A light came on inside the grandstand and three suited men stood in the open double doorway. Perfect targets if Rollo needed shooting practise. He didn't.

The leader of the three newcomers, a tall, blond man, shouted, "Billy, *was ist los*? What is taking so long?"

"End game!" Rollo called and sprinted towards the exit.

Slim and Peewee raced ahead of him through the open gates and ducked into the shadows. Rollo stopped in the first patch of darkness, turned, and leaned against the fence, and pulled one of Pat's toys from inside his jacket. The SUVs had parked metres from the apparently intact armoured truck. Both drivers remained inside their cars. The blond German and his two accomplices edged out of the building, semi-automatic handguns drawn.

They scanned the scene, peering through the rain, clearly having difficulty interpreting what they saw. Ten more paces and they'd reach the blast radius.

Now's the time.

Rollo turned the key to unlock the detonator panel Pat had spent all of five minutes teaching him how to operate. He flipped open the protective cover and threw the first switch.

A string of eight small explosions shook the earth, looking and sounding like supercharged firecrackers. They ripped small chunks of tarmac from the road, starting behind the rearmost Mercedes and finishing in front of the armoured truck. All three vehicles rocked and bucked like small boats in a heavy sea. The German and his mates dived back inside the building. Jobsworth cowered on the top step, but the Goons could do nothing but sit and tremble against the metal stanchion and hope for the best.

Rollo waited for the debris to settle and to make sure the SUV drivers were still safe inside their vehicles before hovering his thumb over the second rocker switch.

Behind him, Slim and Peewee applauded and laughed. Kids on bonfire night had less fun. They both had their mobiles out to take pictures.

"No selfies, guys," he said. "That would be out of order. By the way, either of you want to do the honours?"

He held up the detonator and offered it across.

"No thanks, Colours." Slim chuckled, his phone on camera mode. "Wouldn't want to miss the shot. Can I call 'action'?"

Rollo sighed, rocked the switch, and started walking. They'd parked the Volvo down a quiet, farm lane, five hundred metres from the racecourse. He wanted to make a clean and quick getaway and didn't need to witness the action. He'd seen plenty of explosions in his time, and Pat had told him exactly what to expect.

After their quick recce a few days earlier, the confident Irish genius had created the small, shaped charges designed to create deep holes but throw the debris up. He told Rollo's team where and how deep to plant the devices and also told them the damage the ninth and final device would cause—a deep crater fifteen meters in diameter. No cars could take up pursuit, at least not from the racecourse side. As an added bonus, the final explosion would take out the main power and telephone cables, and mobile signal in the region was patchy at best. With all the mayhem, the local mobile service was bound to be swamped with emergency calls and would give Rollo and his team plenty of time to escape the area.

The detonation, when it finally arrived, made a hell of a lot more noise than all the "firecrackers" put together. The earth shuddered beneath Rollo's boots and the grandstand lights cut out immediately to confirm the accuracy of Pat's predictions.

Rollo dusted off his hands. All in all, a good night's work.

Peewee reached him first, closely followed by his chunky shadow, Slim.

"Bloody hell, Colours," Slim said, studying the video files on his mobile. "A bit disappointing. Nothing but flying earth, turf, and asphalt. Then the lights went out. If I'd paid for tickets, I'd have been really disappointed."

"Yeah," Peewee agreed, "and the signal strength on my mobile just disappeared. Bloody rubbish service around here."

The comedians laughed and, for once, Rollo joined in.

They changed into dry outer clothes and removed their camouflage makeup with alcohol wipes. Rollo took the wheel and drove away from the scene of bloodless mayhem. He kept the speed at a sedate fifty-five mph along the B3400.

After a familiar, sharp right-hander, Peewee and Slim both cackled.

"Bloody hell. Will you look at that?" Peewee shouted, pointing at two bedraggled men in Post Call security uniforms who were banging on the front door of The Coach & Horses, but failing to gain entry.

Between bouts of laughter, Slim said, "Fancy stopping to give our mates a lift?"

Rollo ignored their merriment and fed more diesel into the Volvo's engine.

Next stop, Mike's farm.

Chapter Twenty-Nine

Monday 7th December – Night

The Solent, Off Southampton, England

The last time Kaine had taken a swim in the open sea out of easy sight of land had been on the fateful night he'd taken eighty-three innocent lives. He tried to ignore the harrowing sense of loss and guilt, and focus on the mission, but images of the fireball in the sky off the Humber coast kept forcing their way, unbidden, into his consciousness.

The RIB-safe S-785 powered through the waves, its muscular, twin, Yamaha 250V6, outboard motors driving the V-hulled boat forwards at over fifty knots.

To avoid raising suspicion, Larry steered a course to take them at a thirty-degree angle away from *Andros Freeway* and three miles distant. Judging by the trawler's position on the sonar, his ploy seemed to work. *Andros Freeway*'s skipper maintained his position fifteen miles off the coast, apparently at anchor, apparently in wait.

At a three-mile separation, Larry killed the engine, and the RIB-safe quickly slowed to a stop. Bobbing in the heavy swell, its low profile would have produced an almost-invisible radar return.

Pat checked his equipment and circled his thumb and index finger in the divers' "okay" signal.

Holding tight to the rope handholds attached to the bulwarks, Kaine turned to Larry.

"Hold her here until you receive our signal," he said, having to shout over the howling south-westerly, "and then bring her in at max power. We won't have long before Pat's gizmos have the last word."

Larry nodded. "Right you are, boss. Enjoy your midnight dip and watch out for sharks." He ended with a wink.

"All set, Pat?" Kaine called to his dive buddy.

The Irishman dipped his head and attached a water-proof buoyancy backpack to his webbing straps. "Right as the rain lashing down on us, Captain. Can't wait to dive into that lovely, clear water, now. Looks like the Caribbean in summer."

"Systems check?" Kaine asked, confirming his digital readout. "Nitrox fully charged?"

Pat read his system's pressure gauge. "Check."

"GPS?"

"Synchronised and verified with yours and the RIB-safe's."

"Time. 01:35 and fifteen seconds … now."

"Confirmed."

Kaine circled his fingers. "Stick tight to my right wing. I

don't want you ending up in France. I know what your navigation's like."

"Ah now, that's a bit harsh. Lose your way in the heaviest fog in a decade one time and nobody ever lets you forget it."

"Just keep heading northeast," Larry said, while double-checking the webbing and pressure gauges on both their harnesses, "and you'll end up in Brighton. Can't miss it." Laughing, he pointed due south, to France.

Kaine interrupted the loud guffaw. "Okay, game time, men. Headsets on."

They fitted the hoods and checked the delivery pressure and the seal. The nitrox mix started off cold and dry but would become warm and moist once the rebreather kicked in and started scrubbing carbon dioxide from the system.

"Radio check. Alpha Two?"

Larry gave the okay.

"Alpha Three, do you hear me. Over?"

"*Loud and clear. Over,*" Pat answered, his voice taking on the flat, metallic tone typical of electronic, closed-comms systems.

"Confirmed. Radio silence until we board unless absolutely necessary. Alpha One, out."

Kaine and Pat took their positions on the side tube of the wildly bucking RIB-safe. Kaine gave the signal and they rolled backwards into the sea. After the initial shock of tumbling through space, he hit the water, barely making a splash. The cloak of pressure as the water closed over his head was like an old friend come to pay a visit. He was home.

Kaine bobbed to the surface and waited for Pat to settle at his side before giving the thumbs-down sign. He bled some air out of his dive jacket, reduced the buoyancy of his equipment sack, and slipped under the breaking waves and out of the howling wind.

He descended to the predetermined three metres, opening, and closing his mouth until his ears popped. Maintaining a dive depth above five metres would avoid any decompression problems when they resurfaced.

As he sank through the water, the sound of the wind and the breaking waves disappeared to be replaced by the comforting, deep-throated burble of the Yamaha outboards on idle. The noise vibrated through his chest.

He settled his breathing, balanced the compensator valve, hung vertically in the water, and watched for Pat's ready signal—a double-flash from his torch.

Kaine waited for Pat to take up his wingman position— right shoulder, two metres back—and they struck out towards *Andros Freeway*, using the GPS and the transmitter they planted on the keel of the ninety-five-foot fishing boat the previous afternoon.

They took an indirect course towards the vessel. Nothing would give two divers away faster than making a direct, straight-line approach to their target. A winding, circuitous approach would at least give the impression of two large fish, or maybe seals, wallowing around in search of food, assuming *Andros Freeway*'s sonar was functional and sensitive enough to pick them up.

Despite having to tow the buoyancy-regulated equipment sacks, and without pushing hard, they completed the three-mile swim in a little under an hour, even with the indirect approach. The extra-large fins and the nitrox breathing mix allowed them to power along at a strong, steady pace. The lightweight drysuits, although essential to survive the freezing December seas, would prove highly restrictive in an on-board firefight, but there was no avoiding it.

At the end of the swim, Kaine broke radio silence once, and once only.

Hand signals would have been useless. Visibility at depths below three metres was minimal. Irrespective of Pat's quip, the silt-heavy, chilly waters of the eastern Solent bore as much relationship to the crystal-clear Caribbean as a slurry pit did to a rock pool. Luckily, the receiver in his GPS unit maintained the trace on *Andros Freeway* or they would have swum right past her.

"Surface, surface, surface."

They broke through to air at *Andros Freeway*'s stern. Her diesel engines thrummed, but the props weren't churning up any wake. The boat had to be at anchor, probably awaiting their friends from the Continent, but nothing showed on Kaine's GPS screen. The harsh conditions must have delayed the rendezvous.

The weather could have been better. The stiffened south-westerly increased the chop and tossed them around like corks in a bathtub, but it could have been a whole lot worse, too.

Pat bobbed alongside.

They added more air to their buoyancy bladders and linked arms for stability. Kaine peeled back his hood as did Pat. Freezing rain and sea water slapped his face, shocking him further awake.

Kaine leaned closer. "How many?"

He had to raise his voice above the roar of the wind and the chop of the heavy sea. No danger of their quarry hearing them over the orchestra of wind and wave.

Pat raised the infrared camera to his eye. Kaine tried to hold him steady, but the swell made it impossible.

"Four heat signals, boss. Two in the wheelhouse, one

below deck, and another hanging over the portside. Looks to be puking his ring. A landlubber."

"Are you sure? Corky's intel warned of a five-person team for these pickups."

"That's as may be, but this is showing only four people on that boat. After what you did at the warehouse, I'm assuming Teddy-boy's running a skeleton crew on *Andros Freeway* tonight. One good thing, though."

"What's that?"

"I can't see any illegals in the hold, and you know what that means."

Kaine knew exactly Pat's implication. "You think we should mine the hull and be done with it?"

Pat nodded. "That I do, boss. It'd make our job easier."

"I know, but we've been through this. I'm going aboard, but you're welcome to bow out. Plant your mine but give me time to have a scout around and get clear before you detonate."

Kaine made out Pat's head shake in the glow of the trawler's running lights.

"And miss out on the party? That's not going to happen. Just thought I'd mention the easy option. Didn't have the slightest expectation you'd take it, though."

Kaine paused a moment to gather his thoughts.

"Ready?"

"That I am, boss."

Kaine unlinked his arm from Pat's and pulled the harpoon gun from his shoulder. He confirmed the compressed-air charge, released the safety bar to free the harpoon with the grappling hook tip, and loosened the knotted rope attached. He swam to within five metres of the hull, starboard side. Pat matched his movements and leaned close again.

"No change in their position, boss. The stern's clear."

"Get ready."

Kaine took careful aim, allowing for the irregular swell and the breaking waves—they'd likely only get one chance to board without raising attention. He waited for the next wave to lift them and fired.

The gun hissed and bucked, and the harpoon flew in a graceful arc, dragging the nylon rope as a thin, white tail. The grappling tines sprung open and darted through the guard rail. Kaine pulled and the tines snagged on the lower of the two horizontal rails. Pat grabbed the rope to keep the hook locked in place.

Kaine unbuckled his dive gear and tied it to the rope, then he removed his fins and clipped them to the side of his pack. Minus his bodyweight as ballast, the CCUBA and its attached weapons bag sat on the surface, bobbing in the swell.

Without further word—they'd practised the manoeuvre hundreds of times in their SBS days—Kaine rigged for climbing, the most vulnerable phase of ship boarding. He attached a pair of jumars to the rope—one secured by a loop and carabiner to his climbing harness and the other secured by a longer loop and carabiner to his dominant foot. Once he started climbing, Pat added his weight to hold the rope steady.

Out of the water, the light drysuit was heavy and restrictive, but Kaine completed the short climb in seconds. He took hold of the gunwale and pulled himself up until his eye line drew level with the deck—clear. He released his hold on the rope, levered himself through the rails, and flopped onto the deck, barely breathing hard.

Eyes open and scanning the boat for danger, he twanged the rope. At the signal, Pat let go to release the tension.

Kaine unclipped the jumars from his harness and loosened the grappling hook. He tied off the rope before pulling it, hand over hand, until both equipment bags appeared at the rail.

The wind at his back lessened a fraction.

Kaine sensed rather than saw the movement. He dived to his right as something whistled past his ear and clanged against the handrail, throwing up sparks as metal struck metal.

A man roared, "Bastard!", and raised the iron bar to swing again.

Kaine launched himself forwards. The swinging bar sailed over his head and Kaine snapped out a volley of quick-fire punches, head-belly-head.

The man staggered backwards under the onslaught and lost his balance as *Andros Freeway*'s deck juddered under the impact of a monster wave. He lost his footing, fell, struck his head on an outrigger, and toppled over the railings before Kaine could catch him.

Kaine's earpiece crackled.

"Alpha Three to Alpha One. Was that you? Over."

The worry in Pat's tone cut through the electronic dampening.

Kaine activated his mic. "Alpha One, here. No, I'm fine. Unwanted gatecrasher. Back on plan. Out."

He allowed the driving rain to cool his face before returning to the railings and setting to work.

Once the bags were aboard, he retrieved the caving ladder from his pack, secured it to the rail, and dropped it over the side. Then he unpacked his C8, unplugged the muzzle's waterproof stopper, and tugged on the charging handle. He took a knee and kept guard, covering the deck with slow sweeps of his trusty assault rifle.

Seconds later, Pat's head appeared between the railings above the scuppers. Kaine tapped his shoulder and he slithered aboard, heading straight for his pack to release and make ready his weapon.

"What happened to the unwilling swimmer?" Kaine whispered into Pat's ear.

"Poor fellow sank like a lead brick, and I lost him in the murk."

"Bugger tried to brain me. I would have liked to return the favour."

Pat shrugged, unconcerned. He tugged his backpack into place—the one with the surprise presents for Teddy Tedesco—and gave the ready signal.

Kaine skirted around the open hold and crawled to the starboard side, keeping to the shadows. Pat remained to port. They edged forwards and kneeled on either side of the wheelhouse, listening.

Behind the closed door, a man and woman chatted. They spoke loud enough to be heard clearly and confirm to Kaine his impromptu dance with the bar-wielding ambusher had passed without raising attention.

"…heard about Timothy?" a young woman asked, the Hampshire accent showing her local origins.

"Yeah. Bit of a shock. Black bugger'd been with Teddy ages. Years. No idea why he and Teddy had the fallin' out after that cockup at the warehouse. Two dead and another lost a hand." The man's accent matched the woman's, and the timbre was so similar, they might have been siblings.

"Teddy must've blamed Timothy," she said. "I didn't know Chukka none, but Randy were a decent enough bloke. Always treated me well. Nice buns. Huge big piece of meat he had on him, too. Filled me up, it did."

"Jesus, sis. Don't go there. I can't be hearin' 'bout your sex life. "It ain't right you talkin' to me like that."

"What sex life?" she said through a lewd laugh. "With Randy gone, I'm practically a nun now. Costin' me a fortune in batteries for my dildos."

Pat's expression of distaste matched Kaine's feelings on the matter.

"Jesus, Rainey. That's enough. Turnin' my stomach, it is. An' Christ knows what Dad would say if he heard you. You're what, seventeen? Reckon the old man still thinks you're a virgin."

"Bollocks," Rainey shot back. "He can't hear nothin' from down in the hold. An' I know you ain't gonna tell him nothin' neither, or he might get to know 'bout how you're cuttin' the skank and skimmin' off the profits. And don't think I ain't seen how you take advantage of them pretty, young illegals. So, shut yer fuckin' piehole afore I shut it for you."

"Christ's sake, girl. You're a whore. Worse than your fuckin' mother."

"She were your mother, too," Rainey snapped.

"Shut it. Isaak's gonna hear ya."

"Nah, he's still hangin' over the side. Worst sailor I've ever seen. I reckon he turns green when he's takin' a bath."

They laughed, their quarrel apparently forgotten.

"Rainey, Jack!" A third, deeper voice—from behind and below Kaine and Pat—interrupted the sibling's conversation. "I've cleared away the panels. Any word from Planck?"

Kaine ducked further into the shadows.

"Hang on, Dad!" Jack called out loud and lowered his voice to add, "Check the radar, girl. I'll keep Dad sweet."

"Why do I have to do all the work 'round here just 'cause I'm the girl?"

Kaine had heard more than enough of the sweet, family interchange. He tapped two fingers to his chest and then pointed to the hold, communicating, "*I'll take the dad.*"

With his index finger, he pointed to Pat and turned it to the wheelhouse, giving the order, "*You take the kids.*"

Pat nodded his understanding and edged around the side of the wheelhouse towards the door, rifle raised. Kaine stood and trained his weapon on the black maw that was the open hold. He held up three fingers and counted down.

Three ... two ... one ...

Chapter Thirty

Monday 7th December — Pre-Dawn

Andros Freeway, The Solent, Off Southampton, England

While Kaine covered the hatch to the hold, Pat jumped up, kicked open the wheelhouse door, and yelled, "Armed police! Armed police!"

Rainey screamed.

Jack shouted something Kaine couldn't catch over Pat's single gunshot.

A head covered by a woollen beanie, the father, poked above the rim of the hold, all wide eyes, open mouth, and misaligned teeth. Kaine allowed him to scramble part-way up the ladder—one hand holding the top rung, the other a pistol, which he rested on the deck—before breaking cover.

"That's far enough, Captain Freeway," Kaine shouted.

The man's eyes found Kaine's. He raised his gun, trying to aim and climb out at the same time. Kaine's reaction shot hit the teak deck below the father's face. Pencil-length splinters exploded upwards and buried themselves into Freeway's chin. He howled and reared back. Kaine's second shot whistled past the man's left ear.

Rainey screamed again. "Dad!"

"The next one's a kill shot," Kaine yelled above the howling wind. "Very carefully, lower the gun to the deck and climb up."

Glowering pure hatred, Freeway bent forwards and set the weapon down.

"Slide it away."

Reluctantly, he obeyed. The gun skittered across the weathered planking and fell into the waterlogged scuppers.

"My kids? I-I heard a shot." He looked past Kaine and into the bright light flooding through the open wheelhouse door.

"Concern from the man who brings his son and seventeen-year-old daughter on a smuggling run? How touching."

Kaine lowered his C8. The red target laser picked a spot over the man's heart.

"Alpha Three," he yelled over his shoulder, but without pulling his focus from the father. "Everything okay in there?"

"Yes, boss. Warning shot only. The lass tried reaching for a gun. You?"

"No problem here," Kaine said. "Okay, *Captain* Freeway, out you come. No sudden moves. And don't bother looking for Isaak. He took a midnight dip."

Andros Freeway's skipper climbed fully onto the deck.

Once upright, he stood between the hold and the wheel-house, one hand picking wood from his chin, the other thrown up and out from his side to maintain his balance on the wildly pitching deck.

"Who the fuck are you?"

"Less of the language, *Captain*. I can see where Rainey gets her foul mouth from."

Freeway's scowl knitted his bushy, grey eyebrows together under his woollen hat. His chin dripped blood onto his off-white, roll-neck sweater. A salt-stained donkey jacket, jeans, and heavy boots, all of them black, completed the "hard-working trawler man" disguise. He looked the part, but Kaine wondered when the last time the man had actually pulled any fish from the water.

"You know who you're messin' with? You know who I work for?"

"*Andros Freeway* is registered to one Wayne Gregory Free-way. That's you, *Captain*, but she's actually owned by a company registered in the Channel Islands. A company which, in turn, is owned by a miserable coward named Jerome Tedesco. You'll probably know him as Teddy. Ah, I can see by your reaction I'm right."

Freeway lowered both hands and stretched to his full height, way over six feet. He had broad shoulders, a barrel chest, and a trim waist. Not a man to treat lightly.

"This is an act of piracy," he boomed. "Mr Tedesco's going to tear you apart."

Kaine smiled. "He's already tried that, but I'm still here. Okay, in you go." Kaine stepped to one side and jerked his head towards the wheelhouse. "Don't make any sudden moves. I'd hate for your delightful daughter to see you with a hole in your chest."

Freeway ducked under the metal lintel and twisted

towards Kaine, his face dark and angry. "Leave her out of this. She's an innocent."

Not quite as innocent as you think, Wayne, old man.

"Play nice and no one gets hurt. Now, in you go. Quick as you like."

Kaine removed his finger from the trigger before he prodded the C8's muzzle into Freeway's kidney. The smuggler grunted, grabbed his back, and scrambled into the light. He rushed to hug his daughter. Jack, a slightly shorter and slimmer replica of his father—but without the beanie or the grey flecks in his hair—stood in the corner, eyes fixed on Pat's C8.

Both daughter and son had a slight chin cleft, and their brown eyes, olive skin, and black hair showed a Mediterranean ancestry. She appeared impossibly young and innocent—how misleading looks could be.

"You okay, girl?" Freeway asked.

She nodded, said nothing, but looked up at Kaine through big eyes. No sign of fear. No sign of tears. Calculating her options. Unless Kaine was very much mistaken, she'd be rivalling Tedesco as the firm's head honcho in a few years.

Jack, on the other hand, looked close to breaking down. His lower lip trembled, and he panted, working his way towards hyperventilation. Kaine had seen similar evidence of shock in rookies during their first exposure to battle.

"Take it easy, Jack," Kaine said, keeping his voice calm and low. "Slow your breathing. Nothing bad will happen unless one of you does something stupid. Alpha Three, take the kids below. Captain Freeway and I are going to have a little chinwag."

Pat de-cocked his C8, slung it across his chest, and drew

his Glock. He pointed it at the inner hatch jutting out from the centre of the wheelhouse. "After you, youngsters. And step away from the lower rung when you reach it. I'd surely hate to have to shoot either of you. Away you go, now."

Rainey threw a glance at her father, who nodded. She led the way, closely followed by her brother. Pat waited for them to clear the foot of the ladder before climbing down, his back towards the ladder, facing out. He shut the hatch and slid the top cover closed above him, leaving the two captains to face each other.

Kaine made safe his rifle and hung it over his shoulder. He leaned against the door jamb and smiled. "Take a seat, Wayne. It must be uncomfortable bowing your head like that. Don't build these wheelhouses for people your height, do they."

Freeway swivelled his captain's chair around to face Kaine and climbed into it. He leaned forwards, jutting out his chin. It would have been intimidating if he hadn't winced when the action tugged at his fresh gashes and more blood dripped onto the off-white sweater.

"If your man touches one hair on their—"

"Don't worry, Wayne. Do as you're told, and everything will be hunky-dory. Trust me. Unlike Teddy Tedesco, I'm a man of my word." He glanced at the clock on the wall above the control deck. "Looks like you're behind schedule. Any blips on your radar? Brighten the screen."

Slowly, Freeway rotated a knob on the control panel and the radar screen glowed into green life. In the bottom right quadrant, a tiny, fixed blip showed Larry and the RIB-safe still in its holding position. Ten minutes out, no more. Dozens more blips and trails confirmed the English Channel as one of the world's busiest shipping lanes.

"We're never alone in the Channel, eh?" Kaine asked but received nothing but a glower in reply. "Which one's *MV Schiphol?*"

The boat's name elicited a response. The crinkled brows twitched, as did Freeway's mouth, but still he said nothing.

"Don't be surprised, Wayne. I know all about the meeting and the cargo, but I've been off comms for a while. I'm not privy to any changes in your schedule. Care to enlighten me?"

Freeway sneered. "Fuck off. I'm tellin' you nothin'. I don't talk to pirates."

Kaine sighed. "You want to do this the hard way? Fair enough."

He stripped open the Velcro seal from his drysuit breast pocket, drew out his SIG, and racked the slide in one fast motion. Freeway jerked back, his steel-grey eyes fixed on the gun. Few men in his position would have failed to show at least some fear. Despite the chill inside the compact wheel-house, sweat glistened on Freeway's face. He raised both hands, palms out.

"Now wait a min—"

"No, you wait."

Kaine stood away from the door and rolled in time with the bucking, pitching rhythm of the boat, at ease with the movement, using his ankles, knees, and hips as gimbals to keep his body upright and level. The light of understanding flashed in Freeway's eyes.

"Fuck. You're a sailor?"

"A marine. What gave it away? Rhetorical question, Captain. You don't need to answer." Kaine pursed his lips. "Let me make one thing clear. I detest drug runners. It's the same with people smugglers, pimps, and sex traffickers. You

314

ruin lives, and cause death and destruction in your wake. To me, none of you deserve any sympathy."

He paused to let his words drive home.

"So, this is the way we're going to play it. I ask a question and you answer it to my satisfaction. If you lie, or delay, I'll shoot you. It won't be fatal, but—"

"You wouldn't dar—"

Almost without taking aim, Kaine squeezed the trigger. The back of Freeway's right calf blew apart. The 9mm bullet from a SIG P226 at a range of less than four metres will do terrible damage to skeletal muscle.

Freeway howled, fell from the chair, and thumped to the steel floor. Blood splattered the bulkhead beneath the bench. Rainey yelled again, the sound only slightly muffled by the wooden hatch and the bulkhead.

The top hatch slid back, and Pat poked his head through the opening, leading with his Glock. "You okay up there, boss?"

"No problem for me, Alpha Three. The kids?"

"Tied to the table. One's seething, the other's wetting himself, but both are unharmed. You'll be needing the first aid kit, I imagine?"

Kaine shook his head. "Not necessary. We'll let this one bleed for a while. I'll give him one more chance. If he doesn't take it, you can bring up the lad. Jack, isn't it?"

Pat nodded at Kaine's hidden wink. "Right you are, boss. Let me know and I'll cut him loose for you."

Freeway's head jerked up, eyes pleading.

"No, no, please don't," he begged, all fight apparently gone. He struggled to right himself from the huddle on the floor. Although both hands were wrapped tight around the wound, blood still squeezed between his fingers. "I'll tell you anything you need to know. Just don't hurt my kids."

"Wanting to protect your children is highly laudable, but what of the other people's children hooked on your drugs? And the illegal immigrants you transport? What about them?"

Kaine stepped forwards, hooked a hand under Freeway's armpit, and dumped him unceremoniously into the chair. Sweat poured out of the man. Kaine backed to the doorway and studied the smuggler as he sat hunched over, still trying to reduce the blood loss.

"Don't worry," Kaine said without emotion, "I deliberately missed the artery. You'll probably walk with a limp the rest of your life, but you'll live—assuming you answer the rest of my questions."

Freeway nodded.

A beaten man?

Maybe. Maybe not.

"When's the rendezvous?"

Freeway read the time on the bulkhead clock. 02:57.

"Three fifteen. They were delayed leavin' port and have been battlin' heavy weather." He released a hand long enough to point at a blip on the radar screen. "That's her. That's *MV Schiphol*."

"How many in the crew?"

"Three. The skipper, Laurens Planck, his first mate, and a deck hand."

"How do they make the delivery?"

"She stands off a quarter mile. Planck lowers a lifeboat and ferries the goods across. In this weather, we'll shoot a line over the side and winch up the package. Ain't easy under these conditions, but we've had plenty of practice."

"Do you use a password?"

"Nah," Freeway answered. "Been doin' this every

month or so for three years. We know each other right well. He knows my boy, too. But he don't know you."

Kaine smirked. Freeway's plan was clear. He wanted Jack released. With two topside and free to roam, they'd be more difficult to handle. Freeway probably gambled on Pat not being able to shoot an unarmed girl. He'd be right about that, but Kaine wasn't going to give the captain an opportunity to put up a fight. He didn't want to add any more unnecessary deaths to his tally sheet.

"Don't get your hopes up, Wayne. Jack and Rainey are staying down below, out of harm's way. Think of them as being under my colleague's protection. You're just going to have to convince Captain Planck an injury has forced you to take on a new first mate." Kaine punched a thumb into his chest. "If he asks, you can call me Peter. Peter Sidings. Do you understand?"

Freeway's eyes darted around the wheelhouse, trying to find an alternative escape plan, before his shoulders slumped, and he nodded.

"Yeah, yeah. I understand. Christ, man, I wouldn't want to be in your shoes when Mr Tedesco gets a hold of you. He's gonna make you suffer."

"Let me worry about Teddy Tedesco. What's the cargo?"

"Thirty-five kilos of cocaine, from Bolivia via the Hook of Holland," he answered without hesitation.

"Street value?"

Freeway's expression turned wistful, and he shrugged. "A million, maybe a million and a half. What do I know?"

Kaine imagined the effect losing such an amount of product would have on Teddy's mood so soon after losing his brother. The day was going to be a shocker for the poor man. And yes, he was growing poorer by the hour.

"Far as I'm aware, drug smuggling doesn't operate on credit. What about payment for the cargo?"

Hesitation.

Kaine aimed the SIG at Freeway's left knee.

The smuggler flinched. "In a footlocker inside my cabin," he said through gritted teeth. "There's a waterproof box full of cash—three hundred grand. Used notes. After we've collected the cargo, I attach the money to a buoy and drop it over the side. Captain Planck collects it and then we weigh anchor."

"And if you don't deliver the money?"

"Dunno. Never happened before. Planck will probably go ape-shit and chase us down. He'll be armed to the teeth and his RIB is a damned sight faster than this old tub. He'd overhaul us in seconds. Did I tell you he'd be armed?"

Kaine tapped the webbing strap of his C8. "So am I. What's your fee for this job?"

"Twenty grand."

Kaine snorted. "You can kiss your payday goodbye, Wayne, old man. Anything else coming in apart from drugs?"

"No," Freeway answered, his face pale. The pain in his leg must have kicked in. "We're not expectin' any other cargo tonight."

"When we arrived, you were in the hold. What were you doing down there?"

Freeway grimaced as the boat plunged into a deep trough and jarred him against the control desk. More blood oozed down his calf. "Releasin' the side panels covering the hidden storage lockers. I-I don't like havin' the … cargo exposed one second longer than necessary."

"Excellent. Now you can have that first aid kit. Better patch yourself up before our visitors arrive."

Ordinarily, Kaine didn't like to deviate from a plan unless circumstances demanded it, but he saw an opportunity to deal Tedesco an even more damaging blow—an opportunity far too good to pass up.

"Alpha Three! Do you have a minute?"

Chapter Thirty-One

Monday 7th December – Pre-Dawn

***Andros Freeway, The Solent, Off Southampton,
England***

Kaine didn't have to wait long.

Pat popped his head through the top opening again, smiling brightly. "You called, boss?"

Kaine beckoned him forwards. Pat pushed open the hatch door, skirted around Freeway, and made sure Kaine had an uninterrupted view of the injured man while making his approach through the wheelhouse to the main doorway.

Freeway took a keen interest in Pat's movements.

Kaine raised his SIG. "Don't get any ideas, Wayne. The next bullet destroys a knee."

Without dropping his aim, Kaine backed out of the

wheelhouse doorway with Pat and lowered his voice. "Fancy going for another swim?"

Pat turned his head and cast a disinterested look at the boiling seas. "I'd be delighted, boss. What did you have in mind?"

As Kaine explained his plan, Pat's expression, which started as glum, slid along the scale to inscrutable, and ended up with a mischievous grin.

"Ha, love it, so I do," he said, adding a sly wink. "You can count on me, boss."

Kaine clapped him on the shoulder. "Always knew I could, but before you go, is everything set up down below?"

The grin morphed into a full-blown smile. "Sure, it is. And it'll make a nice little bang when you want it to."

"Excellent. Off you toddle, then. We'll pick you up in the RIB-safe in what, thirty-five minutes?"

Kaine left Pat to retrieve his CCUBA gear from the end of the knotted line and blocked Freeway's view through the doorway. While Kaine was briefing Pat, the smuggler had rolled up his trouser leg and applied a pressure bandage. He looked to have done a half-decent job. Working a fishing boat could be a hazardous occupation and, no doubt, Freeway had tended a good few wounds in his time.

Kaine kept one eye on Freeway and the other on the fast-approaching *MV Schiphol*, which was fighting the headwind and the tide in full flow. Freeway nodded at the scene through the starboard viewing window. *MV Schiphol*'s running lights punched through the spray-filled gloom—green on the left and red on the right indicating an oncoming vessel.

"Why's Planck showing navigation lights?" Kaine asked.

"Why wouldn't he?"

"I'd have thought a boat smuggling drugs would prefer to run dark."

"Shows how much you know 'bout anythin'," Freeway said, taking his turn to sneer. "A fishin' boat this close to shore at night without navigation lights would arouse suspicion, right? Coastguard would likely be here in minutes."

Kaine shrugged. "Makes sense."

"Where'd your mate go?"

"I ask the questions, not you." Kaine jerked up his chin. "Button your jacket. I don't want that blood showing."

Freeway did as he was told after stowing the first aid kit under the bench. For the first time since boarding, the radio crackled into life.

"MV S *to* AF, *receiving? Over.*" Captain Planck's Dutch accent was clear, despite the background noise and the signal interference. For the signal to be so poor over such a short distance, they had to be using a VLF transmitter. Sneaky. Not many coast guard stations were outfitted with the same equipment used to communicate with submarines close to the surface.

Kaine showed Freeway his SIG once again. "A little reminder, Wayne. Take care what you say."

Freeway nodded, picked up the press-to-talk mic, and said, "*AF* to *MV S*. Come ahead. Out." He released the PTT button and returned the mic to its clip.

"That's it?" Kaine asked.

Freeway sniffed. "What d'you expect, a full-blown chat about the state of the smugglin' business?"

"A well-oiled operation. If I didn't know what you were carrying and who you were working for, I'd almost be impressed."

"Teddy's gonna skin you alive. He don't tend to get his

hands dirty these days, but I guess he'll make an exception in your case."

Kaine smiled.

"He'll have to find me first."

He bent at the waist and released his dagger from its sheath. At a mile distant, no one aboard *MV Schiphol* would have seen him wave its honed blade under Freeway's nose.

"See this?"

How could he not?

"I gutted Teddy's little brother with this baby," he said, enjoying the shock and terror his words instilled. Freeway's eyes followed the knife's movements. "I slid this fifteen-centimetre blade between Pony's ribs and sliced open his heart. He wasn't as tough as they say. Bled like anyone else and squealed like everyone I've ever killed."

Kaine spread the "lunatic" vibe a little thick, but the effect was exactly what he wanted—shocked awe and abject fear. People in Wayne Freeway's line of work wouldn't pay attention to "please and thank you". They only knew the hard sell, and Kaine could play the tough man as well as anyone.

"If Teddy wants a piece of my hide, he'll need to find someone better than Pony to get it."

Freeway's mouth hung open, and his eyes bugged. "You? *You* killed Pony Tedesco?"

Kaine stared back, straight faced. "That's what I said."

"Fuck me," Freeway said, swallowing hard. "I heard the rumours but didn't believe it none. Over the years plenty of stories been circulatin' about Pony Tedesco. Figured most of them were bullshit … but, fuck. You killed Pony Tedesco? That's fuckin' … awesome."

Freeway's face broke into a hesitant smile, showing his brown, misaligned teeth.

"Anyone who kills that piece of filth has my respect." He pushed out a hand, offering to shake.

Kaine rejected the submission as another trick. Freeway kept his hand held out for a moment longer but dropped it when Kaine focused his attention on the radar.

Around eight hundred metres off, *MV Schiphol* hove to, turning to starboard and showing *Andros Freeway* her red, navigation light, with the white, masthead light to the rear. The starboard floodlights fired up, illuminating the water and making the port side relatively darker, hiding what was happening from passing traffic. The boats lay parallel in the water, stem to stern, *Andros Freeway* on a northwest heading, *MV Schiphol* pointing southeast. According to the radar's slide indicator, both boats drifted towards the English coast on an eight-knot flow tide.

Kaine shot Freeway a dark look. "Want you and your kids to live past tonight?"

The trawler man swallowed and nodded.

"Do whatever you normally do. There'll be a response, right?"

Freeway nodded again. "I need to move my arm and fire up the rest of the deck lights."

"Go ahead."

Freeway threw another switch on the control panel. The bank of starboard floodlights snapped on, and a brilliant, white arc bloomed over the foam-topped water. The rain had died a little since they'd boarded but, if anything, the wind had strengthened.

"What next?" Kaine asked.

"They lower the RIB. I prepare the harpoon and make ready to collect the … cargo. Jack normally helps me winch it aboard."

"I'll be Jack," Kaine said, grabbing a donkey jacket

hooked to the inside wall and tugging it over his drysuit. "You carry on. Where's the harpoon?"

Freeway's eyes bulged. "Kiddin', right? You fuckin' shot me in the leg. I can't walk, let alone work."

Kaine scoffed. "Suck it up, big guy. I've had worse injuries shaving."

Freeway hesitated for a moment before taking a breath and sliding his injured leg from the footrest and placing his foot on the floor. He hissed out a curse as he stood and added his full weight to the injury.

"Good boy," Kaine said, adding an encouraging smile. "That wasn't too bad now, was it?"

The big, brave, sweaty smuggler spat, "Fuckin' bastard," and held on tight to the back of the chair as *Andros Freeway* plunged into another trough before righting herself on the other side. Being hove to in a heavy sea made the ride more fairground Big Dipper than pleasure boat cruise, but smugglers didn't have the luxury of waiting for a break in the weather.

Poor dears.

Freeway glanced at the radar. He grunted and staggered backwards—counter to the natural sway of the boat—and dived headlong, hoping to catch Kaine off guard.

Kaine sidestepped to his left and raised his knee into Freeway's face. The captain groaned, slumped to the floor, and stayed down on his hands and knees, head shaking. Blood dripped from his nose, mixing with the rainwater lapping on the wheelhouse floor.

"Stupid, stupid move," Kaine said, almost sadly. "Why d'you have to go and do something like that? I'm going to kill you now. Then I'm going to do your brats."

Freeway pushed up from the floor, still kneeling. He threw his hands up, face pleading. "No, no, please don't. I'm sorry, I had to try. Kill me if you like, but please leave my kids alone. Please?"

It would have taken a total sociopath not to be affected by the man's words. If Kaine had intended to kill them, the father's pleas might have made him think twice, but they were unnecessary. He made a great play of looking from Freeway to the blade and back again.

"Nice words, Wayne. Very moving. This is your final warning. Behave yourself. Now get off your knees, wipe your nose, and start working. You're lucky Captain Planck's a bit tardy lowering his boat into the water." He nodded to the radar screen, which showed a tiny, grey-and-white dot peel away from *MV Schiphol*'s port beam. The little boat took a wide, anticlockwise course around the larger vessel's stern, and vectored towards *Andros Freeway*. Kaine judged the boat's ETA at less than three minutes.

He turned his eyes back on Freeway. "If he'd seen your dumb move, I'd have had to scupper this tub without giving you the chance to abandon ship."

"What? You're going to sink my boat?"

"That's what I said. What's wrong? You're insured, aren't you?"

"But …"

"Quit stalling. Where's the harpoon?"

Freeway held a hand to his nose, trying to stem the blood flow. Poor man had spilled a load of claret so far and, judging from its deflection, his nose was broken in at least two places. Still, it wouldn't affect Freeway's looks too badly. It had been broken before and even without the new damage, the man was no oil painting.

"Stowed in the aft locker." Freeway pointed to a rust-stained, metal box bolted to the port bulkhead.

"Okay, then. Go fetch, little doggy."

Kaine stepped back and allowed the man room to go about his work. Freeway hobbled to the locker and removed a gas-powered harpoon gun roughly triple the size of the one they'd used to board *Andros Freeway*. He inserted a tined harpoon with its feather-line attached, scrambled to the starboard gunwale, and waited.

Kaine couldn't avoid associating the image of Wayne Freeway resting the harpoon gun on the railing and pointing, with the memory of the night he took the same position with a rocket launcher and shot down Flight BE1555. He blinked the image away and drove the memories down into the depths. They would resurface later, in the quiet times between sleep and wakefulness, they always did, but right then, he had to concentrate.

The smuggler's RIB approached from the north, cutting into the cone of *Andros Freeway*'s floodlights, bouncing and bucking through the waves, throwing up huge arcs of white spray in its wake. The high-pitched whine of its single Mercury outboard barely cut through the roaring winds and screaming seas. Two occupants. The first sat at the helm, piloting the speedster, presumably Captain Planck. The second sat on one of the bench seats at the stern, holding onto the safety roll bar, an orange box the size of a suitcase clamped between his knees. When no more than fifty metres from *Andros Freeway* and safely in her lee, the pilot throttled back. The little boat stopped almost dead in the water, but the pilot fed in enough power to keep it on an even keel and running level with *Andros Freeway*.

Planck flashed the RIB's searchlight once, and Freeway pulled the trigger.

The harpoon gun hissed, and the one-metre-long dart flew, trailing its thin, white tail. The harpoon arced over the

RIB and disappeared into the murk, but the running line draped itself over the man guarding the orange case.

"Nice shot, Wayne."

While Planck balanced the power to keep the RIB pointing into the waves, his mate tugged on the running line. At the same time, Freeway, with Kaine acting as his helper, fed out the heavier line until it reached the small boat. The mate clipped the heavy line to the case and raised his arm. They were good to go.

Kaine stepped away, giving Freeway room to feed the line onto a powered winch and draw the cargo aboard. It took both of them to haul the case over the rail and dump it onto the deck.

Grudgingly, Kaine had to admit it was a smooth operation. Despite his injury, Freeway worked efficiently. Kaine almost felt sorry to slam his fist into the man's gut and knee him in the face again as he doubled over. Freeway collapsed to the deck alongside the cargo and lay still.

At first, the men in the RIB didn't react. To them, it might have appeared as though Freeway had tripped and fallen, but when Kaine swung the C8 from his back and took aim, their stunned reaction was almost comical. The mate threw himself below the line of the port tube, as though a few millimetres of reinforced rubber would stop a high-powered NATO round. Planck, who had supervised the unloading, clambered over his mate, desperate to reach the pilot seat.

Kaine stepped close to the gunwale, jammed his right thigh tight against the railing, and took as steady an aim as possible in the conditions. The RIB rose and fell, yawed and rolled. Planck's frantic movements made the boat even more erratic and unstable.

Focusing on his vision and ignoring all other sensory

input, Kaine breathed out slowly and decreased his heart rate. He squeezed the trigger. His first shot missed. As did his second, but the next three were more accurate. The third glanced off the stern bulwark, shattering the resin cover, and the fourth and fifth slammed into the Mercury's black, plastic cowling. The motor cut out. Without power to hold it in position, the RIB started drifting towards England's southern shore. Planck's anguished howl broke through the storm's roar. He yanked down the zip on his jacket and reached a hand inside, trying to tug something out from under his arm.

Oh no you don't, Captain.

Kaine took careful aim and fired again. The sixth slug smashed into the control panel next to Planck's right hip. The Dutchman's hand came out empty and he threw his arms in the air. At least he tried to, but the RIB's wild rearing threw him off balance and he ended up joining his mate at the bottom of the boat. The wind must have carried Kaine's belly laugh across the gap, because Planck's head appeared above the port tube, and he waved a clenched fist at Kaine.

Still laughing, Kaine waved back and watched in amusement as Planck shouted instructions at his mate, who ducked down into the boat and reappeared with a pair of short-handled oars. Watching the hapless pair of smugglers battling the waves and the current, and trying to paddle back to *MV Schiphol*, was worth the cold swim out to *Andros Freeway*. With advanced notice, he could have sold tickets.

"No point, Planck, old chap," Kaine yelled, "*MV Schiphol's* going nowhere."

Behind Kaine, Freeway groaned and tried to push himself up from the heaving deck. Once again, blood poured from his flattened nose. Kaine helped the stunned man to his feet, holding him under the armpits.

"Sorry about hitting you without warning, Wayne, but I needed to concentrate. Those weren't the easiest shots I've ever taken."

Freeway blinked and shook his head. "Huh?"

"Never mind. Let's get back into the dry. It's perishing out here, and I need to collect something."

With the knife, he sliced three metres from the end of the running line, grappled the groggy smuggler into the wheelhouse, and dumped him onto the floor. He tied Freeway's hands at the wrists and his wrists to his ankles, and left him sitting in a seawater puddle in the corner.

He opened the forward hatch and descended the ladder. "You kids okay?"

Jack said nothing but scowled at him through red, puffy eyes. On the other hand, Rainey's squawked insult to Kaine's ancestry would have made her ineligible for entry into polite society.

"Thanks for that, Rainey, dear. Won't be long now. Soon let you free. I need to collect something from your dad's cabin first."

Kaine found the waterproof sack of money where Freeway said it would be and carried it through the cabin and up into the wheelhouse, ignoring more of Rainey's high-pitched screeching. If she kept up the haranguing, the girl would strain something.

Back in the open air, Kaine switched on his comms system. "Alpha One to Alpha Two, receiving? Over."

"*Alpha Two, receiving you strength five. Ready for collection? Over.*"

"That's an affirmative, Alpha Two. Alpha Three, receiving? Over."

"*Alpha Three here, boss. Ready when you are. Over.*"

"You have a green light, Alpha Three. Green, green, green. Alpha One, out."

Kaine turned to Freeway. The man's eyes were wide open, and he seemed more aware of his surroundings.

"You might want to take a look at this, Wayne," Kaine said, pointing through the open door. "Crane your neck if you like."

Freeway frowned and shuffled forwards on his backside in time to see *MV Schiphol*'s stern erupt in a ball of fire. Seconds later the muffled crack of a water-suppressed explosion rippled across the sea.

"Fuckin' hell!"

"You asked where my friend had gone. As you can see, I sent him on a little errand."

MV Schiphol had already started to list, her stern and port beam settling deeper into the water. Kaine estimated she had less than thirty minutes to live. Before sending Pat on his impromptu mission, Kaine checked the radar and made sure there was enough depth below the hull that scuttling the Dutch trawler wouldn't prove a future hazard to shipping.

"My friend is very good at his job," Kaine continued. "He's allowed enough time for anyone left aboard to abandon ship. He's done the same for *Andros Freeway*."

Freeway's head snapped around. "What? There's a bomb on board?"

Screaming blue curses, Freeway shuffled and rocked and rolled, fighting to tear his hands free from their bonds.

"Take it easy, Wayne. I know how to tie a knot and the breaking strain of that line is beyond even a man as big as you. As you correctly guessed, my friend has planted a bomb. It's in the engine room. Do you know what a shaped charge is? Most of the force of the explosion will be focused down, into the hull. My friend estimates this boat will sink inside five minutes."

Freeway slumped back against the rust-pocked wall. "Kill me if you like but cut my kids loose, please." Tears rolled down his face, mixing with the semi-congealed blood. "Please?"

"What do you take me for, Wayne? Unlike your employer, I'm not a wanton murderer. You have an inflatable life raft, yes?"

Freeway glanced at the metal locker adjacent to the one that used to contain the harpoon gun and nodded.

"Excellent. I'll cut you free before I leave and give you plenty of time to escape before sinking this tub of rust. How long do you think you'll need?"

"I-I … forty-five minutes?"

"Nah, too long. I don't want you thinking you can disarm the bomb. Believe me, you can't. As I said, my friend is *very* good at his job. You'll have fifteen minutes from when I leave, understood?"

"You're going to be in the water when the bomb goes off?"

Kaine smiled and shook his head. "Thanks for your concern, Wayne, old chap, but look at the radar screen. Can you see it from there?"

The RIB-safe—piloted by the reliable, if under-utilised, Larry Kovaks—showed on the screen as a fast-moving blip headed straight towards them. If he concentrated hard enough, Kaine could almost hear the Yamaha engines' roar growing louder.

"When you land, do one thing for me will you?" Kaine said, being extra pleasant, as though at a restaurant asking a nearby diner to pass the salt.

"What?" Freeway answered, his face a Hallowe'en mask of tear-streaked dirt and part-dried blood.

Kaine patted the bag of money. "Tell Teddy the captain said, 'Thanks for the cash', would you?"

———

LARRY TIMED his approach on the RIB-safe to perfection and reduced the speed long enough to enable Kaine to pull Pat aboard and power away within seconds. Clearly, he hadn't lost any of his piloting skills since leaving the service.

Pat rolled into the bottom of the boat. Kaine left him to remove his CCUBA and used the grab ropes to haul himself forwards.

"Are they clear, Larry?" he shouted over the wind, holding the safety cage to stop himself being bucked out of the speedy, little craft.

Larry, one hand on the wheel, the other on the throttle, strapped securely into his seat with a five-point safety harness, nodded to the small radar screen.

"They're well away now, boss."

A small, green dot indicated a powered inflatable running in a straight line towards Southampton and away from the larger smear that represented *Andros Freeway*. Kaine read the digital clock.

"Well, will you look at that? Only took them nine minutes. I'll give Freeway credit for one thing. He knows how to drill his family in evacuation protocols." He twisted at the waist and gave Pat the okay signal. "Ready when you are, Pat."

The Irishman finished stuffing his gear into the side locker and dropped onto one of the rear bench seats. After fastening the lap strap, he held up a radio detonator. "Sure you don't want to do the honours yourself, boss?"

"No, I'm good, thanks."

Pat hit the red button. Two seconds later, *Andros Freeway* shuddered and the sea beneath her turned white. A soft thump reached Kaine's ears, barely registering over the storm.

Within five minutes, *Andros Freeway* slipped beneath the ragged waves, her starboard floodlights still shining bright, illuminating the grey waters as she headed to the bottom.

Larry turned his head away, Pat had the grace to look glum, and Kaine swallowed. Any sailor alive unmoved by the death of a vessel didn't have a soul. At least *Andros Freeway* had shipped her last cargo of drugs and transported her last group of sex slaves. Kaine chalked one up to the good guys, and clapped Larry on the shoulder.

"Take us in, Larry."

"Okay, boss. I'm looking forward to a nice, hot shower and a decent breakfast."

"Sounds good to me," Kaine said, turning away from the watery gravesite and facing the south coast of England.

"What next, boss?"

"Next, Larry, old chap, some of us are going to play a little bingo."

"Bingo, sir? Are you serious?"

"Open the throttles, Larry. I'll brief everyone at the farm."

Larry tugged on the two levers, the Yamaha outboards roared, and the RIB-safe raced towards the distant shore-line. Kaine wished he could be a fly on the wall of Teddy's penthouse home when he received his messages.

See you soon, Teddy.

Chapter Thirty-Two

Monday 7th December – Jerome Tedesco

Ocean Village, Southampton, Hampshire, England

Teddy slumped over his desk, head in hands.

"Shit! Shit! Shit!"

These days, he hated working through the night. Always put him in a bad mood. Back in the day, pulling all-nighters used to be acceptable, exciting even. Keeping on top of multiple schemes showed he was building a business, showed he was moving and shaking, but when things went wrong …

Fuck!

"Problem, Mr Tedesco?"

Teddy glowered up at Timothy's temporary replacement, the ginger-haired lug.

"What gave that away?"

Ginger had the good sense not to answer. Timothy wouldn't have asked the stupid question in the first place, but Timothy was gone, his body incinerated like the queer, Ashby. Fuck it, why'd the black bastard have to turn greedy all of a sudden? Teddy could have used the man's advice.

Ah well, water under the bridge.

He checked his Rolex. Five nineteen in the morning. Wouldn't be daylight for another two and a half hours. He rubbed his face, trying to drive some life into it, then looked up at the ginger dickhead.

"If you must know, that was Big Gino in London."

Ginger stared back, blank-faced.

"He wondered what happened at Garrett & Stimpson."

"The warehouse?"

"Yeah. He expected to hear from his team by now, but nothing. He ain't a happy bunny. Fucker practically accused me of stitching him up. Thinks I moved on his team. As though I could be bothered to whip up that kind of agro for a few hundred grand's worth of gold baubles. Fucking moron. But he's got juice with a couple of the big players in the Smoke. I could do without any hassle from those arseholes."

Ginger looked interested. "Want me to give—"

The intercom buzzed. He held up a finger to cut Ginger off mid-sentence. Elizabeth knew better than to interrupt him unless it was urgent. He'd never have kept her around if she wasn't such a useful filter. The bitch loved being in the thick of things, too. Came in early when he was busy even though he didn't pay her overtime. All she really wanted was a ring on her finger, and maybe he'd give her one some-time. Maybe. Rewarding loyalty was good for business. He'd read that somewhere. She was a fucking good lay, too.

Always had been. Looked good for her age, as well. A class act.

"What is it?"

"You need to turn on the local news," she said.

"Why?"

"There's been a robbery at the docks. Someone took down Garrett & Stimpson."

Teddy smiled and allowed the tension to ease from his neck and shoulders. Big Gino could stuff his accusations up his big, fat arse. Most likely, his own men were late reporting in. Either that, or they'd done a runner with the goods and Teddy's tribute. In which case, Big Gino would owe Teddy, not the other way around.

The day was starting to improve.

"Don't worry, Elizabeth. I know all about it."

"No, Mr Tedesco, it's not as simple as that. You need to listen to the report."

Teddy clicked off the intercom and dabbed an icon on his computer touchscreen. The radio channel opened up. He scrolled through to BBC local news and listened with growing frustration to the weather forecast.

Fucking rain. Rain and more rain. What else is new?

When the news finally started, Teddy's budding optimism hit the shitter. Despite the lack of an official statement by the plods, the reporters had stitched the information together. Someone had intercepted Big Gino's team. They'd left some dead bodies and others still alive, but bloody and broken for the filth to mop up.

Shit! Shit a fucking brick. The tribute!

"Elizabeth!" he yelled, ignoring the intercom. "Get Big Gino on the line again!"

Teddy hated eating humble pie, especially one that

contained a large dollop of dog turd, but if he played it right, he might still be able to save face.

His desk phone rang. Teddy picked it up. "Okay, Elizabeth. Put it through."

The line clicked and burst into a double ringtone. Big Gino answered on the eighth ring. Teddy took a breath and plastered a smile onto a reluctant face.

"Gino, thanks for taking my call. I'm afraid I have a bit of bad—'

"You fuckwad!" Gino screamed. "I just heard the job's gone to shit and back. I paid the fee in good faith, but you didn't hold up your part of the deal. Either you ain't the man in charge down there, or you got sticky fingers! Which one is it?"

"Gino, Gino, there's really no need for all this animosity," Teddy said, using his most placatory note, the one he'd heard the therapist use so many times. "I can assure you, this had nothing to do with me, or my people. From what the news report said, it sounds like your guys fucked up. My people were doing other things last night. How certain are you of the security at your end? I mean, how many of your people knew about the job?"

"Fuck off, Teddy. Only me and the gang knew about it, and Jonah, the inside man. They ain't likely to stitch themselves up, are they?"

"No, but if they're amateurs, they could—"

"Amateurs! Jesus, you don't have a single fucking clue. The guy in charge is my son-in-law, Val. He's a pro and has been for years. That team is skilled. Never been caught until they try a job on your turf. You know what that tells me, Teddy?"

"No, Gino. What does it tell you?"

Teddy knew what was coming, but the anger bubbling

in his gut and threatening to eat through his stomach wall wouldn't let him back down to a fat, London-based, Italian prick. Who did he think he was, talking to Teddy Tedesco like he was a jumped-up guttersnipe from the East End? He was Teddy-fucking-Tedesco, the man people feared. The man who could snuff out a person's life as easy as snapping his fingers.

"It tells me you're past your sell-by date. It tells me you're finished."

"Now listen to me, Gino, you fat fuck. I reckon you've been trying to stitch me up for years. You've been poaching my men, haven't you, fuckwit? Ginger was fucking right. You set Captain Arsewipe on me and got the inside shtick from Timothy, didn't you!"

"What? You've popped a rivet!" Big Gino roared. "Captain Arsewipe? Timothy? I got no idea what the fuck you're—"

Teddy lowered his voice, made it menacing. "I'm gonna spread the word Big Gino's a lying, backstabbing, Wop bastard. I'm gonna tear you a new one!"

He slammed the phone into its cradle and rubbed his hands together, trying to wipe away the anger and the sweat.

Ginger replaced the handset of the extension and raised his eyebrows.

"Nice one, boss. You told him good."

"Don't give a toss what you think, dickhead. What I do want is for you to find out what happened at that warehouse. I'll put you in touch with one of my contacts from the Boys in Blue, and you can go 'help the police with their inquiries'. Got it?"

Ginger's eyebrows knitted together.

"What's up?"

"Don't like the idea of talking to the filth. Goes against the grain. They're evil fuckers. Ain't one of them can be trusted."

"In the words of the Prime Minister at PM's Questions, I refer you to the comment I made a short time ago."

"Huh?"

"I don't give a rat's arse what you think. You wanted Timothy's job. Do as you're told, and we'll make it permanent."

"Didn't realise it was temporary."

Ginger's frown made him look like a slapped arse. Christ. Couldn't get half-decent staff these days.

Teddy picked up his internal line and dialled Mother. The poor love didn't sleep well these days and appreciated his call whenever he had a moment.

As usual, she took an age to answer.

Teddy turned his back on the ginger fucker to maintain his privacy but didn't lose sight of him in the glass door of his drinks cabinet. No one was going to sneak up on Teddy Tedesco.

"Jerome, my darling boy," Mother said, her soothing and gentle voice making his morning just a tiny bit more palatable.

"Sleep well, Mother?"

"As well as can be expected for an old woman close to meeting her Maker. I had another dream about your father. He's looking forward to seeing me again in the Afterlife."

"Mother, I wish you'd stop talking like that," Teddy said, keeping his voice low enough for Ginger not to think he was turning soft. "You're in the prime of your life. And how many times do I have to tell you, my name's Teddy. No one calls me Jerome."

"Your brother calls you Jerome."

Not anymore, he doesn't.

"That's only when he's trying to annoy me, Mother. You know what he's like. Always trying to get a rise out of people."

"Yes, dear. That's his way. No harm in him really. Antonio always was a highly strung boy."

"Yes, Mother. Highly strung. That's a good way of describing him."

Highly strung? Strung out's more like it.

"That reminds me, dear. Where is he?"

"Where's who?"

"Antonio. I haven't seen your brother for ages. Days. It really isn't like him to ignore his mother for so long. When he calls, I'll give him a piece of my—"

"Mother, I'll get him to call next time I see him."

No point upsetting her with news of Pony's condition, or lack of it. He needed to break it to her gently.

"Thank you, darling. What time is it? Oh Lord, it's not even six o'clock. What are you doing up so early? Or didn't you sleep last night? You can't keep these late hours anymore. You aren't as young as you used to be. Remember what happened to your dear father. Worked himself into an early grave. You're not far off the age he was when he passed. His poor heart gave out, sitting at his office desk. I do worry for—"

"Mother, I eat healthily and take plenty of exercise. You don't have to worry about me."

She never learned how the old boy really passed, and Teddy certainly wasn't going to tell her.

"But you're my little boy. Of course I'm going to worry about you, dear. Actually, you sound a little tense."

"Maybe a little, Mother. It's why I'm up so early. The world of international finance never sleeps. In fact, I'm waiting on a call from my broker in Hong Kong. The Hang Seng is in a state of flux right now. Oil prices are down, too. I might have to sell some stocks to cover a shortfall."

He hated lying to Mother, but if she learned the truth it would kill her. Out of sight of Ginger, he crossed his fingers.

Mother never could pick up on his fibs. "Why don't you take a break this afternoon and join me at bingo? It's been ages since we played together, and the mental challenge will help you take your mind off your business troubles."

Bingo? Why couldn't she give it a rest?

Oh crap!

Dread struck him hard. Why hadn't he thought of it earlier? The one place she was vulnerable was at the bingo hall. If Captain Arsewipe and Big Gino couldn't get to Teddy directly, what was stopping them getting to him through Mother? Dread brought on a cold sweat.

"I'm sorry, Mother, but that's completely out of the question, and, to be honest, I'd really rather you stayed home for the next few days."

"Absolutely not. It's my one pleasure in life. Why would you want me to stop playing? I thought you loved me?"

"I do, Mother. I love you very much, but the … weather is looking really treacherous over the next week. Hang on, I tell you what. Why don't you sign onto one of those online sites? They have bingo running all day, every day. You could play to your heart's content."

"Electronic bingo? Oh dear me, no," Mother scoffed. "Not the same thing at all. There's no atmosphere, and I'd miss Barry Mandel. Such a funny man, he does so make me laugh. And I'd miss my friends, too."

"But Mother!"

"No, no, I won't hear of it. Don't ask again."

Fuck!

"Okay, okay," he said, desperately trying to think of an alternative. "How about I send someone else to help look after you? Your driver, what's his name?"

"Henry, dear. Nice man, but a little gruff. Not much of a conversationalist."

I pay him for his brawn, not his wit.

"And he's rather large and not very attractive. He intimidates the other ladies when he stands over me. Some of them have stopped sitting beside me."

"That's as maybe, but Henry's a good, safe driver. Never had an accident, but he did say there were a few unsavoury-looking characters hanging around the hall on Friday. Delinquents, he called them. Coloured boys. I'd feel a lot better if I could send someone else along to help Henry. Would you mind?"

She tutted. "Oh very well, but only if he's pleasant-looking. What about that nice, young German fellow? He's presentable and rather nicely spoken."

Teddy smiled at the mental image of the Kraut wowing a group of wizened, old crones at bingo. It would serve him right for being such a pretty boy and for sucking up to Mother. That being said, the fact he'd behaved well under fire at the fuckup at the Yellow Diamond warehouse was a point in his favour, and the Kraut still had some credit saved up from locating the Shafer woman.

Yes. Schechter would go down well with the old dears. And he'd send a few more bruisers as out-of-sight backup.

"Okay, Mother. I'll have Hardy Schechter escort you to bingo every day until the weather improves."

Ginger's reflection in the glass door waved its arm. Teddy swivelled his chair. The redheaded one looked worried, thoughtful. The mutt held up his mobile and waggled it in the air.

343

"Mother, the call from my broker just came in. I'm going to have to go, but promise me one thing, will you?"

"What's that, Jerome?"

"You must do what Mr Schechter and Henry tell you. They know how to protect you from the delinquents. Do we have a deal?"

Mother sighed, feigning annoyance—he recognised the pretence. "Yes, dear. We have a deal so long as you don't work too hard."

"I won't, Mother. I'll pop down to see you before you leave, and we'll have a nice cuppa. Bye-bye now. Bye-bye. Love you."

He ended the call before she could say anything else and looked across to the other side of the room.

"This had better be important for you to interrupt me talking to Mother."

"It is, Mr Tedesco," the redhead answered, pointing to a string of texts on his mobile. "It's Schechter out at the track."

"What? What the fuck's up now?"

"They've been hit, boss."

"What!"

"They've been hit. Sounds like three men hit the place. The access road's been blown up and—"

"Three men?"

"Yes, sir."

"Three men overpowered nine of my guys—all of them heavily armed—and the Post Call clowns, and then they took my money?"

Ginger dithered. "Er, not really, sir." His twisted upper lip made him look constipated.

"How much did they get away with?"

"It's all gone. A little over two-point-three million. But they didn't exactly take it."

"What d'you fucking mean, 'They didn't exactly take it'? What the fuck *did* they do with it?"

"They, er … torched it, Mr Tedesco. With a fire-bomb. Actually, with two fire-bombs according to Schechter."

"Jesus H Christ. Two-point-three million up in smoke?"

"Yes, Mr Tedesco."

"What happened to my men? All dead?"

"No, sir. They were left … safe and sound and … four were tied to a post in the middle of the winner's enclosure. Barely a mark on any of them, but the racecourse is a mess. Hundreds of thousands of pounds worth of structural damage."

"Fucking Jesus! When did this happen?"

"Round about two in the morning, sir."

"What? That's more than three hours ago and they're only just calling it in?"

"The place is a disaster area, Mr Tedesco. The phone lines and internet were down, as was the mobile phone system. Took them ages to call the fire brigade, and they couldn't get close enough to fight the fire. Everything's destroyed—grandstand, offices, stables, the lot. Schechter had to leg it across the fields to the nearest working mobile phone on a local farm. He's only just gotten through."

Stunned, Teddy flopped back in his chair.

"You're telling me that three men destroyed the racecourse and all my cash, and the fuckers I pay big money for just stood around with their fingers stuck up their arses? Is that what you're saying?"

Ginger shrugged. "Just reporting what I've been told, Mr Tedesco."

Teddy stood and picked up his computer monitor. He

threatened to throw it across the room but managed to hold himself in check. He dropped it back to the desk and slumped into his chair.

"Fuck! Think yourself lucky I'm not a Roman senator, you redheaded shit-for-brains!"

The big man frowned and stared over Teddy's head, clearly not understanding the reference.

"They used to kill the messengers who brought bad news, Ginger. Didn't you know that?"

"Did they, Mr Tedesco?"

"Either the Romans or the ancient Greeks, or the fucking Krauts. Who the fuck knows? It's all ancient history. Maybe it's in one of these books."

"Kind of like what you did with Johnno Ashby, you mean, Mr Tedesco?"

Teddy stopped ranting long enough to take a breath and think. "You know what, Ginger? You aren't as thick as you look. That's exactly right. Maybe I'm channelling a Roman senator."

"Or an ancient Greek one, Mr Tedesco?"

Teddy shot out of his chair, planted his fists on the desktop, and stared down the red-haired, red-faced clown. "You taking the piss?"

The merest flicker of the man's thin lips showed something—what? Annoyance? Anger? Fear? All three? It had better be fear, or the ginger mutt might be getting uppity, and Teddy wasn't having that. For now, Ginger would keep, but something else gnawed at him, like he'd forgotten something.

Shit.

"Where's Isaak?"

"I don't know, Mr Tedesco. Didn't answer the radio this morning, and I haven't heard from him."

"What the fuck? It's pushing six o'clock. Where is he?"

"He went out on the boat last night, sir. You sent him to monitor the merchandise."

"I know that. He isn't back yet?"

"No, Mr Tedesco."

"What the fucking hell's going on? Things are turning to shit and no one's telling me anything."

The intercom clicked again.

"Mr Tedesco," Elizabeth said, "I have Captain Freeway on the line. He says it's urgent."

Shit-a-brick. Now what?

Chapter Thirty-Three

Wednesday 9th December – Early Afternoon

New Century Bingo Hall, Southampton, Hampshire, England

Kaine hunched his shoulders to lose a couple of inches in height and blend a little better with the aging crowd. At his side, Lara did the same. They edged forwards in the queue.

The New Century Bingo Hall had seen better days. The bull-nosed, Art Deco façade could have used a fresh coat of plaster and paint, and the windows were either in need of a good clean or replacement glass. However, the grime didn't seem to worry the constant stream of little, old ladies filtering through the rotating doors. Those unable to climb the flight of ten concrete steps to the entrance used the sloping ramp, some pausing occasionally to recover their breath between excited chatter. Willing helpers pushed the wheelchair-bound up the retro-fitted slope. All were wrapped up against the biting wind in warm coats, hats, and scarves. Umbrellas pointed into the stiff breeze. Stalwart British matriarchs battling their way to the games with every bit as much determination as the spectators filing in to watch the gladiators of Rome, Kaine imagined.

A few of the congregation, the bingo-worshippers, were below pensionable age, and a few were men, but the youngsters stood out against the crowd of blue-rinse women.

Being part of the crowd was not Kaine's preferred option, but short of sending Mike in his place—which was never going to happen—he couldn't think of a better alternative. With Lara on his arm, her hair streaked with grey and wearing padding around the waist, old-fashioned court shoes, and an unflattering, woollen coat, they blended in with a crowd eager to take their seats before the three o'clock commencement.

Inside, the place was nicer, warm, and with cream-coloured walls picked out with green piping. The ticket collectors did a roaring trade, as did the tea and cake shop in the corner.

Kaine hadn't played bingo before and neither had Lara, but Mike—whose wife used to be an aficionado—had given them a crash course. It seemed simple enough. The player buys as many randomly numbered grids as they can afford or reasonably monitor. A caller pulls table tennis balls from a bent metal cage, shouts out a cunning code related to the numbers written on the balls, and the players dot out squares on a grid. Prizes are paid to the first player who fills in all the corner numbers, lines, or the whole grid.

How difficult could it be?

After Mike's five-minute overview, Danny described the

game as, "Nothing too taxing, and nothing to get worked up over. A few quid in prize money will hardly raise anyone's blood pressure."

Mike's response, giving numerous examples of grand-mothers coming to blows over decisions in the heat of battle, raised hoots of laughter from Kaine's hard-bitten warriors.

Kaine and Lara followed the stream of ladies through a large, wooden door and into the auditorium. He held back, leaning against the tiled wall beside the door, breathing heavily, scanning the place for their targets. It didn't take long to spot them. Far corner, front row, with the best view of the stage. Two men in dark suits stood either side of a fire exit, guarding a grandmotherly woman seated at a table on her own.

From his elevated position, Kaine watched her spread out twelve purple grids, lined in three horizontal rows. None of the other women in the hall had anywhere near that number. The closest Kaine could find was an old dear with a dowa-ger's hump, seated third row back in the centre who was flanked by ladies of a similar vintage. The woman planned to work nine grids. According to Mike, anyone playing more than eight grids could be considered a Bingo Grand Master.

He turned Lara to face him. "Listen carefully," he said, keeping his voice well below the enthusiastic hum of the pre-match crowd. "You know I hate having to use you in a live operation, but I had no choice. Follow the plan. Do not deviate. If things go wrong, head for the front entrance, and do exactly what Rollo tells you. Agreed?"

Lara looked at him through Mike's late wife's horn-rimmed glasses and nodded. Even with greyed teeth and the ageing makeup, pancaked in place by Bobbie using the skills picked up in her drama classes, Lara was gorgeous. Her eyes shone, and she oozed vitality. A mature woman, but still stunningly beautiful.

"Don't worry, Ryan. I know what I'm doing. Your plan is fool proof."

"Jesus, Lara have you learned nothing? No plan is fool proof. This is a live mission, and those men in the dark suits will be armed. Anything can happen."

She smiled and squeezed his arm. "Ryan, we're in a room full of septuagenarians playing bingo. The worst thing that can happen here is if someone interrupts the game, and that's the last thing we're going to do."

"I don't want you getting hurt."

"Yes, I know, and I will take care. Did I ever tell you how distinguished you look with white hair?"

Kaine growled. "I've been going grey for years, and having you along isn't helping."

"And that walking stick really works for you, along with the flat cap and the half-moon glasses. Gives me a good idea what you'd look like as a granddad."

Doubt I'll live that long.

Lara's smile faded. She closed her eyes and trembled under his touch.

"You're putting on a brave front, aren't you?"

She nodded. "Truth is, I'm terrified."

"Good. Fear will keep you awake and aware. Adrenaline is your friend. Use it. You can do this."

"I know."

The bud in Kaine's ear buzzed. With no shortage of hearing aids in the crowd, he blended right in. He listened to the message, clicked the PPT button on his thumb mic twice, and smiled at Lara.

"Are the others in position?" she asked, making sure not to look at the men in dark suits.

"They are indeed. And Rollo's team has all three of Tedesco's outside men under surveillance."

Before he could say anything else, the PA system crackled into surround-sound life. "Ladies and gentlemen, please take your seats. The first game will start in five minutes."

For people who'd struggled to climb the steps, the stragglers could move remarkably quickly when forced to. Less than the allotted time later, the players had found their spots, most of the tables were full, and an expectant hush descended. The house lights dimmed and a dark yellow spotlight—that was probably meant to be gold—sliced through the air, illuminating the centre of the stage with an oval cone. The announcer took his time to introduce the caller as though he was bringing an A-list celeb into the fold. Barry "The Man" Mandel stepped into the spotlight, basking in the uproarious applause. The fake tan showed off whitened teeth, and he started working the crowd.

While Barry babbled on, Kaine and Lara hobbled around the outside of the hall. They ignored the vacant tables at the back and edged towards the solo player. By the time Barry took up his position behind his magic apparatus, Kaine and Lara had dropped into the vacant chairs beside their target.

When the houselights faded up again, Barry started calling, and a deathly hush filled the room, broken only by Barry's silky monologue, and the dabbing of thick, felt pens on pieces of card. If any of the players bothered to look up from their grids, they might have noticed a subtle change in the composition of the two men in dark suits. Whereas before the lights came back up, the one on the right had dirty-blond hair and was taller than his partner, they were now of similar height. The replacement bodyguards, Slim Simms and Pat O'Hara, stood straight and tall, hands clasped in front of their buttoned jackets. Neither smiled. Neither drew the attention of anyone in the room, but Kaine and Lara. Slim wore a blond wig and, despite the mocking banter from the rest of the men when he first put it on, the look actually suited him.

After a few minutes of drawn-out tension, a yell of, "Bingo," from the back of the hall, followed by a loud groan from a number of the players, interrupted Barry's flow. The oppressive silence lifted, and Barry called on his glamorous assistant to check the numbers. The floor walker—a squat woman of indeterminate age wearing an overlarge blazer with the logo of the establishment on its breast pocket— marched towards the potential winner with all the pomp and ceremony befitting her status.

As arranged, Lara turned to the elderly lady on her right, the former soloist. "Thank goodness. I need a rest," she said, breathing heavily and flapping a white-gloved hand in front of her face. The gloves hid the smooth skin of hands in their mid-thirties—a dead giveaway.

Still breathless, Lara continued her charm offensive.

"It's been years since I played. Exciting, but I'd quite forgotten how exhausting it is." She looked at the woman's cards. "I really don't know how you can manage so many grids. It's all I can do to concentrate on these three. Even so, I'm absolutely certain I missed a few numbers."

Mother Tedesco lowered her reading glasses. Her round face wrinkled into a benign smile.

"Why not check them on the board, dear?' she asked, referencing the large electronic screen on the wall behind

Barry. "I'll help you if you like. I did notice you were getting rather flustered."

Lara shook her head. "I wouldn't want to put you off your game."

"Nonsense, dear," she said, dabbing her felt tip on three numbers on Lara's upper card, and two more on the lower. "It's nice to have some company. Normally, I play alone. Not by choice, though. My over-protective son thinks I shouldn't leave the house, let alone mix with others."

"Surely not?"

"It's true, dear. See those two young men behind me, the ones in the suits?" she asked without turning away from Lara. "Would you believe they're my bodyguards?"

Lara placed her hand to her chest. "Really? Your son must be very important, and he clearly loves you very much."

Mother Tedesco's smile broadened. "He does. He does indeed. So much more than ... sorry, never mind. I do love him dearly, but sometimes I wish he wouldn't be so over-protective. Honestly, the way he behaves with his security men and making me ride in armoured limousines, anyone would think he was Chancellor of the Exchequer or the Prime Minister."

Making a five-star production of the process, Barry double-checked the numbers with the woman in the blazer and awarded the relevant prize for a horizontal line—ten percent off the price of the winner's next grid. The audience applauded and, after the tumult died, Barry resumed his calling. Two minutes later, an elderly man in the middle of a group of women claimed a diagonal and the checking process began again.

"Is that what your son is?" Lara asked, making the most of the opportunity. "A politician?"

"No, dear. He's a successful businessman. In fact, he owns this hall and a number of other businesses in Southampton." She leaned forwards and lowered her voice. "My Jerome owns a casino and a racecourse, too. I'm so very proud of him. I think he's a multi-millionaire, but he's ever so humble. He's bought me my own flat, you know. There's a maid and a nurse. Everything." She held out a wrinkled hand. "Veronica Tedesco. I'm ever so pleased to meet you, dear."

Lara took the hand and they shook. "I'm Edith, Edith Johansson. Please forgive the gloves, I have terrible dermatitis." She released her grip, turned to Kaine, and tapped his arm. He jerked his head up to simulate waking from a nap. "Albert, say hello to Veronica."

Kaine cupped a hand to his ear. "Sorry? What was that, love?"

Lara lowered her head and spoke into his chest pocket. "Say hello to Veronica. She's helping me to fill in my card."

Kaine screwed up his face and peered over his half-moons. "Nice to meet you, m'dear." He stood, groaning, and shook Mrs Tedesco's hand before addressing Lara. "I'm sorry, pet. Having trouble with the ... bally acoustics in here. He tapped a finger to his earpiece. "Mind if I find the nearest ... quiet spot?"

Lara's shoulders dropped. "If you must, dear. But no more than two whiskies before supper. Promise?"

"Of course. Far too early in the day for more than two."

He kissed her cheek and took his leave of Tedesco's mother. On his shuffling way to the fire exit, he smiled at Lara's excuse for him. "Poor lamb struggles in crowds. So proud. Hates to admit he's losing his hearing."

"My dear father was the same," Mrs Tedesco said, "and they call women vain."

Lara laughed and shot Kaine a hidden wink before putting her head down in search of something called a full house.

Leaning heavily on his stick, Kaine limped towards his men and paused in front of them long enough to blow his nose on a hankie.

"Any problems, Pat?" he asked quietly, not looking up at either man.

"Not many, boss. Schechter tried putting up a bit of a fight. The other one came quietly. Meek and mild as a three-day-old kitten, he was. Rollo's team has dealt with the external guards."

"Excellent." Kaine fixed Pat and then Slim with a steely eye. "If anything dodgy happens here, the doc takes absolute priority. Protect her first. Got that?"

Both men nodded.

"You can rely on us, boss," Slim said, firm and assured.

"That's why you're here." Kaine nodded and pushed through the door after taking one final look at Lara and his enemy's innocent mother.

He kept in character through the building and out to the car park but dropped it on climbing into the front passenger seat of the Peugeot Boxer hired specifically for the task. He nodded at Danny, who sat behind the wheel, wearing full battle gear, including chest and leg armour.

"Afternoon, Captain."

"Afternoon, Sergeant. How are our guests?"

Kaine twisted in his seat to face the cargo space. Dressed the same as Danny, Rollo sat on an ammo box, Glock in hand, guarding two of the prisoners.

As per Kaine's instructions, Rollo and Danny had bound the unnamed man's wrists and ankles together with cable ties. They'd also thrown a black, cotton hood over his head and secured it at the neck with duct tape. The hood expanded and contracted with the man's panicked breathing, but the material was porous. If he didn't hyperventilate, he'd be fine.

The second man, Schechter, was similarly trussed, only he was hood free, but gagged with a rag held in place with tape. Eyes wide and breathing as quickly as his mate, the German stared as Kaine removed his grey wig, false teeth, and glasses. Danny handed Kaine a damp cloth and he removed the old-man makeup.

"That's better," he said, dropping the cloth into a black, plastic bag for later disposal. "So, Mr Hardy Schechter"— the German stiffened at the use of his name, but Kaine carried on talking—"I imagine you're wondering what happens now?"

Schechter tried to swallow—not an easy thing to do when gagged and trussed much like an oven-ready Christmas turkey.

"I'm going to be honest with you, Hardy. If you hadn't saved the cameraman the other day, what was his name, Pickford? Yes, that's right, Pickford. If you hadn't dragged him to safety, you'd be dead already. Nod if you understand what I'm saying."

Schechter nodded vigorously. Sweat poured off him, dripping from the tip of his nose onto his trousers.

Kaine continued, driving home his message. "Bear in mind, I still haven't decided your fate. I haven't forgotten what you did to the dog at Breaker's Folly."

This time, Schechter didn't nod. He lowered his head— just about the only part of him he could move.

"Look at me, Hardy."

Schechter's eyes rolled up and locked with Kaine's.

"Good, that's better. Now, I'm about to ask you a series

of questions. Answer them to my satisfaction and you might survive to return to Hamburg and live out the rest of your life in tranquillity."

The man wearing the hood screamed something unintelligible and strained against his bonds.

Kaine nodded to Rollo, who removed a stun gun from his jacket pocket, pressed the terminals into the man's neck, and fired. The man bucked and spasmed before collapsing on his side in the foetal position.

"That really is hilarious," Rollo said, blowing on the terminals as if it were the muzzle of a six-gun.

"I imagine your friend was trying to tell you something," Kaine said. "Was he one of the men lined up at the warehouse to ambush me?"

Schechter grunted and closed his eyes.

"I'll take that as a yes. Okay, I'm going to have my friend remove your gag. If you yell, he'll zap you and you'll have given up your chance at life."

Kaine gave Rollo the signal. He put away the stun gun and pulled the dagger from the sheath on his right calf.

"Hold still now, son," Rollo said. "Wouldn't want to end up like Vincent van Gogh, now would we?"

He slid the tip of the knife under the tape in front of Schechter's ear, sliced it open, and ripped it away. Schechter winced, and blood flowed from a split lower lip. He licked the wound.

"Thank you," he said, voice cracked and dry. "M-Might I say something?"

"You just did."

"Excuse me? Oh … I see. The woman, Mrs Shafer … please believe me. … Until he mentioned sending his brother, I had no idea what Mr Tedesco intended to do to her. I thought he would order someone to bribe or intimidate her into keeping quiet. He has done that sort of thing before. I … am so sorry."

Kaine couldn't tell whether the man was lying through his teeth, but he moved on anyway. They had less than ninety minutes before the afternoon bingo session ended. Mrs Tedesco was a creature of habit. He doubted Lara could convince her to stay for tea and cake.

"Are you going to answer my questions?"

"*Ja*. Yes. After what Mr Tedesco had Ginger do to Randy and Chukka at the warehouse, I have no love for the man. You are The Captain, *ja*?"

Kaine nodded.

"Please ask your questions. I will answer them to the best of my abilities."

"How many bodyguards does Teddy have right now? How are they armed, and what's their current deployment?"

"Excluding Ginger, who stays at Mr Tedesco's side, there are"—he closed his eyes and creased his face to access his memory—"six men and one woman inside the building. All of the men carry semi-automatic weapons. As for the woman, Mr Tedesco's personal assistant, Elizabeth, I doubt she is armed, but I cannot be certain …"

Kaine spent five minutes pumping Schechter dry. In terms of the tower block's internal structure and layout, Kaine already had most of the answers, but he used the German to confirm Corky's most recent intel on the organisational structure. Schechter added a few valuable details—the day's passcode for the dedicated lift to the penthouse, for example. Not that Kaine intended going up to Tedesco. He had a different plan in mind.

This time, Teddy Tedesco would definitely be coming to him.

Chapter Thirty-Four

Wednesday 9th December – Jerome Tedesco

Ocean Village, Southampton, Hampshire, England

Teddy knocked back his second tumbler of whisky. So what if it was still early? He'd barely slept for two days. His body clock didn't know whether it was early morning or the middle of the night.

He stared through the rain-spattered window at the grey afternoon, hoping, for what? Inspiration? Bollocks. Watching the Solent, the dangerous stretch of water between the coast and the Isle of Wight, often had the power to sooth his spirits, but not today. Not since the bitch, Angela Shafer, and her damned mutt stuck their noses into his business. No, that wasn't right, it wasn't her, it was that bastard. Captain Arsewipe.

Teddy'd been on edge since Captain Arsewipe killed Pony and tore Teddy's carefully constructed organisation into ribbons.

By rights, he should have been feeling guilty about Pony's demise and what a cock-up that had been. Teddy'd given his fuck-up baby brother a simple task. "Disappear" a single middle-aged woman. How difficult should that have been? A quick in and out, slice and dice, and hide the body. That's all Teddy wanted, but no, Pony had to play silly buggers. He had to drag it out and use that psychological torture bullshit to earn his jollies. And then he'd molested her. Stupid fuckwit. Why couldn't he have just killed the bitch and be done with it? Absolute moron.

Teddy should have known better. Pony had always been a liability. A loose cannon. A pain in the arse.

Pony, the lunatic, wouldn't be missed by anyone with any sense—anyone except Mother.

Don't go there, Teddy. Leave Mother out of it.

In the end, Captain Arsewipe had done him a favour, not that Teddy could let it slide. If he didn't get payback, he'd lose face, and that would lead to disaster. Lose face in his game and he would take his turn on the slippery slope to oblivion.

Fuck, what a ball-ache.

What the hell was going on in the world when an honest businessman with a tight organisation and a small army could be picked off by a few morons with guns? And to cap it all, the tell-tale tightening at the front of his head warned of an oncoming migraine. His first for years.

All I need.

Gorge rose to Teddy's throat. The last time he'd felt so helpless was when Jerzy Harrow's mob murdered Father. It had taken three weeks to earn payback. Those three weeks had been the most frustrating of his life, until now. At least back then, he knew the people responsible for Father's demise, but this situation—the one with Captain Arsewipe and his pack of hyenas—turned out worse, far worse. He had no idea who or where the bugger was, or what his end game might be.

Captain Arsewipe didn't really give a toss about protecting some random, middle-aged cow who'd witnessed a body dump and had been on the receiving end of Pony's twisted, little game, did he? No, it had to be something else, something more. The arsehole had to be working for Big Gino, who'd been after a slice of Teddy's south coast pie for years. Fuck that. Over Teddy's dead body would he let Gino Dragoni move in on his territory.

And that was another thing. He probably shouldn't have blown up at Big Gino like that. Disrespecting a man with Gino's connections might end up biting Teddy on the bum. Maybe he ought to send an olive branch. Extend the hand of friendship.

Fuck it.

Plenty of time for that bollocks.

Scowling, he turned his back on the uninspiring view, pushed away from the window, and marched to his desk. He leaned over and hit the intercom button.

"Ginger. Get in here now!"

The office door swung open, and the redheaded assassin-cum-bodyguard entered. At her desk in the outer office, Elizabeth manned the phones, fielding calls and keeping the day-to-day business, the legal stuff, purring. Sitting sideways to his office she wore one of her severe, grey, skirt suits, professional-looking and glacier cool. Tasty. He'd make her a partner one day—or so he kept promising her.

"Yes, Mr Tedesco?" Ginger said, staring hard, eager to please, but as thick as a side of beef.

He might've been an efficient killer, but he didn't have a fraction of Timothy's intellect.

"What's happening?"

"Sorry, sir?"

Christ, give me strength.

"What's happening with the search? Where's Captain Arsewipe?"

Teddy paused for a moment, but before Ginger could answer, he continued.

"Millions," he said, quietly seething. "Two nights ago, that bastard cost me millions. He dropped me in the shit with both the Dutch and Big Gino, and then he just disappears into … where? The stratosphere? I've heard nothing for two stinking days! What are you doing to find him, hey? Like I told you, I want the fucker's bollocks toasted and on a dinner plate, right here."

He stabbed a finger at the leather insert in the real, antique desk.

The bodyguard's cheeks bunched. He looked pained. "He seems to have … gone to ground, sir. Disappeared. I talked to your contacts in the police, and they don't have a Scooby. The description Wayne Freeway gave them is just about useless." He frowned in concentration. "Slim build, average height, forty-something, with a neatly trimmed, dark beard, and wearing a wetsuit. Could be any beach bum on the south coast. Freeway couldn't describe his partner either, except to say he set the bombs and had an Irish accent. Shit, one of the pigs, Detective Sergeant Anderson, muttered something about it having all the hallmarks of The Provisional IRA." Ginger snorted. "Total bollocks, of course. The Provos haven't had the infrastructure in place to carry out something like this on the mainland for the best part of fifteen years."

"Go on," Teddy said when Ginger stopped talking to look at the screen of his mobile.

"It's the same crappy description with the teams at the racecourse and the warehouse, only they were in combat gear and wore camouflage makeup. Three teams of three, nine men in total. All highly skilled and the raids were coordinated, timed to coincide with each other. The cops reckon they're probably ex-military, maybe mercenaries."

Teddy dropped into his chair, causing it to bounce and squeak. He poured another drink. Ginger stared longingly at the bottle and the full glass.

Dream on, fool. This is the good stuff. Not for the likes of you.

"So, the cops think they're 'probably ex-military, maybe mercenaries,' do they?" he said, allowing his words to bleed sarcasm. "That's what they think, is it?"

Ginger opened his mouth to answer but Teddy's angry snarl silenced whatever facile remark he was about to spew into the world.

"If that's all the filth can come up with despite their state-of-the-art equipment and the money they take from honest taxpayers, it's no fucking wonder the crime figures are skyrocketing. A bloody cretin could have worked that out. Military uniforms, weapons, and explosives? Of course they're shitting ex-military mercenaries!"

He knocked back another sizeable portion of whisky and allowed the fiery warmth to settle his heart rate before signalling Ginger to continue.

"I've got feelers out, Mr Tedesco. Every man and woman on the payroll and every rat in the county is on the lookout for the fucker and his people but, like I said, he's in hiding. I don't know what else to do except wait for him to make his next move. I've hired six more men, like you said, and doubled the door security at all the casinos and night clubs. They'll be starting next week. I've also made contingency plans to double the guard during the next cash collection. And I'll supervise that one myself."

While Teddy mulled over his response to Ginger's so-called initiative, the mobile in the redhead's hand buzzed. He looked at Teddy, asking permission to answer. Teddy stared back at him, watching his latest right-hand man squirm.

"Who is it?"

"A text, sir."

"Better check it, then. Could be useful."

Ginger read the screen, frowning and scrolling through a long text. The delay gave Teddy time to think.

Why had all this crud fallen on his shoulders? Normally, things rumbled along nicely with only a few pimples and ruts in the road to upset the smooth progress of the business. Teddy preferred not to interfere. Liked to consider himself a good boss, easy to get along with unless forced to protect his interests. Why would anyone want to mess with the equilibrium? Why?

Ginger raised his head. "It's Birdy out at the track."

"What the fuck's up now?"

"They've been hit again, boss."

The dread returned, deeper and darker, turning the inside of his mouth to dust.

"You're kidding, right? What's left to hit? The fucking place is in ruins."

Ginger's face resumed its normal, vacant expression.

"Birdy says every time they try to fix something, it's bombed again. Yesterday, the contractors patched the biggest hole in the road, the one near the main gates. Last night another bomb went off. Undid the repairs. Same thing with the phone lines. Someone keeps cutting the bastard things." He shrugged apologetically and added, "Birdy reckons the saboteurs are trying to delay the rebuild."

"Really? With that insight, Birdy should apply to join the cops."

"Huh?"

"Never mind."

"What should I tell Birdy?"

"Tell him to set guards. I want the place up and running for the next meeting in March."

"With all the injuries and desertions, we're running light on men, Mr Tedesco."

"Well, hire more, you clown!" Teddy screamed. "Do I have to think of everything?"

Another shrug from the dumb ox nearly had Teddy reach for the gun in his desk drawer and shoot the fucker in the face, but before he could say anything else, the private phone rang.

The world stopped spinning.

Couldn't be Pony and Mother would never interrupt bingo to make a call.

"It's him," Teddy said, "Captain Arsewipe. Get on the extension."

Ginger hurried across the room to the spare desk and waited, right hand hovering over the handset.

Teddy nodded, and they picked up the phones at the same time.

"Yeah?" Teddy asked, playing it cool.

"Hello, Teddy," Captain Arsewipe answered, calm and relaxed. "How are you today?"

"What do you want?"

"No pleasantries? Suits me." The voice hardened, turning to steel. "You've had enough time to stew. I thought it was about time we had another of our pleasant, little chats."

"So? Chat away."

Teddy could play the hard man, too.

"In person, Teddy. We need to meet face-to-face. And this time, you won't bottle out and send lackeys to ambush me. You don't have enough men left. No, this time, you'll come in person."

"And why would I do that? I'm happy enough here in my office where it's warm and safe."

Captain Arsewipe's mocking laugh grated on Teddy's nerves, but he held himself in check rather than ranting pathetically at a disembodied voice.

"Think you're safe, do you?"

"Try coming in here and see how far you get."

Ginger smiled and gave Teddy an encouraging thumbs-up—as though he needed it. He gave Ginger a dead-eyed stare in return. The redheaded man's smile dropped away and he lowered his hand.

"Teddy, Teddy, Teddy," the mocking bastard said, sounding disappointed, "I have a rocket launcher aimed at your office right now. One press of a button will remove the top two storeys of that block, and I won't have to dirty my hands."

Fuck, is he serious?

One glance at the blood draining from Ginger's already pale face told Teddy all he needed to know.

"Don't talk bollocks," Teddy said. "If you had something like that, we wouldn't be having this conversation. This building would be a ruin and I'd already be dead. You're lying."

Despite resorting to bravado, his standard response to threats, Teddy's words sounded hollow, even to himself.

"I never lie about such things. I'm guessing your ugly mate, the backstabbing Ginger, is listening on the extension in your private office?"

Christ, the man knew everything.

How?

"What of it?" Teddy asked, trying to keep calm, but the sweat running down his forehead and stinging his eyes gave him away.

"Are you there, Ginger? Or would you prefer Geoffrey Hendricks?"

Ginger's jaw dropped. "How the fuck—"

"I know many things. So, is it Geoffrey or Ginger?"

Ginger looked at Teddy, once again asking permission to speak. Teddy nodded.

"Either will do, scumbag."

"Ginger it is then. So, tell me Ginger, before your dishonourable discharge from 2 PARA, did you ever have the chance to test fire a PAAS-3?"

Ginger swallowed hard and his shoulders jerked back.

"For the benefit of your ignorant boss, tell Teddy what a PAAS-3 is, Ginger. Go on. I'll wait."

Teddy hit mute on the phone. "What the fuck's he talking about? What's a pas-thingy?"

"It's a Portable Air-Attack System, Mark III. A shoulder-mounted rocket launcher," he answered quietly. "Civilians used to call them Bazookas."

"Dangerous? Can it do what he says it can?"

Still holding the phone to his ear, Ginger jumped up

and crossed to the edge of the window. He leaned to one side just enough for one eye to peer past the frame and see through the glass.

"And some," he answered.

"See anything down there?"

"No, but the PAAS-3 is highly accurate over its full, twenty-mile range. With a laser target lock, the bugger could fire it in Winchester and still be guaranteed to hit us."

"Hello?" Captain Arsewipe said. "Has Ginger confirmed what I told you?"

Teddy released the mute button. "Yeah, he did, and so what? If you really had one of those things, you'd have used it by now. You're bluffing."

"Oh Teddy, Teddy," he said, mocking again, "unless I'm playing poker, the one thing I never do is bluff. The only thing stopping me from pushing the button is not being able to see you die. In short, it would be too quick for you. If I blow up that building, I'll never hear you beg for mercy. I'll never record your babbling apology to Angela Shafer for what Pony did to her. She needs closure, and your pre-death confession is going to give it to her."

Teddy clamped his knees together to stop them knocking. The captain wasn't just an arsehole, he was a stone-cold killer. A raving lunatic. He even made Pony look stable. Teddy took a breath, trying to steady his nerves.

"Well, in that case, what's stopping me staying here until the police or my men find you and kill you? You said it yourself, I'm safe as houses in here. You aren't going to touch me. And I doubt you'll be able to stop me taking in supplies. I can order food online and stay in here forever. So, fuck you, *Captain*."

"Teddy, can I ask you a question?"

"If you like," Teddy asked, dialling up the generosity.

No point holding back the smug. He was staying put and there wasn't a thing Captain Arsewipe could do about it.

"When was the last time you spoke to your mother?"

Oh Jesus. Oh fucking Jesus.

Chapter Thirty-Five

Wednesday 9th December – Jerome Tedesco

Ocean Village, Southampton, Hampshire, England

Teddy dropped the phone and jumped out of his chair. He skirted around the desk, heading towards the second office door, the one leading downstairs to Mother's rooms, but no …

What was he thinking? Mother wasn't home. She was at bingo.

Fucking hell! Bingo!

Christ, if anything happened to her …

Still standing, he snatched up the phone, hit mute again, and screamed towards the office door, "Elizabeth, call Schechter! Ask him if Mother's okay."

"Mr Tedesco," Ginger whispered, waving the extension at him. "The captain ... he's still talking."

Teddy rested a fist on the desk, released the mute button, and pressed the phone to his ear.

"...couldn't protect her. Shall I put him on the line?"

Captain Arsewipe stopped speaking, obviously waiting for an answer.

"What? What was that? Repeat yourself, man!"

Captain Arsewipe sighed. "Okay, just this once. I understand you've had quite a shock. I'd also be upset if someone kidnapped my mother and threatened to torture the old dear."

Oh God. No!

"Harm my mother and I'll make you wish you'd never been—"

"Yes, yes. You keep threatening me, but here I am, still breathing. Still a thorn in your side. Funny that, eh? Whether or not I start hurting your mother depends entirely on you, Teddy, my man. What I said before was, don't bother asking Elizabeth to contact Hardy, I have him here with me. Would you like to speak to him? He's still conscious, just about. And, by the way, we've also taken care of your backup men. You know, the ones you had guarding the perimeter of the bingo hall."

Teddy tried to stop panting, but his nervous system was running on overdrive and wouldn't obey his commands.

"Yes," he said eventually, barely able to speak.

"Yes what?"

"Put Schechter on the line."

Captain Arsewipe laughed. The madman actually fucking laughed. He had Mother at his mercy and was laughing about it. Teddy sat. He clenched his arms tight against his sides, balled his free hand into a fist, and rocked slowly backwards and forwards.

"Say please." Again, Captain Arsewipe mocked.

"What?"

"You heard me. I said, 'Say please.'"

Fucking bastard. The absolute fucking shit.

"Put Schechter on the line. *Please*."

"Very well, as you asked so nicely, here he is. … Hardy, old chap, you can talk now."

Something scratched against the mouthpiece on the other end of the line, causing a loud crackle. A man coughed.

"M-Mr … Tedesco?"

A German accent. Schechter!

He sounded weak, his voice was muffled as though talking through swollen lips. Oh God. Teddy's stomach lurched. It was true. They *did* have Mother.

He fought the need to retch.

"Schechter, is that you?"

"Y-Yes, Mr Tedesco … I am s-sorry. Too many of them … overpowered us. T-They killed Henry. Shot him in the throat. I-I tried to stop them but—"

A fizz, like an electric buzzer, was followed by a yelp and a thump—like a body falling. The scratching returned and then stopped.

"That's more than enough of him," Captain Arsewipe said, a sneer clear in his voice. "Never could stand to hear a man whining. It's so unbecoming. Okay, Teddy, what's it to be? A meeting man-to-man, or shall I start sending your dear mother back to you one small piece at a time. Maybe I'll start with a big toe. Or an ear?"

Teddy nearly cried out, begged him to stop, but showing any weakness at this stage would be fatal to Mother and to him. Could anyone be so vicious to an old lady? Could the man be bluffing?

"Mother's old and frail. She's never hurt anyo—"

"Neither has Angela Shafer!" Captain Arsewipe snapped, showing seething anger for the first time. "But you still sent Pony after her."

Teddy shut his mouth. He'd miscalculated badly.

In the call's background a man screamed. Schechter? A second scream. Captain Arsewipe followed his muffled, "That's enough for now," with a clearer, "Did you hear that, Tedesco?"

Teddy couldn't bring himself to respond. He threw all his efforts into thinking of a way out. He needed a plan—a plan of action.

"That wasn't a rhetorical question, Teddy. Answer me, damn you."

"Yes, yes. I heard it."

"That's what it sounds like when a man's having his thumbs removed with a pair of garden secateurs. The next screams you hear will come from Mother."

Teddy fought the need to scream himself, but he wasn't beaten. Not beaten.

Play him, Teddy. You'll find a way out. You have to.

"No, stop. Don't hurt her, I'll meet you. Tell me where and when."

"The basement carpark of your building. You have ten minutes."

The car park. A nugget formed, far off. Yes, there it was—the idea. He just needed time. Time to work it through.

"Christ. Ten minutes? I-I …"

"Clock's ticking, Teddy. Mother will be very upset if you're late."

The line clicked dead. Teddy threw the phone down and turned to Ginger.

"The bastard thinks he's given me no time to plan." He depressed the switch on the intercom. "Elizabeth, call every man in the building. Tell them to meet me by the lifts on the second floor right away. Make sure they're fully armed. They're going to earn their keep for once, plus a bonus for killing a miserable, shit-faced clown. You stay here and keep your head down."

"Yes, Teddy. Please be careful."

"Don't worry about me, love. I'm the man with the plan." He turned to Ginger. "Want to earn yourself half a million quid?"

"To kill him?" Ginger nodded to the phone on Teddy's desk.

"Yeah, that's right. The second he releases Mother, you off the son-of-a-bitch."

"What about you? Where will you be?"

"I'm going down to the basement to keep him occupied."

Ginger looked from him to the office door and back again. Teddy read doubt and fear in the pale blue eyes.

"Half a million pounds, Ginger," Teddy said. "Think about it."

Greed replaced the fear, and Ginger nodded slowly. "How am I gonna get the drop on him?"

Gotcha. Greed beats fear every time.

"There's a private lift down to the basement car park. No one knows about it but me and Mother, and now you. It opens into the janitor's storeroom."

"Why don't you use that way to sneak up on him yourself?"

Teddy stood and opened the panel hiding the safe.

"Can't do that," he said, dialling in the combination. "The bastard's going to keep hold of Mother until he sees me."

The safe door sprang open, scraping slightly, despite the expensive repairs. Teddy reached in, removed the stacks, and threw them on the desk.

"There you are. Ten stacks, each with ten bundles of fifty-pound notes. Quarter of a million pounds. You'll get the second half when the captain's dead."

Ginger smiled. "Got a bag in there?"

"Stick them in your pockets, up your arse, I don't give a fuck."

Teddy reached into the safe once more and took hold of the Glock. It was heavy in his hand but felt good. Powerful.

Ginger finished packing away the money, stuffing every pocket. His smart, well-tailored jacket bulged at the seams. It made him look like a fat man wearing a suit two sizes too small.

Teddy checked the load on his Glock. Seventeen rounds. It would have to be enough.

He rushed towards the door leading to Mother's rooms, opened it, and signalled for Ginger to follow.

"The lift is at the end of the corridor. Passcode is 1-9-4-9. The year Mother was born. Express lift. It'll take you straight down to the basement. No dings, no bells, no announcements. Got it?"

"Yeah, I got it, but what makes you think the captain's going to go through with the exchange? If I were him, I'd just shoot you on sight."

Teddy sneered. "Yeah, me too, but I reckon Captain Arsewipe's different. Despite what he says and what he did to the Kraut's thumbs, I'm betting he's squeamish when it comes to innocent civilians. Look at the way he's protecting the Shafer bitch and her daughter. And he let the Freeways go, didn't he? I reckon he only killed Isaak 'cause Isaak was armed. And none of the men at the racetrack or the warehouse were seriously injured, remember."

"What about the bloke at the warehouse. The inside man. They murdered him, didn't they?"

"No, I'm pretty sure the London mob did that, not Captain Arsewipe's crew. I'm betting the prick's a boy scout at heart. I'll go meet him and wangle a swap, me for Mother. As soon as you see her free and clear, kill the fucker and anyone else you see. The rest of his mob will likely scarper the moment he hits the floor."

"Fair enough," Ginger said, removing his weapon from its shoulder holster and working a bullet into the chamber. "I'll see you later for the rest of my money."

Yeah, right.

"Do your job and you'll get your cash. You have my word."

Ginger sniffed, wiped his nose with the back of his empty hand, and headed through into the corridor without a backwards glance. Teddy closed the door quietly behind him and gave up a silent prayer.

Mother's life rested in the hands of a mercenary who couldn't even be bothered to carry a handkerchief. If things worked out as planned, he'd be forever in Ginger's debt.

Teddy hated the idea of owing anyone anything. In the end, he'd have to clean house. Half a million quid? Why the fuck should he pay a man extra for doing the job he was employed for? No bloody way.

First things first. Save Mother. Kill Captain Arsewipe, then get shot of a greedy, red-headed coward.

He checked his watch. Five minutes to go. Time to move.

"Elizabeth," he said, pushing through the door to the outer office and striding towards the lift, "are they ready?"

"Yes, Teddy. Six men, all armed and waiting for you, as you ordered."

Teddy checked his Glock again. The textured handle was slippery with his sweat, but the action worked well as he locked and loaded. Adrenaline coursed through his system, and he rode the natural, heart-thumping high. Before the week started, it had been ages since he'd killed personally, but after Ashby and Timothy, he was getting the chance to relive the process. The excitement of anticipation gave him a raging hard-on. Despite the stakes, and his fear for Mother, the thrill was intoxicating.

"Wish me luck, Lizzie."

"Kill them dead, Teddy. Kill them all dead."

He kissed her roughly, mashing his lips against hers the way she liked it, and headed to the lift.

Chapter Thirty-Six

Wednesday 9th December – Angela Shafer

Mike's Farm, Long Buckby, Northants, England

Angela's jaw still ached a little when she chewed, but it was improving all the time, and she could talk and even smile without too much pain. That she could even think of smiling so soon after so vicious an attack, showed the value of feeling safe, and being under the care of a good doctor.

Lara, the good doctor who wasn't actually a doctor, had been surprised that Pig hadn't broken her jaw. The swelling had started to go down, and the bruising on her stomach and legs was fading quickly, turning all sorts of weird colours. Bobbie would probably call it body art.

The very worst part of the ordeal was the way Bobbie and the men, and even Lara, looked at her with pity. All except the leader, Ryan Kaine. Such a strange, sad man. His eyes carried pain and love and sadness and anger in equal measure. When he looked at Lara, the love was obvious. The pain came on the rare occasion when Angela caught him alone. Was he thinking of the eighty-three people he killed on the plane—Jackie included? She saw the hate in Ryan's dark brown eyes and a cold, flinty expression hardened his face whenever he talked about Tedesco and discussed his plans to take the man down. The sadness lingered permanently, deep and sorrowful.

Angela recognised two different men behind the mask Ryan Kaine presented to the world. The kind, gentle, caring man she saw when he was attending to her and Bobbie's needs. The quietly spoken man quick to laugh and joke with his men. And she saw the second man, the stern, unflappable soldier. The fighter. To survive in Ryan Kaine's world, he needed the second, but he still tried desperately hard to hold onto the first.

To be the man she'd come to know and respect, he needed the humanity. He needed the support and friendship he found in his men, and also the love he found in the intelligent woman he called "Doc" in public, and "Lara" when he thought no one else could hear.

Without those things, he would be nothing more than the terrorist killer of Jackie and eighty-two others the newsreaders said he was.

Despite the traumatic circumstances, Angela was glad she'd had the chance to meet him, face-to-face, to understand who he was and why he did what he did.

Bobbie knocked on the door and entered the bedroom without waiting for a response, as was her way. Quickly, Angela covered herself with the bath towel, not wanting Bobbie to see the bruising again.

Too late.

Bobbie's lower lip trembled, but she fought back the tears.

"How are you, Mum?"

"Better, darling. Getting stronger every day."

Bobbie nodded and added a sad smile. "You do look better. I was going to make coffee. Fancy a cup?"

"Tea, I think. Afternoon tea with some of those fancy biscuits the nice, young man rather likes. What was his name again? Corporal Something-or-other."

Bobbie shook her head in exasperation. "You know very well what his name is, Mum. Stop your teasing. And he's a sergeant now. Sergeant Danny Pinkerton, but don't even think of calling him 'Pinkie'."

Angela smiled and managed to do so without wincing. "Wouldn't dream of it, darling. He seems like such a nice man."

"He is, Mum. Very nice."

"And you seem rather smitten."

"Too early for that, but …"

A worry clouded her face. Angela had seen the look so many times in Bobbie's life. A worrier to the core. "What is it, love? You're worried about him?"

"Of course I am. I'm worried for all of them, but especially Danny. They're putting themselves at risk to help us and I'd hate for anything—"

"I talked to Mike this morning," Angela interrupted, knowing exactly what Bobbie meant and feeling precisely the same way. "He told me a little about the captain and his men. Very highly trained, they know what they're doing, and Ryan would never take unnecessary risks. Although you're right to be concerned, of course, there's nothing to be gained by it, love. Nothing at all."

She reached for Bobbie's hand and gripped it tight to her bruised chest. "We need to be strong. Ryan's trying to help us rebuild our lives and … Oh dear, the waiting's horrible, isn't it?"

Bobbie nodded and kissed Angela's swollen cheek softly enough for it not to hurt.

"As usual, you're totally right. Must be an age thing. The waiting's driving me nuts, and Mike won't let me in the room with all the radios. You know that's what he's doing, don't you? He's listening to the feed from Tedesco's penthouse bunker. That's why I wanted to make coffee. I was going to take one into Mike, maybe get a chance to eavesdrop. What do you think? Fancy joining me?"

"Anything's better than sitting in this room, not knowing. Put the kettle on, and I'll be right with you."

Bobbie smiled. "Great. Mike would never say no to you. Hurry up, though. I've been waiting long enough already."

She rushed from the room, giving Angela the chance to throw on jeans and a jumper, and add a little concealer to cover the most exposed bruises. Angela took her time descending the stairs—her stomach and legs objecting to the enforced exercise the whole way down—and reached the kitchen as Bobbie finished pouring boiling water over the tea leaves. She replaced the lid on the pot and added a tea cosy. She'd already loaded the tray with mugs, the biscuit barrel, and a jug of milk. No one took sugar.

"Ready?" Bobbie asked, picking up the tray.

"When you are, love."

She followed Bobbie through the kitchen door, and they struck out across the mud-spattered courtyard. A weak sun threw out a bright, yellow light but little heat, and a bitter wind drove through the gap between farmhouse and barn, whipping dead leaves into the air. In the main paddock,

Dynamite whinnied a greeting. Angela smiled but didn't make the detour to nuzzle the beautiful beast as she wanted to.

By the time they reached the barn, she shivered and regretted not throwing a jacket over her shoulders. She knocked and snapped the lock on the small door inset into the larger, double barn doors.

"Mike?" she called, knowing better than to startle an old military man. "It's Angela and Bobbie. We've brought tea and bickies."

Darkness inside the barn made picking their way around tractors and rusted equipment difficult, but she led Bobbie to the rickety-looking wooden steps running up the far wall. They climbed to the loft space Ryan and Mike had converted into an operations centre. Halfway up the creaking staircase, she heard the disembodied, electronically enhanced words of a man and woman talking. Angela didn't recognise either voice. She stopped and listened.

"*Elizabeth. Are they ready?*" the man asked.

"*Yes, Teddy. Six men, all armed and waiting for you, as you ordered.*"

"*Wish me luck, Lizzie.*"

"*Kill them dead, Teddy. Kill them all dead.*"

Behind her, Bobbie gasped. "Teddy? Is that Tedesco?"

Tea mugs rattled on the tray. Angela's heart fluttered. She raced up the last five steps and burst into the room.

Ahead of her, Mike—a phone clamped to his ear—sat, leaning forwards, in front of a bank of computer screens. Some were powered off, others showed windows with the horizontal squiggly lines of voice traces.

Bobbie stepped behind Angela, accidentally bumping her with the tray. Mike turned and stared at them, a look of pure dread on his craggy face.

"Mike," she cried. "What's wrong?"

"It's Ryan and the men. They're walking into a trap."

"Call them. Call them now!"

"I'm trying, but they're operational, on local radio comms only. They've gone dark. Nobody's picking up."

Bobbie cried out. The tray crashed to the floor. Shards of crockery flew. Hot tea splashed Angela's ankles. She barely felt it.

Chapter Thirty-Seven

Ocean Village, Southampton, Hampshire, England

Kaine clicked the PTT button on his thumb. "Alpha One to all. The lift will be here in two minutes. Hold your positions. No firing until my orders unless they shoot first. No comms response necessary. Alpha One, out."

The underground car park looked and smelled like every other garage he'd ever had the displeasure of visiting. Poorly lit, with dark patches where the strip lights either failed to pierce the gloom or were burned out and hadn't yet been replaced. The smell, stale air mixed with exhaust fumes and scorched oil, was offensive.

Ten minutes was a long time to wait ahead of battle, but the delay served two purposes. It gave him enough time to work out the optimal deployment, without allowing Tedesco the opportunity to think, or call in more troops.

For the umpteenth time, Kaine tried to figure out what he'd missed.

With Pat and Slim protecting Lara at the bingo hall, Kaine commanded six loyal, battle-hardened, and highly skilled men. The opposition consisted of Tedesco, Ginger, and six hired hands. All were unknown quantities apart from Ginger, and Kaine had a special place set aside in Hell for that particular lowlife.

According to Schechter, the building's one lift could hold no more than four men. Teddy would have to split his troops. Anyone who'd studied military tactics—from Sun Tzu to Field Marshal Montgomery—knew it was a bad idea, as an overconfident General George Custer found out at Little Bighorn.

Under every scenario Kaine could envisage, he had the upper hand, but still the doubt remained.

He reviewed his deployment one more time.

In the darkening streets outside, he'd stationed Cough and Stefan. They wore police uniforms and were tasked with preventing civilians entering the building during the operation. They also had orders to take down any of Tedesco's men who managed to evade the trap and make it outside—unlikely, but not completely out of the question.

Kaine held the centre ground, hidden behind a concrete support pillar with a perfect view of the lift and the doors to and from the emergency staircase.

Rollo and Larry took Kaine's left flank, both hiding behind cars and both with a one-eighty-degree firing arc. The remaining two, Danny and Peewee, covered Kaine's right flank, their view partially restricted by the right-angled projection in the corner formed by the two jutting walls of the janitor's storeroom.

The white descent light above the lift doors flashed on, and an electronic bell dinged. Kaine ratcheted the slide on his SIG. No need for rifles in such a confined space. All his men were armed with handguns of their choice, Glocks and SIGs. Each weapon untraceable, provided by Rollo, and each expertly maintained and prepared. Kaine heard four other semi-automatics rack and load.

Time for action.

The lift dinged again, but the doors remained stubbornly shut.

"Captain?" Tedesco shouted from inside the lift. "Can you hear me?"

"Yes, Teddy. I hear you. Are you coming out, or do you want me to start posting bits of your dear, old mother through the letterbox out front?"

Kaine winced at the words, but needs must.

"The door to the staircase is about to open," Tedesco shouted. "It's some of my men. They're coming in to give me cover and protect Mother. They have orders not to shoot unless you do."

Damn it.

Kaine was impressed. It seemed as though Tedesco had read *Art of War.* The translators of Sun Tzu had a lot to answer for if even lowlife scum could learn from the best.

"Okay," Kaine shouted. "They can come out."

The staircase door opened. Three beefy men filed out. They wore ballistic vests and crouched behind transparent, police riot shields.

Crap.

Kaine hadn't seen that coming either. Tedesco clearly had the building—his bolt hole—set up to repel his rivals' incursions. No matter. As long as Tedesco thought Kaine had his mother, Kaine had the upper hand.

As a single unit, the three men shuffled sideways until they covered the lift door. Once in position, the man in the centre reached behind him and hammered on the door panel with the butt of his gun. Only then did the lift doors slide open to reveal three more men, who also wore ballistic vests. They were tall. So tall, they hid Tedesco.

"Nice work, Teddy," Kaine called. "I should have expected you'd be too scared to show your face."

"Can't see you out there, Captain. So, who's the coward?"

Kaine stepped out from behind the support column and leaned against its cold, solid bulk. He held his SIG against his chest, in full view, pointing it towards the low ceiling.

"Here I am, Teddy. Where are you?"

His plan required Tedesco to step out of the lift and for the lift door to close behind him. Without it, there would be a stand-off. The plan also relied on Rollo's timing, and Kaine had total faith in the big man.

Rollo's position had him twenty metres from his target with a perfect view of the lift.

Tedesco said something too quiet for Kaine to hear and the three men behind the shields stepped forwards one pace. This allowed room for the three in the lift to exit and fan out alongside their colleagues in a protective arc.

Again, Kaine was impressed. It looked as though the men had been drilled in the very manoeuvre.

A shadow moved inside the lift, but Kaine couldn't see what caused it until the guard behind the central screen dropped to one knee and revealed the man himself—Jerome "Teddy" Tedesco.

Although slimmer and pastier, and a full head shorter

than his monstrous, younger brother, Kaine would have recognised him anywhere.

The man of the hour scowled from behind his Perspex barrier.

"Well, I'm here. Where's Mother?"

Kaine smiled and shook his head. "Not yet, Teddy. First, I want to talk to your men."

"What? We're not here to fucking jabber. I want Mother here and I want her here right now, or my men will—"

"Start firing?" Kaine barked. "Really? What are they going to aim at? No, just hold your water for a while, Teddy, old chap. We'll get you your dear, old Mumsie in a minute."

The six men in front of Tedesco, only three of whom were protected by riot shields, looked at each other. The shields wobbled as three pairs of shoulders moved.

"You men listen to me," Kaine said, speaking slowly to make sure they could all hear what he had to say. "Teddy Tedesco is a lying piece of crap who sent his brother to rape and murder an innocent woman and her daughter."

"He's lying," Tedesco shouted.

"It's the truth. Whatever he's paying you isn't enough to die for. I have ten men in this garage, and they're all armed with armour-piercing shells. Your shields are useless and so are those ballistic vests."

Tedesco's defensive line shuffled again, their resolve clearly weakening.

"Leave the building now and you have my word no one will stop you."

"Nobody's fucking moving!" Tedesco screamed. He stepped one pace forwards and pressed the muzzle of his gun into the back of the neck of the man holding the middle screen. The lift doors closed behind him.

"Where's Mother. Where is she?"

"Now!" Kaine shouted.

Rollo pressed the detonator. A muffled pop behind the man standing on the far right of the screen made him duck. A small puff of smoke rose from the lift's control panel.

Tedesco spun. "What was that?"

"That, Teddy," Kaine said, "was the sound of my man disabling the lift controls. The lift's dead and you're stuck down here. No place to run. Okay, boys, last chance. I'm going to count to three. Anyone left in front of Tedesco leaves this garage in a body bag. One … two …"

The guard in the centre—the one with a gunmetal-blue jaw who'd felt the muzzle of Tedesco's weapon against his neck—dropped his shield, jumped up, and slammed Tedesco backwards into the lift doors. In the same movement, the guard, Blue, dropped his gun and threw his hands in the air.

"Don't shoot. I don't work for rapists. I've had enough."

The man to his right broke next. He lowered his gun to the floor and stood. Behind him, Tedesco shook his head, clearly stunned at the turn of events.

He screamed, "No!" His gun hand moved, but Blue and his mate spun and grabbed Teddy's arms. They twisted them up and behind his back, which proved the catalyst for the remaining four guards. They de-cocked their weapons and surrendered.

Well, that was easier than expected.

Teddy, struggling against his captors, screamed, "Where's Mother? Where's my mother?"

Kaine strolled forwards, checking his watch. "Probably playing her last frame of bingo."

"What? She's … what?"

Kaine stopped within arm's reach of the beaten man.

"Far as I know, she's safe and sound and still playing bingo. Unlike you, Teddy, I don't make war on women."

"You bastar—"

To Kaine's right, a door opened.

Kaine spun.

A gunshot echoed through the parking garage, the harsh sound bounced off the bare walls.

Peewee grunted, slid down the concrete wall, and slumped in a heap on the floor between two cars. Blood smeared the wall and flowed from a wound, but Kaine couldn't see its point of origin.

Danny stood alongside Peewee, eyes wide, arms outstretched, hands empty. An arm encircled his neck and a gun pressed against his temple. Behind him, partly hidden by Danny's head and raised shoulder, stared a blue eye in a pale face beneath a mess of flame-red hair.

Ginger!

"Anyone so much as moves, and this fucker's brains decorate the garage!"

Chapter Thirty-Eight

Wednesday 9th December – Afternoon

Ocean Village, Southampton, Hampshire, England

Options raced through Kaine's head.

Distance to target? Five and a half metres, maybe less.

Lighting? Poor, but adequate.

Atmospheric conditions? Not a factor.

With his gun still cocked and ready to fire, what were the odds of hitting Ginger's Glock with a snapshot under these conditions? Good but not excellent.

Chances of pulling off the shot before Ginger pulled the trigger? Zero.

With a gun pressed against Danny's temple, things looked bad.

Peewee moved, groaned. Still alive, thank God, but in no condition to help Danny.

What could he do?

"Sorry, boss," Danny said, struggling to talk as Ginger tightened the arm lock around his throat. "My fault. Bastard sneaked up behind us."

Ginger backed away, pulling Danny with him until stopped by the wall. His head turned, searching for a way out. He crabbed sideways, heading for the exit grill, sliding his left foot along the floor, searching for trip hazards. The gun at Danny's temple remained locked in place, pressed hard. No chance of him missing.

Kaine slowed his breathing. Danny needed his best work. In Ginger's careful movements, he saw a possibility. One slight chance. A gamble, but he was out of options.

Sorry, Danny. There's no alternative.

Kaine locked eyes with Danny, shouted, "You always were a fucking liability, *Corporal*," and turned to his captor.

"Shoot the useless fucker for all I care, or I will," Kaine continued, "but you're going nowhere."

One chance, Kaine. Take it.

Kaine raised his SIG and took careful aim at the centre of Danny's chest. Less need for a snapshot now. He held the weapon steady, waiting for Ginger's reaction, praying he wouldn't panic.

Ginger stopped under a flickering strip light, his crow's-feet wrinkles deepened for a second as his eyes met Kaine's.

Kaine hardened himself to Danny's shocked and hurt, "Boss?"

"Don't you 'Boss' me, you useless piece of shit. Never could rely on you. One job, that's all. You had one job, and you blew it. Peewee's dead, and it's all your fault. I've been carrying your useless bones for fucking years, and I've had enough. Hear me? Enough."

Ginger ducked lower behind Danny's shoulder, giving Kaine even less of a target. The handle of the Glock angled downwards as a result. It still promised death, but at least he'd created some movement.

"You know what, *Captain*," Ginger jeered. "I don't fucking believe you. I heard what you told Teddy-boy just now. You're one of those bleeding hearts. A lily-livered bastard dedicated to protecting the weak and the innocent. Pathetic. Wouldn't last ten minutes in a real firefight. You'd no more shoot your own man than I'd give myself up. I'm getting out of here and no one's gonna stop me."

He started moving again, dragging a reluctant Danny sideways. Kaine slowed his breathing further. Under no illusions, the minute Ginger escaped the car park, Danny's life was forfeit. With Peewee's blood pooling on the garage floor and no idea how serious his wound was, Kaine had to act fast. No one else was in a position to help.

Ginger and Danny reached Peewee's prone form. The redhead lifted his foot to step over the injured man. The Glock's muzzle slipped away from Danny's temple.

Forgive me, Danny.

Kaine fired twice.

The first shot slammed into the lower-left quadrant of Danny's ballistic vest near his gut. He grunted and jerked forwards at the waist. The second shot tore through the top of Danny's trapezius—the muscle between shoulder and neck. The bullet continued, its impetus barely slowed by the soft tissue and the vest's webbing strap. It smashed through the centre of Ginger's face, emerged through the back of his skull, and smacked into the concrete, its power finally spent.

Slowly, the corpse that had once been Ginger collapsed to the floor, taking Danny with it. Kaine raced forwards, caught his friend before he hit the deck, and clamped a hand over the gently bleeding wound.

"Two!" Kaine yelled to Rollo. "I need a medic here, double-quick."

"Yes, sir. I already called. Doc's on the way."

Some part of Kaine's consciousness registered activity in his periphery. Rollo, with Larry as his backup, barked orders at Tedesco and his remaining men. With things under control, Kaine allowed himself to concentrate on Danny.

The lad groaned, struggled to sit up, but Kaine, on his haunches, kept a tight hold.

"Danny," he whispered, "I'm so sorry, son. There was no other way."

"Don't believe it," Danny said, his breathing fast and shallow, but his speech strong. "I don't bloody believe it."

Kaine ground his teeth together, guilt and worry fighting for supremacy.

"I couldn't let him take you outside. He'd have killed you. How are you?"

"Dunno, boss. Stunned, to be honest."

Kaine shifted his hand to check the wound. It didn't look too bad, not as much blood as he'd first feared. His second bullet had torn through the webbing of Danny's ballistic vest and drilled a small hole through a few layers of skin and muscle, but hadn't hit an artery or smashed a bone. He pulled in a breath and let it out slowly.

"Shooting you was the only way to kill the bugger clean. Nothing else I could do."

Danny lifted his head. Slowly, a pained smile spread

across his sweat-shiny face. "That's not what I'm shocked about, boss."

"No?"

"All your effing and blinding? Never heard you swear like that before. Ought to be ashamed of yourself, boss. Setting a bad example for the troops. And what would the doc say?" He clapped Kaine on the upper arm. "Where's Peewee?"

Peewee!

How the hell could he have forgotten Peewee? Movement caught Kaine's peripheral vision. He spun.

Cough and Stefan burst into the garage, C8s raised and sweeping for danger.

"Four," Kaine called out, "check on Seven. Five, report to Two."

Without breaking stride, they separated to follow his instructions.

Cough fell to his knees in front of a groaning Peewee.

Stefan raced to help Rollo and Larry, but they had full control of the situation. Rollo had separated Tedesco from his armed guards. He was on his knees in front of the lift, hands on top of his head, fingers interlaced. He silently stared down the barrel of Rollo's Glock.

Lined up five metres to the right of their boss, and in a similar kneeling, hand-locked posture, the guards only had eyes for Kaine. Their awed, stunned voices rose above the background din.

"Did you see that?"

"The bastard shot his own man."

"Yeah, yeah, I saw it. Shot him to get to Ginger. Murdering fucker."

"Who, the bastard?"

"No, Ginger."

"What? I'm confused."

Rollo shouted for silence. The men clamped their mouths shut. They weren't that stupid.

Peewee groaned and struggled to sit. Cough, holding cloth to the back of his head, helped him up and leaned him against the wall.

"Not serious, sir." Cough announced. "Head laceration. Looks worse than it is."

"Okay, Seven?" Kaine called to Peewee. "You had us all worried for a minute."

"Not me," Danny said. "I had other things on my mind."

Peewee winced and gave Danny the finger.

"Don't worry about me, boss," he said, his speech pained but clear. "Hit my head on the bloody wall when the bugger back-shot me. My vest stopped the bullet, but I must have split my scalp open. Stunned me a little. Bleeding like a pig, it is." He kicked Ginger's lifeless torso. "I was only playing dead. Had the bastard in my sights and was waiting for him to get past me, but you got to him first. Bloody good shot, by the way, boss. I reckon some of the blood on my vest is Ginger's. Bits of brain matter, too. Nasty."

"Yeah," Danny said, heavily. "Don't worry about him, boss. He'll be cool. Never uses his head, anyway."

"Up yours, Three," Peewee snapped. "I'm in pain here."

"Me too," Danny said, smiling. "Bet I hurt more than you. You were only shot the once."

"Yeah, touché. You got me there."

Kaine nearly burst out laughing in relief but held it back for fear of it coming across as hysteria. Danny struggled against him.

"Boss, if you'll help me up, we can mop up here before someone outside calls the local plods."

"Good idea. I'm glad one of us is still thinking straight."

Kaine climbed to his feet, pulling Danny up with him and propping him against the wall. He took Danny's right hand and pressed it to the wound. "Keep the pressure on it until the doc can clean and stitch it up. Your shoulder's going to be a little stiff for a while. … Seven, did you lose consciousness?"

Peewee started to shake his head but flinched and tensed his shoulders. "Dunno, boss. Possibly. But not for long. Can't remember seeing the fucker take Dan—I mean Three."

"In that case, stay where you are for the moment. Four" —he looked at Cough—"organise someone to help escort him to the van. He's not to be left alone until the doc checks him out back at the RV point. I don't want him falling over and making more of a mess on the floor."

Peewee's grimace turned into a wry grin. "Thank you, boss. You're all heart."

Cough patted Peewee's shoulder, said, "Don't bloody move," and called to Stefan. "Five, gimme a hand here, would you? Our little mate's leaking all over himself."

Kaine gave them room to operate, left Danny where he stood after confirming he wasn't likely to keel over from blood loss, and looked down at his own hand. Red and sticky with Danny's blood, he was surprised to see it steady. No post-adrenaline tremble yet, but it would come soon enough. Hopefully later—when he was alone.

He wiped the hand clean on a trouser leg before dabbing the "activate" button on his earpiece.

"Alpha One to Team Bingo, receiving? Over."

"*Bingo One receiving. ETA, around seven minutes. Over,*" Slim said, sounding tense. In the background, Kaine could clearly make out Lara, urging him to hurry.

"*Ryan,*" she shouted, probably screaming into poor Slim's ear. "*Are you hurt?*"

"Bingo One, abort. I repeat, abort. The situation here is stable. No serious casualties. Continue to the original RV point. I repeat, head for the original RV point. Alpha One, out."

Kaine killed the comms link before Lara could try to override his command. She wasn't above playing the "medic takes precedence" card, and he didn't want to put Slim or Pat in an awkward position. Drawing a line under the ongoing discipline situation for the time being, he inhaled deeply and let the breath out slowly. He leaned closer to Danny and spoke quietly. "Sure you're okay, Sergeant?"

"And now I'm a sergeant again? You demoted me just now—when you were talking to Ginger. Up and down like a bloody yo-yo. I wish you'd make up your mind."

"That was a warning signal, to make sure you were ready for my move."

"Yes, boss, I did get it, but being shot's never fun. Next time, do you mind if we reverse roles?"

Danny's forgiving smile did almost as much to improve Kaine's mood as knowing Lara was safe and not heading straight to a crime scene.

"You mean next time I allow a bad guy to sneak up behind me and take me hostage, *Sergeant?*"

The smile vanished in an instant, replaced by an embarrassed grimace.

"Ah, yes. I take your point, boss. Fair play, I fucked up. My turn to apologise."

"I should think so, too. Stay there until we're ready to move out."

He left them to it and hurried across to Rollo and Larry.

"What now, boss?" Rollo asked without taking his eyes from the captives.

Kaine crossed his arms and stood over the kneeling men. All but Tedesco returned his look with a mixture of hope and fear.

"You," he said, pointing to Blue, the first one to have broken rank. "I gave you a promise, yes?"

Blue swivelled his head right and left, looking for support from his friends. He received none.

"What did I say?" Kaine prompted.

"You said if we lowered our weapons you'd let us go."

"So, what are you waiting for? Off you toddle."

Nobody moved until Kaine nodded to Larry, who turned his weapon away from the group and onto Tedesco.

"Not you, though, Teddy," Rollo snarled. "You stay right where you are, you piece of filth."

The six men hesitated for a moment, none wanting to be the first to test the truth of Kaine's promise. As expected, they took their lead from Blue and followed when he jumped up and raced away. For men who'd spent at least five minutes kneeling on a freezing, concrete floor, they moved quickly.

"That went tits-up for a bit," Rollo said, talking through the side of his mouth. "What now?"

"Now," Kaine answered, "we tidy up."

Tedesco unlinked his fingers and held up his hands. "Money? You want money. I-I can pay. Millions. I've got cash in my safe. And Ginger." He waved a quivering hand at the crumpled body. "Look in his pockets. He's got folding money. Lots of it."

"Four!" Kaine shouted without looking away. "Check the body. What's he carrying?"

Cough left Peewee to Stefan's tender care and patted Ginger down. He pulled something from a jacket pocket and held it up.

"Bloody hell. Cash, sir. Bundles of fifties. Loads of them. The bugger was a walking ATM."

Danny pushed away from the wall, a beaming smile showing the recuperative properties of certain kinds of paper.

"How much?" he asked, stepping closer to Cough.

"Dunno." Cough dived in again and kept pulling out more bundles. "Loads."

"Quarter of a million quid," Tedesco said, staring hard at Kaine. "There's more upstairs in Mother's rooms. Let me go and you can have it all. Take it. I'll disappear. Forget all about the Shafer women. I promise."

Kaine shook his head. "Think I'd trust the word of a man like you? The Shafers will never be safe as long as you're alive."

"So, what you gonna do? Shoot me in cold blood? Murder an unarmed man?" The idea took hold, and his voice grew more confident. "No, no. You won't do that. Don't have it in you. You've already proved that by not taking Mother. So, what's next? The police? I'll take my chances with the filth. There's no evidence against me. Elizabeth will be upstairs in the office right now, wiping the files. Sanitising the system. Nothing's going to trace back to me."

A gleam of triumph flashed in his eyes and a mocking smile formed. His nostrils flared. The man was triumphant. He'd beaten Kaine. Or so he thought.

"What you gonna do?" Tedesco repeated, folding his arms and leaning against the lift doors. "Nothing. Look around you. It's a battle scene. Blood, a dead body, and your men did it all. There's nothing to say I'm not the victim of an attempted kidnap. Your men's DNA will be all over the place. Nah, you're the one who's in trouble, not me."

Kaine turned his head to look at Rollo. "What do you think, Two? Are you scared yet?"

Without drawing his eyes from the prisoner or lowering his Glock, Rollo grinned. "Not me, boss. Are you?"

Kaine coughed a laugh. "Scared of Teddy's posturing and his empty threat? Not going to hap—"

The storeroom door burst open. A woman raced through the doorway. A silver gun glinted in her hand.

She screamed, "Teddy, I'm coming!" and fired wildly.

Bullets hit the roof, the floor, a wall, and ricocheted around the garage.

Kaine dived in front of Rollo. No thought, only action. A lance of fire sliced through his upper arm.

Two shots boomed from different points in the garage. Two men aimed and shot in lightning reaction. Each bullet hit the woman.

Two black holes, tightly grouped, punctured Elizabeth's pearl-white blouse. She staggered, stopped. Red patches spread from the black centres.

She looked down, then up. Confusion spread with the blood. Her mouth opened, and she tried to speak, but the words wouldn't form. She searched the garage until she found Tedesco and smiled, before crumpling in slow motion to the floor.

"Why?" Kaine asked, struggling to his feet, but rejecting Rollo's offer to help. "What the hell was she thinking?"

Damn it, what's wrong with people?

Tedesco dropped his hands to his sides and stared at the

fallen woman, his expression impassive. "Stupid bitch loved me. Can't blame her, though. Who wouldn't?"

Kaine snapped. He grabbed Tedesco by the lapels and slammed him into the lift doors. A head butt to the nose, a gut punch, and a knee to the groin put Tedesco on the floor, gasping for breath and spitting teeth and blood onto the concrete. Kaine wanted to tear, pound, mash the bastard's face into a bloody pulp, but Rollo pulled him off.

"Easy, boss. We wouldn't want to ruin the surprise."

Kaine struggled against him, but the red mist, the mist he rarely allowed to take control, dispersed and the moment passed.

"The surprise," Kaine said, nodding and forcing a deep breath in. "Thanks. I'd almost forgotten."

Rollo took hold of Kaine's left elbow and inspected the new wound. A thin, black, scorch mark cut through the jacket sleeve showing where one of the dead woman's bullets had creased his biceps. Blood dampened the material, its colour partially masked by the jacket's black dye.

"You okay, boss?"

"A scratch," Kaine said, tearing his arm from Rollo's grip.

"That bullet was meant for me," Rollo said, his words quiet, the thanks unspoken.

Kaine shrugged. "Had to make up for Danny."

Rollo nodded.

No more to be said.

Tedesco's whooping, rattling breaths slowed. He turned his head to look up at Kaine. Even with the smashed nose, split upper lip, broken teeth, and—no doubt—badly mashed testicles, he managed a mocking smile.

He tried to say, "Fucking bastard," but the sibilant lisp weakened the impact. "Still can't kill an unarmed man.

That's why I'm coming back. Nothing's gonna stop me. Hear? Nothing!"

"Threats don't sound as powerful through broken teeth and a mashed nose, Teddy," Danny said and burst out laughing, holstering his smoking SIG before clamping his gun hand to his damaged wing.

Larry made safe his Glock and brayed in delight. Soon, every man in the garage joined him, more in relief than humour. All but Kaine. He'd come too close to allowing his demons free rein and didn't feel much like smiling, let alone wailing like a banshee.

"Enough," he shouted. "I want this place sanitised inside five minutes. Move!"

The laughter died in an instant and the team kicked into action, policing brass and clearing debris. Rollo meshed his fingers in Tedesco's hair and jerked him to his feet. Tedesco squealed, holding onto Rollo's fist in an effort to reduce the load on his scalp.

"Where are you taking me?"

Kaine de-cocked his SIG, slid it into its holster, and fastened the retaining strap.

"You're going nowhere, Teddy. You're staying right here, in fact."

Rollo dragged his captive to the support column Kaine had used earlier as a shield and slammed him into it, face first.

Tedesco screamed. More blood and another tooth flew from his mouth.

"What are you doing?" Panic rose, speeding his words.

Kaine ignored the question and snapped one half of a pair of handcuffs to Tedesco's right wrist. Rollo did the same to the left wrist and they wrapped Tedesco's arms around the concrete column. As expected, the column was too large to allow the separate cuffs to meet around the far side.

While Tedesco screamed and yelled and fought impotently for his freedom, Kaine slid a chain he'd brought specifically for the purpose through the free loop of each manacle and pulled. He left only enough slack on Tedesco's arms to allow him room to breathe.

Finally, Rollo fastened the chain with a brass padlock. They stepped back to admire their handiwork.

"What do you think?" he asked Rollo.

"Doesn't look too comfortable. What do you reckon, Three?"

Danny stepped up and studied the scene. "Rather him than me, boss."

With his left cheek squeezed against the concrete, Tedesco fought his restraints until the moment of realisation hit. He was trapped, and he finally knew it. For the first time, fear—sweat-producing, stomach-churning, bowel-loosening fear—showed on his bloodied face.

"Surprise," Tedesco lisped. "You said something about a surprise. What—"

"I wondered when you'd twig," Kaine said, making sure Tedesco could see the look in his eyes. "Over the years, you've upset a lot of people. Funnily enough, they all want payback."

"Who? What's happening?" Teddy asked, dribbling blood from mouth and nose.

"Under normal circumstances," Kaine continued, ignoring Tedesco's questions, "I'd compile irrefutable evidence against you and send it to the proper authorities, but"—he scratched his beard—"circumstances aren't exactly normal. For various reasons, my trust in the UK's judicial system has been sorely tested recently. You see, I can't risk the possibility that you'll get off, or be given a ridiculously light sentence. And a man with money has a long reach, even if he is behind bars."

The van's reverse warning beeped, and its taillights illuminated the garage in a cherry-red glow. Cough jumped from the driver's side, opened the rear doors, and reached inside for the flame thrower.

Kaine paused in his explanation and turned to Rollo. "I have this now, Two. Make sure they do a good job. Nothing can come back to any of us."

Rollo nodded. "Consider it done."

"Pony said it before I sliced him open," Kaine continued, talking louder while Cough worked the flame thrower, incinerating the evidence. "He said he was protected. He said you would never leave Angela or her daughter alone. They'd never be able to live a normal life. With you around and active, they'd live in fear for the rest of their lives. I can't have that." He patted Tedesco's exposed cheek with his gloved hand. He had no fear of leaving evidence on Teddy for the forensic teams.

"So," Kaine said, through a sigh, "you see my dilemma. I killed Pony even though he was cuffed and restrained, but you're right. I hated it. Not my way at all. If you'd come out to fight, face-to-face, it would have been different, but you cowered in your top-floor fortress, and I had to find another way to end this."

Rollo gave the signal. He'd finished. The men piled into the van.

"Nearly time to go. Where was I? … Oh yes. In case you're wondering, I was prepared for a firefight here in the garage but didn't really want to kill your men. As you said, I'm 'weak' that way."

"You're going to leave me here like this?"

"Yes, exactly."

"That's your surprise?"

Kaine shook his head. "Nope. Someone would eventually call the police and you'd spin them a line. They'd probably let you go, and you'd be free to terrorise the Shafers and continue in business. No, I can't let that happen, I'm afraid. As I kept telling you, Angela and Bobbie Shafer are my responsibility. I promised to keep them safe."

Tedesco swallowed. Not an easy task with broken teeth, a broken nose, and his head pinned against a concrete pillar. "What … what are you going to do?"

"I'm going to make a simple phone call. After that, you'll never see me again."

Kaine pulled a single-use-only burner phone from his jacket and hit the pre-programmed number. The call connected almost instantly. He looked into Teddy Tedesco's eyes as he delivered his message to the call's recipient.

"Hello, Big Gino. The package is ready for you now."

Tedesco's eyes bulged, fear widened the pupils. "What? No. You can't. No. You fucking—"

Kaine blocked his ears to the sibilant ranting, disconnected the call, and dropped the mobile to the concrete.

He turned and marched to the van.

Chapter Thirty-Nine

Saturday 12th December – Morning

Mike's Farm, Long Buckby, Northants, England

"It's safe," Kaine said with absolute certainty, showing Angela a confident smile. "You can go home now."

For the first time since the assault, Angela fell apart, as Kaine feared she might. She'd been wound tight, holding herself together during the operation but, with the pressure released, the inevitable happened. She collapsed into the sofa, her body convulsed, tears flowed, and she wept into her fists. Kaine hated the helplessness of watching the poor woman disintegrate before his eyes. A woman he'd vowed to help. Until that point, she'd been so strong, so brave.

Bobbie fell beside her, wrapping her mother in her arms, crying, too.

"Mum," she said, looking up at Kaine and Lara for help, "please don't cry. We'll be—"

"I can't," Angela said, through the sobs wracking her body. "Please don't make me go back there. Can't we stay here?"

She searched the room for Mike, who stood close by, eyes glassy.

"Mike, please. Can we stay here?" she repeated, reaching out to him with one hand while holding tight to Bobbie with the other. "You need help running the farm, don't you?"

Mike stepped close and took her outstretched hand in both of his. "Aye, lass. Stay as long as you like, but the captain's right, it's safe to go home. You'll always be welcome to visit, but you need to return to your life, and Bobbie has school."

"University," Bobbie corrected. "It's years since I went to school."

Mike grinned. "See what I mean? Can't stand to be corrected in my own home, me. Such a nit-picker, your daughter. It'll be good to have some peace and quiet around here. All these hooligans scuffing up my well-ordered home. So many mouths to feed. Too much for an old man to put up with for long."

His gentle delivery belied the gruff words, and everyone in the room knew how he felt. Rollo and Danny stood in the kitchen out of the way. Both looked uncomfortable, but Danny's reaction to Bobbie's distress was a picture. Still wearing a sling, he stood balanced on the balls of his feet, ready to leap forwards and offer the women anything they needed.

According to Lara, the sling was probably unnecessary. Kaine suspected he wore it to elicit sympathy in Bobbie and to generate guilt in Kaine. If Bobbie's reaction to seeing the wounded hero on his return to the farm was any indication, the ploy had worked a treat. Kaine tempered his guilt over shooting Danny with the knowledge of what would have happened if Ginger had escaped, but the self-reproach was there, nonetheless.

Lara, holding herself stiff but close enough to Kaine for them to brush arms, spoke next. "Angela, if Ryan says you'll be safe, you can believe him. He'd never suggest you go home if there was any danger." She turned to face him, her eyes pleading. "Tell them, Ryan. Explain how you can be so certain."

Kaine didn't like exposing his methods or risking his team but found it impossible to resist Lara's plea. Besides, Angela and Bobbie needed an explanation. They deserved the truth.

Without seeking Mike's permission, and risking his benign wrath, he sat in the chair facing the sofa—Mike's chair—and leaned forwards. He took a moment to gather his thoughts.

"Without naming names or going into details," he said, focusing his attention on Angela, who needed the reassurance more than Bobbie, "I have two friends who know their way around computer systems."

Angela dabbed her tears with a tissue. She'd stopped crying and her shaking had subsided, but the fear remained, bubbling close to the surface. It wouldn't take much for her to break down again.

"I set one of them the task of wiping all trace of you from Tedesco's IT system. After he was finished, and independently, I asked the other to search the same files for any mention of you. She found nothing. Call it a failsafe, built-in, redundancy measure. I also asked them both to interrogate the Hampshire police files to adjust one or two things. Names, dates, and so on. No one will ever know you were involved in anything to do with Breaker's Folly."

He stopped talking to allow Angela and Bobbie to absorb the implications.

"You can do that?" Angela asked, her voice breaking. "I thought it was impossible to remove information from the internet once it was created."

"Difficult," Kaine agreed, smiling, "but not impossible. I don't have a clue how it's done, but my … friends do."

"What about the cloud?" Bobbie asked, still holding tight to Angela. "These days, most people back up their data to the cloud."

Kaine gave her the benefit of a wry grin. "Apparently, that particular cloud dumped its rain somewhere over the Indian Ocean. As I said, I don't have the details, but I do know nothing will ever come back to you or your mother."

Angela tilted her head to look up at Lara, whose confident nod seemed to give her encouragement. "At Tedesco's office, were there any paper files? Notes. That sort of thing?"

"Good question," Kaine said, relaxing against the back of the chair until Mike's growled warning showed he could only take so many liberties with a long-standing friendship. Kaine sat forwards again.

"Didn't I tell you about that terrible fire in Tedesco's office on the day he … disappeared? How remiss of me. An accident with a Cuban cigar, apparently. You can never be too careful with a naked flame."

Angela's faltering smile, when it arrived, showed promise. She had a long journey ahead, but she'd already shown her strength. With time and help, she'd recover. Never back to exactly the way she was before, but she would recover.

Mike broke the growing silence with a deep-throated cough. "If you've quite finished flapping your gums, I think we could all benefit from a cuppa." He glowered at his chair. "And I'm absolutely certain you could do with stretching your legs. Yes?"

"Correct, as usual, Mike. On both counts."

Kaine jumped to his feet and, winking at Lara, he bent to dust off the seat of Mike's chair, making a big show of doing it.

"Ryan?" Angela asked, her voice a little stronger, but still uncertain. "When do we have to leave?"

"Mike and I were talking earlier. There's no rush. A day, a week, a month. It's up to you. I just wanted to explain the situation and give you time to prepare."

"Are you staying here, too?"

"Not for long. I'm still a wanted man in the UK and a danger to anyone near me. I need to go."

"As do I," Lara announced. "Ryan and I have things to do, places to be. Don't we, Ryan."

Her tone made it clear she wasn't asking.

"Yes, boss," he said, pretending to be pressurised into accepting her constant presence against his will. "Angela, I'm sorry, but there is one thing I need to ask of you and Bobbie."

"If you want us to promise not to tell anyone about you and what your men did for us, that's a given. We'll say nothing. You have our word. Doesn't he, Bobbie?"

"We owe you everything, Captain," Bobbie said. She sat up straight and crossed a finger over her heart. "Our lips are sealed."

"No, that's not it at all. It's just that … well, at first, when you reach home, you're bound to feel a little uncertain. At least for a while. I was wondering whether you'd be prepared to put up with one of my men as an extended house guest? A minder?"

In the kitchen doorway, Danny opened his mouth to speak, but Rollo silenced him with an elbow to the ribs. Lara, standing sideways to Angela and Bobbie, hid a grin behind her hand.

Bobbie clamped her mouth shut and looked into the glowing ashes. A red flush coloured her neck and bloomed on her cheeks.

"The 83 Trust would cover his salary and expenses, and I'd make sure he was well behaved."

Angela, clearly having seen Bobbie and Danny's reaction, dabbed her eyes again, taking her time to answer. "And who did you have in mind?"

"I don't know," Kaine said, playing along. "Peewee's injured but recovering. Slim and Larry are on their way to the Bahamas to spend some of their pay and soak up a little sun. Cough, Stefan, or Pat might be available, but I'd have to ask for a volunteer."

Danny, unable to contain himself any longer, threw up a hand. "I'll do it, boss. Happy to."

Rollo whispered in his ear, loud enough for everyone to hear. "Idiot. Won't you ever learn? A good marine never volunteers for anything."

Kaine sighed. "Sorry, Danny. Not possible. I can't put an injured man on guard duty."

Danny's reaction was a pure delight. He frowned and followed every eye in the room back to his sling. Realisation soon hit.

"You mean this?" he asked, throwing his right hand across to his left shoulder and flapping his injured wing. "Give me a couple of days, and I'll be one hundred percent."

When Kaine didn't respond, Danny turned to Angela.

"What do you say, Mrs Shafer? I'd be honoured to offer my security services."

Angela turned to her daughter. "Bobbie, could you stand to have him under our feet for a few weeks?"

Bobbie shot back an instant answer. "Suppose I could get used to it. After a while," she said, looking at Danny, rather than her mother.

Danny stepped further into the living room. "I'd be no bother, Mrs Shafer. You'd hardly know I was there."

Brow knitted, lips pursed, Angela paused again before nodding. "Okay then. But you'll have to sleep downstairs in the spare room. Our landing squeaks worse than the one in this place, and I'll need my sleep."

Bobbie's eyes popped. "Mum, please! You're embarrassing Danny."

Angela's laugh sliced through the tension, and everyone started talking at once. Bobbie let go of her mother, and took Danny to one side. On tiptoes, she kissed his cheek, and he shot a glance at Kaine, silently asking permission. Kaine turned his back, giving his tacit approval.

When Mike disappeared into the kitchen to return seconds later with a bottle of bubbly and champagne flutes on a silver tray, the impromptu party started. The champagne didn't last long, but Mike countered by opening the drinks cabinet and offering everyone rum, which Kaine and Rollo declined. Too early in the day for Rollo, and Kaine was still on duty. He'd always be on duty.

———

AN HOUR LATER, with the conversation turning to food and a celebratory visit to a local restaurant, and Kaine's face aching from all the unaccustomed smiling, Lara slipped her hand into his.

"I promised Mike I'd feed Dynamite," she said, smiling. "Join me?"

He tore his eyes away from hers and glanced through the window. The winter sun sliced through a thin sheet of cloud, but the wind shook the bare oaks, and it looked bitter. Completely perfect.

"Fair enough. The rain's stopped, and it's a good time for a walk. And if Danny mentions being the victim of friendly fire one more time, I'll have to land him one."

He helped her into a heavy coat, and they strolled to the stables. She fed and groomed the mighty beast. Kaine stood back, watching the action, the flowing lines, and firm curves with keen interest. Occasionally, he glanced at the horse.

It took the best part of an hour to finish and for Lara to lower the latch on the stall door.

"Enjoy that?" he asked.

"Yes. Did you?"

"Very much."

"I saw you staring."

"Why wouldn't I stare? He's a magnificent beast. And his vet's passable."

With daylight fading and the stable lights not offering much in the way of illumination, he had difficulty seeing her expression. He hoped it was a smile.

"Ryan Liam Kaine, you're such an old romantic."

"Who me? No idea what you mean," Kaine said, pulling her into a hug. "Hard as nails, me. No time for romance."

"I'm talking about Danny and Bobbie. You could easily have made things difficult for them."

"Kidding, right? I've seen the way they are with each

other. What sort of a friend would I be to stand in their way?"

Lara stepped closer. Fresh from brushing and feeding the horse, heat poured off her.

"Still," she said, "one word from you and he'd have backed down. You know that, don't you?"

"Yes, I know. I expect he was worried I'd shoot him again."

She smacked his arm.

"Ouch. Careful, that hurt. Danny wasn't the only one on the receiving end of a bullet, you know." He rubbed the area.

"Idiot," she said, "it was a scratch and on the other arm."

"Was it? Oh yes, you're right. My memory's playing up. Must be the company."

She pulled him close and rested her head on his shoulder. Kaine wrapped his arms around her.

"What's happening with us, Ryan?"

He flinched and pulled her closer. "What do you mean?"

"When are you going to take me home?"

Damn it.

Working with the horse must have reminded her of all she'd lost. Corky and Sabrina had found nothing in their searches to suggest anyone, either official or unofficial, was looking for Lara, which suggested her Lincolnshire clinic might be safe. His stomach lurched. Lara could return to her old life, but he'd have to give her up.

"Home. You mean your clinic?"

"No, the villa. I think of it as home, don't you?"

Bloody hell. Don't think, man. React.

"Lara Orchard," he said, burying his face in her hair. "To me, home is right here with you."

She jerked her head away and stared at him, eyes dancing. "Now that's what I call romantic. Kiss me."

Kaine hesitated.

"Ryan, what's wrong. Don't you want to kiss me?"

"I do, but …"

"But what?"

"Every time we've been alone together, something's interrupted me. I half-expected my mobile to buzz."

Her laughter made his heart race.

"I can't hear any ringing, Captain Kaine. Do as you're told and kiss me."

"Yes, ma'am."

Some orders were easier to obey than others.

The END.

Next in the Ryan Kaine series

vinci-books.com/onthemoney

Justice is coming, no matter the cost.

A death leads Kaine and Lara into a dangerous underworld.
When the stakes get deadly, they'll risk everything to stop a ruthless
gang.

Turn the page for a preview…

On The Money: Chapter One

Tuesday 26th January - Byron Codell

Brooke Street, Walthamstow, London, England

Thou shalt not steal.

Bible said it loud and clear, and Bible was Goddamned fucking right. One of them Ten Commandment things.

Byron Arlon "Barcode" Codell didn't know which Commandment exactly, but that didn't matter a damn. What it meant mattered. Mattered big time.

Steal something, anything, food to survive even, and the thief would suffer the flames of hell for all eternity. Thieving fuckers would burn forever. That's what Bible said.

Yeah, that's right, stealing did a person's soul no good in

the afterlife, no good at all. But who gave a shit for souls? If that same thief took from Barcode, bad things would happen in the here and now. Right away. No one stole from Barcode.

Ain't no one gonna mess with Barcode no more. The ink lines on the back of his neck were a permanent reminder of what happened to anyone who tried to fuck him over. Barcode wasn't never gonna take no disrespect. Not no more.

Which was why he was aiming to climb up on the garage roof in the middle of the night.

Some fucker were dipping his greasy fingers into Barcode's pie, and that certain someone was gonna lose more than the same sticky fingers. The thieving pig-fucker was going to die.

Wrapped up in his heaviest parka and dressed all in black, apart from the white lines on his trainers, Barcode pulled the fur-lined hood over his shaved head. He cinched the drawstring tight under his nose to cover his mouth. Side flaps and fur threw his face into deep shadow.

He stuck his head over the top of the shoulder-high, wooden fence, and checked out the sloping back garden.

Nothing much had changed since the last time he'd been there, or since the old man kicked the bucket. Such a shame, but old people died, didn't they? Nothing shocking in that. Nothing at all.

Unlike last time he'd climbed the fence, the crib stood dark as night.

No lights shone from the kitchen window over the shitty patch of land that had once been an okay back garden, with flowers and vegetables and shit. Back before the old man took ill and his wheelchair became his legs.

Stupid, old man thought he was still relevant, still worthy of respect. Not in Barcode's books. Cripples was a waste of space. A waste of oxygen. A blight on the world. Should be swiped from the area, moved into homes. Culled or something.

But the old geezer were pushing up the daisies now. Gone to his Maker. Nothing mattered to him no more.

The old man's grandson, Darwin Moore. He mattered, though. Still stayed in the house, but only on weekends. Never on a Tuesday. Darwin, the college boy geek, spent the week studying somewhere up north, which were the reason the house stood empty.

Perfect.

Even if the old boy had still been alive—sitting behind his net curtains, in front of his TV—he'd have been lost in his favourite soap. For the old, TV stood in for "product", the street drugs Barcode and his posse shifted by the baggie load. Gramps woulda been sitting with his back to the window and the sound turned up loud enough for a deaf dog to hear the dialogue from a couple houses away. Nah, the old sod wouldn't have noticed an armed assault force scrambling over his garden fence, let alone a stealthy black dude with a barcode tattoo on the back of his neck.

After pulling on his leather gloves, Barcode grabbed the top of the fence and vaulted over, landing in a patch of soft, sticky mud. He scuffed his tracks as he headed down the slight hill. Although the old bastard hadn't been in the back garden for years before he croaked, on account of his wheelchair, no telling when Darwin would venture out for a look-see. Didn't make no sense to leave a clear trail.

The crib—a two-bedroomed, end-of-terrace house—had to be worth a fucking mint, even in a shitty area like

Brooke Street. Darwin shoulda sold up soon as Gramps kicked the bucket. Fuck knew why he didn't. Probably wanted to keep it in memory of his dear, departed grandpa and his poor, murdered mother. Stupid, sentimental fuckwit should be living for the moment, not dwelling on the past. No profit in it.

The mother weren't all that bright neither. Shouldn't have left the crippled, old man on his own to fly off on a hen's night. And why Amsterdam, for fuck's sake? What was wrong with London? Bitch coulda had a good time down the West End for the same scratch as flying to Dutch-land.

Paid the price though, didn't she? Mrs Moore and the others who died on that flight. Served her right. Served them all right. Blown outta the sky in a fireball.

Barcode smiled. Wished he coulda seen the boom for real and not just on some shaky phone footage.

Must've been a hell of a firework show.

Eighty-three dead. Either burned to charcoal, crushed on impact or—much worse—drowned in the freezing North Sea.

Yeah, Barcode woulda loved to have seen it in real life. Such a buzz.

Ah well. Can't do nothin' 'bout it now.

Keeping close to the fence, staying in the deep shadow, Barcode crept around the garden, the tall grass swishing up to his knees, soaking the legs of his jeans. He made it to the rear of the garage. The metal wheelbarrow was exactly where he'd left it, leaning against the garage wall. He used it to boost himself onto the flat roof.

Again, keeping close to the end wall of the house, Barcode scrambled on hands and knees to the front of the garage and squatted.

Simples.

Gave him the perfect view.

One of his own crew, fucking scumbag, had been dipping his fingers in the till, which meant the total take was coming up five percent short. Not much, but significant. In any other business, the shortfall mighta been explained away by bad weather keeping the punters off the streets and outta the shops. But in his industry, clients would crawl over shattered glass and sell their babies as sex slaves to raise the cash to cover the next fix.

Nah, a drop in revenue meant only one thing.

Thievery. Plain and simple.

He'd first noticed the shortage a couple days ago.

Up front, he thought about running to Top Man, but that would only have reflected badly on Barcode. It would probably have dropped him well and truly in the slime. No telling what TM woulda done. The invisible fucker might even put the evil eye on Barcode for dropping the ball. After all, the thievery was happening on one of Barcode's pitches. Made him responsible for clearing up his own mess. In the end, Barcode made up the shortfall from his personal cut, but that couldn't last forever. If the thieving fuck kept getting away with it, he'd only get greedier. Eventually, Barcode wouldn't be able to cover the losses and that wouldn't do. Not at all.

It had to stop, and stop right away.

If he didn't flush out the scumbag and deal with the prick before TM sussed out the losses, TM would probably decide Barcode wasn't up to the task of running his own crew. And that would put a cramp on his plans to move up in the Tribe and reach his ultimate goal.

Move TM aside and take over.

Complete and utter domination. The only thing that

mattered to Barcode. But he was smarter than them mugs who tried to take over by playing hardball, all gung-ho but no smarts. Barcode played the long game. Over time, stealth were better than shock tactics.

He sucked air between his teeth, smiled, and settled down to study one third of his crew. That week's evening shift. If he'd worked it out right, it wouldn't take long to prove.

Barcode pulled a pair of stolen binoculars from the pocket of his parka and sat cross-legged on the tar-covered roof, hidden deep in the shadows. He raised them to his eyes and started in on the spying.

As he watched, his anger built.

He fed on it. Used it. Enjoyed it. Anger kept him warm.

If emotions made the man, Barcode was a man built of fire and rage. World saw him for what he was—big, powerful, angry. But there was more. Below the surface, hidden deep, lay ambition and a brain to take him to where he wanted to be. And a street-level, middle manager wasn't nearly the final destination.

He'd go further. Much further.

Barcode was going to the top. Wouldn't be easy. There were plenty of faces standing between him and TM's spot. Yeah, plenty of wannabes, but none with Barcode's patience or smarts.

To TM and his lieutenants, the Heavies, Barcode weren't nothing special, not yet. But he was worth more than they knew. Even his handle meant more than he let on. The tat on the back of his neck—the barcode that gave him his tag—actually meant something. It wasn't just a random load of fat and thin vertical lines. No way.

At aged twelve, he'd been turned on by a movie about a hired assassin who wore a barcode tattoo on the back of his neck. The young Byron wanted a tat just like it. Thought it would be cool. Saved up his hard-earned for months and spent hours each week in the school gym, building his muscles with weights, and his reflexes with the speed bags.

According to the rat-faced, broken-toothed tattoo artist who inked him, the vertical, black lines he'd etched into young Byron's dark skin displayed nothing but his name, his handle—Hitman #48—and his date of birth.

"Barcode" was reborn that day, and he was totally fucking psyched. But, weeks later and after the scabs had healed, when he ran a Tesco's barcode reader over the lines, the code gave a different result. It spewed out an insult to his mother and her love life. Even though he was fired up and spitting bullets, Barcode never told no one about how he'd been screwed over. Kept it to himself. Never allowed no one to run a scanner over the tat again, neither. Nobody could never accuse Barcode of being shit at keeping secrets.

Months later, someone out walking found the same rat-faced, heartless fucker who thought it funny to play games with his needle gun and mess with a teenage kid. Found him floating face down in the Thames, missing his eyes—and his heart.

Barcode didn't tell no one he'd done the deed, neither. Yeah, Barcode could keep a secret all right.

Later, the filth tried to finger him for the deed. They call him in to "help with they enquiries". Yeah, right. The fuck with that. Barcode were too smart for them. Ran rings around them during the interrogation, and they still didn't have no clue.

Since then, he coulda paid another inker to cover the lines, change them, but he left it untouched as a lesson to himself not to be so stupid again. And besides, Barcode was, as the tat actually said, a Big Black Bastard.

Too fuckin' right I is. And nobody's ever gonna say different.

In the dark and the cold, Barcode watched and waited. And he smiled.

———

BRUTUS.

Yep.

Had to be Brutus.

Couldn't've been no one else. No one else on his crew had the balls, or the stupidity.

The minute he discovered the pilferage, Barcode knew it had to be Brutus, the third mini-leader of his posse.

It had only taken a few seconds to rule out everyone else.

First, he cleared Petey. No way his blood, his brother, would do nothing to drop Barcode in the brown stuff. They'd known each other since nursery. Grown up together. Petey was as honest as any dealer had a right to be. Petey would die for Barcode and Barcode would let him.

Ha!

As for Rhino, the second stringer, Barcode cleared him almost as fast as he cleared Petey. Rhino didn't have the stones, or the need. The musclebound cretin didn't partake of the product, not even occasionally. Fine, upstanding member of the Tribe, he was. Didn't even smoke normal cigarettes. Treated his body as a fucking temple, and worshiped his pregnant squeeze, Ariel. Top of all that was the clincher—Rhino, the scar-faced bugger, didn't have the smarts to rip no one off without giving himself away in seconds.

That left Brutus. The third wheel. The third deputy.

The bastard in charge of the pitch Barcode were watching through the binoculars.

Brutus.

You stupid, greedy, selfish fucker.

He had to go, but …

Barcode couldn't deal with the thief without proof. The Tribe had its rules, and any member who pointed an accusing finger without proof was liable to find himself in as much trouble as the tribesman he accused.

Nah, Barcode needed evidence, which was how come he ended up sitting, cross-legged, on the flat, garage roof freezing his nuts off, risking butt cramp and piles.

As it happened, it only took twenty-five minutes to eyeball the act.

Slimy bastard!

Barcode spotted it when the fifth customer of the evening handed across her small bundle of creased notes— probably earned from lying on her back and spreading her scrawny legs. As the bitch scurried away, her fix held tight in a grimy fist, Brutus handed the cash to his rider, Lil' Aran, who slid the notes into his backpack.

Lil' Aran, ten years old, no more, spent the shift pedalling up and down the lanes between all the pitches, ready to make a lightning split the moment the bacon shoved they noses into Tribe business.

The routine was slick and simple. Barcode designed it for the purpose and it worked real well.

Customer arrives.

Money passes from customer to dealer—in this case, Brutus.

Dealer tips the nod to rider.

Rider—Lil' Aran—rolls up on his BMX, takes cash,

hands product to Brutus, and buggers off up the lane in a flat-out, wheel-spinning sprint.

Dealer passes product to customer.

Junkie buggers off, happy as shit, transaction complete, and no outsider any the wiser.

Only this time, while the client buggers off, baggie in her hot, little fist, and Lil' Aran sprints away, Brutus stoops to tie his shoelace.

Again, no real issue, but, through the high-powered binoculars, Barcode couldn't see nothing wrong with the laces in the first place. They sure didn't seem loose to him.

First time it happened, Barcode didn't think nothing of it. After all, no self-respecting crewman would allow his brilliant, white laces to go slopping in the puddles, but seven deals later, same thing happened, this time with the other shoe.

Once was all right, twice maybe, but it kept happening. Over the course of two hours, Brutus tied his laces five fucking times.

The big guy either hadn't learned to tie his laces proper, which meant they kept coming undone, or he had another reason to fiddle with his sneakers.

Yeah. Another reason, right enough.

So fucking simple. When Barcode first sussed the shortfall, he'd credited Brutus with more brains. He expected the bastard to hand off the stolen money to an accomplice or an unwitting stooge. Maybe even hide it under a rock for a pickup in the middle of the night when even the hardest-bitten junkies crawled into their shitholes, and the Tribe had shut up shop for the day. He didn't expect something so blatant. How long did the fucker think he'd get away with it for?

So simple and so stupid.

A fiver here and a tenner there, but over a week, it would mount up. In the two months since Top Man gave Barcode the pitch, the fucker coulda syphoned off fucking hundreds.

Plain, old, sleight of hand—or rather of foot. No accomplice. His fucking shoe! How careless to have missed it for so long.

Jesus fuck.

Barcode chewed his thumbnail down to the skin.

Disrespect.

Brutus was dissing him. Laughing at him.

For Brutus to treat Barcode that way showed more than greed. It showed contempt. Contempt for the Tribe and, worse still, contempt for Barcode.

Brutus is gone. End of.

Barcode crawled backwards along the roof and retraced his steps through the garden.

———

BARCODE TIMED HIS APPROACH SO LIL' Aran was heading towards the furthest point on his ride but before making his turn. The rider would be far enough away not to interfere if he was working the scam with Brutus, but close enough to act as witness and confirm Barcode didn't plant the cash.

No point taking chances.

"Hey, blood," Barcode called, smiling as he loped along the lane towards the pitch. "How's it hangin'?"

He waved with his left hand, keeping his right tucked tight against his side.

Brutus, as wide as he was tall, nineteen stones of pure

beef—and a bucket load of it between the ears—looked up. The thief's eyebrows shot up.

His smile was as forced as any TV presenter Barcode had ever watched.

"Hey, blood. You early, man. Weren't expectin' you for a couple hours."

Yeah, and that's the whole point, fucker.

Brutus ripped the beanie from his head and used it to shoo away a mealy-mouthed, shit-for-brains regular who couldn't pay the full fee. The yellow streetlight shone on Brutus' polished dome.

Barcode stopped at arm's length and pushed out his left fist—the sign things were cool. They bumped. All sweet and friendly, like.

"Thought I'd come see how shit was hangin'. Apart from that dickwad"—he tilted his head towards the disappearing, failed customer—"how's trade?"

Brutus pulled the beanie back on and tucked his head into his shoulders. "Cold as fuck out here, man. I'm thinkin' we should relocate the store. Maybe we could take over one of them houses and set up shop in the warm and the dry." With his chin, he pointed at the street behind Barcode.

Taking care not to show Brutus his back, Barcode turned sideways and observed the row of houses running across from the alley, the closest had the garage he'd just been using. Above the fencing, the terrace stretched away and stopped when it reached the more expensive, semi-detached homes closer to the High Street. Each house showed lights. Each were lived in.

"Good idea, Brutus. Whose house we gonna occupy? How 'bout number fifteen? Yo' Auntie Grace live there, right? You reckon we gonna set up in her front room? And what happens when the bacon come a-callin'? You'll be holdin', and the riders won't have time to scoot nowhere. Nah, this shit's what we do, and this here station's where we stayin'."

Brutus lowered his head even more. He shuffled from one foot to the other, all nervous.

"Wazzup, man? You need the toilet?"

"Nah, freezin' my ass off, innit."

The runt, Barcode's real-life cousin, Lil' Aran, stopped outta earshot, balanced on his pedals, flashing his pure, bike-handling skills. Looked like he could tell something were off and didn't want no part in it.

Smart boy.

Any time now, Lil' Aran might be due a promotion, despite his youth.

Barcode pointed to the rider. "What's happenin' with Lil' Aran?"

As expected, Brutus turned to look.

Barcode stepped back a pace, grabbed the handle of the baseball bat, and pulled it from the deep pocket his Auntie May had sewn into the lining of his parka. He swung a hard uppercut, stepping into the blow—adding his full body-weight to increase the power of the swing.

The fat end of the bat landed between Brutus' legs with enough force to crush his dick, and take the rascal clean off his feet.

Brutus screamed, doubled over, and crumpled to his knees. Slowly, he toppled forwards to land face first in a grimy puddle. Barcode smiled at the effect of the under-hand blow, surprised he could generate so much power.

"Man, that's gotta hurt bad," he said, resting the fat end of the bat on the back of Brutus' neck. The blow had knocked the beanie clean off of the thief's head, and it floated on top of the puddle. "I can't tell if you pissed yo'self, or if that damp patch in yo' kecks is blood, blood. You feel me?"

Barcode flashed a glance up the alley. Lil' Aran's jaw dropped. The rider planted a foot on the ground to stop himself toppling.

To add to the bad vibes, a hard, cold rain started dropping. Before long, it poured down with all the force of a power shower. Spluttering, struggling to breathe, Brutus tried to pull his head clear of the water, but Barcode wasn't having it. He planted a foot into the middle of Brutus' back, forcing him down hard. Bubbles frothed around the drowning fucker's head. His arms and legs thrashed.

Barcode let him splash and buck for a count of twenty before releasing the pressure and stepping away.

Brutus exploded outta the water and rolled away, coughing and spluttering. Gagging like a bitch. He scrambled away on his thieving butt and fetched up against the rusted, chain-link fence, where he curled into a tight ball, face creased in hurt, eyes closed.

Yeah, now you know what pain feels like, blood.

"W-What the f-fuck you do that for, man?" he squeaked.

Barcode was impressed the fucker could speak at all after the crunching blow. Musta had balls of steel. Mashed steel now, though. Barcode couldn't hold back a snicker. He signalled with the bat for Lil' Aran to come as witness, but the rider didn't budge. Couldn't blame him none. Musta been scared shitless, thinking Barcode had totally lost his shit.

"Take off them sneakers," he ordered Brutus, speaking loud enough for Lil' Aran to hear.

When the fucker didn't move, Barcode ran the head of the bat along the fence above Brutus' head. It made an aggressive rattle and meshed well with the splashing rain.

The crumpled man turned his head up and rain sluiced into his pained eyes. "What? What you say?"

"You hear me, blood. Kick off them sneakers 'fore I drop you, fucker."

Still twitching and shivering, the big man's shoulders tensed in realisation. "You … you trippin', blood. Had too much product. You bust my balls and tell me to—"

Brutus screamed again as Barcode slammed the bat down on the top of his shoulder. The satisfying crunch of a shattering collar bone buzzed up through the handle.

Barcode yelled, "Shut the fuck up, you mutha!" and raised the bat high, holding it aloft but not completing the downswing. "Lil' Aran, come here, cuz!"

The young rider shook his head. "No way, man. You flipped."

Breathing hard, as much to steady his nerves as from the exercise, Barcode lowered the bat slowly and rested it on Brutus' bad shoulder. The thief squealed.

"Nah, lil' man. Things is cool. Come here, I need you as a witness. You safe from me, unless you part of it."

"Part o' what?"

"The thievery."

Lil' Aran sat up straighter in the saddle. Rain ran down his face and dripped off his chin like it was pouring out the spout of a teapot.

"You know me, BC. I ain't no t'ief!" he shouted above the whistling wind, the driving rain, and Brutus' groaning and crying.

"So, do as I tell you. Come here and rip off this fucker's sneakers!"

Lil' Aran paused a moment, considering. He threw a glance at his escape route, then looked at Brutus before pushing down on the pedal. The bike edged closer, not gaining much speed.

"Hurry, man. I's gettin' soaked here."

The rider pedalled harder, throwing up spray as the low-slung bike splashed through the growing pools of filthy water. Five metres away, he skidded to a sideways stop, jumped off his ride, and propped it against the fence. Then he approached the newly made cripple.

"Take off his sneakers."

Brutus raised his head to stare at Lil' Aran, "Don't touch me you mutha—"

Another scream cut off Brutus' cuss as Barcode pressed the bat harder into the smashed shoulder.

"Who give you permission to speak, fucker? Go on, Lil' Aran. Let's see what he hidin' inside them flashy Pitch Blacks."

Brutus tried to scrunch away but, crowded by Barcode on one side, Lil' Aran on the other, and tight against the fence, there wasn't nowhere he could squirm to.

Lil' Aran squatted in front of the fallen soldier and looked up at Barcode. "Okay if I takes out my cutter? Don't wanna mess with wet knots."

Barcode nodded. "Go for it, cuz."

The little rider pulled out a butterfly knife and flicked it open like he'd practised in his bedroom for hours. Musta been studying Gerard, the smooth-talking, French Heavy, but he didn't get the action quite so slick.

Lil' Aran sliced through the laces and ripped the right sneaker from Brutus' foot.

Using his fingertips, the rider fished inside the soft cuff. They came out with a bunch of crumpled banknotes. Lil' Aran gasped and shook his head.

"How much he got in there, cuz?"

Lil' Aran smoothed out the paper and sorted them into tens and fives. He counted them slowly. "Thirty-five quid."

"Check the other shoe."

The rider repeated the process.

"Fifty-five. That's … er," he said, scrunching up his eyes to work the maths.

"Ninety, cuz," Barcode said, saving him the work. "He got ninety quid stuffed into them sneakers."

Lil' Aran stood and brushed water and gravel from the knees of his jeans. "Where'd he come up with that cash, BC?"

"Fucker's been rippin' off the Tribe. I been watchin' him for the last couple hours."

Brutus shook his head. "Nah, man. You got it all wrong. I'm clean. That's my stash. I put it there for safe keepin'. Honest."

He released one fist from his crushed junk and held it up to Barcode, hand open, begging.

Barcode sniffed, turned, and strolled away, all cool, like. Lil' Aran followed, stuffing the paper into his backpack. He collected his bike, and walked alongside Barcode.

"You just leavin' him there, BC?"

"What you want me to do?"

The rider shrugged. "Kill the fucker? He'll run, right?"

"Nah, lil' man. He ain't runnin' nowhere with bruised nuts and a smashed shoulder."

Barcode stopped walking and turned to face the pool of light. Somehow, Brutus had pulled himself to his feet. He leaned against the fence, hunched over, unable to stand straight. Barcode doubted the fucker'd be able to stand straight for weeks.

"I ain't killin' no one. That up to TM, not me."

"You sure, BC?" Lil' Aran asked, still looking up, blinking the rain outta his eyes. "I'll back yo' action."

"Thanks, cuz, but I's sure. Way I see it, TM's gonna send a posse o' Heavies to Brutus' crib. If he there, they likely do the job for me. If he gone, *no problemo*. He'll turn up soon enough. My job's to push product and take care o' business. Not my place to dish out punishment without orders. Me? I's just a foot soldier, cuz."

For now.

Grab your copy…
vinci-books.com/onthemoney

About Kerry J Donovan

#1 International Best-seller with *Ryan Kaine: On the Run*, Kerry was born in Dublin. He currently lives with Margaret in a bungalow in Nottinghamshire. He has three children and four grandchildren.

Kerry earned a first-class honours degree in Human Biology and has a PhD in Sport and Exercise Sciences. A former scientific advisor to The Office of the Deputy Prime Minister, he helped UK emergency first-responders prepare for chemical attacks in the wake of 9/11. He is also a former furniture designer/maker.

kerryjdonovan.com